LARGE PRINT EDITION

RANDOM HOUSE

*Also available*
*in Random House Large Print*

THE LOST WORLD
DISCLOSURE

# MICHAEL CRICHTON

# AIRFRAME

Published by Random House Large Print
in association with Alfred A. Knopf, Inc.
New York    1996

CIP information is available from
the Library of Congress.

ISBN 0-679-75898-4

Random House Web Address: http://www.randomhouse.com/
PRINTED IN THE UNITED STATES OF AMERICA
FIRST LARGE PRINT EDITION

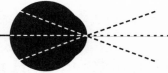

This Large Print Book carries the
Seal of Approval of N.A.V.H.

*The damn things weigh half a million pounds, fly a third of the way around the world, and they carry passengers in greater comfort and safety than any vehicle in the history of mankind. Now, are you fellas really going to stand there and tell us you know how to do the job better? Are you going to pretend you know anything about it at all? 'Cause it looks to me like you boys are just stirring folks up for your own reasons.*

> Aviation legend Charley Norton, 78, speaking to reporters in 1970 after an airplane crash

*The irony of the Information Age is that it has given new respectability to uninformed opinion.*

> Veteran reporter John Lawton, 68, speaking to the American Association of Broadcast Journalists in 1995

# MONDAY

# ABOARD TPA 545

5:18 A.M.

Emily Jansen sighed in relief. The long flight was nearing an end. Morning sunlight streamed through the windows of the airplane. In her lap, little Sarah squinted in the unaccustomed brightness as she noisily sucked the last of her bottle, and pushed it away with tiny fists. "That was good, wasn't it?" Emily said. "Okay . . . up we go . . ."

She raised the infant onto her shoulder, began to pat her back. The baby gave a gurgling belch, and her body relaxed.

In the next seat, Tim Jansen yawned and rubbed his eyes. He had slept through the night, all the way from Hong Kong. Emily never slept on planes; she was too nervous.

"Morning," Tim said, looking at his watch. "Just a couple of hours more, hon. Any sign of breakfast?"

"Not yet," Emily said, shaking her head. They had taken TransPacific Airlines, a charter from Hong Kong. The money they saved would be useful when they set up housekeeping at the University of Colorado, where Tim was going to be an assistant professor. The flight had been pleasant enough— they were in the front of the plane—but the stewardesses seemed disorganized, the meals coming at odd times. Emily had turned down dinner because Tim was asleep, and she couldn't eat with Sarah sleeping in her lap.

And even now, Emily was surprised by the casual behavior of the crew. They left the cockpit door open during the flight. She knew Asian crews often did that, but it still struck her as inappropriate; too informal, too relaxed. The pilots strolled around the plane at night, kibitzing with the stewardesses. One was leaving right now, walking to the back of the plane. Of course, they were probably stretching their legs. Stay alert, all of that. And certainly the fact that the crew was Chinese didn't trouble her. After a year in China, she admired the efficiency and attention to detail of the Chinese. But somehow, the whole flight just made her nervous.

Emily put Sarah back down in her lap. The baby stared at Tim and beamed.

"Hey, I should get this," Tim said. Fumbling in the bag under his seat, he brought out a video camera, trained it on his daughter. He waggled his free hand to get her attention. "Sarah . . . Sar-ah . . . Smile for Daddy. Smi-le . . ."

Sarah smiled, and made a gurgling sound.

"How does it feel to be going to America, Sarah? Ready to see where your parents are from?"

Sarah gurgled again. She waved her tiny hands in the air.

"She'll probably think everybody in America looks weird," Emily said. Their daughter had been born seven months ago in Hunan, where Tim had studied Chinese medicine.

Emily saw the camera lens pointed at her. "And

what about you, Mom?" Tim said. "Are you glad to be going home?"

"Oh, Tim," she said. "Please." She must look like hell, she thought. All those hours.

"Come on, Em. What are you thinking?"

She needed to comb her hair. She needed to pee.

She said, "Well, what I really want—what I have dreamed about for months—is a cheeseburger."

"With Xu-xiang hot bean sauce?" Tim said.

"God *no*. A cheeseburger," she said, "with onions and tomatoes and lettuce and pickles and mayonnaise. *Mayonnaise,* God. And French's mustard."

"You want a cheeseburger too, Sarah?" Tim said, turning the camera back to their daughter.

Sarah was tugging at her toes with one tiny fist. She pulled her foot into her mouth, and looked up at Tim.

"Taste good?" Tim said, laughing. The camera shook as he laughed. "Is that breakfast for you, Sarah? Not waiting for the stewardess on this flight?"

Emily heard a low rumbling sound, almost a vibration, that seemed to come from the wing. She snapped her head around. "What was that?"

"Take it easy, Em," Tim said, still laughing.

Sarah laughed, too, giggling delightfully.

"We're almost home, honey," Tim said.

But even as he spoke, the plane seemed to shudder, the nose of the plane turning down. Suddenly everything tilted at a crazy angle. Emily felt Sarah sliding forward off her lap. She clutched at her daughter, pulling her close. Now it felt like the plane was going *straight down,* and then suddenly it was going up, and her stomach was pressed into the seat. Her daughter was a lead weight against her.

Tim said, "What the hell?"

Abruptly she was lifted off the seat, her seat belt cutting into her thighs. She felt light and sick to her stomach. She saw Tim bounce out of his seat, his head slamming into the luggage compartments overhead, the camera flying past her face.

From the cockpit, Emily heard buzzing, insistent alarms and a metallic voice that said, "Stall! Stall!" She glimpsed the blue-suited arms of the pilots moving swiftly over the controls; they were shouting in Chinese. All over the aircraft, people were screaming, hysterical. There was the sound of shattering glass.

The plane went into another steep dive. An elderly Chinese woman slid down the aisle on her back, screaming. A teenage boy followed, tumbling head over heels. Emily looked at Tim, but her husband wasn't in his seat any more. Yellow oxygen masks were dropping, one swinging in front of her face, but she could not reach for it because she was clutching her baby.

She was pressed back into her seat as the plane descended steeply, an incredibly loud whining dive. Shoes and purses ricocheted across the cabin, clanging and banging; bodies thumped against seats, the floor.

Tim was gone. Emily turned, looking for him, and

suddenly a heavy bag struck her in the head—a sudden jolt, pain, blackness, and stars. She felt dizzy and faint. The alarms continued to sound. The passengers continued to scream. The plane was still in a dive.

Emily lowered her head, clutched her infant daughter to her chest, and for the first time in her life, began to pray.

## SOCAL APPROACH CONTROL

### 5:43 A.M.

"Socal Approach, this is TransPacific 545. We have an emergency."

In the darkened building that housed Southern California Air Traffic Approach Control, senior controller Dave Marshall heard the pilot's call and glanced at his radar screen. TransPacific 545 was inbound from Hong Kong to Denver. The flight had been handed over to him from Oakland ARINC a few minutes earlier: a perfectly normal flight. Marshall touched the microphone at his cheek and said, "Go ahead, 545."

"Request priority clearance for emergency landing in Los Angeles."

The pilot sounded calm. Marshall stared at the shifting green data blocks that identified each aircraft in the air. TPA 545 was approaching the California coastline. Soon it would pass over Marina Del Rey. It was still half an hour out of LAX.

Marshall said, "Okay, 545, understand you request priority clearance to land. Say the nature of your emergency."

"We have a passenger emergency," the pilot said. "We need ambulances on the ground. I would say thirty or forty ambulances. Maybe more."

Marshall was stunned. "TPA 545, say again. Are you asking for *forty* ambulances?"

"Affirmative. We encountered severe turbulence during flight. We have injuries of passengers and flight crew."

Marshall thought, Why the hell didn't you tell me this before? He spun in his chair, beckoned to his supervisor, Jane Levine, who picked up the extra headset, punched in, and listened.

Marshall said, "TransPacific, I copy your ground request for forty ambulances."

"Jesus," Levine said, making a face. "*Forty?*"

The pilot was still calm as he replied, "Ah, roger, Approach. Forty."

"Do you need medical personnel, too? What is the nature of the injuries you are bringing in?"

"I am not sure."

Levine made a spinning gesture: Keep the pilot talking. Marshall said, "Can you give us an estimate?"

"I am sorry, no. An estimate is not possible."

"Is anyone unconscious?"

"No, I do not think so," the pilot answered. "But two are dead."

"Holy shit," Jane Levine said. "Nice of him to tell us. Who is this guy?"

Marshall hit a key on his panel, opening a data block in the upper corner of the screen. It listed the manifest for TPA 545. "Captain's John Chang. Senior pilot for TransPacific."

"Let's not have any more surprises," Levine said. "Is the aircraft all right?"

Marshall said, "TPA 545, what is the condition of your aircraft?"

"We have damage to the passenger cabin," the pilot said. "Minor damage only."

"What is the condition of the flight deck?" Marshall said.

"Flight deck is operational. FDAU is nominal." That was the Flight Data Acquisition Unit, which tracked faults within the aircraft. If it said the plane was okay, it probably was.

Marshall said, "I copy that, 545. What is the condition of your flight crew?"

"Captain and first officer in good condition."

"Ah, 545, you said there were injuries to the crew."

"Yes. Two stewardesses have been hurt."

"Can you specify the nature of the injuries?"

"I am sorry, no. One is not conscious. The other one, I don't know."

Marshall was shaking his head. "He just told us nobody was unconscious."

"I'm not buying any of this," Levine said. She picked up the red phone. "Put a fire crew on level one alert. Get the ambulances. Order neuro and ortho teams to meet the plane and have Medical notify the Westside hospitals." She looked at her watch. "I'll call the LA FSDO. This'll make his damn day."

## LAX

### 5:57 A.M.

Daniel Greene was the duty officer at the FAA Flight Standards District Office on Imperial Highway, half a mile from LAX. The local FSDOs—or Fizdos, as they were called—supervised the flight operations of commercial carriers, checking everything from aircraft maintenance to pilot training. Greene had come in early to clear the paper off his desk; his secretary had quit the week before, and the office manager refused to replace her, citing orders from Washington to absorb attrition. So now Greene went to work, muttering. Congress was slashing the FAA budget, telling them to do more with less, pretending the problem was productivity and not workload. But passenger traffic was up four percent a year, and the commercial fleet wasn't getting younger. The combination made for a lot more work on the ground. Of course, the FSDOs weren't the only ones who were strapped. Even the NTSB was broke; the Safety Board only got a million dollars a year for aircraft accidents, and—

The red phone on his desk rang, the emergency line. He picked it up; it was a woman at traffic control.

"We've just been informed of an incident on an inbound foreign carrier," she said.

"Uh-huh." Greene reached for a notepad. "Incident" had a specific meaning to the FAA, referring to the lower category of flight problems that carriers were required to report. "Accidents" involved deaths or structural damage to the aircraft and were always serious, but with incidents, you never knew. "Go ahead."

"It's TransPacific Flight 545, incoming from Hong Kong to Denver. Pilot's requested emergency landing at LAX. Says they encountered turbulence during flight."

"Is the plane airworthy?"

"They say it is," Levine said. "They've got injuries, and they've requested forty ambulances."

"*Forty?*"

"They've also got two stiffs."

"Great." Greene got up from his desk. "When's it due in?"

"Eighteen minutes."

"Eighteen minutes—Jeez, why am I getting this so late?"

"Hey, the captain just told us, we're telling you. I've notified EMS and alerted the fire crews."

"Fire crews? I thought you said the plane's okay."

"Who knows?" the woman said. "The pilot is not making much sense. Sounds like he might be in shock. We hand off to the tower in seven minutes."

"Okay," Greene said. "I'm on my way."

He grabbed his badge and his cell phone and went

out the door. As he passed Karen, the receptionist, he said, "Have we got anybody at the international terminal?"

"Kevin's there."

"Beep him," Greene said. "Tell him to get on TPA 545, inbound Hong Kong, landing in fifteen. Tell him to stay at the gate—and *don't let the flight crew leave.*"

"Got it," she said, reaching for the phone.

Greene roared down Sepulveda Boulevard toward the airport. Just before the highway ran beneath the runway, he looked up and saw the big TransPacific Airlines widebody, identifiable by its bright yellow tail insignia, taxiing toward the gate. TransPacific was a Hong Kong–based charter carrier. Most of the problems the FAA had with foreign airlines occurred with charters. Many were low-budget operators that didn't match the rigorous safety standards of the scheduled carriers. But TransPacific had an excellent reputation.

At least the bird was on the ground, Greene thought. And he couldn't see any structural damage to the widebody. The plane was an N-22, built by Norton Aircraft in Burbank. The plane had been in revenue service five years, with an enviable dispatch and safety record.

Greene stepped on the gas and rushed into the tunnel, passing beneath the giant aircraft.

He sprinted through the international building. Through the windows, he saw the TransPacific jet pulled up to the gate, and the ambulances lined up on the concrete below. The first of them was already driving out, its siren whining.

Greene came to the gate, flashed his badge, and ran down the ramp. Passengers were disembarking, pale and frightened. Many limped, their clothes torn and bloody. On each side of the ramp, paramedics clustered around the injured.

As he neared the plane, the nauseating odor of vomit grew stronger. A frightened TransPac stewardess pushed him back at the door, chattering at him rapidly in Chinese. He showed her his badge and said, "FAA! Official business! FAA!" The stewardess stepped back, and Greene slid past a mother clutching an infant and stepped into the plane.

He looked at the interior, and stopped. "Oh my God," he said softly. *"What happened to this plane?"*

## GLENDALE, CALIFORNIA

### 6:00 A.M.

"Mom? Who do you like better, Mickey Mouse or Minnie Mouse?"

Standing in the kitchen of her bungalow, still wearing her jogging shorts from her five-mile morning run, Casey Singleton finished making a tuna sandwich and put it in her daughter's lunch box. Singleton was thirty-six years old, a vice-president at Norton Aircraft in Burbank. Her daughter sat at the breakfast table, eating cereal.

"Well?" Allison said. "Who do you like better, Mickey Mouse or Minnie Mouse?" She was seven, and she ranked everything.

"I like them both," Casey said.

"I know, Mom," Allison said, exasperated. "But who do you like *better*?"

"Minnie."

"Me, too," she said, pushing the carton away.

Casey put a banana and a thermos of juice in the lunch box, closed the lid. "Finish eating, Allison, we have to get ready."

"What's quart?"

"Quart? It's a measure of liquid."

"No, Mom, *Qua-urt*," she said.

Casey looked over and saw that her daughter had picked up her new laminated plant ID badge, which had Casey's picture, and beneath that C. SINGLE-TON and then in large blue letters, QA/IRT.

"What's *Qua-urt*?"

"It's my new job at the plant. I'm the Quality Assurance rep on the Incident Review Team."

"Are you still making airplanes?" Ever since the divorce Allison had been extremely attentive to change. Even a minor alteration in Casey's hairstyle prompted repeated discussions, the subject brought up again and again, over many days. So it wasn't surprising she had noticed the new badge.

"Yes, Allie," she said, "I'm still making airplanes. Everything's the same. I just got a promotion."

"Are you still a BUM?" she said.

Allison had been delighted, the year before, to learn that Casey was a Business Unit Manager, a BUM. "Mom's a bum," she'd tell her friends' parents, to great effect.

"No, Allie. Now get your shoes on. Your dad'll be picking you up any minute."

"No, he won't," Allison said. "Dad's always late. What's your promotion?"

Casey bent over and began pulling on her daughter's sneakers. "Well," she said, "I still work at QA, but I don't check the planes in the factory any more. I check them after they leave the plant."

"To make sure they fly?"

"Yes, honey. We check them and fix any problems."

"They better fly," Allison said, "or else they'll crash!" She began to laugh. "They'll all fall out of the sky! And hit everybody in their houses, right while they're eating their cereal! That wouldn't be too good, would it, Mom?"

Casey laughed with her. "No, that wouldn't be good at all. The people at the plant would be *very* upset." She finished tying the laces, swung her daughter's feet away. "Now where's your sweatshirt?"

"I don't need it."

"Allison—"

"Mom, it's not even cold!"

"It may be cold later in the week. Get your sweatshirt, please."

She heard a horn honk on the street outside, saw Jim's black Lexus in front of the house. Jim was behind the wheel, smoking a cigarette. He was wearing a jacket and tie. Perhaps he had a job interview, she thought.

Allison stomped around her room, banging drawers. She came back looking unhappy, the sweatshirt hanging from the corner of her backpack. "How come you're always so tense when Dad picks me up?"

Casey opened the door, and they walked to the car in the hazy morning sunshine. Allison cried, "Hi, Daddy!" and broke into a run. Jim waved back, with a boozy grin.

Casey walked over to Jim's window. "No smoking with Allison in the car, right?"

Jim stared at her sullenly. "Good morning to you, too." His voice was raspy. He looked hung over, his face puffy and sallow.

"We had an agreement about smoking around our daughter, Jim."

"Do you see me smoking?"

"I'm just saying."

"And you've said it before, Katherine," he said. "I've heard it a million times. For Christ's sake."

Casey sighed. She was determined not to fight in front of Allison. The therapist had said that was the reason Allison had begun stuttering. The stuttering was better now, and Casey always made an effort not to argue with Jim, even though he didn't reciprocate. On the contrary: he seemed to take special pleasure in making every contact as difficult as possible.

"Okay," Casey said, forcing a smile. "See you Sunday."

Their arrangement was that Allison stayed with her father one week a month, leaving Monday and returning the following Sunday.

"Sunday." Jim nodded curtly. "Same as always."

"Sunday at six."

"Oh, Christ."

"I'm just checking, Jim."

"No, you're not. You're controlling, the way you always do—"

"Jim," she said. "Please. Let's not."

"Fine with me," he snapped.

She bent over. "Bye, Allie."

Allison said, "Bye, Mom," but her eyes were already distant, her voice cool; she had transferred her allegiance to her father, even before her seat belt was fastened. Then Jim stepped on the gas, and the Lexus drove away, leaving her standing there on the sidewalk. The car rounded the corner, and was gone.

Down at the end of the street, she saw the hunched figure of her neighbor Amos, taking his snarly dog for a morning walk. Like Casey, Amos worked at the plant. She waved to him, and he waved back.

Casey was turning to go back inside to dress for work, when her eye caught a blue sedan parked across the street. There were two men inside. One was reading a newspaper; the other stared out the window. She paused: her neighbor Mrs. Alvarez had been robbed recently. Who were these men? They weren't gang bangers; they were in their twenties with a clean-cut, vaguely military appearance.

Casey was thinking about taking down the license plate when her beeper went off, with an electronic squeal. She unclipped it from her shorts and read:

***JM IRT 0700 WR BTOYA

She sighed. Three stars signaled an urgent message: John Marder, who ran the factory, was calling an IRT meeting for 7 A.M. in the War Room. That was a full hour before the regular Morning Call; something was up. The final notation confirmed it, in plant slang—BTOYA.

Be There Or It's Your Ass.

# BURBANK AIRPORT

### 6:32 A.M.

Rush hour traffic crept forward in the pale morning light. Casey twisted her rearview mirror, and leaned over to check her makeup. With her short dark hair, she was appealing in a tomboyish sort of way—long limbed and athletic. She played first base on the plant softball team. Men were comfortable around her; they treated her like a kid sister, which served her well at the plant.

In fact, Casey had had few problems there. She had grown up in the suburbs of Detroit, the only daughter of an editor at the Detroit *News*. Her two older brothers were both engineers at Ford. Her mother died when she was an infant, so she had been raised in a household of men. She had never been what her father used to call "a girly girl."

After she graduated from Southern Illinois in journalism, Casey had followed her brothers to Ford. But she found writing press releases uninteresting, so she took advantage of the company's continuing education program to get an MBA from Wayne State. Along the way, she married Jim, a Ford engineer, and had a child.

But Allison's arrival had ended the marriage: confronted by diapers and feeding schedules, Jim started drinking, staying out late. Eventually they separated. When Jim announced he was moving to the West Coast to work for Toyota, she decided to move out, too. Casey wanted Allison to grow up seeing her father. She was tired of the politics at Ford, and the bleak Detroit winters. California offered a fresh start: she imagined herself driving a convertible, living in a sunny house near the beach, with palm trees outside her window; she imagined her daughter growing up tanned and healthy.

Instead, she lived in Glendale, an hour and a half inland from the beach. Casey had indeed bought a convertible, but she never put the top down. And although the section of Glendale where they lived was charming, gang territories began only a few blocks away. Sometimes at night, while her daughter slept, she heard the faint pop of gunfire. Casey worried about Allison's safety. She worried about her education in a school system where fifty languages were spoken. And she worried about the future, because the California economy was still depressed, jobs scarce. Jim had been out of work for two years now, since Toyota fired him for drinking. And Casey had survived wave after wave of layoffs at Norton, where production had slumped thanks to the global recession.

She had never imagined she would work for an aircraft company, but to her surprise she had found that her plainspoken, midwestern pragmatism was perfectly suited to the culture of engineers that dominated the company. Jim considered her rigid and "by the book," but her attention to detail had served her well at Norton, where she had for the last year been a vice-president of Quality Assurance.

She liked QA, even though the division had a nearly impossible mission. Norton Aircraft was divided into two great factions—production and engineering—which were perpetually at war. Quality Assurance stood uneasily between the two. QA was involved in all aspects of production; the division signed off every step of fabrication and assembly. When a problem emerged, QA was expected to get to the bottom of it. That rarely endeared them to mechanics on the line, or the engineers.

At the same time, QA was expected to deal with customer support problems. Customers were often unhappy with decisions they themselves had made, blaming Norton if the galleys they had ordered were in the wrong place, or if there were too few toilets on the plane. It took patience and political skill to keep everybody happy and get the problems resolved. Casey, a born peacemaker, was especially good at this.

In return for walking a political tightrope, workers in QA had the run of the plant. As a vice-president, Casey was involved in every aspect of the company's work; she had a lot of freedom and wide-ranging responsibility.

She knew her title was more impressive than the job she held; Norton Aircraft was awash in vice-presidents. Her division alone had four veeps, and competition among them was fierce. But now John Marder had just promoted her to liaison for the IRT. This was a position of considerable visibility—and it put her in line to head the division. Marder didn't make such appointments casually. She knew he had a good reason for doing it.

She turned her Mustang convertible off the Golden State Freeway onto Empire Avenue, following the chain-link fence that marked the south perimeter of Burbank Airport. She headed toward the commercial complexes—Rockwell, Lockheed, and Norton Aircraft. From a distance, she could see the rows of hangars, each with the winged Norton logo painted above—

Her car phone rang.

"Casey? It's Norma. You know about the meeting?"

Norma was her secretary. "I'm on my way," she said. "What's going on?"

"Nobody knows anything," Norma said. "But it must be bad. Marder's been screaming at the engineering heads, and he's pushed up the IRT."

John Marder was the chief operating officer at Norton. Marder had been program manager on the N-22, which meant he supervised the manufacture of that aircraft. He was a ruthless and occasionally reckless man, but he got results. Marder was also married to Charley Norton's only daughter. In recent years, he'd had a lot to say about sales. That made Marder the second most powerful man in the company after the president. It was Marder who had moved Casey up, and it was—

". . . do with your assistant?" Norma said.

"My what?"

"Your new assistant. What do you want me to do with him? He's waiting in your office. You haven't forgotten?"

"Oh, right." The truth was, she had forgotten. Some nephew of the Norton family was working his way through the divisions. Marder had assigned the kid to Casey, which meant she'd have to babysit him for the next six weeks. "What's he like, Norma?"

"Well, he's not drooling."

"Norma."

"He's better than the last one."

That wasn't saying much: the last one had fallen off a wing in major join and had nearly electrocuted himself in radio rack. "How much better?"

"I'm looking at his resume," Norma said. "Yale law school and a year at GM. But he's been in Marketing for the last three months, and he doesn't know anything about production. You're going to have to start him from the beginning."

"Right," Casey said, sighing. Marder would expect her to bring him to the meeting. "Have the kid meet me in front of Administration in ten minutes. And make sure he doesn't get lost, okay?"

"You want me to walk him down?"

"Yeah, you better."

Casey hung up and glanced at her watch. Traffic was moving slowly. Still ten minutes to the plant. She drummed her fingers on the dashboard impatiently. What could the meeting be about? There might have been an accident, or a crash.

She turned on the radio to see if it was on the news. She got a talk station, a caller saying, "—not fair to make kids wear uniforms to school. It's elitist and discriminatory—"

Casey pushed a button, changing the station.

"—trying to force their personal morality on the rest of us. I don't believe a fetus is a human being—"

She pushed another button.

"—these media attacks are all coming from people who don't like free speech—"

Where, she thought, is the *news?* Had an airplane crashed or not?

She had a sudden image of her father, reading a

big stack of newspapers from all over the country every Sunday after church, muttering to himself, "That's not the story, *that's* not the story!" as he dropped the pages in an untidy heap around his living room chair. Of course, her father had been a print journalist, back in the 1960s. It was a different world now. Now, everything was on television. Television, and the mindless chatter on the radio.

Up ahead, she saw the main gate of the Norton plant. She clicked the radio off.

Norton Aircraft was one of the great names of American aviation. The company had been started by aviation pioneer Charley Norton in 1935; during World War II it made the legendary B-22 bomber, the P-27 Tigercat fighter, and the C-12 transport for the Air Force. In recent years, Norton had weathered the hard times that had driven Lockheed out of the commercial transport business. Now it was one of just four companies that still built large aircraft for the global market. The others were Boeing in Seattle, McDonnell Douglas in Long Beach, and the European consortium Airbus in Toulouse.

She drove through acres of parking lots to Gate 7, pausing at the barrier while security checked her badge. As always, she felt a lift driving into the plant, with its three-shift energy, the yellow tugs hauling bins of parts. It wasn't a factory so much as a small city, with its own hospital, newspaper, and police force. Sixty thousand people had worked here when she first came to the company. The recession had trimmed that to thirty thousand, but the plant was still huge, covering sixteen square miles. Here they built the N-20, the narrow-body twinjet; the N-22, the widebody; and the KC-22, the Air Force fuel tanker. She could see the principal assembly buildings, each more than a mile in length.

She headed for the glass Administration building, in the center of the plant. Pulling into her parking space, she left the engine running. She saw a young man, looking collegiate in a sport coat and tie, khaki slacks, and penny loafers. The kid waved diffidently as she got out of the car.

# BLDG 64

### 6:45 A.M.

"Bob Richman," he said. "I'm your new assistant." His handshake was polite, reserved. She couldn't remember which side of the Norton family he was from, but she recognized the type. Plenty of money, divorced parents, an indifferent record at good schools, and an unshakable sense of entitlement.

"Casey Singleton," she said. "Get in. We're late."

"Late," Richman said, as he climbed into the car. "It's not even seven."

"First shift starts at six," Casey said. "Most of us in QA work the factory schedule. Don't they do that at GM?"

"I wouldn't know," he said. "I was in Legal."

"Spend any time on the floor?"

"As little as possible."

Casey sighed. It was going to be a long six weeks with this guy, she thought. "You've been over in Marketing so far?"

"Yeah, a few months." He shrugged. "But selling isn't really my thing."

She drove south toward Building 64, the huge structure where the widebody was built. Casey said, "By the way, what do you drive?"

"A BMW," Richman said.

"You might want to trade it in," she said, "for an American car."

"Why? It's made here."

"It's *assembled* here," she said. "It's not made here. The value added's overseas. The mechanics in the plant know the difference; they're all UAW. They don't like to see a Beamer in the parking lot."

Richman stared out the window. "What are you saying, something might happen to it?"

"Guaranteed," she said. "These guys don't screw around."

"I'll think about it," Richman said. He suppressed a yawn. "Jesus, it's early. What are we rushing to?"

"The IRT. It's been pushed up to seven," she said.

"IRT?"

"The Incident Review Team. Every time something happens to one of our planes, the IRT meets to figure out what happened, and what we should do about it."

"How often do you meet?"

"Roughly every two months."

"That often," the kid said.

*You're going to have to start him from the beginning.*

"Actually," Casey said, "two months is pretty infrequent. We have three thousand aircraft in revenue service around the world. With that many birds in the air, things happen. And we're serious about customer support. So every morning we hold a conference call with the service reps around the world. They report everything that caused a dispatch delay the day before. Most of it's minor stuff: a lav door jammed; a cockpit light failed. But we track it in QA, do a trend analysis, and pass that on to Product Support."

"Uh-huh . . ." He sounded bored.

"Then," Casey said, "once in a while, we hit a problem that warrants an IRT. It has to be serious, something that affects flight safety. Apparently we've got one today. If Marder's pushed the meeting up to seven, you can bet it's not a bird strike."

"Marder?"

"John Marder was the program manager for the widebody, before he became chief operating officer. So it's probably an incident involving the N-22."

She pulled over and parked in the shadow of Building 64. The gray hangar loomed above them, eight stories high and nearly a mile long. The asphalt in front of the building was strewn with disposable earplugs, which the mechanics wore so they wouldn't go deaf from the rivet guns.

They walked through the side doors and entered an interior corridor that ran around the perimeter of the building. The corridor was dotted with food dispensers, in clusters a quarter of a mile apart. Richman said, "We got time for a cup of coffee?"

She shook her head. "Coffee's not allowed on the floor."

"No coffee?" He groaned. "Why not? It's made overseas?"

"Coffee's corrosive. Aluminum doesn't like it."

Casey led Richman through another door, onto the production floor.

"Jesus," Richman said.

The huge, partially assembled widebody jets gleamed under halogen lights. Fifteen aircraft in various stages of construction were arranged in two long rows under the vaulted roof. Directly ahead of them, she saw mechanics installing cargo doors in the fuselage sections. The barrels of the fuselage were surrounded by scaffolding. Beyond the fuselage stood a forest of assembly jigs—immense tools, painted bright blue. Richman walked under one of the jigs and looked up, openmouthed. It was as wide as a house and six stories tall.

"Amazing," he said. He pointed upward at a broad flat surface. "Is that the wing?"

"The vertical stabilizer," Casey said.

"The what?"

"It's the tail, Bob."

"That's the *tail*?" Richman said.

Casey nodded. "The wing is over there," she said,

pointing across the floor. "It's two hundred feet long—almost as long as a football field."

A Klaxon sounded. One of the overhead cranes began to move. Richman turned to look.

"This your first time on the floor?"

"Yeah . . ." Richman was turning around, looking in all directions. "Awesome," he said.

"They're big," Casey said.

"Why are they all lime green?"

"We coat the structural elements with epoxy to prevent corrosion. And the aluminum skins are covered so they don't get dinged during assembly. The skins are highly polished and very expensive. So we leave that coating on until Paint Shed."

"Sure doesn't look like GM," Richman said, still turning and looking.

"That's right," Casey said. "Compared to these aircraft, cars are a joke."

Richman turned to her, surprised. "A *joke*?"

"Think about it," she said. "A Pontiac has five thousand parts, and you can build one in two shifts. Sixteen hours. That's nothing. But these things"— she gestured to the aircraft looming high above them—"are a completely different animal. The widebody has one million parts and a span time of seventy-five days. No other manufactured product in the world has the complexity of a commercial aircraft. Nothing even comes close. And nothing is built to be as durable. You take a Pontiac and run it all day every day and see what happens. It'll fall apart in a few months. But we design our jets to fly for twenty years of trouble-free service, and we build them to twice the service life."

"Forty years?" Richman said, incredulous. "You build them to last forty years?"

Casey nodded. "We've still got lots of N-5s in service around the world—and we stopped building them in 1946. We've got planes that have accumulated four times their design life—the equivalent of eighty years of service. Norton planes will do that. Douglas planes will do that. But no one else's birds will do that. You understand what I'm saying?"

"Wow," Richman said, swallowing.

"We call this the bird farm," Casey said. "The planes're so big, it's hard to get a sense of the scale." She pointed to one aircraft to their right, where small clusters of people worked at various positions, with portable lights shining up on the metal. "Doesn't look like many people, right?"

"No, not many."

"There's probably two hundred mechanics working on that plane—enough to run an entire automobile line. But this is just one position on our line—and we have fifteen positions in all. There's five thousand people in this building, right now."

The kid was shaking his head, amazed. "It looks sort of empty."

"Unfortunately," Casey said, "it *is* sort of empty. The widebody line's running at sixty percent capacity—and three of those birds are white-tails."

"White-tails?"

"Planes we're building without customers. We build at a minimum rate to keep the line open, and we haven't got all the orders we want. The Pacific Rim's the growth sector but with Japan in recession, that market's not placing orders. And everybody else is flying their planes longer. So business is very competitive. This way."

She started up a flight of metal stairs, walking quickly. Richman followed her, footsteps clanging. They came to a landing, went up another flight. "I'm telling you this," she said, "so you'll understand the meeting we're going into. We build the hell out of these planes. People here are proud of what they do. And they don't like it when something goes wrong."

They arrived at a catwalk high above the assembly floor, and walked toward a glass-walled room that seemed to be suspended from the roof. They came to the door. Casey opened it.

"And this," she said, "is the War Room."

## WAR ROOM

### 7:01 A.M.

She saw it freshly, through his eyes: a large conference room with gray indoor-outdoor carpeting, a round Formica table, tubular metal chairs. The walls were covered with bulletin boards, maps, and engineering charts. The far wall was glass, and overlooked the assembly line.

Five men in ties and shirtsleeves were there, a secretary with a notepad, and John Marder, wearing a blue suit. She was surprised he was here; the COO rarely chaired IRTs. In person, Marder was dark, intense, in his mid forties, with slicked-back hair. He looked like a cobra about to strike.

Casey said, "This is my new assistant, Bob Richman."

Marder stood up and said, "Bob, welcome," and shook the kid's hand. He gave a rare smile. Apparently Marder, with his finely tuned sense of corporate politics, was ready to fawn over any Norton family member, even a nephew on loan. It made Casey wonder if this kid was more important than she thought he was.

Marder introduced Richman to the others at the table. "Doug Doherty, in charge of structure and mechanical . . ." He gestured to an overweight man of forty-five, with a potbelly, bad complexion, and thick glasses. Doherty lived in a state of perpetual gloom; he spoke in a mournful monotone, and could always be counted on to report that everything was bad, and getting worse. Today he wore a checked shirt and a striped tie; he must have gotten out of the house before his wife saw him. Doherty gave Richman a sad, thoughtful nod.

"Nguyen Van Trung, avionics . . ." Trung was thirty, trim and quiet, self-contained. Casey liked him. The Vietnamese were the hardest-working people at the plant. The avionics guys were MIS specialists, involved with the aircraft computer programs. They represented the new wave at Norton: younger, better educated, better manners.

"Ken Burne, powerplant . . ." Kenny was red haired and freckled; his chin thrust forward, ready to fight. Notoriously profane and abusive, he was known in the plant as Easy Burne because of his quick temper.

"Ron Smith, electrical . . ." Bald and timid, nervously fingering pens in his pocket. Ron was extremely competent; it often seemed he carried the schematics for the aircraft around in his head. But he was painfully shy. He lived with his invalid mother in Pasadena.

"Mike Lee, who represents the carrier . . ." A well dressed man of fifty, gray hair cropped short, in a blue blazer with a striped tie. Mike was a former Air Force pilot, a retired one-star general. He was TransPacific's rep at the plant.

"And Barbara Ross, with the notepad." The IRT secretary was in her forties, and overweight. She glared at Casey with open hostility. Casey ignored her.

Marder waved the kid to a seat, and Casey sat down beside him. "First item," Marder said. "Casey is now liaising QA to the IRT. Considering the way she handled the RTO at DFW, she'll be our press spokesman from now on. Any questions?"

Richman looked bewildered, shaking his head. Marder turned to him, and explained: "Singleton did a good job with the press on a rejected takeoff at Dallas–Fort Worth last month. So she'll handle any press inquiries we get. Okay? We all on the same page? Let's get started. Barbara?" The secretary handed around stapled packets of paper.

"TransPacific Flight 545," Marder said. "An N-22, fuse number 271. Flight originated at Kaitak Hong Kong at 2200 hours yesterday. Uneventful takeoff, uneventful flight until approximately 0500 hours this morning, when the aircraft encountered what the pilot described as severe turbulence—"

There were groans throughout the room. "Turbulence!" The engineers shook their heads.

"—severe turbulence, producing extreme pitch excursions in flight."

"Ah, Christ," Burne said.

"The aircraft," Marder continued, "made an emergency landing at LAX, and medical units were on hand. Our preliminary report indicates fifty-six injured, and three dead."

"Oh that's very bad," Doug Doherty said in a sad monotone, blinking behind his thick glasses. "I suppose this means we've got the NTSB on our backs," he said.

Casey leaned over to Richman and whispered, "National Transportation Safety Board usually gets involved when there are fatalities."

"Not in this case," Marder said. "This is a foreign carrier, and the incident occurred in international airspace. NTSB has its hands full with the Colombia crash. We think they're going to pass on this one."

"Turbulence," Kenny Burne said, snorting. "Is there any confirmation?"

"No," Marder said. "The plane was at thirty-seven-thousand feet when the incident took place. No other aircraft at that altitude and position reported weather problems."

"Satellite weather maps?" Casey said.

"Coming."

"What about the passengers?" she said. "Did the captain make an announcement? Was the seat-belt sign on?"

"Nobody's interviewed the passengers yet. But our preliminary information suggests no announcement was made."

Richman was looking bewildered again. Casey scribbled a note on her yellow pad, tilted it so he could read: *No Turbulence.*

Trung said, "Have we debriefed the pilot?"

"No," Marder said. "The flight crew caught a connecting flight out, and left the country."

"Oh great," Kenny Burne said, throwing his pencil on the table. "Just great. We got a damn hit-and-run."

"Hold on, now," Mike Lee said, in a cool tone. "On behalf of the carrier, I think we have to recognize the flight crew acted responsibly. They have no liability here; but they face possible litigation from the civil aviation authorities in Hong Kong, and they went home to deal with it."

Casey wrote: *Flight Crew Unavailable.*

"Do, uh, we know who the captain was?" Ron Smith asked timidly.

"We do," Mike Lee said. He consulted a leather notebook. "His name is John Chang. Forty-five years old, resident of Hong Kong, six thousand hours' experience. He's TransPacific's senior pilot for the N-22. Very skilled."

"Oh yeah?" Burne said, leaning forward across the table. "And when was he last recertified?"

"Three months ago."

"Where?"

"Right here," Mike Lee said. "On Norton flight simulators, by Norton instructors."

Burne sat back, snorting unhappily.

"Do we know how he was rated?" Casey asked.

"Outstanding," Lee said. "You can check your records."

Casey wrote: *Not Human Error (?)*

Marder said to Lee, "Do you think we can get an interview with him, Mike? Will he talk to our service rep at Kaitak?"

"I'm sure the crew will cooperate," Lee said. "Especially if you submit written questions . . . I'm sure I can get them answered within ten days."

"Hmm." Marder said, distressed. "That long . . ."

"Unless we get a pilot interview," Van Trung said, "we may have a problem. The incident occurred one hour prior to landing. The cockpit voice recorder only stores the last twenty-five minutes of conversation. So in this case the CVR is useless."

"True. But you still have the FDR."

Casey wrote: *Flight Data Recorder.*

"Yes, we have the FDR," Trung said. But this clearly didn't assuage his concerns, and Casey knew why. Flight recorders were notoriously unreliable. In the media, they were the mysterious black boxes that revealed all the secrets of a flight. But in reality, they often didn't work.

"I'll do what I can," Mike Lee promised.

Casey said, "What do we know about the aircraft?"

"Aircraft's brand-new," Marder said. "Three years' service. It's got four thousand hours and nine hundred cycles."

Casey wrote: *Cycles = Takeoffs and Landings.*

"What about inspections?" Doherty asked gloomily. "I suppose we'll have to wait weeks for the records . . ."

"It had a C check in March."

"Where?"

"LAX."

"So maintenance was probably good," Casey said.

"Correct," Marder said. "As a first cut, we can't attribute this to weather, human factors, or maintenance. So we're in the trenches. Let's run the fault tree. Did anything about this aircraft cause behavior that looks like turbulence? Structural?"

"Oh sure," Doherty said miserably. "A slats deploy would do it. We'll function hydraulics on all the control surfaces."

"Avionics?"

Trung was scribbling notes. "Right now I'm wondering why the autopilot didn't override the pilot. Soon as I get the FDR download, I'll know more."

"Electrical?"

"It's possible we got a slats deploy from a sneak circuit," Ron Smith said, shaking his head. "I mean, it's *possible . . .*"

"Powerplant?"

"Yeah, powerplant could be involved," Burne said, running his hand through his red hair. "The thrust reversers could have deployed in flight. That'd make the plane nose over and roll. But if the reversers deployed, there'll be residual damage. We'll check the sleeves."

Casey looked down at her pad. She had written:

*Structural — Slats Deploy*
*Hydraulics — Slats Deploy*
*Avionics — Autopilot*
*Electrical — Sneak Circuit*
*Powerplant — Thrust Reversers*

That was basically every system on the aircraft.

"You've got a lot of ground to cover," Marder said, standing and gathering his papers together. "Don't let me keep you."

"Oh hell," Burne said. "We'll nail this in a month, John. I'm not worried."

"I am," Marder said. "Because we don't have a month. We have a week."

Cries around the table. "A week!"

"Jeez, John!"

"Come on, John, you know an IRT always takes a month."

"Not this time," Marder said. "Last Thursday our president, Hal Edgarton, received an LOI from the Beijing government to purchase fifty N-22s, with an option for another thirty. First delivery in eighteen months."

There was stunned silence.

The men all looked at each other. A big China sale had been rumored for months. The deal had been reported as "imminent" in various news accounts. But nobody at Norton really believed it.

"It's true," Marder said. "And I don't need to tell you what it means. It's an eight-billion-dollar order from the fastest-growing airframe market in the world. It's four years of full-capacity production. It'll put this company on solid financial footing into the twenty-first century. It'll fund development for the N-22 stretch and the advanced N-XX widebody. Hal and I agree: this sale means the difference between life and death for the company." Marder placed the papers in his briefcase and snapped it shut.

"I fly to Beijing Sunday, to join Hal and sign the letter of intent with the minister of transport. He's going to want to know what happened to Flight 545. And I better be able to tell him, or he'll turn around and sign with Airbus. In which case I'm in deep shit, this company is in deep shit—and everybody at this table is out of a job. The future of Norton Aircraft is riding on this investigation. So I don't want to hear anything but answers. And I want them inside a week. See you tomorrow."

He turned on his heel and walked out of the room.

# WAR ROOM

7:27 A.M.

"What an asshole," Burne said. "This is his idea of motivating the troops? Fuck him."

Trung shrugged. "It's the way he always is."

"What do you think?" Smith said. "I mean, this could be great, *great* news. Has Edgarton really got an LOI from China?"

"I bet he does," Trung said. "Because the plant's been quietly gearing up. They've made another set of tools to fab the wing; the tools are about to be shipped to Atlanta. I'll bet he's got a deal."

"What he's got," said Burne, "is a major case of cover my ass."

"Meaning?"

"Edgarton might have a tentative from Beijing. But eight billion dollars is a big order from a big gorilla. Boeing, Douglas, and Airbus are all chasing that order. The Chinese could give it to any of them at the last minute. That's their style. They do it all the time. So Edgarton's shitting rivets, worrying he won't close the deal and he'll have to tell the board he lost the big one. So what does he do? He lays it on Marder. And what does Marder do?"

"Makes it our fault," Trung said.

"Right. This TPA flight puts them in perfect position. If they close with Beijing, they're heroes. But if the deal falls apart . . ."

"It's because we blew it," Trung said.

"Right. We're the reason an eight-billion-dollar deal cratered."

"Well," Trung said, standing, "I think we better look at that plane."

# ADMINISTRATION

9:12 A.M.

Harold Edgarton, the newly appointed president of Norton Aircraft, was in his office on the tenth floor, staring out the window overlooking the plant, when John Marder walked in. Edgarton was a big man, an ex-fullback, with a ready smile and cold, watchful eyes. He had previously worked at Boeing, and had been brought in three months earlier to improve Norton's marketing.

Edgarton turned, and frowned at Marder. "This is a hell of a mess," he said. "How many died?"

"Three," Marder said.

"Christ," Edgarton said. He shook his head. "Of all the times for this to happen. Did you brief the investigation team on the LOI? Tell them how urgent this is?"

"I briefed them."

"And you'll clear it up this week?"

"I'm chairing the group myself. I'll get it done," Marder said.

"What about press?" Edgarton was still worried. "I don't want Media Relations handling this one. Benson's a drunk, the reporters all hate him. And the engineers can't do it. They don't speak English, for Christ's sake—"

"I've got it handled, Hal."

"You do? I don't want you talking to the fucking press. You're grounded."

"I understand," Marder said. "I've arranged for Singleton to do the press."

"Singleton? That QA woman?" Edgarton said. "I looked at that tape you gave me, where she talked to the reporters about the Dallas thing. She's pretty enough, but she comes off as a straight arrow."

"Well, that's what we want, isn't it?" Marder said. "We want honest all-American, no-nonsense. And she's good on her feet, Hal."

"She'd better be," Edgarton said. "If the shit hits the fan, she has to perform."

"She will," Marder said.

"I don't want anything to undermine this China deal."

"Nobody does, Hal."

Edgarton looked at Marder thoughtfully for a moment. Then he said, "You better be real clear about that," he said. "Because I don't give a damn who you're married to—if this deal doesn't close, a lot of people are going to get taken out. Not just me. A lot of other heads will roll."

"I understand," Marder said.

"You picked the woman. She's your call. The Board knows it. If anything goes wrong with her, or the IRT—you're out on your ass."

"Nothing will go wrong," Marder said. "It's under control."

"It damn well better be," Edgarton said, and turned away again to look out the window.

Marder left the room.

# LAX MAINTENANCE HANGAR 21

## 9:48 A.M.

The blue minivan crossed the runway and raced toward the line of maintenance hangars at Los Angeles Airport. From the rear of the nearest hangar, the yellow tail of the TransPacific widebody protruded, its emblem shining in the sun.

The engineers began to talk excitedly as soon as they saw the plane. The minivan rolled into the hangar and came to a stop beneath the wing; the engineers piled out. The RAMS team was already at work, a half-dozen mechanics up on the wing, wearing harnesses, scrabbling on their hands and knees.

"Let's do it!" Burne shouted, as he climbed a ladder to the wing. He made it sound like a battle cry. The other engineers scrambled up after him. Doherty followed last, climbing the ladder with a dejected air.

Casey stepped out of the van with Richman. "They all go right to the wing," Richman said.

"That's right. The wing's the most important part of an aircraft, and the most complicated structure.

They'll look at it first, then do a visual inspect on the rest of the exterior. This way."

"Where are we going?"

"Inside."

Casey walked to the nose, and climbed a roll-in staircase to the forward cabin door, just behind the cockpit. As she came to the entrance, she smelled the nauseating odor of vomit.

"Jesus," Richman said, behind her.

Casey went inside.

She knew the forward cabin would have the least damage, but even here some of the seat backs were broken. Armrests had torn free and swung into the aisles. Overhead luggage bins were cracked, the doors hanging open. Oxygen masks dangled from the ceiling, some missing. There was blood on the carpet, blood on the ceiling. Puddles of vomit on the seats.

"My God," Richman said, covering his nose. He looked pale. "This happened because of *turbulence?*"

"No," she said. "Almost certainly not."

"Then why would the pilot—"

"We don't know yet," she said.

Casey went forward to the flight deck. The cockpit door was latched open, and the flight deck appeared normal. All the logs and paperwork were missing. A tiny infant's shoe was on the floor. Bending to look at it, she noticed a mass of crumpled black metal wedged beneath the cockpit door. A video camera. She pulled it free, and it broke apart in her hands, an untidy heap of circuit boards, silver motors, and loops of tape hanging from a cracked cassette. She gave it to Richman.

"What do I do with this?"

"Keep it."

Casey headed aft, knowing it would be worse in the back. Already she was forming a picture in her mind of what had happened on this flight. "There's no question: this aircraft underwent severe pitch oscillations. That's when the plane noses up and down," she explained.

"How do you know?" Richman said.

"Because that's what makes passengers vomit. They can take yaw and roll. But pitching makes them puke."

"Why are the oxygen masks missing?" Richman said.

"People grabbed them as they fell," she said. It must have happened that way. "And the seat backs are broken—do you know how much force it takes to break an airplane seat? They're designed to withstand an impact of sixteen Gs. People in this cabin bounced around like dice in a cup. And from the damage, it looks like it went on for a while."

"How long?"

"At least two minutes," she said. An eternity for an incident like this, she thought.

Passing a shattered midships galley, they came into the center cabin. Here damage was much worse. Many seats were broken. There was a broad swath of blood across the ceiling. The aisles were cluttered with debris—shoes, torn clothing, children's toys.

A cleanup crew in blue uniforms marked NORTON IRT was collecting the personal belongings, putting them into big plastic bags. Casey turned to a woman. "Have you found any cameras?"

"Five or six, so far," the woman said. "Couple of video cameras. There's all sorts of stuff here." She reached under a seat, came out with a brown rubber diaphragm. "Like I said."

Stepping carefully over the litter in the aisles, Casey moved farther aft. She passed another divider and entered the aft cabin, near the tail.

Richman sucked in his breath.

It looked as if a giant hand had smashed the interior. Seats were crushed flat. Overhead bins hung down, almost touching the floor; ceiling panels had split apart, exposing wiring and silver insulation. There was blood everywhere; some of the seats were soaked deep maroon. The aft lavs were ripped apart, mirrors shattered, stainless-steel drawers hanging open, twisted.

Casey's attention was drawn to the left of the cabin, where six paramedics were struggling to hold a heavy shape, wrapped in white nylon mesh, that hung near a ceiling bin. The paramedics adjusted their position, the nylon webbing shifted, and suddenly a man's head flopped out of the mesh—the face gray, mouth open, eyes sightless, wisps of hair dangling.

"Oh God," Richman said. He turned and fled.

Casey went over to the paramedics. The corpse

was a middle-aged Chinese man. "What's the problem here?" she said.

"Sorry, ma'am," one of the medics said. "But we can't get him out. We found him wedged here, and he's stuck pretty good. His left leg."

One of the paramedics shined a light upward. The left leg was jammed through the overhead bin, into the silver insulation above the window panel. She tried to remember what cabling ran there, whether it was flight critical. "Just be careful getting him out," she said.

From the galley, she heard a cleanup woman say, "Strangest damn thing I ever saw."

Another woman said, "How'd it get here?"

"Damned if I know, honey."

Casey went over to see what they were talking about. The cleaning woman was holding a blue pilot's cap. It had a bloody footprint on the top.

Casey reached for it. "Where'd you find this?"

"Right here," the cleaning woman said. "Outside the aft galley. Long way from the cockpit, isn't it?"

"Yes." Casey turned the cap in her hands. Silver wings on the front, the yellow TransPacific medallion in the center. It was a pilot's cap, with a stripe for a captain, so it probably belonged to one of the backup crew. If this plane carried a backup crew; she didn't know that yet.

"Oh dear me this is awful just awful."

She heard the distinctive monotone, and looked up to see Doug Doherty, the structural engineer, striding into the aft cabin.

"What did they do to my beautiful plane?" he moaned. Then he saw Casey. "You know what this is, don't you. It's not turbulence. They were *porpoising*."

"Maybe," Casey said. "Porpoising" was the term for a series of dives and climbs. Like a porpoise leaping in water.

"Oh yes," Doherty said, gloomily. "That's what happened. They lost control. Terrible, just terrible . . ."

One of the paramedics said, "Mr. Doherty?"

Doherty looked over. "Oh don't tell me," he said. "*This* is where the guy got wedged?"

"Yes, sir . . ."

"Wouldn't you know," he said, gloomily, moving closer. "It had to be the aft bulkhead. Right where every flight-critical system comes together to— okay, let me see. What is it, his foot?"

"Yes, sir." They shone the light for him. Doherty pushed up against the body, which swayed in the harness.

"Can you hold him? Okay . . . anybody got a knife or something? You probably don't but—"

One of the paramedics gave him a pair of scissors, and Doherty began to cut. Bits of silver insulation floated to the ground. Doherty cut again and again, his hand moving quickly. Finally he stopped. "Okay. He missed the A59 cable run. He missed the A47 cable run. He's left of the hydraulic lines, left of the avionics pack . . . Okay, I can't see he hurt the plane in any way."

The paramedics, holding the dead body, stared at Doherty. One of them said, "Can we cut him out, sir?"

Doherty was still looking intently. "What? Oh yeah sure. Cut him out."

He stepped back, and the paramedics applied the big metal jaws to the upper portion of the plane. They wedged the jaws between the overhead luggage bins and the ceiling, then opened them. There was a loud cracking sound as the plastic broke.

Doherty turned away. "I can't watch," he said. "I can't watch them tear up my beautiful aircraft." He headed back to the nose. The paramedics stared as he left.

Richman came back, looking slightly embarrassed. He pointed out the windows. "What're those guys doing on the wing?"

Casey bent down, looked through the windows at the engineers on the wing. "They're inspecting the slats," she said. "Leading edge control surfaces."

"And what do slats do?"

*You'll have to start him from the beginning.*

Casey said, "You know anything about aerodynamics? No? Well, an aircraft flies because of the shape of the wing." The wing looked simple, she explained, but it was actually the most complicated physical component of the aircraft, and it took the longest to build. By comparison, the fuse—the fuselage—was simple, just a lot of round barrels riveted together. And the tail was just a fixed vertical vane, with control surfaces. But a wing was a work of art. Nearly two hundred feet long, it was incredibly strong, capable of bearing the weight of the plane. But at the same time, precisely shaped to within a hundredth of an inch.

"The shape," Casey said, "is what's crucial: it's curved on top, flat on the bottom. That means air going across the top of the wing has to move faster, and because of Bernoulli's principle—"

"I went to law school," he reminded her.

"Bernoulli's principle says the faster a gas moves, the lower its pressure. So the pressure within a moving stream is less than the air surrounding it," she said. "Since air moves faster across the top of the wing, it creates a vacuum which sucks the wing upward. The wing is strong enough to support the fuselage, so the whole plane is lifted up. That's what makes a plane fly."

"Okay . . ."

"Now. Two factors determine how much lift is created—the speed the wing moves through the air, and the amount of curvature. The greater the curvature, the greater the lift."

"Okay."

"When the wing is moving fast, during flight, going maybe point eight Mach, it doesn't need much curvature. It actually wants to be almost flat. But when the aircraft is moving slower, during takeoff and landing, the wing needs greater curvature to maintain lift. So, at those times we increase the curvature, by extending sections in the front and back—flaps at the back, and slats at the leading edge."

"Slats are like flaps, but in the front?"

"Right."

"I never noticed them before," Richman said, looking out the window.

"Smaller planes don't have them," Casey said. "But this aircraft weighs close to three-quarters of a million pounds, fully loaded. You've got to have slats on a plane this size."

As they watched, the first of the slats moved outward, then tilted down. The men on the wing stuck their hands in their pockets and watched.

Richman said, "Why are the slats so important?"

"Because," Casey said, "one possible cause of 'turbulence' is slat extension in mid flight. Remember at cruise speed, the wing should be almost flat. If the slats extend, the plane may become unstable."

"And what would make the slats extend?"

"Pilot error," Casey said. "That's the usual cause."

"But supposedly this plane had a very good pilot."

"Right. Supposedly."

"And if it wasn't pilot error?"

She hesitated. "There is a condition called uncommanded slats deployment. It means the slats extend without warning, all by themselves."

Richman frowned. "Can that happen?"

"It's been known to occur," she said. "But we don't think it's possible on this aircraft." She wasn't going to get into the details with this kid. Not now.

Richman still frowned. "If it's not possible, why are they checking?"

"Because it might have happened, and our job is to check everything. Maybe there's a problem with this particular aircraft. Maybe the control cables aren't properly rigged. Maybe there's an electrical fault in the hydraulics actuators. Maybe the proximity sensors failed. Maybe the avionics code is buggy. We'll check every system, until we find out what happened, and why. And right now, we haven't got a clue."

Four men were squeezed into the cockpit, hunched over the controls. Van Trung, who was certified for the aircraft, sat in the captain's seat; Kenny Burne was in the first officer's seat on the right. Trung was functioning the control surfaces, one after another—flaps, slats, elevators, rudder. With each test, the flight deck instrumentation was verified visually.

Casey stood outside the cockpit with Richman. She said, "You got anything, Van?"

"Nothing yet," Trung said.

"We've got diddly-squat," Kenny Burne said. "This bird is cherry. There's nothing wrong with this plane."

Richman said, "Then maybe turbulence caused it, after all."

"Turbulence my ass," Burne said. "Who said that? Is that the kid?"

"Yes," Richman said.

"Straighten the kid out, Casey," Burne said, glancing over his shoulder.

"Turbulence," Casey said to Richman, "is a famous catchall for anything that goes wrong on the flight deck. Turbulence certainly occurs, and in the old days, planes had some rough times. But these days turbulence bad enough to cause injuries is unusual."

"Because?"

"Radar, pal," Burne snapped. "Commercial aircraft are all equipped with weather radar. Pilots can see weather formations ahead and avoid them. They've also got much better communications between aircraft. If a plane hits rough weather at your flight level two hundred miles ahead of you, you'll hear about the sigmet, and get a course change. So the days of serious turbulence are over."

Richman was annoyed by Burne's tone. "I don't know," he said. "I've been on planes where turbulence got pretty rough—"

"Ever see anybody get *killed* on one of those planes?"

"Well, no . . ."

"Seen people thrown from their seats?"

"No . . ."

"Seen injuries of any kind?"

"No," Richman said, "I haven't."

"That's right," Burne said.

"But surely it is possible that—"

"Possible?" Burne said. "You mean like in court, where anything is possible?"

"No, but—"

"You're a lawyer, right?"

"Yes, I am, but—"

"Well you better get one thing straight, right now. We're not doing law, here. Law is a bunch of bullshit. This is an *aircraft*. It's a *machine*. And either something happened to this machine, or it didn't. It's not a matter of *opinion*. So why don't you shut the fuck up and let us work?"

Richman winced, but didn't back down. "Fine," he said, "but if it wasn't turbulence, there'll be evidence—"

"That's right," Burne said, "the seat-belt sign. Pilot hits turbulence, the first thing he does is flash the seat-belt sign, and make an announcement. Everybody buckles up, and nobody gets hurt. This guy never made an announcement."

"Maybe the sign doesn't work."

"Look up." With a ping, the seat-belt sign came on above their heads.

"Maybe the announcement doesn't—"

Burne's amplified voice said, "Working, working, you better believe it's working." The PA clicked off.

Dan Greene, the chubby operations inspector from the FSDO, came on board, puffing from the climb up the metal stairs. "Hey, guys, I got your certificate to ferry the plane to Burbank. I figured you want to take the bird to the plant."

"Yeah, we do," Casey said.

"Hey, Dan," Kenny Burne called. "Nice job keeping the flight crew here."

"Fuck you," Greene said. "I had my guy at the gate a minute after the plane arrived. The crew was already gone." He turned to Casey. "They get the stiff out?"

"Not yet, Dan. He's wedged in pretty tight."

"We got the other dead bodies off, and sent the seriously injured to Westside hospitals. Here's the list." He handed a sheet of paper to Casey. "Only a few are still at the 'port infirmary."

Casey said, "How many are still here?"

"Six or seven. Including a couple of stewardesses."

Casey said, "Can I talk to them?"

"Don't see why not," Greene said.

Casey said, "Van? How much longer?"

"Figure an hour, minimum."

"Okay," she said. "I'm going to take the car."

"And take fucking Clarence Darrow with you," Burne said.

# LAX

### 10:42 A.M.

Driving in the van, Richman gave a long exhale. "Jeez," he said. "Are they always so friendly?"

Casey shrugged. "They're engineers," she said. She was thinking, What did he expect? He must have dealt with engineers at GM. "Emotionally, they're all thirteen years old, stuck at the age just before boys stop playing with toys, because they've discovered girls. They're all still playing with toys. They have poor social skills, dress badly—but they're extremely intelligent and well trained, and they are very arrogant in their way. Outsiders are definitely not allowed to play."

"Especially lawyers . . ."

"Anybody. They're like chess masters. They don't waste time with amateurs. And they're under a lot of pressure now."

"You're not an engineer?"

"Me? No. And I'm a woman. And I'm from QA. Three reasons why I don't count. Now Marder's made me IRT liaison to the press, which is another strike. The engineers all hate the press."

"Will there be press on this?"

"Probably not," she said. "It's a foreign carrier, foreigners died, the incident didn't occur in the United States. And they don't have visuals. They won't pay any attention."

"But it seems so serious . . ."

"Serious isn't a criterion," she said. "Last year, there were twenty-five accidents involving substantial airframe damage. Twenty-three occurred overseas. Which ones do you remember?"

Richman frowned.

"The crash in Abu Dhabi that killed fifty-six people?" Casey said. "The crash in Indonesia that killed two hundred? Bogotá, that killed a hundred and fifty-three? You remember any of those?"

"No," Richman said, "but wasn't there something in Atlanta?"

"That's right," she said. "A DC-9 in Atlanta. How many people were killed? None. How many were injured? None. Why do you remember it? Because there was film at eleven."

The van left the runway, went through the chain-link gate, and out onto the street. They turned onto Sepulveda, and headed toward the rounded blue contours of the Centinela Hospital.

"Anyway," Casey said. "We have other things to worry about now." She handed Richman a tape recorder, clipped a microphone to his lapel, and told him what they were going to do.

## CENTINELA HOSPITAL

### 12:06 P.M.

"You want to know what happened?" the bearded man said, in an irritable voice. His name was Bennett; he was forty years old, a distributor for Guess jeans; he had gone to Hong Kong to visit the factory; he went four times a year, and always flew TransPacific. Now he was sitting up in bed, in one of the curtained-off infirmary cubicles. His head and right arm were bandaged. "The plane almost crashed, that's what happened."

"I see," Casey said. "I was wondering if—"

"Who the hell are you people, anyway?" he said. She handed him her card, introduced herself again. "Norton Aircraft? What do you have to do with it?"

"We build the airplane, Mr. Bennett."

"That piece of shit? Fuck you, lady." He threw the card back at her. "Get the fuck out of here, both of you."

"Mr. Bennett—"

"Go on, get out! Get out!"

• • •

Outside the curtained cubicle, Casey looked at Richman. "I have a way with people," she said ruefully.

Casey went to the next cubicle, and paused. Behind the curtain, she heard Chinese being spoken rapidly, first a woman's voice, and then a man's voice responding.

She decided to move on to the next bed. She opened the curtains and saw a sleeping Chinese woman in a plaster neck brace. A nurse in the room looked up, held her finger to her lips.

Casey went on to the next cubicle.

It was one of the flight attendants, a twenty-eight-year-old woman named Kay Liang. She had a large abrasion on her face and neck, the skin raw and red. She sat in a chair by the empty bed, thumbing through a six-month-old issue of *Vogue*. She explained that she had remained in the hospital to stay with Sha-Yan Hao, another stewardess, who was in the next cubicle.

"She is my cousin," she said. "I'm afraid she was hurt badly. They will not let me be in the room with her." She spoke English well, with a British accent.

When Casey introduced herself, Kay Liang looked confused. "You're from the manufacturer?" she said. "But a man was just here . . ."

"What man?"

"A Chinese man. He was here a few minutes ago."

"I don't know about that," Casey said, frowning. "But we'd like to ask you some questions."

"Of course." She put the magazine aside, folded her hands in her lap, composed.

"How long have you been with TransPacific?" Casey asked.

Three years, Kay Liang answered. And before that, three years with Cathay Pacific. She always flew international routes, she explained, because she had languages, English and French, as well as Chinese.

"And where were you when this incident occurred?"

"In the midcabin galley. Just behind business class." The flight attendants were preparing break- fast, she explained. It was about five A.M., perhaps a few minutes later.

"And what happened?"

"The plane began to climb," she said. "I know that, because I was setting out drinks, and they start- ed to slide off the trolley. Then almost immediately, there was a very steep descent."

"What did you do?"

She could do nothing, she explained, except hold on. The descent was steep. All the food and drinks fell. She thought the descent lasted about ten sec- onds, but she wasn't sure. Then there was another climb, extremely steep, and then another steep descent. On the second descent, she struck her head against the bulkhead.

"Did you lose consciousness?"

"No. But that was when I scraped my face." She gestured to her injury.

"And what happened next?"

She was not sure, she said. She was confused because the second stewardess in the galley, Miss Jiao, fell against her, and they were both knocked to the floor. "We could hear the cries of the passengers," she said. "And of course we saw them in the aisles."

Afterward, she said, the plane became level again. She was able to get up and help the passengers. The situation was very bad, she said, particularly aft. "Many injured and many bleeding, in pain. The flight attendants were overwhelmed. Also, Miss Hao, my cousin, was not conscious. She had been in the aft galley. This upset the other stewardesses. And three passengers were dead. The situation was very distressing."

"What did you do?"

"I got the emergency medical kits to care for the passengers. Then I went to the cockpit." She wanted to see if the flight crew was all right. "And I wanted to tell them the first officer had been injured in the aft galley."

"The first officer was in the aft galley when the incident occurred?" Casey said.

Kay Liang blinked. "Of the relief crew, yes."

"Not the flight crew?"

"No. The first officer of the relief crew."

"You had two crews on board?"

"Yes."

"When did the crews change?"

"Perhaps three hours earlier. During the night."

"What was the name of the injured first officer?" Casey asked.

Again, she hesitated. "I . . . I am not sure. I had not flown with the relief crew before."

"I see. And when you went to the cockpit?"

"Captain Chang had the plane in control. The crew was shaken, but not injured. Captain Chang told me that he had requested an emergency landing at Los Angeles."

"You've flown with Captain Chang before?"

"Yes. He is a very good captain. Excellent captain. I like him very much."

Protesting too much, Casey thought. The stewardess, previously calm, now appeared uneasy. Liang glanced at Casey, then looked away.

"Did there appear to be any damage to the flight deck?" Casey asked.

The stewardess frowned, thinking. "No," she said. "The flight deck appeared normal in every respect."

"Did Captain Chang say anything else?"

"Yes. He said they had an uncommanded slats deployment," she said. "He said that had caused the upset, and the situation was now under control."

Uh-oh, Casey thought. This was not going to make the engineers happy. But Casey was troubled by the stewardess's technical phrasing. She thought it unlikely that a flight attendant would know about uncommanded slats deployment. But perhaps she was just repeating what the captain had said.

"Did Captain Chang say why the slats deployed?"

"He just said, uncommanded slats deployment."

"I see," Casey said. "And do you know where the slats control is located?"

Kay Liang nodded. "It is a lever in the center pillar, between the chairs."

That was correct, Casey thought.

"Did you notice the lever at that time? While you were in the cockpit?"

"Yes. It was in the up and locked position."

Again, Casey noted the terminology. A pilot would say, Up and locked. Would a flight attendant?

"Did he say anything else?"

"He was concerned about the autopilot. He said the autopilot kept trying to cut in, to take over the plane. He said 'I had to fight the autopilot for control.'"

"I see. And what was Captain Chang's manner at this time?"

"He was calm, as always. He is a very good captain."

The girl's eyes flickered nervously. She twisted her hands in her lap. Casey decided to wait for a moment. It was an old interrogator's trick: let the subject break the silence.

"Captain Chang comes from a family of pilots," Kay Liang said, swallowing. "His father was a pilot during the war. And his son is a pilot as well. His son."

"I see . . ."

The flight attendant lapsed into silence again. There was a pause. She looked down at her hands, then back up. "So. Is there anything else I can tell you?"

Outside the cubicle, Richman said, "Isn't this the thing you said couldn't happen? Uncommanded slats deployment?"

"I didn't say it couldn't happen. I said I didn't believe it was possible on this aircraft. And if it did, it raises more questions than it answers."

"And what about the autopilot—"

"Too early to tell," she said, and went into the next cubicle.

"It must have been around six o'clock," Emily Jansen said, shaking her head. She was a slender woman of thirty, with a purple bruise on her cheek. An infant slept on her lap. Her husband lay in the bed behind her; a metal brace ran from his shoulders to his chin. She said his jaw was broken.

"I had just fed the baby. I was talking to my husband. And then I heard a sound."

"What sort of a sound?"

"A rumbling or a grinding sound. I thought it came from the wing."

Not good, Casey thought.

"So I looked out the window. At the wing."

"Did you see anything unusual?"

"No. It all looked normal. I thought the sound might be coming from the engine, but the engine looked normal, too."

"Where was the sun that morning?"

"On my side. Shining in on my side."

"So was there sunlight on the wing?"

"Yes."

"Reflecting back at you?"

Emily Jansen shook her head. "I don't really remember."

"Was the seat-belt sign on?"

"No. Never."

"Did the captain make an announcement?"

"No."

"Going back to this sound—you described it as a rumble?"

"Something like that. I don't know if I heard it, or felt it. It was almost like a vibration."

*Like a vibration.*

"How long did this vibration last?"

"Several seconds."

"Five seconds?"

"Longer. I would say ten or twelve seconds."

A classic description of a slats deployment in flight, Casey thought.

"Okay," she said. "And then?"

"The plane started going down." Jansen gestured with the flat of her hand. "Like that."

Casey continued to make notes, but she no longer really listened. She was trying to put together the sequence of events, trying to decide how the engineers should proceed. There was no question that both witnesses were telling a story consistent with slats deployment. First, rumbling for twelve seconds—exactly the time it took the slats to extend. Then a slight nose up, which would occur next. And then porpoising, as the crew tried to stabilize the aircraft.

What a mess, she thought.

Emily Jansen was saying, "Since the cockpit door was open, I could hear all the alarms. There were warning sounds—and voices in English that sounded recorded."

"Do you remember what they said?"

"It sounded like 'Fall . . . fall.' Something like that."

It was the stall alarm, Casey thought. And the audio reminder was saying, "Stall, stall."

*Damn.*

She stayed with Emily Jansen a few minutes more and then went back outside.

In the corridor, Richman said, "Does that rumbling sound mean the slats deployed?"

"It might," she said. She was tense, edgy. She wanted to get back to the aircraft, and talk to the engineers.

From one of the curtained cubicles farther down the corridor, she saw a stocky gray-haired figure emerge. She was surprised to see it was Mike Lee. She felt a burst of irritation: What the hell was the carrier rep doing talking to passengers? It was very inappropriate. Lee had no business being here.

She remembered what Kay Liang had said: *A Chinese man was just here.*

Lee came up toward them, shaking his head.

"Mike," she said. "I'm surprised to see you here."

"Why? You should give me a medal," he said. "A couple of the passengers were considering lawsuits. I talked them out of it."

"But Mike," she said. "You talked to crew members before we did. That's not right."

"What do you think, I fed them a story? Hell, they gave *me* the story. And there's not much doubt about what happened." Lee stared at her. "I'm sorry, Casey, but Flight 545 had an uncommanded slats deploy, and that means you've still got problems on the N-22."

Walking back to the van, Richman said, "What did he mean, you've still got problems?"

Casey sighed. No point in holding back now. She said, "We've had some incidents of slats deployment on the N-22."

"Wait a minute," Richman said. "You mean *this has happened before*?"

"Not like this," she said. "We've never had serious injuries. But yes, we've had problems with slats."

## EN ROUTE

1:05 P.M.

"The first episode occurred four years ago, on a flight to San Juan," Casey said, as they drove back. "Slats extended in mid flight. At first, we thought it was an anomaly, but then there were two additional incidents within a couple of months. When we investigated, we found that in every case the slats had deployed during a period of flight deck activity: right after a crew change, or when they punched in coordinates for the next leg of the flight, or something like that. We finally realized the slats lever was getting knocked loose by the crews, banged by clipboards, caught on uniform sleeves—"

"You're kidding," Richman said.

"No," she said. "We'd built a locking slot for the lever, like 'park' on an automobile transmission. But despite the slot, the lever was still being accidentally dislodged."

Richman was staring at her with the skeptical expression of a prosecuting attorney. "So the N-22 *does* have problems."

"It was a new aircraft," she said, "and all aircraft have problems when they're first introduced. You can't build a machine with a million parts and not have snags. We do everything we can to avoid them. First we design, then we test the design. Then we build, then we flight test. But there are always going to be problems. The question is how to resolve them."

"How do you resolve them?"

"Whenever we discover a problem, we send the operators a heads-up, called a Service Bulletin, which describes our recommended fix. But we don't have the authority to mandate compliance. Some carriers implement, some don't. If the problem persists, the FAA gets into the act and issues an

Airworthiness Directive to the carriers, requiring them to fix the planes in service within a specified time. But there are *always* ADs, for every model aircraft. We're proud of the fact that Norton has fewer than anyone else."

"So you say."

"Go look it up. They're all on file at Oak City."

"At what?"

"Every AD that's ever been issued is on file at the FAA's Technical Center in Oklahoma City."

"So you had one of these ADs on the N-22? Is that what you're telling me?"

"We issued a Service Bulletin recommending the carriers install a hinged metal cover that sits over the lever. That meant the captain had to flip up the cover before he could deploy the slats, but it solved the problem. As usual, some carriers made the fix, others didn't. So the FAA issued an AD making it mandatory. That was four years ago. There's been only one incident since then, but that involved an Indonesian carrier who didn't install the cover. In this country, the FAA requires carriers to comply, but abroad . . ." She shrugged. "The carriers do what they want."

"That's it? That's the whole history?"

"That's the whole history. The IRT investigated, the metal covers were installed on the fleet, and there haven't been any more slats problems on the N-22."

"Until now," Richman said.

"That's right. Until now."

# LAX MAINTENANCE HANGAR

1:22 P.M.

"A *what?*" Kenny Burne said, shouting from the cockpit of TransPacific 545. "They said it was *what?*"

"Uncommanded slats deployment," Richman said.

"Aw, blow me," Burne said. He started climbing out of the seat. "What a crock of *shit.* Hey! Clarence, come in here. See that seat? That's the first officer's seat. Sit down there."

Richman was hesitant.

"Come on, Clarence, get in the damn seat."

Awkwardly, Richman squeezed between the other men in the cockpit, and got into the first officer's chair on the right.

"Okay," Burne said. "You comfy in there, Clarence? You're not a pilot, by any chance?"

"No," Richman said.

"Okay, good. So, here you are, all set to fly the plane. Now, you see straight ahead"—he pointed to the control panel directly in front of Richman, which consisted of three video screens, each four inches square—"you got your three color CRTs showing your primary flight display, navigation display, and on the left, systems display. All those little semicircles represent a different system. All green, meaning everything's fine. Now, on the roof above your head, that's your overhead instrument panel. All the lights are out, which means everything is fine. It's dark unless there's a problem. Now, to your left is what we call the pedestal."

Burne pointed to a boxy structure that protruded between the two seats. There were a half-dozen levers in slots on the pedestal. "Now, from right to left, flaps–slats, two throttles for the engines, spoilers, brakes, thrusters. Slats and flaps are controlled by that lever nearest you, the one with the little metal cover over it. See it?"

"I see it," Richman said.

"Good. Flip up the cover, and engage the slats."

"Engage the . . ."

"Pull the slats lever down," Burne said.

Richman flicked up the cover, and struggled for a moment to move the lever.

"No, no. Grab it firmly, pull it up, then right, then down," Burne said. "Just like a gearshift on a car."

Richman closed his fingers around the handle. He pulled the lever up, across, and down. There was a distant hum.

"Good," Burne said. "Now, look at your display. See that amber SLATS EXTD indicator? It's telling you the slats are coming out of the leading edge. Okay? Takes twelve seconds to fully extend. Now they're out, and the indicator is white and says SLATS."

"I see," Richman said.

"Okay. Now retract the slats."

Richman reversed his actions, pushing the lever up, sliding it left and down to locked position, then closing the cover over the handle.

"That," Burne said, "is a commanded slats extension."

"Okay," Richman said.

"Now, let's perform an *uncommanded* slats extension."

"How do I do that?"

"Any way you can, pal. For starters, hit it with the side of your hand."

Richman reached across the pedestal, brushing the lever with his left hand. But the cover protected it. Nothing happened.

"Come on, hit that sucker."

Richman swung his hand laterally back and forth, banging against the metal. He hit it harder and harder each time, but nothing happened. The cover protected the handle; the slats lever remained up and locked.

"Maybe you could knock it with your elbow," Burne said. "Or tell you what, try this clipboard here," he said, pulling a clipboard from between the seats, and giving it to Richman. "Go on, give it a good whack. I'm looking for an accident here."

Richman struck the lever with the clipboard. It clanged against the metal. He turned the clipboard and pushed the lever with one edge. Nothing happened.

"You want to keep trying?" Burne said. "Or are you starting to get the point? *It can't be done,* Clarence. Not with that cover in place."

"Maybe the cover wasn't in place," Richman said.

"Hey," Burne said, "that's good thinking. Maybe

you can knock the cover up, by accident. Try that with your clipboard, Clarence."

Richman swung the clipboard at the edge of the cover. But the surface was smoothly curved, and the clipboard just slid off. The cover remained closed.

"No way to do it," Burne said. "Not by accident. So. What's the next thought?"

"Maybe the cover was already up."

"Good idea," Burne said. "They're not supposed to be flying with the cover up, but who the hell knows what they did. Go ahead and lift the cover up."

Richman lifted the cover up on its hinge. The handle was now exposed.

"Okay, Clarence. Go to it."

Richman swung his clipboard at the handle, banging it hard, but with most lateral movements, the raised cover still acted as a protection. The clipboard hit the cover before it struck the handle. Several times on impact, the cover dropped back down again. Richman had to keep stopping to lift the cover up again before he could proceed.

"Maybe if you used your hand," Burne suggested.

Richman tried swiping at the handle with his palm. In a few moments, the side of his hand was red, and the lever remained firmly up and locked.

"Okay," he said, sitting back in the seat. "I get the point."

"It can't be done," Burne said. "It simply can't be done. An uncommanded slats deploy is impossible on this aircraft. Period."

From outside the cockpit, Doherty said, "Are you

guys finished screwing around? Because I want to pull the recorders and go home."

As they came out of the cockpit, Burne touched Casey on the shoulder and said, "See you a minute?"

"Sure," she said.

He led her back in the plane, out of earshot of the others. He leaned close to her and said, "What do you know about that kid?"

Casey shrugged. "He's a Norton relative."

"What else?"

"Marder assigned him to me."

"You check him out?"

"No," Casey said. "If Marder sent him, I assume he's fine."

"Well, I talked to my friends in Marketing," Burne said. "They say he's a weasel. They say, don't turn your back on him."

"Kenny . . ."

"I'm telling you, something's wrong with that kid, Casey. Check him out."

With a metallic whir from the power screwdrivers, the floor panels came away, revealing a maze of cables and boxes under the cockpit.

"Jesus," Richman said, staring.

Ron Smith was directing the operation, running his hand over his bald head nervously. "That's fine," he said. "Now get the panel to the left."

"How many boxes we got on this bird, Ron?" Doherty said.

"A hundred and fifty-two," Smith said. Anybody else, Casey knew, would have to thumb through a thick sheaf of schematics before he answered. But Smith knew the electrical system by heart.

"What're we pulling?" Doherty said.

"Pull the CVR, the DFDR, and the QAR if they got one," Smith said.

"You don't know if there's a QAR?" Doherty said, teasing him.

"Optional," Smith said. "It's a customer install. I don't think they put one in. Usually on the N-22 it's in the tail, but I looked, and didn't find one."

Richman turned to Casey; he was looking puzzled again. "I thought they were getting the black boxes."

"We are," Smith said.

"There's *a hundred and fifty-two* black boxes?"

"Oh hell," Smith said, "they're all over the aircraft. But we're only after the main ones now—the ten or twelve NVMs that count."

"NVMs," Richman repeated.

"You got it," Smith said, and he turned away, bending over the panels.

It was left to Casey to explain. The public perception of an aircraft was that it was a big mechanical device, with pulleys and levers that moved control surfaces up and down. In the midst of this machinery were two magic black boxes, recording events in the flight. These were the black boxes that were always talked about on news programs. The CVR, the cockpit voice recorder, was essentially a very sturdy tape deck; it recorded the last half hour of cockpit conversation on a continuous loop of magnetic tape. Then there was the DFDR, the digital flight data recorder, which stored details of the behavior of the airplane, so that investigators could discover what had happened after an accident.

But this image of an aircraft, Casey explained, was inaccurate for a large commercial transport. Commercial jets had very few pulleys and levers—indeed, few mechanical systems of any sort. Nearly everything was hydraulic and electrical. The pilot in the cockpit didn't move the ailerons or flaps by force of muscle. Instead, the arrangement was like power steering on an automobile: when the pilot moved the control stick and pedals, he sent electrical impulses to actuate hydraulic systems, which in turn moved the control surfaces.

The truth was that a commercial airliner was controlled by a network of extraordinarily sophisticated electronics—dozens of computer systems, linked together by hundreds of miles of wiring. There were computers for flight management, for navigation, for communication. Computers regulated the engines, the control surfaces, the cabin environment.

Each major computer system controlled a whole array of sub-systems. Thus the navigation system ran the ILS for instrument landing; the DME for distance measuring; the ATC for air traffic control; the TCAS for collision avoidance; the GPWS for ground proximity warning.

In this complex electronic environment, it was

relatively easy to install a digital flight data recorder. Since all the commands were already electronic, they were simply routed through the DFDR and stored on magnetic media. "A modern DFDR records eighty separate flight parameters every second of the flight."

"Every second? How big is this thing?" Richman said.

"It's right there," Casey said, pointing. Ron was pulling an orange-and-black striped box from the radio rack. It was the size of a large shoe box. He set it on the floor, and replaced it with a new box, for the ferry flight back to Burbank.

Richman bent over, and lifted the DFDR by one stainless-steel handle. "Heavy."

"That's the crash-resistant housing," Ron said. "The actual doohickey weighs maybe six ounces."

"And the other boxes? What about them?"

The other boxes existed, Casey said, to facilitate maintenance. Because the electronic systems of the aircraft were so complicated, it was necessary to monitor the behavior of each system in case of errors, or faults, during flight. Each system tracked its own performance, in what was called Non Volatile Memory. "That's NVM."

They would download eight NVM systems today: the Flight Management Computer, which stored data on the flight plan and the pilot-entered waypoints; the Digital Engine Controller, which managed fuel burn and powerplant; the Digital Air Data

Computer, which recorded airspeed, altitude, and overspeed warnings . . .

"Okay," Richman said. "I think I get the point."

"None of this would be necessary," Ron Smith said, "if we had the QAR."

"QAR?"

"It's another maintenance item," Casey said. "Maintenance crews need to come on board after the plane lands, and get a fast readout of anything that went wrong on the last leg."

"Don't they ask the pilots?"

"Pilots will report problems, but with a complex aircraft, there may be faults that never come to their attention, particularly since these aircraft are built with redundant systems. For any important system like hydraulics, there's always a backup—and usually a third as well. A fault in the second or third backup may not show in the cockpit. So the maintenance crews come on board, and go to the Quick Access Recorder, which spits out data from the previous flight. They get a fast profile, and do the repairs on the spot."

"But there's no Quick Access Recorder on this plane?"

"Apparently not," she said. "It's not required. FAA regulations require a CVR and a DFDR. The Quick Access Recorder is optional. Looks like the carrier didn't put one on this plane."

"At least, I can't find it," Ron said. "But it could be anywhere."

He was down on his hands and knees, bent over a laptop computer plugged into the electrical panels. Data scrolled down the screen.

```
A/S PWR TEST      0 0 0 0 0 0 1 0 0 0 0
AIL SERVO COMP    0 0 0 0 1 0 0 1 0 0 0
AOA INV           1 0 2 0 0 0 1 0 0 0 1
CFDS SENS FAIL    0 0 0 0 0 0 1 0 0 0 0
CRZ CMD MON INV   1 0 0 0 0 0 2 0 1 0 0
EL SERVO COMP     0 0 0 0 0 0 0 0 0 1 0
EPR/N1 TRA-1      0 0 0 0 0 0 1 0 0 0 0
FMS SPEED INV     0 0 0 0 0 0 4 0 0 0 0
PRESS ALT INV     0 0 0 0 0 0 3 0 0 0 0
G/S SPEED ANG     0 0 0 0 0 0 1 0 0 0 0
SLAT XSIT T/O     0 0 0 0 0 0 0 0 0 0 0
G/S DEV INV       0 0 1 0 0 0 5 0 0 0 1
GND SPD INV       0 0 0 0 0 0 2 1 0 0 0
TAS INV           0 0 0 0 1 0 1 0 0 0 0
```

"This looks like data from the flight control computer," Casey said. "Most of the faults occurred on one leg, when the incident occurred."

"But how do you interpret this?" Richman said.

"Not our problem," Ron Smith said. "We just offload it and bring it back to Norton. The kids in Digital feed it to mainframes, and convert it to a video of the flight."

"We hope," Casey said. She straightened. "How much longer, Ron?"

"Ten minutes, max," Smith said.

"Oh sure," Doherty said, from inside the cockpit. "Ten minutes max, oh sure. Not that it matters. I wanted to beat rush hour traffic but now I guess I can't. It's my kid's birthday, and I won't be home for the party. My wife's going to give me hell."

Ron Smith was starting to laugh. "Can you think of anything else that might go wrong, Doug?"

"Oh sure. Lots of things. Salmonella in the cake. All the kids poisoned," Doherty said.

Casey looked out the door. The maintenance people had all climbed off the wing. Burne was finishing up his inspection of the engines. Trung was loading the DFDR into the van.

It was time to go home.

As she started down the stairs, she noticed three Norton Security vans parked in a corner of the hangar. There were about twenty security guards standing around the plane, and in various parts of the hangar.

Richman noticed, too. "What's this about?" he said, gesturing to the guards.

"We always put security on the plane, until it's ferried to the plant," she said.

"That's a lot of security."

"Yeah, well." Casey shrugged. "It's an important plane."

But she noticed that the guards all wore sidearms. Casey couldn't remember seeing armed guards before. A hangar at LAX was a secure facility. There wasn't any need for the guards to be armed.

Was there?

# BLDG 64

4:30 P.M.

Casey was walking through the northeast corner of Building 64, past the huge tools on which the wing was built. The tools were crisscrossed blue steel scaffolding, rising twenty feet above the ground. Although they were the size of a small apartment building, the tools were precisely aligned to within a thousandth of an inch. Up on the platform formed by the tools, eighty people were walking around, putting the wing together.

To the right, she saw groups of men packing tools into large wooden crates. "What's all that?" Richman said.

"Looks like rotables," Casey said.

"Rotables?"

"Spare tooling that we rotate into the line if something goes wrong with the first set. We built them to gear up for the China sale. The wing's the most time-consuming part to build; so the plan is to build the wings in our facility in Atlanta, and ship them back here."

She noticed a figure in a shirt and tie, shirtsleeves rolled up, standing among the men working on the crates. It was Don Brull, the president of the UAW local. He saw Casey, called to her, and started toward her. He made a flicking gesture with his hand; she knew what he wanted.

Casey said to Richman, "Give me a minute. I'll see you back at the office."

"Who is that?" Richman said.

"I'll meet you back at the office."

Richman remained standing there, as Brull came closer. "Maybe you want me to stay and—"

"Bob," she said. "Get lost."

Reluctantly, Richman headed back toward the office. He kept glancing over his shoulder as he walked away.

Brull shook her hand. The UAW president was a short and solidly built man, an ex-boxer with a broken nose. He spoke in a soft voice. "You know, Casey, I always liked you."

"Thanks, Don," she said. "Feeling's mutual."

"Those years when you were on the floor, I always kept my eye on you. Kept you out of trouble."

"I know that, Don." She waited. Brull was notorious for long windups.

"I always thought, Casey isn't like the others."

"What's going on, Don?" she said.

"We got some problems with this China sale," Brull said.

"What kind of problems?"

"Problems with the offset."

"What about it?" she said, shrugging. "You know there's always offset with a big sale." In recent years, airframe manufacturers had been obliged to send portions of the fabrication overseas, to the countries ordering planes. A country that ordered fifty planes expected to get a piece of the action. It was standard procedure.

"I know," Brull said. "But in the past, you guys sent part of the tail, maybe the nose, maybe some interior fab. Just parts."

"That's right."

"But these tools we're crating up," he said, "are for the wing. And the Teamsters on the loading dock are telling us these crates aren't going to Atlanta—they're going to Shanghai. The company's going to give the wing to China."

"I don't know the details of the agreement," she said. "But I doubt that—"

"The *wing,* Casey," he said. "That's core technology. Nobody ever gives away the wing. Not Boeing, nobody. You give the Chinese the wing, you give away the store. They don't need us any more. They can build the next generation of planes on their own. Ten years from now, nobody here has a job."

"Don," she said, "I'll check into this, but I can't believe the wing is part of the offset agreement."

Brull spread his hands. "I'm telling you it is."

"Don. I'll check for you. But right now I'm pretty busy with this 545 incident, and—"

"You're not listening, Casey. The local's got a problem with the China sale."

"I understand that, but—"

"A *big problem.*" He paused, looked at her. "Understand?"

She did. The UAW workers on the floor had absolute control over production. They could slow down, sick out, break tooling, and create hundreds of other intractable problems. "I'll talk to Marder," she said. "I'm sure he doesn't want a problem on the line."

"Marder *is* the problem."

Casey sighed. Typical union misinformation, she thought. The China sale had been made by Hal Edgarton and the Marketing team. Marder was just the COO. He ran the plant. He didn't have anything to do with sales.

"I'll get back to you tomorrow, Don."

"That's fine," Brull said. "But I'm telling you, Casey. Personally. I'd hate to see anything happen."

"Don," she said. "Are you threatening me?"

"No, no," Brull said quickly, with a pained expression. "Don't misunderstand. But I hear that if the 545 thing isn't cleared up fast, it could kill the China sale."

"That's true."

"And you're speaking for the IRT."

"That's true, too."

Brull shrugged. "So, I'm telling you. Feelings are strong against the sale. Some of the guys are pretty hot about it. I was you, I'd take a week off."

"I can't do that. I'm right in the middle of the investigation."

Brull looked at her.

"Don. I'll talk to Marder about the wing," she said. "But I have to do my job."

"In that case," Brull said, putting his hand on her arm, "you take real good care, honey."

# ADMINISTRATION

4:40 P.M.

"No, no," Marder said, pacing in his office. "This is nonsense, Casey. There's no way we'd send the wing to Shanghai. What do they think, we're crazy? That'd be the end of the company."

"But Brull said—"

"The Teamsters are screwing with the UAW, that's all. You know how rumors run through the plant. Remember when they all decided composites made you sterile? Damn guys wouldn't come to work for a month. But it wasn't true. And this one's not true, either. Those tools are going to Atlanta," he said. "And for one very good reason. We're fabbing the wing in Atlanta so that the senator from Georgia will stop messing with us every time we go to the Ex-Im Bank for a big loan. It's a jobs program for the senior senator from Georgia. Got it?"

"Then somebody better get the word out," Casey said.

"Christ," Marder said. "They know this. The union reps sit in on all the management meetings. It's usually Brull himself."

"But he didn't sit in on the China negotiations."

"I'll speak to him," Marder said.

Casey said, "I'd like to see the offset agreement."

"And you will, as soon as it's final."

"What are we giving them?"

"Part of the nose, and the empennage," Marder

said. "Same as we did for France. Hell, we can't give them anything else, they're not competent to build it."

"Brull was talking about interfering with the IRT. To stop the China sale."

"Interfering how?" Marder said, frowning at her. "Did he threaten you?"

Casey shrugged.

"What did he say?"

"He recommended a week's vacation."

"Oh, for Christ's sake," Marder said, throwing up his hands. "This is ridiculous. I'll talk to him tonight, straighten him out. Don't worry about this. Just stay focused on the job. Okay?"

"Okay."

"Thanks for the heads-up. I'll take care of this for you."

## NORTON QA

### 4:53 P.M.

Casey rode the elevator from the ninth floor down to her own offices, on the fourth floor. She replayed the meeting with Marder, and decided he wasn't lying. His exasperation had been genuine. And it was true what Marder said—rumors flew through the plant, all the time. A couple of years back, there was a week when the UAW guys had all come up to her, asking solicitously, "How do you feel?" It was days before she learned there was a rumor she had cancer.

Just a rumor. Another rumor.

She walked down the corridor, past the photographs of famous Norton aircraft from the past, with a celebrity posed in front: Franklin Delano Roosevelt beside the B-22 that carried him to Yalta; Errol Flynn, with smiling girls in the tropics, in front of an N-5; Henry Kissinger, on the N-12 that had taken him to China in 1972. The photographs were sepia-toned, to convey a sense of age, and the stability of the company.

She opened the doors to her offices: frosted glass, with raised lettering: "Quality Assurance Division." She came into a large open room. The secretaries sat in the bullpen; executive offices lined the walls.

Norma sat by the door, a heavyset woman of indeterminate age, with blue-rinse hair, and a cigarette dangling from her mouth. It was against regulations to smoke in the building, but Norma did as she pleased. She had been with the company as long as anyone could remember; it was rumored that she had been one of the girls in the picture with Errol Flynn, and that she had had a hot affair with Charley Norton back in the fifties. Whether any of that was true or not, she certainly knew where all the bodies were buried. Within the company, she was treated with a deference bordering on fear. Even Marder was cautious around her.

Casey said, "What've we got, Norma?"

"The usual panic," Norma said. "Telexes are flying." She handed a stack to Casey. "The Fizer in Hong Kong phoned three times for you, but he's gone home now. Fizer in Vancouver was on the horn half an hour ago. You can probably still get him."

Casey nodded. It was not surprising that the Flight Service Representatives in the major hubs would be checking in. The FSRs were Norton employees assigned to the carriers, and the carriers would be worried about the incident.

"And, let's see," Norma said. "The Washington office is all atwitter, they've heard the JAA is going to exploit this on Airbus's behalf. What a surprise. Fizer in Düsseldorf wants a confirm it was pilot error. Fizer in Milan wants information. Fizer in Abu Dhabi wants a week in Milan. Fizer in Bombay heard engine failure. I straightened him out. And your daughter said to tell you she did not need her sweatshirt."

"Great."

Casey took the faxes back to her office. She found Richman sitting at her desk. He looked up in surprise, and rose quickly from her chair. "Sorry."

Casey said, "Didn't Norma find you an office?"

"Yes, I have one," Richman said, walking around the desk. "I was just, ah, just wondering what you wanted me to do with this." He held up a plastic bag with the video camera they had found on the plane.

"I'll take it."

He gave it to her. "So. What happens now?"

She dropped the stack of telexes on her desk. "I'd say you're through for the day," she said. "Be here tomorrow at seven."

He left, and she sat down in her chair. Everything seemed to be as she had left it. But she noticed that the second drawer on the desk was not quite closed. Had Richman been going through her desk?

Casey pulled the drawer open, revealing boxes of computer disks, stationery, a pair of scissors, some felt-tip pens in a tray. It all looked undisturbed. But still . . .

She heard Richman leave, then went back down the hall to Norma's desk. "That kid," she said, "was sitting behind my desk."

"Tell me," Norma said. "The little twerp asked me to get him coffee."

"I'm surprised Marketing didn't straighten him out," Casey said. "They had him a couple of months."

"As a matter of fact," Norma said, "I was talking to Jean over there, and she says they hardly ever saw him. He was always on the road."

"On the road? A new kid, a Norton relative? Marketing would never send him on the road. Where'd he go?"

Norma shook her head. "Jean didn't know. You want me to call Travel, and find out?"

"Yeah," Casey said. "I do."

Back in her office, she turned to the plastic bag on the desk, opened it, and pulled the videotape from the shattered camera. She set the tape to one side. Then she dialed Jim's number, hoping to talk to Allison, but she got the answering machine. She hung up without leaving a message.

She thumbed through the telexes. The only one

that interested her was from the FSR in Hong Kong. As always, he was way behind the curve.

```
FROM: RICK RAKOSKI, FSR HK
TO: CASEY SINGLETON, QA/IRT
    NORTON BBK

TRANSPACIFIC AIRLINES TODAY REPORTS
FLIGHT 545, AN N-22, FUSE 271,
FOREIGN REGISTRY 098/443/HB09,
FLYING FROM HK TO DENVER EXPERIENCED
A TURBULENCE UPSET DURING CRUISE
FL370 APPROXIMATELY 0524 UTC
POSITION 39 NORTH/170 EAST. SOME
PASSENGERS AND CREW SUFFERED MINOR
INJURIES. AIRCRAFT MADE EMERGENCY
LANDING LAX.

FLIGHT PLAN, PASSENGER AND CREW MAN-
IFEST ATTACHED. PLS ADVISE SOONEST.
```

The telex was followed by four pages of passenger manifest and crew list. She glanced at the crew list:

```
JOHN ZHEN CHANG, CAPTAIN        5/7/51
LEU ZAN PING, FIRST OFFICER     3/11/59
RICHARD YONG, FIRST OFFICER     9/9/61
GERHARD REIMANN, FIRST OFFICER 7/23/49
HENRI MARCHAND, ENGINEER        4/25/69
THOMAS CHANG, ENGINEER          6/29/70
ROBERT SHENG, ENGINEER          6/13/62
```

It was an international crew, of the kind that often flew for charter companies. Hong Kong crews had often flown for the Royal Air Force and were extremely well trained.

She counted the names: seven people. Such a large flight crew was not strictly necessary. The N-22 was designed to be flown by a two-man crew, just a captain and first officer. But all the Asian carriers were expanding rapidly, and they generally carried larger crews for extra training hours.

Casey went on. The next telex was from the FSR in Vancouver.

```
FROM: S. NIETO, FSR VANC
TO: C. SINGLETON, QA/IRT

FYI FLIGHT CREW TPA 545 DEADHEAD ON
TPA 832, FROM LAX TO VANCOUVER,
FIRST OFFICER LU ZAN PING TAKEN OFF
THE AIRCRAFT AT VANCOUVER MEDICAL
EMERGENCY DUE TO PREVIOUSLY
UNRECOGNIZED HEAD INJURY. F/O
COMATOSE IN VANC GEN HOSP, DETAILS
TF. REMAINING CREW OF TPA 545
TRANSIT BACK TO HONG KONG TODAY.
```

So the first officer had been seriously injured, after all. He must have been in the tail when the incident occurred. The man whose cap they had found.

Casey dictated a telex to the FSR in Vancouver, asking him to interview the first officer as soon as possible. She dictated another to the FSR in Hong

Kong, suggesting an interview with Captain Chang on his return.

Norma buzzed her. "No luck on the kid," she said.

"Why not?"

"I talked to Maria in Travel. They didn't make Richman's arrangements. His trips were charged to a special company account, a set-aside for foreign, off-budget stuff. But she heard the kid ran up a hell of a big charge."

"How big?" Casey said.

"She didn't know." Norma sighed. "But I'm having lunch tomorrow with Evelyn in Accounting. She'll give me everything."

"Okay. Thanks, Norma."

Casey turned back to the telexes on her desk. They were all other business:

Steve Young, from the FAA's Certification office, asking about fire-retardant test results on seat cushions the previous December.

A query from Mitsubishi about burnouts of their five-inch displays in the first-class section of American N-22 widebodies.

A list of revisions to the N-20 Aircraft Maintenance Manual (MP. 06-62-02).

A revision of the prototype Virtual Heads-Up Display units, to be delivered in the next two days.

A memo from Honeywell advising replacement of the D-2 electrical bus on all FDAU units numbered A-505/9 through A-609/8.

Casey sighed, and went to work.

# GLENDALE

7:40 P.M.

She was tired when she got home. The house seemed empty without Allison's lively chatter. Too tired to cook, Casey went into the kitchen and ate a cup of yogurt. Allison's colorful drawings were taped on the refrigerator door. Casey considered calling her; but it was right around her bedtime, and she didn't want to interrupt if Jim was putting her to sleep.

She also didn't want Jim to think she was checking up on him. That was a sore point between them. He always felt she was checking.

Casey went into the bathroom and turned on the shower. She heard the phone ring, and went back into the kitchen to answer it. It was probably Jim. She picked up the receiver. "Hello, Jim—"

"Don't be stupid, bitch," a voice said. "You want trouble, you'll get it. Accidents happen. We're watching you *right now.*"

*Click.*

She stood in the kitchen, holding the phone in her hand. Casey had always thought of herself as levelheaded, but her heart was pounding. She forced herself to take a deep breath as she hung up the receiver. She knew these calls happened sometimes. She'd heard of other vice-presidents getting threatening calls at night. But it had never happened to her, and she was surprised at how frightened she felt. She took another deep breath, tried to shrug it off. She picked up her yogurt, stared at it, put it down. She was suddenly aware that she was alone in a house with all the blinds open.

She went around the living room, closing the blinds. When she came to the front window, she looked out at the street. In the light of the overhead street lamps, she saw a blue sedan parked a few yards up from her house.

There were two men inside.

She could see their faces clearly, through the windshield. The men stared at her as she stood at the window.

*Shit.*

She went to the front door, bolted it, locked the security chain. She set the burglar alarm, her fingers trembling and clumsy as she punched in the code. Then she flicked off the living room lights, pressed her body to the wall, and peered out the window.

The men were still in the car. They were talking now. As she watched, one of them pointed toward her house.

She went back to the kitchen, fumbled in her purse, found her pepper spray. She clicked off the safety. With her other hand she grabbed the phone, and pulled it on the long cord back to the dining room. Still watching the men, she called the police.

"Glendale police."

She gave her name and address. "There are men parked outside my house. They've been here since this morning. I've just gotten a threatening call."

"Okay, ma'am. Is anybody in the house with you now?"

"No. I'm alone."

"Okay, ma'am. Lock your door and set the alarm if you have one. A car is on the way."

"Hurry," she said.

On the street, the men were getting out of the car. And walking toward her house.

They were dressed casually, in polo shirts and slacks, but they looked grim and tough. As they came forward they split up, one walking onto the lawn, the other heading toward the back of the house. Casey felt her heart thump in her chest. Had she locked the back door? Gripping the pepper spray, she moved back to the kitchen, turning off the light there, then past the bedroom to the back door. Looking through the window in the door, she saw one of the men standing in the back alley. He was looking around cautiously. Then his gaze turned toward the back door. She crouched down, slipped the chain across the door.

She heard the sound of soft footsteps, coming closer to the house. She looked up at the wall, just above her head. There was a keypad for the alarm, and a big red button marked EMERGENCY. If she hit that button, a screeching alarm would sound. Would that scare him away? She wasn't sure. Where were the damned police, anyway? How long had it been?

She realized she could not hear the footsteps any more. Cautiously, she raised her head until she could peer out the bottom corner of the window.

The man was walking down the alley away from her now. Then he turned, circling the house. Heading back to the street.

Staying low, Casey ran back to the front of the bungalow, to the dining room. The first man was no longer on her lawn. She felt panic: Where was he? The second man appeared on the lawn, squinted at the front of her house, then headed back toward the car. She saw the first man was already in the car, sitting in the passenger seat. The second man opened the door and got in behind the wheel. Moments later, a black-and-white squad car pulled up behind the blue sedan. The men in the car seemed surprised, but they didn't do anything. The squad car turned on its spotlight, and one officer got out, moving cautiously forward. He talked to the men in the sedan for a moment. Then the two men got out. They all walked up the steps to her front door—the policeman and the two men from the car.

She heard the doorbell ring, and answered it.

A young police officer said, "Ma'am, is your name Singleton?"

"Yes," she said.

"You work for Norton Aircraft?"

"Yes, I do . . ."

"These gentlemen are Norton Security. They say they're guarding you."

Casey said, "What?"

"Would you like to see their credentials?"

"Yes," she said. "I would."

The policeman shone a flashlight while the two

men each held out their wallets for her. She recognized credentials for Norton Security Services.

"We're sorry, ma'am," one of the guards said. "We thought you knew. We've been told to check the house every hour. Is that all right with you?"

"Yes," she said. "It's fine."

The policeman said to her, "Is there anything else?"

She felt embarrassed; she mumbled thanks, and went back inside.

"Make sure you lock that door, ma'am," the guards said politely.

"Yeah, I got 'em parked in front of my house, too," Kenny Burne said. "Scared the hell out of Mary. What's going on, anyway? Labor negotiations aren't for another two years."

"I'll call Marder," she said.

"Everybody gets guards," Marder said, on the phone. "The union threatens one of our team, we detail guards. Don't worry about it."

"Did you talk to Brull?" she said.

"Yeah, I straightened him out. But it'll take a while for the word to filter down to the rank and file. Until it does, everybody gets guards."

"Okay," she said.

"This is a precaution," Marder said. "Nothing more."

"Okay," she said.

"Get some sleep," Marder said, and hung up.

# TUESDAY

# GLENDALE

### 5:45 A.M.

She awoke uneasily, before the alarm went off. She pulled on a bathrobe, walked to the kitchen to turn on the coffee, and looked out the front window. The blue sedan was still parked on the street, the men inside. She considered taking her five-mile run, she needed that exercise to start her day, but decided against it. She knew she shouldn't feel intimidated. But there was no point in taking chances.

She poured a cup of coffee, sat in the living room. Everything looked different to her today. Yesterday, her little bungalow felt cozy; today, it felt small, defenseless, isolated. She was glad Allison was spending the week with Jim.

Casey had lived through periods of labor tension in the past; she knew that the threats usually came to nothing. But it was wise to be cautious. One of the first lessons Casey had learned at Norton was that the factory floor was a very tough world—tougher even than the assembly line at Ford. Norton was one of the few remaining places where an unskilled high school graduate could earn $80,000 a year, with overtime. Jobs like that were scarce, and getting scarcer. The competition to get those jobs, and to keep them, was fierce. If the union thought the China sale was going to cost jobs, they could very well act ruthlessly to stop it.

She sat with the coffee cup on her lap and realized

she dreaded going to the factory. But of course she had to go. Casey pushed the cup away, and went into the bedroom to dress.

When she came outside and got into her Mustang, she saw a second sedan pull up behind the first. As she drove down the street, the first car pulled out, following her.

So Marder had ordered two sets of guards. One to watch her house, and one to follow her.

Things must be worse than she thought.

She drove into the plant with an uncharacteristic feeling of unease. First shift had already started; the parking lots were full, acres and acres of cars. The blue sedan stayed right behind her as Casey pulled up to the security guard at Gate 7. The guard waved her through and, by some unseen signal, allowed the blue sedan to follow directly, without putting the barrier down. The sedan stayed behind her until she parked at her spot in Administration.

She got out of the car. One of the guards leaned out the window. "Have a nice day, ma'am," he said.

"Thanks. I will."

The guard waved. The sedan sped off.

Casey looked around at the huge gray buildings: Building 64, to the south. Building 57 to the east, where the twinjet was built. Building 121, the Paint Shed. The maintenance hangars in a row off to the west, lit by the sun rising over the San Fernando Mountains. It was a familiar landscape; she'd spent five years here. But today she was uncomfortably aware of the vast dimensions, the emptiness of the place in early morning. She saw two secretaries walking into the Administration building. No one else. She felt alone.

She shrugged her shoulders, shaking off her fears. She was being silly, she told herself. It was time to go to work.

## NORTON AIRCRAFT

### 6:34 A.M.

Rob Wong, the young programmer at Norton Digital Information Systems, turned away from the video monitors and said, "Sorry, Casey. We got the flight recorder data—but there's a problem."

She sighed. "Don't tell me."

"Yeah. There is."

She was not really surprised to hear it. Flight data recorders rarely performed correctly. In the press, these failures were explained as the consequence of crash impacts. After an airplane hit the ground at five hundred miles an hour, it seemed reasonable to think that a tape deck might not be working.

But within the aerospace industry, the perception was different. Everyone knew flight data recorders failed at a very high rate, even when the aircraft didn't crash. The reason was that the FAA did not require they be checked before every flight. In practice, they were usually function-checked about once a year. The consequence was predictable: the flight recorders rarely work.

Everybody knew about the problem: the FAA, the NTSB, the airlines, and the manufacturers. Norton had conducted a study a few years back, a random check of DFDRs in active service. Casey had been on that study committee. They'd found that only one recorder in six worked properly.

Why the FAA would mandate the installation of FDRs, without also requiring that they be in working order before each flight, was a frequent subject of late-night discussion in aerospace bars from Seattle to Long Beach. The cynical view was that malfunctioning FDRs were in everybody's interest. In a nation besieged by rabid lawyers and a sensational press, the industry saw little advantage to providing an objective, reliable record of what had gone wrong.

"We're doing the best we can, Casey," Rob Wong said. "But the flight recorder data is anomalous."

"Meaning what?"

"It looks like the number-three bus blew about twenty hours before the incident, so the frame syncs are out on the subsequent data."

"The frame syncs?"

"Yeah. See, the FDR records all the parameters in rotation, in data blocks called frames. You get a reading for, say, airspeed, and then you get another reading four blocks later. Airspeed readings should be continuous across the frames. If they're not, the frames are out of sync, and we can't build the flight. I'll show you."

He turned to the screen, pressing keys. "Normally, we can take the DFDR and generate the airplane in tri-axis. There's the plane, ready to go."

A wire-frame image of the Norton N-22 wide-body appeared on the screen. As she watched, the wire frame filled in, until it took on the appearance of an actual aircraft in flight.

"Okay, now we feed it your flight recorder data . . ."

The airplane seemed to ripple. It vanished from the screen, then reappeared. It vanished again, and when it reappeared the left wing was separated from the fuselage. The wing twisted ninety degrees, while the rest of the airplane rolled to the right. Then the tail vanished. The entire plane vanished, reappeared again, vanished again.

"See, the mainframe's trying to draw the aircraft," Rob said, "but it keeps hitting discontinuities. The wing data doesn't fit the fuse data which doesn't fit the tail data. So it breaks up."

"What do we do?" she said.

"Resync the frames, but that'll take time."

"How long? Marder's on my back."

"It could be a while, Casey. The data's pretty bad. What about the QAR?"

"There isn't one."

"Well, if you're really stuck, I'd take this data to Flight Sims. They have some sophisticated programs there. They may be able to fill in the blanks faster, and tell you what happened."

"But Rob—"

"No promises, Casey," he said. "Not with this data. Sorry."

# BLDG 64

### 6:50 A.M.

Casey met Richman outside Building 64. They walked together in the early-morning light toward the building. Richman yawned.

"You were in Marketing, weren't you?"

"That's right," Richman said. "We sure didn't keep these hours."

"What did you do there?"

"Not much," he said. "Edgarton had the whole department doing a full court press on the China deal. Very hush-hush, no outsiders allowed. They threw me a little legal work on the Iberian negotiation."

"Any travel?"

Richman smirked. "Just personal."

"How's that?" she said.

"Well, since Marketing had nothing for me to do, I went skiing."

"Sounds like fun. Where'd you go?" Casey said.

"You ski?" Richman said. "Personally, I think the best skiing outside of Gstaad is Sun Valley. That's my favorite. You know, if you have to ski in the States."

She realized he hadn't answered her question. By then they had walked through the side door, into

Building 64. Casey noticed the workers were openly hostile, the atmosphere distinctly chilly.

"What's this?" Richman said. "We got rabies
today?"

"Union thinks we're selling them out on China."

"Selling them out? How?"

"They think management's shipping the wing to
Shanghai. I asked Marder. He says no."

A Klaxon sounded, echoing through the building.
Directly ahead, the big yellow overhead crane
cranked to life, and Casey saw the first of the huge
crates containing the wing tooling rise five feet up
into the air on thick cables. The crate was constructed of reinforced plywood. It was as broad as a
house, and probably weighed five tons. A dozen
workers walked alongside the crate like pallbearers,
hands up, steadying the load as it moved toward one
of the side doors and a waiting flatbed truck.

"If Marder says no," Richman said, "then what's
the problem?"

"They don't believe him."

"Really? Why not?"

Casey glanced to her left, where other tools were
being crated for shipment. The huge blue tools were
first packed in foam, then braced internally, and then
crated. All that padding and bracing was essential,
she knew. Because even though the tools were twenty feet in length, they were calibrated to thousandths
of an inch. Transporting them was an art in itself.
She looked back at the crate, moving on the hoist.

All the men standing beneath it were gone.

The crate was still moving laterally, ten yards from where they stood.

"Uh-oh," she said.

"What?" Richman said.

She was already pushing him. *"Go!"* she said, shoving Richman to the right, toward the shelter of the scaffolding that stood beneath a partially assembled fuselage. Richman resisted; he didn't seem to understand that—

*"Run!"* she shouted. "It's going to break loose!"

He ran. Behind her, Casey heard the creak of rending plywood, and a metallic *twang!* as the first of the hoist cables snapped, and the giant crate began to slide from its harness. They had just reached the fuselage scaffolding when she heard another *twang!* and the crate smashed down onto the concrete floor. Slivers of plywood exploded in all directions, whistling through the air. They were followed by a thunderous *whomp!* as the crate toppled over on its side. The sound reverberated through the building.

"Jesus *Christ*," Richman said, turning to look back at her. "What was *that?*"

"That," she said, "is what we call a job action."

Men were running forward, hazy forms in the cloud of lingering dust. There were shouts, and calls for help. The medic alarm sounded, ringing through the building. At the opposite side of the building, she saw Doug Doherty, shaking his head mournfully.

Richman looked over his shoulder, and pulled a

four-inch splinter of plywood from the back of his jacket. "Jeez," he said. He took the jacket off, inspected the tear, putting his finger through the hole.

"That was a warning," Casey said. "And they've also wrecked the tool. Now it'll have to be uncrated and rebuilt. This means weeks of delay."

Floor supervisors in white shirts and ties ran forward into the group around the fallen crate. "What happens now?" Richman said.

"They'll take names and kick ass," Casey said. "But it won't do any good. There'll be another incident tomorrow. There's no way to stop it."

"This was a warning?" Richman said. He put the jacket back on.

"To the IRT," she said. "A clear signal: Watch your backs, watch your heads. We'll see falling wrenches, all sorts of accidents, whenever we're on the floor. We'll have to be careful."

Two workmen broke away from the group around the crate, and started walking toward Casey. One man was burly, wearing jeans and a red-checked work shirt. The other was taller, and wore a baseball cap. The man in the work shirt held a steel drill-press stanchion in his hand, swinging it at his side like a metal club.

"Uh, Casey," Richman said.

"I see them," she said. She was not going to get rattled by a couple of floor goons.

The men walked steadily toward her. Suddenly a supervisor appeared in front of them, holding his clipboard, demanding the men show their badges. The men stopped to talk to the supervisor, glaring at Casey over his head.

"We won't have any trouble with them," she said. "An hour from now, they'll be gone." She went back to the scaffolding, picked up her briefcase. "Come on," she said to Richman. "We're late."

# BLDG 64/IRT

7:00 A.M.

Chairs scraped as everyone pulled up to the Formica table. "Okay," Marder said, "let's get started. We're having some union activity, aimed at stalling this investigation. Don't let it get to you. Keep your eye on the ball. First item: weather data."

The secretary passed sheets around the room. It was a report from the LA Traffic Control Center on a form marked "Federal Aviation Administration / REPORT OF AIRCRAFT ACCIDENT."

Casey read:

### WEATHER DATA

CONDITIONS IN ACCIDENT AREA AT TIME OF ACCIDENT

JAL054 a B747/R was 15 minutes ahead of TPA545 on the same route and 1000′ above. JAL054 made no report of turbulence.

## REPORT JUST PRIOR TO ACCIDENT

UAL829 a B747/R reported moderate chop at the FIR 40.00 North/165.00 East at FL350. This was 120 miles north and 14 minutes ahead of TPA545. UAL829 made no other reports of turbulence.

## FIRST REPORT SUBSEQUENT TO ACCIDENT

AAL722 reported continuous light chop at 39 North/170 East at FL350. AAL722 was on the same route, 2000' below, and approximately 29 minutes behind TPA545. AAL722 made no report of turbulence.

"We still have satellite data coming, but I think the evidence speaks for itself. The three aircraft nearest in time and location to TransPacific report no weather except light chop. I'm ruling out turbulence as a cause of this accident."

There were nods around the table. No one disagreed.

"Anything else for the record?"

"Yes," Casey said. "Passenger and crew interviews agree the seat-belt sign was never illuminated."

"Okay. Then we're done with weather. Whatever happened to that plane wasn't turbulence. Flight recorder?"

"Data's anomalous," Casey said. "They're working on it."

"Visual inspection of the plane?"

"The interior was severely damaged," Doherty said, "but the exterior was fine. Cherry."

"Leading edge?"

"No problem we could see. We'll have the aircraft here today, and I'll look at the drive tracks and latches. But so far, nothing."

"You test the control surfaces?"

"No problem."

"Instrumentation?"

"Bravo Zulu."

"How many times you test 'em?"

"After we heard the passenger's story from Casey, we did ten extensions. Trying to get a disagree. But everything's normal."

"What story? Casey? You got something from the interviews?"

"Yes," she said. "One passenger gave a report of a slight rumble coming from the wing, lasting ten to twelve seconds . . ."

"*Shit,*" Marder said.

". . . followed by a slight nose up, then a dive . . ."

"God*damn* it!"

". . . and then a series of violent pitch excursions."

Marder glared at her. "Are you telling me it's the slats again? Have we still got a slats problem on this aircraft?"

"I don't know," Casey said. "One of the flight attendants reported that the captain said he had an uncommanded slats deployment, and that he'd had problems with the autopilot."

"Christ. *And* problems with the autopilot?"

"Screw him," Burne said. "This captain changes his story every five minutes. Tells Traffic Control he's got turbulence, tells the stewardess he's got slats. Right now I bet he's telling the carrier a whole different story. Fact is, we don't know what happened in that cockpit."

"It's obviously slats," Marder said.

"No, it's not," Burne said. "The passenger Casey talked to said the rumbling sound came from the wing or the engines, isn't that right?"

"Right," Casey said.

"But when she looked at the wing, she didn't see the slats extend. Which she would have seen, if it happened."

"Also true," Casey said.

"But she couldn't have seen the engines, because they'd be hidden by the wing. It's possible the thrust reversers deployed," Burne said. "At cruise speed that'd produce a definite rumble. Followed by a sudden drop in airspeed, probably a roll. The pilot shits, tries to compensate, overreacts—bingo!"

"Any confirmation thrusters deployed?" Marder said. "Damage to the sleeves? Unusual rubstrips?"

"We looked yesterday," Burne said, "and we didn't find anything. We'll do ultrasound and X rays today. If there's something there, we'll find it."

"Okay," Marder said. "So we're looking at slats and thrusters, and we need more data. What about the NVMs? Ron? The faults suggest anything?"

They turned to Ron Smith. Under their gaze, Ron

hunched lower in his seat, as if trying to pull his head between his shoulders. He cleared his throat.

"Well?" Marder said.

"Uh, yeah, John. We have a slats disagree on the FDAU printout."

"So the slats *did* deploy."

"Well, actually—"

"And the plane started porpoising, beat hell out of the passengers, and killed three. Is that what you're telling me?"

No one spoke.

"*Jesus,*" Marder said. "What is the *matter* with you people? This problem was supposed to be fixed four years ago! Now you're telling me it *wasn't?*"

The group fell silent and stared at the table, embarrassed and intimidated by Marder's rage.

"God*damn* it!" Marder said.

"John, let's not get carried away." It was Trung, the avionics head, speaking quietly. "We're overlooking a very important factor. The autopilot."

There was a long silence.

Marder glared at him. "What about it?" he snapped.

"Even if the slats extend in cruise flight," Trung said, "the autopilot will maintain perfect stability. It's programmed to compensate for errors like that. The slats extend; the AP adjusts; the captain sees the warning and retracts them. Meanwhile the plane continues, no problem."

"Maybe he went out of autopilot."

"He must have. But why?"

"Maybe your autopilot's screwed up," Marder said. "Maybe you got a bug in your code."

Trung looked skeptical.

"It's happened," Marder said. "There was an autopilot problem on that USAir flight in Charlotte last year. Put the plane into an uncommanded roll."

"Yes," Trung said, "but that wasn't caused by a bug in the code. Maintenance pulled the 'A' flight control computer to repair it, and when they reinstalled it, they didn't push it in the shelf far enough to fully engage the connector pins. The thing kept making intermittent electrical connection, that's all."

"But on Flight 545, the stewardess said the captain had to fight the autopilot for control."

"And I'd expect that," Trung said. "Once the aircraft exceeds flight params, the autopilot actively attempts to take over. It sees erratic behavior, and assumes nobody is flying the plane."

"Did that show up on the fault records?"

"Yes. They indicate the autopilot tried to kick in, every three seconds. I assume the captain kept overriding it, insisting on flying the plane himself."

"But this is an experienced captain."

"Which is why I think Kenny is right," Trung said. "We have no idea what took place in that cockpit."

They all turned to Mike Lee, the carrier representative. "How about it, Mike?" Marder said. "Can we get an interview or not?"

Lee sighed philosophically. "You know," he said,

"I've spent a lot of time in meetings like this. And the tendency is always to blame the guy who's not there. It's human nature. I've already explained to you why the flight crew left the country. Your own records confirm the captain is a first-rate pilot. It's possible he made an error. But given the history of problems with this aircraft—slats problems—I'd look first at the aircraft. And I'd look hard."

"We will," Marder said. "Of course we will, but—"

"Because it's to no one's advantage," Lee said, "to get into a pissing match. You are focused on your pending deal with Beijing. Fine, I understand. But I would remind you TransPacific is also a valued customer of this company. We've bought ten planes to date, and we have twelve more on order. We're expanding our routes, and we are negotiating a feeder deal with a domestic carrier. We don't need any bad press at the moment. Not for the planes we've bought from you, and certainly not for our pilots. I hope I'm being clear."

"Clear as a fucking bell," Marder said. "I couldn't have said it better myself. Guys, you have your marching orders. Get on with it. I want *answers.*"

## BLDG 202/FSIM

7:59 A.M.

"Flight 545?" Felix Wallerstein said. "It's very disturbing. Very disturbing indeed." Wallerstein was a silver-haired, courtly man from Munich. He ran the

Norton Flight Simulator and Pilot Training program with Germanic efficiency.

Casey said, "Why do you say 545 is disturbing?"

"Because," he shrugged. "How could it happen? It does not seem possible."

They walked through the large main room of Building 202. The two flight simulators, one for each model in service, stood above them. They appeared to be truncated nose sections of the aircraft, held up by a spidery array of hydraulic lifts.

"Did you get the data from the flight recorder? Rob said you might be able to read it."

"I tried," he said. "With no success. I hesitate to say it is useless, but—what about the QAR?"

"No QAR, Felix."

"Ah." Wallerstein sighed.

They came to the command console, a series of video screens and keyboards to one side of the building. Here the instructors sat while they monitored the pilots being trained in the simulator. Two of the simulators were being used as they watched.

Casey said, "Felix, we're concerned the slats extended in cruise flight. Or possibly the thrust reversers."

"So?" he said. "Why should that matter?"

"We've had problems with slats before . . ."

"Yes, but that is long since fixed, Casey. And slats cannot explain such a terrible accident. Where people are killed? No, no. Not from slats, Casey."

"You're sure?"

"Absolutely. I will show you." He turned to one of

the instructors at the console. "Who's flying the N-22 now?"

"Ingram. First officer from Northwest."

"Any good?"

"Average. He's got about thirty hours."

On the closed-circuit video screen, Casey saw a man in his mid thirties, sitting in the pilot's seat of the simulator.

"And where is he now?" Felix said.

"Uh, let's see," the instructor said, consulting his panels. "He's over the mid-Atlantic, FL three-thirty, point eight Mach."

"Good," Felix said. "So he's at thirty-three thousand feet, eight-tenths the speed of sound. He's been there awhile, and everything seems to be fine. He's relaxed, maybe a little lazy."

"Yes, sir."

"Good. Deploy Mr. Ingram's slats."

The instructor reached over and pushed a button.

Felix turned to Casey. "Watch carefully, please."

On the video screen, the pilot remained casual, unconcerned. But a few seconds later, he leaned forward, suddenly alert, frowning at his controls.

Felix pointed to the instructor's console, and the array of screens. "Here you can see what he is seeing. On his Flight Management display, the slats indicator is flashing. And he's noticed it. Meanwhile, you see the plane gives a slight nose up . . ."

The hydraulics whirred, and the big cone of the simulator tilted upward a few degrees.

"Mr. Ingram now checks his slats lever, as he should. He finds it is up and locked, which is puzzling, since it means he has an uncommanded slats deploy . . ."

The simulator remained tilted up.

"So Mr. Ingram is thinking it over. He has plenty of time to decide what to do. The aircraft is quite stable on autopilot. Let's see what he decides. Ah. He decides to play with his controls. He pulls the slats lever down, then up . . . He's trying to clear the warning. But that doesn't change anything. So. He now realizes he has a system problem on his aircraft. But he remains calm. He's still thinking . . . What will he do? . . . He changes the autopilot params . . . he descends to a lower altitude, and reduces his airspeed . . . absolutely correct . . . He is still in the nose-up attitude, but now at more favorable conditions of altitude and speed. He decides to try the slats lever again . . ."

The instructor said, "Should I let him off the hook?"

"Why not?" Felix said. "I believe we have made the point."

The instructor punched a button. The simulator tilted back to level.

"And so," Felix said, "Mr. Ingram is restored to normal flight. He makes a note of his problem for the maintenance crews, and he continues on his way to London."

"But he stayed in the autopilot," Casey said. "What if he went out of it?"

"Why should he do that? He's in cruise flight; the autopilot has been operating the plane for at least half an hour."

"But suppose he did."

Felix shrugged, turned to the instructor. "Fail his autopilot."

"Yes, sir."

An audible alarm sounded. On the video screen, they saw the pilot look at the controls and take the stick in his hands. The audible alarm ended; the cockpit became silent. The pilot continued to hold the stick.

"Is he flying the plane now?" Felix asked.

"Yes, sir," the instructor said. "He's at FL two-ninety, point seven-one Mach, with autopilot disabled."

"Okay," Felix said. "Deploy his slats."

The instructor pushed a button.

On the systems monitor in the training console, the slats warning flashed, first amber, then white. Casey looked at the adjacent video screen and saw the pilot leaning forward. He had noticed the warning in the cockpit.

"Now," Felix said. "Once again we see the aircraft nose-up, but this time Mr. Ingram must control it himself . . . So he brings the stick back . . . very slightly, very delicately . . . Good . . . and now he is stable."

He turned to Casey. "You see?" He shrugged. "It is very puzzling. Whatever happened to that TransPacific flight, it cannot be the slats. And not thrusters either. In either case, the autopilot will compensate and maintain control. I tell you, Casey, what happened to that aircraft is a mystery."

Back in the sunlight, Felix walked over to his Jeep, with a surfboard on top. "I have a new Henley board," he said. "Like to see it?"

"Felix," she said. "Marder is starting to scream."

"So? Let him. He enjoys it."

"What do you think happened to 545?"

"Well. Let us be frank. Flight characteristics of an N-22 are such that if slats deploy at cruise speed, and the captain goes out of the autopilot, the aircraft is rather sensitive. You remember, Casey. You did the study on it, three years ago. Right after we made the final fix on the slats."

"That's right," she said, thinking back. "We put together a special team to review flight stability issues on the N-22. But we concluded there wasn't a control-sensitivity problem, Felix."

"And you were correct," Felix said. "There is no problem. All modern aircraft maintain flight stability with computers. A jet fighter cannot be flown at all without computers. Fighters are inherently unstable. Commercial transports are less sensitive, but even so, computers shift fuel, adjust attitude, adjust CG, adjust thrust on the engines. Moment to moment, the computers continuously make small changes, to stabilize the aircraft."

"Yes," Casey said, "but the planes can be flown out of autopilot as well."

"Absolutely," Felix said. "And we train our captains to do that. Because the aircraft is sensitive, when the nose goes up, the captain must *very gently* bring it back again. If he corrects too strongly, the plane noses over. In that case he must pull up, but again, very gently, or he is likely to overcorrect, so the plane would climb sharply then nose down once more. And this is precisely the pattern that occurred on the TransPacific flight."

"You're saying it was pilot error."

"Ordinarily I would think so, except the pilot was John Chang."

"He's a good pilot?"

"No," Felix said. "John Chang is a *superb* pilot. I see a lot of pilots here, and some are truly gifted. It's more than quick reflexes and knowledge and experience. It's more than skill. It's a kind of instinct. John Chang is one of the five or six best captains I have ever trained on this aircraft, Casey. So whatever happened to Flight 545, it cannot be pilot error. Not with John Chang in the chair. I am sorry, but in this case, it has to be a problem with the aircraft, Casey. It *has* to be that aircraft."

## TO HANGAR 5

9:15 A.M.

As they walked back across the vast parking lot, Casey was lost in thought.

"So," Richman said, after a while. "Where are we?"

"Nowhere."

No matter how she put the evidence together, that was the conclusion she came to. They had nothing solid so far. The pilot had said it was turbulence, but it wasn't turbulence. A passenger gave a story consistent with slats deployment, but slats deployment couldn't explain the terrible damage to the passengers. The stewardess said the captain fought the autopilot, which Trung said only an incompetent captain would do. Felix said the captain was superb.

Nowhere.

They were nowhere.

Beside her, Richman trudged along, not saying anything. He had been quiet all morning. It was as if the puzzle of Flight 545, so intriguing to him yesterday, had now proven too complex.

But Casey was not discouraged. She had come to this point many times before. It was no surprise the early evidence appeared to conflict. Because aircraft accidents were rarely caused by a single event or error. The IR teams expected to find event cascades: one thing leading to another, and then another. In the end, the final story would be complex: a system failed; a pilot responded; the aircraft reacted unexpectedly, and the plane got in trouble.

Always a cascade.

A long chain of small errors and minor mishaps.

She heard the whine of a jet. Looking up, she saw a Norton widebody silhouetted against the sun. As it passed over her, she saw the yellow TransPacific insignia on the tail. It was the ferry flight from LAX. The big jet landed gently, puffed smoke at the wheels, and headed toward Maintenance Hangar 5.

Her beeper went off. She unclipped it from her belt.

> ***N-22 ROTR BURST MIAMI
> TV NOW BTOYA

"Oh hell," she said. "Let's find a TV."

"Why? What's the matter?" Richman said.

"We have trouble."

# BLDG 64/IRT

9:20 A.M.

"This was the scene just moments ago at Miami International Airport when a Sunstar Airlines jet burst into flames, after its left starboard engine exploded without warning, showering the crowded runway with a hail of deadly shrapnel."

"Aw, blow me!" Kenny Burne shouted. A half-dozen engineers were crowded around the TV set, blocking Casey's view as she came into the room.

"Miraculously, none of the two hundred and seventy passengers on board were injured. The N-22 Norton widebody was revving for takeoff when passengers noticed clouds of black smoke coming from the engine. Seconds later, the plane was rocked by an explosion as the left starboard engine literally blew to pieces, and was quickly engulfed in flames."

The screen didn't show that, it just showed an

N-22 aircraft, seen from a distance, with dense black smoke gushing from beneath the wing.

"Left starboard engine," Burne snarled. "As opposed to the *right* starboard engine, you silly twit?"

The TV now showed close-ups of passengers milling around the terminal. There were quick cuts. A young boy of seven or eight said, "All the people got excited, because of the smoke." Then they cut to a teenage girl who shook her head, tossing her hair over her shoulder, and said, "It was rully, rully scary. I just saw the smoke and, like, I was rully scared." The interviewer said, "What were your thoughts when you heard the explosion?" "I was rully scared," the girl said. "Did you think it was a bomb?" she was asked. "Absolutely," she said. "A terrorist bomb."

Kenny Burne spun on his heel, throwing his hands in the air. "Do you believe this shit? They're asking *kids* what they *thought*. This is the news. 'What did you think?' 'Golly, I swallowed my popsicle.'" He snorted. "Airplanes that kill—and the travelers who love them!"

On the screen, the TV program now showed an elderly woman who said, "Yes, I thought I was going to die. Of course, you have to think that." Then a middle-aged man: "My wife and I prayed. Our whole family knelt down on the runway and thanked the Lord." "Were you frightened?" the interviewer asked. "We thought we were going to die," the man said. "The cabin was filled with smoke—it's a miracle we escaped with our lives."

Burne was yelling again: "You asshole! In a *car* you would have died. In a *nightclub* you would have died. But not in a Norton widebody! We designed it so you'd escape with your miserable fucking life!"

"Calm down," Casey said. "I want to hear this." She was listening intently, waiting to see how far they'd take the story.

A strikingly beautiful Hispanic woman in a beige Armani suit stood facing the camera, holding up a microphone: "While passengers now appear to be recovering from their ordeal, their fate was far from certain earlier this afternoon, when a Norton widebody blew up on the runway, orange flames shooting high into the sky . . ."

The TV again showed the earlier telephoto shot of the plane on the runway, with smoke billowing from under the wing. It looked about as dangerous as a doused campfire.

"Wait a minute, wait a minute!" Kenny said. "A *Norton widebody* exploded? A *Sunstar piece-of-shit engine* exploded." He pointed to the screen image. "That's a goddamn rotor burst, and the blade fragments broke through the cowling *which is just what I told them would happen!*"

Casey said, "You told them?"

"Hell yes," Kenny said. "I know all about this. Sunstar bought six engines from AeroCivicas last year. I was the Norton consultant on the deal. I borescoped the engines and found a shitload of damage—blade notch breakouts and vane cracks. So I told Sunstar to reject them." Kenny was waving his hands. "But why pass up a bargain?" he said. "Sunstar rebuilt them instead. During teardown, we found a lot of corrosion, so the paper on the overseas overhauls was probably faked. I told them again: Junk 'em. But Sunstar put them on the planes. So now the rotor blows—big fucking surprise—and the fragments cut into the wing, so that nonflammable hydraulic fluid is *smoking*. It ain't on fire because the fluid won't burn. And it's *our* fault?"

He spun, pointing back to the screen.

". . . seriously frightening all two hundred and seventy passengers on board. Fortunately, there were no injuries . . ."

"That's right," Burne said. "No penetration of the fuse, lady. No injury to anybody. The wing absorbed it—our wing!"

". . . and we are waiting to speak to officials from the airline about this frightening tragedy. More later. Back to you, Ed."

The camera cut back to the newsroom, where a sleek anchorman said, "Thank you, Alicia, for that up-to-the-minute report on the shocking explosion at Miami Airport. We'll have more details as they emerge. Now back to our regularly scheduled program."

Casey sighed, relieved.

"I can't believe this *horseshit!*" Kenny Burne shouted. He turned and stomped out of the room, banging the door behind him.

"What's his problem?" Richman said.

"For once, I'd say he's justified," Casey said. "The fact is, if there's an engine problem, it's not Norton's fault."

"What do you mean? He said he was the consultant—"

"Look," Casey said. "You have to understand: We build airframes. We don't build engines and we don't repair them. We have nothing to do with engines."

"Nothing? I hardly think—"

"Our engines are supplied by other companies— GE, Pratt and Whitney, Rolls-Royce. But reporters never understand that distinction."

Richman looked skeptical. "It seems like a fine point . . ."

"It's nothing of the sort. If your electricity goes out, do you call the gas company? If your tires blow, do you blame the car maker?"

"Of course not," Richman said, "but it's still your airplane—engines and all."

"No, it's not," Casey said. "We build the plane, and then install the brand of engine the customer selects. Just the way you can put any one of several brands of tires on your car. But if Michelin makes a batch of bad tires, and they blow out, that's not Ford's fault. If you let your tires go bald and get in an accident, that's not Ford's fault. And it's exactly the same with us."

Richman was still looking unconvinced.

"All we can do," Casey said, "is certify that our

planes fly safely with the engines we install. But we can't force carriers to maintain those engines properly over the life of the aircraft. That's not our job— and understanding that is fundamental to knowing what actually occurred. The fact is, the reporter got the story backward."

"Backward? Why?"

"That aircraft had a rotor burst," Casey said. "Fan blades broke off the rotor disk and the cowling around the engine didn't contain the fragments. The engine blew because it wasn't correctly maintained. It should never have happened. But our wing absorbed the flying fragments, protecting passengers in the cabin. So the real meaning of this event is that Norton aircraft are so well built that they protected two hundred and seventy passengers from a bad engine. We're actually heroes—but Norton stock will fall tomorrow. And some of the public may be afraid to fly on a Norton aircraft. Is that an appropriate response to what actually happened? No. But it's an appropriate response to what's being reported. That's frustrating for people here."

"Well," Richman said, "at least they didn't mention TransPacific."

Casey nodded. That had been her first concern, the reason she had rushed across the parking lot to the TV set. She wanted to know if the news reports would link the Miami rotor burst to the TPA in-flight incident the day before. That hadn't happened—at least not yet. But sooner or later, it would.

"We'll start getting calls now," she said. "The cat is out of the bag."

## HANGAR 5

9:40 A.M.

There were a dozen security guards standing outside Hangar 5, where the TransPacific jet was being inspected. But this was standard procedure whenever a RAMS team from Recovery and Maintenance Services entered the plant. RAMS teams circled the globe, troubleshooting stranded aircraft; they were FAA-licensed to repair them in the field. But since members were chosen for expertise rather than seniority, they were non-union; and there was often friction when they came into the factory.

Within the hangar, the TransPacific widebody stood in the glare of halogen lights, nearly hidden behind a gridwork of roll-up scaffolding. Technicians swarmed over every part of the plane. Casey saw Kenny Burne working the engines, cursing his powerplant crew. They had deployed the two thrust reverser sleeves that flared out from the nacelle, and were doing fluorescent and conductivity tests on the curved metal cowls.

Ron Smith and the electrical team were standing on a raised platform beneath the midships belly. Higher up, she saw Van Trung through the cockpit windows, his crew testing the avionics.

And Doherty was out on the wing, leading the

structure team. His group had used a crane to remove an eight-foot aluminum section, one of the inboard slats.

"Big bones," Casey said to Richman. "They inspect the biggest components first."

"It looks like they're tearing it apart," Richman said.

A voice behind them. "It's called destroying the evidence!"

Casey turned. Ted Rawley, one of the flight test pilots, sauntered up. He was wearing cowboy boots, a western shirt, dark sunglasses. Like most of the test pilots, Teddy cultivated an air of dangerous glamour.

"This is our chief test pilot," Casey said. "Teddy Rawley. They call him Rack 'em Rawley."

"Hey," Teddy protested. "I haven't drilled a hole yet. Anyway, it's better than Casey and the Seven Dwarfs."

"Is that what they call her?" Richman said, suddenly interested.

"Yeah. Casey and her dwarfs." Rawley gestured vaguely to the engineers. "The little fellas. Heigh-ho, heigh-ho." He turned away from the plane, punched Casey on the shoulder. "So: How you doing, kid? I called you the other day."

"I know," she said. "I've been busy."

"I'll bet you have," Teddy said. "I bet Marder's got the screws on everybody. So: What've the engineers found? Wait a minute, let me guess—they found absolutely nothing, right? Their beautiful plane is *perfect*. So: Must be pilot error, am I right?"

Casey said nothing. Richman looked uncomfortable.

"Hey," Teddy said. "Don't be shy. I've heard it all before. Let's face it, the engineers are all card-carrying members of the Screw the Pilots Club. That's why they design planes to be practically automatic. They just *hate* the idea that somebody might actually *fly* them. It's so untidy, to have a warm body in the seat. Makes 'em crazy. And of course, if anything bad happens, it must be the pilot. Gotta be the pilot. Am I right?"

"Come on, Teddy," she said. "You know the statistics. The overwhelming majority of accidents are caused by—"

It was at that point that Doug Doherty, crouched on the wing above them, leaned over and said dolefully, "Casey, bad news. You'll want to see this."

"What is it?"

"I'm pretty sure I know what went wrong on Flight 545."

She climbed the scaffolding and walked out on the wing. Doherty was crouched over the leading edge. The slats were now removed, exposing the innards of the wing structure.

She got down on her hands and knees next to him, and looked.

The space for the slats was marked by a series of drive tracks—little rails, spaced three feet apart, that the slats slid out on, driven by hydraulic pistons. At the forward end of the rail was a rocker pin, which allowed the slats to tilt downward. At the back of the compartment she saw the folding pistons which drove the slats along the tracks. With the slats removed, the pistons were just metal arms poking out into space. As always, whenever she saw the innards of an aircraft, she had a sense of enormous complexity.

"What is it?" she said.

"Here," Doug said.

He bent over one of the protruding arms, pointing to a tiny metal flange at the back, curved into a hook. The part was not much larger than her thumb.

"Yes?"

Doherty reached down, pushed the flange back with his hand. It flicked forward again. "That's the locking pin for the slats," he said. "It's spring-loaded, actuated by a solenoid back inside. When the slats retract, the pin snaps over, holds them in place."

"Yes?"

"Look at it," he said, shaking his head. "It's bent."

She frowned. If it was bent, she couldn't see it. It looked straight to her eye. "Doug . . ."

"No. Look." He set a metal ruler against the pin, showing her that the metal was bent a few millimeters to the left. "And that's not all," he said. "Look at the action surface of the hinge. It's been worn. See it?"

He handed her a magnifying glass. Thirty feet above the ground, she leaned over the leading edge and peered at the part. There was wear, all right. She saw a ragged surface on the locking hook. But you would expect a certain amount of wear, where the metal of the latch engaged the slats. "Doug, do you really think this is significant?"

"Oh yes," he said, in a funereal tone. "You got maybe two, three millimeters of wear here."

"How many pins hold the slat?"

"Just one," he said.

"And if this one is bad?"

"The slats could pop loose in flight. They wouldn't necessarily fully extend. They wouldn't have to. Remember, these are low-speed control surfaces. At cruise speed the effect magnifies: a slight extension would change the aerodynamics."

Casey frowned, squinting at the little part through the magnifying glass. "But why would the lock suddenly open, two-thirds of the way through the flight?"

He was shaking his head. "Look at the other pins," Doherty said, pointing down the wing. "There's no wear on the action surface."

"Maybe the others were changed out, and this one wasn't?"

"No," he said. "I think the others are original. This one was changed. Look at the next pin down. See the parts stamp at the base?"

She saw a tiny embossed figure, an *H* in a triangle, with a sequence of numbers. All parts manufacturers stamped their parts with these symbols. "Yeah . . ."

"Now look at this pin. See the difference? On this

part, the triangle is upside down. This is a counter-feit part, Casey."

For aircraft manufacturers, counterfeiting was the single biggest problem they faced as they approached the twenty-first century. Media attention focused mostly on counterfeit consumer items, like watches, CDs, and computer software. But there was a booming business in all sorts of manufactured items, including auto parts and air-plane parts. Here the problem of counterfeiting took a new and ominous turn. Unlike a phony Cartier watch, a phony airplane part could kill you.

"Okay," she said. "I'll check the maintenance records, find out where it came from."

The FAA required commercial carriers to keep extraordinarily detailed maintenance records. Every time a part was changed out, it was noted in a maintenance log. In addition, the manufacturers, though not required to, maintained an exhaustive ship's record of every part originally on the plane, and who had manufactured it. All this paperwork meant that every one of the aircraft's one million parts could be traced back to its origin. If a part was swapped out from one plane to another, that was known. If a part was taken off and repaired, that was known. Each part on a plane had a history of its own. Given enough time, they could find out exact-ly where this part had come from, who had installed it, and when.

She pointed to the locking pin in the wing. "Have you photographed it?"

"Oh sure. We're fully documented."

"Then pull it," she said. "I'll take it to Metals. By the way, could this situation give you a slats disagree warning?"

Doherty gave a rare smile. "Yes, it could. And my guess is, it did. You got a nonstandard part, Casey, and it failed the aircraft."

Coming off the wing, Richman was chattering excitedly. "So, is that it? It's a bad part? Is that what happened? It's solved?"

He was getting on her nerves. "One thing at a time," she said. "We have to check."

"Check? What do we have to check? Check how?"

"First of all, we have to find out where that part came from," she said. "Go back to the office. Tell Norma to make sure the maintenance records are coming from LAX. And have her telex the Fizer in Hong Kong to ask for the carrier's records. Tell him the FAA requested them and we want to look at them first."

"Okay," Richman said.

He headed off toward the open doors of Hangar 5, out into the sunlight. He walked with a sort of swagger, as if he were a person of importance, in possession of valuable information.

But Casey wasn't sure that they knew anything at all.

At least, not yet.

# OUTSIDE HANGAR 5

10:00 A.M.

She came out of the hangar, blinking in the morning sun. She saw Don Brull getting out of his car, over by Building 121. She headed toward him.

"Hello, Casey," he said, as he slammed the door. "I was wondering when you'd get back to me."

"I talked to Marder," she said. "He swears the wing isn't being offset to China."

Brull nodded. "He called me last night. Said the same thing." He didn't sound happy.

"Marder insists it's just a rumor."

"He's lying," Brull said. "He's doing it."

"No way," Casey said. "It doesn't make sense."

"Look," Brull said. "It doesn't matter to me, personally. They close this plant in ten years, I'll be retired. But that'll be about the time your kid starts college. You'll be looking at those big tuition payments, and you won't have a job. You thought about that?"

"Don," she said. "You said it yourself, it doesn't make sense to offset the wing. It'd be pretty reckless to—"

"Marder's reckless." He squinted at her in the sunlight. "You know that. You know what he's capable of."

"Don—"

"Look," Brull said. "I know what I'm talking about. Those tools aren't being shipped to Atlanta,

Casey. They're going to San Pedro—to the port. And down in San Pedro, they're building special marine containers for shipment."

So that was how the union was putting it together, she thought. "Those are oversize tools, Don," she said. "We can't ship them by road or rail. Big tools always go by boat. They're building containers so they can send them through the Panama Canal. That's the only way to get them to Atlanta."

Brull was shaking his head. "I've seen the bills of lading. They don't say Atlanta. They say Seoul, Korea."

"Korea?" she said, frowning.

"That's right."

"Don, that *really* doesn't make sense—"

"Yes, it does. Because it's a cover," Brull said. "They'll send them to Korea, then transship from Korea to Shanghai."

"You have copies of the bills?" she said.

"Not with me."

"I'd like to see them," she said.

Brull sighed. "I can do that, Casey. I can get them for you. But you're putting me in a very difficult situation here. The guys aren't going to let this sale happen. Marder tells me to calm 'em down—but what can I do? I run the local, not the plant."

"What do you mean?"

"It's out of my hands," he said.

"Don—"

"I always liked you, Casey," he said. "But you hang around here, I can't help you."

And he walked away.

# OUTSIDE HANGAR 5

10:04 A.M.

The morning sun was shining; the plant around her was cheerfully busy, mechanics riding their bicycles from one building to another. There was no sense of threat, or danger. But Casey knew what Brull had meant: she was now in no-man's land. Anxious, she pulled out her cell phone to call Marder when she saw the heavyset figure of Jack Rogers coming toward her.

Jack covered aerospace for the *Telegraph-Star,* an Orange County paper. In his late fifties, he was a good, solid reporter, a reminder of an earlier generation of print journalists who knew as much about their beat as the people they interviewed. He gave her a casual wave.

"Hi, Jack," she said. "What's up?"

"I came over," he said, "about that wing tool accident this morning in 64. The one the crane dropped."

"Tough break," she said.

"They had another accident with the AJs this morning. Tool was loaded onto the flatbed truck, but the driver took a turn too fast over by Building 94. Tool slid off onto the ground. Big mess."

"Uh-huh," Casey said.

"This is obviously a job action," Rogers said. "My sources tell me the union's opposed to the China sale."

"I've heard that," she said, nodding.

"Because the wing's going to be offset to Shanghai as part of the sales agreement?"

"Come on, Jack," she said. "That's ridiculous."

"You know that for a fact?"

She took a step back from him. "Jack," she said. "You know I can't discuss the sale. No one can, until the ink's dry."

"Okay," Rogers said. He took out his notepad. "It does seem like a pretty crazy rumor. No company's ever offset the wing. It'd be suicide."

"Exactly," she said. In the end, she kept coming back to that same question. Why would Edgarton offset the wing? Why would any company offset the wing? It just made no sense.

Rogers glanced up from his pad. "I wonder why the union thinks the wing's being sent offshore?"

She shrugged. "You'll have to ask them." He had sources in the union. Certainly Brull. Probably others as well.

"I hear they've got documents that prove it."

Casey said, "They show them to you?"

Rogers shook his head. "No."

"I can't imagine why not, if they have them."

Rogers smiled. He made another note. "Shame about the rotor burst in Miami."

"All I know is what I saw on television."

"You think it will affect the public perception of the N-22?" He had his pen out, ready to take down what she said.

"I don't see why. The problem was powerplant, not airframe. My guess is, they're going to find it was a bad compressor disk that burst."

"I wouldn't doubt it," he said. "I was talking to Don Peterson over at the FAA. He told me that incident at SFO was a sixth-stage compressor disk that blew. The disk had brittle nitrogen pockets."

"Alpha inclusions?" she said.

"That's right," Jack said. "And there was also dwell-time fatigue."

Casey nodded. Engine parts operated at a temperature of 2500 degrees Fahrenheit, well above the melt temperature of most alloys, which turned to soup at 2200 degrees. So they were manufactured of titanium alloys, using the most advanced procedures. Fabricating some of the parts was an art—the fan blades were essentially "grown" as a single crystal of metal, making them phenomenally strong. But even in skilled hands, the manufacturing process was inherently delicate. Dwell-time fatigue was a condition in which the titanium used to make rotor disks clumped into microstructure colonies, rendering them vulnerable to fatigue cracks.

"And how about the TransPacific flight," Rogers said. "Was that an engine problem, too?"

"TransPacific happened yesterday, Jack. We just started our investigation."

"You're QA on the IRT, right?"

"Right, yes."

"Are you pleased with how the investigation is going?"

"Jack, I can't comment on the TransPacific investigation. It's much too early."

"Not too early for speculation to start," Rogers said. "You know how these things go, Casey. Lot of idle talk. Misinformation that can be difficult to clear up later. I'd just like to set the record straight. Have you ruled out engines?"

"Jack," she said, "I can't comment."

"Then you haven't ruled out engines?"

"No comment, Jack."

He made a note on his pad. Without looking up, he said, "And I suppose you're looking at slats, too."

"We're looking at everything, Jack," she said.

"Given the 22 has a history of slats problems . . ."

"Ancient history," she said. "We fixed the problem years ago. You wrote a story about it, if I recall."

"But now you've had two incidents in two days. Are you worried that the flying public will start to think the N-22 is a troubled aircraft?"

She could see the direction his story was going to take. She didn't want to comment, but he was telling her what he would write if she didn't. It was a standard, if minor, form of press blackmail.

"Jack," she said, "we've got three hundred N-22s in service around the world. The model has an outstanding safety record." In fact, in five years of service there had been no fatalities involving the aircraft until yesterday. That was a reason for pride, but she decided not to mention it, because she could see his lead: *The first fatalities to occur on a Norton N-22 aircraft happened yesterday . . .*

Instead she said, "The public is best served by getting accurate information. And at the moment, we have no information to offer. To speculate would be irresponsible."

That did it. He took his pen away. "Okay. You want to go off?"

"Sure." She knew she could trust him. "Off the record, 545 underwent very severe pitch oscillations. We think the plane porpoised. We don't know why. The FDR's anomalous. It'll take days to reconstruct the data. We're working as fast as we can."

"Will it affect the China sale?"

"I hope not."

"Pilot was Chinese, wasn't he? Chang?"

"He was from Hong Kong. I don't know his nationality."

"Does that make it awkward if it's pilot error?"

"You know how these investigations are, Jack. Whatever the cause turns out to be, it's going to be awkward for somebody. We can't worry about that. We just have to let the chips fall where they fall."

"Of course," he said. "By the way, is that China sale firm? I keep hearing it's not."

She shrugged. "I honestly don't know."

"Has Marder talked to you about it?"

"Not to me personally," she said. Her reply was carefully worded; she hoped he wouldn't follow up on it. He didn't.

"Okay, Casey," he said. "I'll leave this alone, but what've you got? I need to file today."

"How come you're not doing Cheapskate Airlines?" she said, using the derogatory in-house term for one of the low-cost carriers. "Nobody's done that story yet."

"Are you kidding?" Rogers said. "Everybody and his brother's covering that one."

"Yeah, but nobody's doing the real story," she said. "Super-cheap carriers are a stock scam."

"A stock scam?"

"Sure," Casey said. "You buy some aircraft so old and poorly maintained no reputable carrier will use them for spares. Then you subcontract maintenance to limit your liability. Then you offer cheap fares, and use the cash to buy new routes. It's a pyramid scheme but on paper it looks great. Volume's up, revenue's up, and Wall Street loves you. You're saving so much on maintenance that your earnings skyrocket. Your stock price doubles and doubles again. By the time the bodies start piling up, as you know they will, you've made your fortune off the stock, and can afford the best counsel. That's the genius of deregulation, Jack. When the bill comes, nobody pays."

"Except the passengers."

"Exactly," Casey said. "Flight safety's always been an honor system. The FAA's set up to monitor the carriers, not to police them. So if deregulation's going to change the rules, we ought to warn the public. Or triple FAA funding. One or the other."

Rogers nodded. "Barry Jordan over at the LA

*Times* told me he's doing the safety angle. But that
takes a lot of resources—lead time, lawyers going
over your copy. My paper can't afford it. I need
something I can use tonight."

"Off the record," Casey said, "I've got a good
lead, but you can't source it."

"Sure," Rogers said.

"The engine that blew was one of six that Sunstar
bought from AeroCivicas," Casey said. "Kenny
Burne was our consultant. He borescoped the
engines and found a lot of damage."

"What kind of damage?"

"Blade notch breakouts and vane cracks."

Rogers said, "They had fatigue cracks *in the fan
blades?*"

"That's right," Casey said. "Kenny told them to
reject the engines, but Sunstar rebuilt them and put
them on the planes. When that engine blew, Kenny
was furious. So you might get a name at Sunstar
from Kenny. But we can't be the source, Jack. We
have to do business with these people."

"I understand," Rogers said. "Thanks. But my
editor's going to want to know about the accidents
on the floor today. So tell me. Are you convinced the
China offset stories are groundless?"

"Are we back on?" she said.

"Yes."

"I'm not the person to ask," she said. "You'll have
to talk to Edgarton."

"I called, but his office says he's out of town.
Where is he? Beijing?"

"I can't comment."

"And what about Marder?" Rogers said.

"What about him?"

Rogers shrugged. "Everybody knows Marder and Edgarton are at each other's throats. Marder expected to be named president, but the Board passed him over. But they gave Edgarton a one-year contract—so he's got only twelve months to produce. And I hear Marder's undercutting Edgarton, every way he can."

"I wouldn't know about that," she said. Casey had, of course, heard such rumors. It was no secret that Marder was bitterly disappointed about Edgarton's appointment. What Marder could do about it was another story. Marder's wife controlled eleven percent of company stock. With Marder's connections, he could probably pull together five percent more. But sixteen percent wasn't enough to call the shots, particularly since Edgarton had the strong support of the Board.

So most people in the plant thought that Marder had no choice except to go along with Edgarton's agenda—at least for the moment. Marder might be unhappy, but he had no option. The company had a cash-flow problem. They were already building planes without buyers. Yet they needed billions of dollars, if they hoped to develop the next generation of planes, and stay in business in the future.

So the situation was clear. The company needed the sale. And everybody knew it. Including Marder.

Rogers said, "You haven't heard Marder's under-cutting Edgarton?"

"No comment," Casey said. "But off the record, it makes no sense. Everybody in the company wants this sale, Jack. Including Marder. Right now, Marder's pushing us hard to solve 545, so the sale goes through."

"Do you think the image of the company will be hurt by the rivalry between its two top officers?"

"I couldn't say."

"Okay," he said finally, closing his notepad. "Call me if you get a break on 545, okay?"

"Sure, Jack."

"Thanks, Casey."

Walking away from him, she realized she was exhausted by the effort of the interview. Talking to a reporter these days was like a deadly chess match; you had to think several steps ahead; you had to imagine all the possible ways a reporter might distort your statement. The atmosphere was relentlessly adversarial.

It hadn't always been that way. There was a time when reporters wanted information, their questions directed to an underlying event. They wanted an accurate picture of a situation, and to do that they had to make the effort to see things your way, to understand how you were thinking about it. They might not agree with you in the end, but it was a matter of pride that they could accurately state your view, before rejecting it. The interviewing process was not very personal, because the focus was on the event they were trying to understand.

But now reporters came to the story with the lead fixed in their minds; they saw their job as proving what they already knew. They didn't want information so much as evidence of villainy. In this mode, they were openly skeptical of your point of view, since they assumed you were just being evasive. They proceeded from a presumption of universal guilt, in an atmosphere of muted hostility and suspicion. This new mode was intensely personal: they wanted to trip you up, to catch you in a small error, or in a foolish statement—or just a phrase that could be taken out of context and made to look silly or insensitive.

Because the focus was so personal, the reporters asked continuously for personal speculations. Do you think an event will be damaging? Do you think the company will suffer? Such speculation had been irrelevant to the earlier generation of reporters, who focused on the underlying events. Modern journalism was intensely subjective—"interpretive"—and speculation was its lifeblood. But she found it exhausting.

And Jack Rogers, she thought, was one of the better ones. The print reporters were all better. It was the television reporters you really had to watch out for. They were the really dangerous ones.

# OUTSIDE HANGAR 5

### 10:15 A.M.

Crossing the plant, she fished her cell phone out of her purse, and called Marder. His assistant, Eileen, said he was in a meeting.

"I just left Jack Rogers," Casey said. "I think he's planning a story that says we're shipping the wing to China, and there's trouble in the executive suite."

"Uh-oh," Eileen said. "That's not good."

"Edgarton better talk to him, and put it to rest."

"Edgarton isn't doing any press," Eileen said. "John will be back at six o'clock. You want to talk to him then?"

"I better, yes."

"I'll put you down," Eileen said.

# PROOF TEST

### 10:19 A.M.

It looked like an aviation junkyard: old fuselages, tails, and wing sections littered the landscape, raised up on rusty scaffolding. But the air was filled with the steady hum of compressors, and heavy tubing ran to the airplane parts, like intravenous lines to a patient. This was Proof Test, also known as Twist-and-Shout, the domain of the infamous Amos Peters.

Casey saw him off to the right, a hunched figure in shirtsleeves and baggy pants, bent over a readout stand, beneath an aft fuselage section of the Norton widebody.

"Amos," she called, waving as she walked over to him.

He turned, glanced at her. "Go away."

Amos was a legend at Norton. Reclusive and obstinate, he was nearly seventy, long past mandatory retirement age, yet he continued to work because he was vital to the company. His specialty was the arcane field of damage tolerance, or fatigue testing. And fatigue testing was of vastly greater importance than it had been ten years before.

Since deregulation, the carriers were flying aircraft longer than anybody ever expected. Three thousand aircraft in the domestic fleet were now more than twenty years old. That number would double in five years. Nobody really knew what would happen to all those aircraft as they continued to age.

Except Amos.

It was Amos who had been brought in by the NTSB as a consultant on the famous Aloha 737 accident, back in 1988. Aloha was an interisland carrier in Hawaii. One of their airplanes was cruising at 24,000 feet when suddenly eighteen feet of the airplane's outer skin peeled off the fuselage, from the cabin door to the wing; the cabin decompressed, and a stewardess was sucked out and killed. Despite the explosive pressure loss, the plane managed to land safely at Maui, where it was scrapped on the spot.

The rest of Aloha's fleet was examined for corrosion and fatigue damage. Two more high-time 737's were scrapped, and a third underwent months of repairs. All three had extensive skin cracks and other corrosion damage. When the FAA issued an Airworthiness Directive mandating inspections of the rest of the 737 fleet, forty-nine more planes, operated by eighteen different carriers, were found to have extensive cracking.

Industry observers were perplexed by the accident, because Boeing, Aloha, and the FAA were supposedly all watching the carrier's 737 fleet. Corrosion cracking was a known problem on some early-production 737s; Boeing had already warned Aloha that the salty, humid Hawaiian climate was a "severe" corrosion environment.

Afterward, the investigation found multiple causes for the accident. It turned out that Aloha, making short hops between islands, was accumulating flight cycles of takeoff and landing at a faster rate than maintenance was scheduled to handle. This stress, combined with corrosion from ocean air, produced a series of small cracks in the aircraft skin. These were unnoticed by Aloha, because they were short of trained personnel. The FAA didn't catch them because they were overworked and understaffed. The FAA's principal maintenance inspector in Honolulu supervised nine carriers and seven repair stations around the Pacific, from China to Singapore to the Philippines. Eventually, a flight occurred in which the cracks extended and the structure failed.

Following the incident, Aloha, Boeing, and the FAA formed a circular firing squad. The undetected structural damage in Aloha's fleet was variously attributed to poor management, poor maintenance, poor FAA inspection, poor engineering. Accusations ricocheted back and forth for years afterward.

But the Aloha flight had also focused industry attention on the problem of aging aircraft, and it had made Amos famous within Norton. He'd convinced management to begin buying more old aircraft, turning wings and fuselages into proof test articles. Day after day, his test fixtures applied repetitive pressures to aging aircraft, stressing them to simulate takeoffs and landings, wind shear and turbulence, so Amos could study how and where they cracked.

"Amos," she said, coming up to him, "it's me. Casey Singleton."

He blinked myopically. "Oh. Casey. Didn't recognize you." He squinted at her. "Doctor gave me a new prescription . . . Oh. Huh. How are you?" He gestured for her to walk with him, and he headed toward a small building a few yards away.

No one at Norton could understand how Casey was able to get along with Amos, but they were neighbors; he lived alone with his pug dog, and she had taken to cooking him a meal every month or so. In return, Amos regaled her with stories of aircraft accidents he'd worked on, going back to the first BOAC Comet crashes in the 1950s. Amos had an encyclopedic knowledge of airplanes. She had learned a tremendous amount from him, and he had become a sort of adviser to her.

"Didn't I see you the other morning?" he said.

"Yes. With my daughter."

"Thought so. Want coffee?" He opened the door to a shed, and she smelled the sharp odor of burned grounds. His coffee was always terrible.

"Sounds great, Amos," she said.

He poured her a cup. "Hope black is okay. Ran out of that creamer stuff."

"Black is fine, Amos." He hadn't had creamer for a year.

Amos poured a cup for himself in a stained mug, and waved her to a battered chair, facing his desk. The desk was piled high with thick reports. *FAA/NASA International Symposium on Advanced Structural Integrity. Airframe Durability and Damage Tolerance. Thermographic Inspection Techniques. Corrosion Control and Structures Technology.*

He put his feet up on the desk, cleared a path through the journals, so he could see her. "I tell you, Casey. It's tedious working with these old hulks. I long for the day when we have another T2 article in here."

"T2?" she said.

"Of course you wouldn't know," Amos said. "You've been here five years, and we haven't made a new model aircraft in all that time. But when there's a new aircraft, the first one off the line is called T1. Test Article 1. It goes to Static Test—we put it on the test bed and shake it to pieces. Find out where the weaknesses are. The second plane off the line is T2. It's used for fatigue testing—a more difficult problem. Over time, metal loses tensile strength, gets brittle. So we take T2, put it in a jig, and accelerate fatigue testing. Day after day, year after year, we simulate takeoffs and landings. Norton's policy is we fatigue test to more than twice the design life of the aircraft. If the engineers design an aircraft for a twenty-year life span—say, fifty thousand hours and twenty thousand cycles—we'll do more than twice that in the pit, before we ever deliver to a customer. We know the planes will stand up. How's your coffee?"

She took a small sip, managed not to wince. Amos ran water through the same old grinds, all day long. That was how it got this distinctive flavor. "Good, Amos."

"Just ask. There's more where that came from. Anyway, most manufacturers test to twice the design life. We test up to four times the spec. That's why we always say, the other companies make doughnuts, Norton makes croissants."

Casey said, "And John Marder always says, That's why the others make money, and we don't."

"Marder." Amos snorted. "It's all money with him, all bottom line. In the old days, the front office told us, Make the best damn airplane you can. Now they say, Make the best airplane you can for a price. Different instruction, you know what I mean?" He slurped his coffee. "So. What is it, Casey—545?"

She nodded.

"Can't help you there," he said.

"Why do you say that?"

"The plane's new. Fatigue's not a factor."

"There's a question about a part, Amos," she said. She showed him the pin, in a plastic bag.

"Hmm." He turned it over in his hands, held it up to the light. "This would be—don't tell me—this would be an anterior locking pin for the second inboard slat."

"That's right."

"Of course it's right." He frowned. "But this part's bad."

"Yes, I know."

"So what's your question?"

"Doherty thinks it failed the aircraft. Could it?"

"Well . . ." Amos stared at the ceiling, thinking. "No. I got a hundred bucks says it *didn't* fail the aircraft."

Casey sighed. She was back to square one. They had no leads.

"Discouraged?" Amos said.

"Yes, frankly."

"Then you're not paying attention," he said. "This is a very valuable lead."

"But why? You just said yourself—it didn't fail the aircraft."

"Casey, Casey." Amos shook his head. *"Think."*

She tried to think, sitting there, smelling his bad coffee. She tried to see what he was driving at. But her mind was blank. She looked at him across the desk. "Just tell me. What am I missing?"

"Were the other locking pins replaced?"

"No."

"Just this one?"

"Yes."

"Why just this one, Casey?" he said.

"I don't know."

"Find out," he said.

"Why? What good will that do?"

Amos threw up his hands. "Casey. Come on, now. Think it through. You have a problem with slats on 545. That's a wing problem."

"Correct."

"Now you've found a part that's been replaced on the wing."

"Correct."

"Why was it replaced?"

"I don't know . . ."

"Was that wing damaged in the past? Did something happen to it, so that this part had to be replaced? Were other parts replaced as well? Are there other bad parts on the wing? Is there residual damage to the wing?"

"Not that you can see."

Amos shook his head impatiently. "Forget what you can *see,* Casey. Look at the ship's record and the maintenance records. Trace this part, and get a history of the wing. Because something else is wrong."

"My guess is you'll find more fake parts." Amos stood, sighing. "More and more planes have fake parts, these days. I suppose it's to be expected.

These days, everybody seems to believe in Santa Claus."

"How's that?"

"Because they believe in something for nothing," Amos said. "You know: government deregulates the airlines, and everybody cheers. We got cheaper fares: everybody cheers. But the carriers have to cut costs. So the food is awful. That's okay. There are fewer direct flights, more hubs. That's okay. The planes look grubby, because they redo the interiors less often. That's okay. But still the carriers have to cut more costs. So they run the planes longer, buy fewer new ones. The fleet ages. That'll be okay—for a while. Eventually it won't be. And meanwhile, cost pressures continue. So where else do they cut? Maintenance? Parts? What? It can't go on indefinitely. Just can't. Of course, now Congress is helping them out, by cutting appropriations for the FAA, so there'll be less oversight. Carriers can ease up on maintenance because nobody's watching. And the public doesn't care, because for thirty years this country's had the best aviation safety record in the world. But the thing is, we *paid* for it. We paid to have new, safe planes and we paid for the oversight to make sure they were well maintained. But those days are over. Now, everybody believes in something for nothing."

"So where's it going to end?" she said.

"I got a hundred bucks," he said, "they'll reregulate within ten years. There'll be a string of crashes, and they'll do it. The free marketeers will scream, but the fact is, free markets don't provide safety. Only regulation does that. You want safe food, you better have inspectors. You want safe water, you better have an EPA. You want a safe stock market, you better have the SEC. And you want safe airlines, you better regulate them, too. Believe me, they will."

"And on 545 . . ."

Amos shrugged. "Foreign carriers operate with much less stringent regulation. It's pretty loosey-goosey out there. Look at the maintenance records—and look hard at the paper for any part you're suspicious of."

She started to leave.

"But Casey . . ."

She turned back. "Yes?"

"You understand the situation, don't you? To check that part, you'll have to start with the ship's record."

"I know."

"That's in Building 64. I wouldn't go there, right now. At least not alone."

"Come on, Amos," she said. "I used to work on the floor. I'll be okay."

Amos was shaking his head. "Flight 545's a hot potato. You know how the guys think. If they can mess up the investigation, they will—any way they can. Be careful."

"I will."

"Be very, very careful."

# BLDG 64

11:45 A.M.

Running down the center of Building 64 was a series of one-story chain-link cages that housed parts for the line, and terminal workstations. The workstations were placed inside small partitions, each containing a microfiche reader, a parts terminal, and a main system terminal.

In the parts cage, Casey bent over a microfiche reader, scrolling through photocopies of the ship's record for Fuse 271, which was the original factory designation for the aircraft involved in the TPA accident.

Jerry Jenkins, the parts flow control manager on the floor, stood beside her nervously, tapping his pen on the table and saying, "Find it yet? Find it yet?"

"Jerry," she said, "take it easy."

"I'm easy," he said, glancing around the floor. "I'm just thinking, you know, you could have done this between shifts."

Between shifts would have drawn less attention.

"Jerry," she said, "we're in kind of a rush here."

He tapped his pen. "Everybody's pretty hot about the China sale. What do I tell the guys?"

"You tell the guys," she said, "that if we lose that China sale, then this line will shut down, and everybody will be out of a job."

Jerry swallowed. "That true? Because I hear—"

"Jerry, let me look at the record, will you?"

The ship's record consisted of the mass of documentation—a million pieces of paper, one for every part on the aircraft—used to assemble the aircraft. This paper, and the even more extensive documentation required for FAA type certification, contained Norton proprietary information. So the FAA didn't store these records, because if they did, competitors could obtain it under the Freedom of Information Act. So Norton warehoused five thousand pounds of paper, running eighty feet of shelf space for each aircraft, in a vast building in Compton. All this was copied onto microfiche, for access at these readers on the floor. But finding the paper for a single part was time-consuming, she thought, and—

"Find it yet? Find it?"

"Yeah," she said at last. "I got it."

She was staring at a photocopy of a sheet of paper from Hoffman Metal Works, in Montclair, California. The slats locking pin was described in a code that matched the engineering drawings: A/908/ B-2117L (2) Ant Sl Ltch. SS/HT. A typed date of manufacture, a stamped date of delivery to the factory, and a date of installation. Followed by two stamps—one signed by the mechanic who installed the part on the aircraft, and a second by the QA inspector who approved the work.

"So," he said. "That the OEM or what?"

"Yeah, it's the OEM." Hoffman was the original equipment manufacturer. The part had come direct from them. No distributor was involved.

Jerry was looking out through the chain link at the factory floor beyond. Nobody seemed to be paying any attention, but Casey knew that they were being watched.

Jerry said, "You leaving now?"

"Yes, Jerry. I'm leaving now."

She headed across the floor, staying on the aisle that ran by the parts cages. Away from the overhead cranes. Glancing up at the overhead walkways to be sure nobody was up there. Nobody was. So far, they were leaving her alone.

What she had learned so far was clear: The original installed part on TPA 545 had come direct from a reputable supplier. The original part was good; the part Doherty found on the wing was bad.

So Amos was right.

Something had happened to that wing, causing it to be repaired, sometime in the past.

But what?

She still had more work to do.

And very little time to do it.

# NORTON QA

### 12:30 P.M.

If the part was bad, where had it come from? She needed maintenance records, and they hadn't arrived yet. Where was Richman? Back in her office, she flipped through a stack of telexes. All the FSRs around the world were asking for information about the N-22. One from the Flight Service Rep in Madrid was typical.

```
FROM: S. RAMONES, FSR MADRID
TO: C. SINGLETON, QA/IRT

PERSISTENT REPORTS VIA MY IBERIA
CONTACT B. ALONSO THAT DUE TO MIAMI
INCIDENT JAA WILL ANNOUNCE CONTINUED
DELAY OF CERTIFICATION OF N-22
AIRCRAFT CITING "AIRWORTHINESS
CONCERNS"

PLS ADVISE.
```

She sighed. What the FSR was reporting was entirely predictable. The JAA was the Joint Aviation Authority, the European equivalent of the FAA. Recently, American manufacturers had had a good deal of difficulty with it. The JAA was flexing new regulatory muscles, and the agency had many bureaucrats who didn't clearly distinguish between negotiated trade advantage and airworthiness issues. For some time now, the JAA had been making special efforts to force the American manufacturers to use European jet engines. The Americans had resisted, so it was logical that the JAA would take advantage of the rotor burst in Miami to put greater pressure on Norton, by withholding certification.

But in the end, it was a political problem, not her area. She went to the next telex:

```
FROM: S. NIETO, FSR VANC
TO: C. SINGLETON, QA/IRT

FIRST OFFICER LU ZAN PING UNDERWENT
EMERGENCY SURGERY FOR SUBDURAL
HEMATOMA AT VANC GEN HOSPITAL 0400
HRS TODAY. F/O NOT AVAILABLE FOR
QUESTIONS AT LEAST 48 HRS. FURTHER
DETAILS TF.
```

Casey had been hoping for an interview with the injured first officer sooner than that. She wanted to know why he was in the back of the plane, and not in the cockpit. But it seemed an answer to that question would have to wait until the end of the week.

She came to the next telex, and stared in astonishment.

```
FROM: RICK RAKOSKI, FSR HK
TO: CASEY SINGLETON, QA/IRT

RECEIVED YOUR REQUEST MAINTENANCE
RECORDS FOR TPA FLIGHT 545, FUSE
271, FOREIGN REGISTRY 098/443/HB09
AND PASSED IT ON TO THE CARRIER.

IN RESPONSE TO FAA REQUEST
TRANSPACIFIC RELEASED ALL RECORDS
FROM REPAIR STATION KAITAK HK,
```

REPAIR STATION SINGAPORE, REPAIR
STATION MELBOURNE. THESE UPLOADED TO
NORTON ONLINE SYSTEMS AS OF 2210
LOCAL TIME. STILL WORKING ON CREW
INTERVIEWS. MUCH MORE DIFFICULT.
DETAILS TF.


A smart move by the carrier, she thought. Since
they didn't want to grant crew interviews, they had
decided to provide everything else, in an apparent
display of cooperation.

Norma came into her office. "Records from LAX
are coming in now," she said. "And Hong Kong
already delivered."

"I see that. Have you got the storage address?"

"Right here." She handed her a slip of paper, and
Casey typed it into the terminal behind her desk.
There was a delay for the call to the mainframe, and
then a screen flashed up.

MAINT REC N-22 / FUSE 271 / FR
   098/443/HB09

DD 5/14   AS 6/19   MOD 8/12

< RS KAITAK    —      MAINT REC (A—C)
< RS SNGPOR    —      MAINT REC (B ONLY)
< RS MELB      —      MAINT REC (A, B ONLY)

"All *right,*" she said.
She went to work.


It was the better part of an hour before Casey had

her answers. But at the end of that time, she had a good picture of what had happened to the slats locking pin on the TransPacific aircraft.

On November 10 of the previous year, on a flight from Bombay to Melbourne, the TransPacific aircraft had experienced a problem with radio communications. The pilot made an unscheduled stop on the island of Java, in Indonesia. There, the radio was repaired without difficulty (a blown circuit panel was changed out), and Javanese ground crews refueled the plane for the continuing flight to Melbourne.

After the aircraft landed in Melbourne, Australian ground crews noted that the right wing was damaged.

Thank you, Amos.

The wing was damaged.

Mechanics in Melbourne noted that the fuel coupling was bent on the right wing, and the adjacent slats locking pin was slightly damaged. This was thought to have been caused by ground personnel in Java during the previous fueling stop.

The fuel line couplings on the N-22 were located on the underside of the wing, just behind the leading edge. An inexperienced ground person had used the wrong power lift truck for the N-22 and had jammed the platform railing into the fuel hose while the hose was hooked into the wing. This bent the hose bracket into the wing coupler, bent the coupler plate, and damaged the nearby slats pin.

Slats locking pins were an infrequent change item, and Melbourne repair station did not have one in stock. Rather than delay the aircraft in Australia, it was decided to allow the plane to continue to Singapore and change the part there. However, a sharp-eyed maintenance person in Singapore noticed that the paper on their replacement locking pin appeared suspect. Maintenance crews were uncertain whether the replacement pin was genuine or not.

Since the part already in place functioned normally, Singapore elected not to replace it, and the aircraft was sent on to Hong Kong, the home terminal for TransPacific, where a genuine replacement part was assured. Hong Kong Repair Station—fully aware they were located in a world center for counterfeiting—took special precautions to insure their spare aviation parts were genuine. They ordered parts directly from the original equipment manufacturers in the United States. On November 13 of the previous year, a brand-new slats locking pin was installed on the aircraft.

Paper for the part appeared to be proper; a photocopy came up on Casey's screen. The part had come from Hoffman Metal Works in Montclair, California—Norton's original supplier. But Casey knew the paper was fake, because the part itself was fake. She would run it down later, and find out where the part had actually come from.

But right now, the only question was the one Amos had posed:

*Were other parts replaced, as well?*

Sitting at her terminal, Casey scrolled through the maintenance summary records for Hong Kong

Repair Station for November 13, to find what else had been done to the aircraft that day.

It was slow going; she had to look at photocopies of maintenance cards, with scrawled handwritten notations after each checkbox. But eventually she found a list of work that had been done on the wing.

There were three notations.

CHG RT LDLT FZ-7. Change the right landing light fuse 7.

CHG RT SLTS LK PIN. Change the right slats locking pin.

CK ASS EQ PKG. Check the associated equipment package. This was followed by a mechanic's notation NRML. Meaning it was checked and normal.

The associated equipment package was a maintenance subgrouping of related parts that had to be checked whenever a faulty part was detected. For example, if seals on the right fuel lines were found to be worn, it was standard practice to check seals on the left side as well, since they were part of the associated equipment package.

Changing the slats locking pin had triggered a maintenance check of associated equipment.

But which equipment?

She knew the associated equipment packages were specified by Norton. But she couldn't pull up the list on her office computer. To do that, she would have to go back to the terminal on the floor.

She pushed away from her desk.

# BLDG 64

2:40 P.M.

Building 64 was nearly deserted, the widebody line seemingly abandoned between shifts. There was a one-hour delay between first and second shifts, because it took that long for the parking lots to clear. First shift ended at 2:30 P.M. Second shift started at 3:30.

This was the time that Jerry Jenkins had said she should examine the records because there wouldn't be an audience. She had to admit he was right. There was nobody around now.

Casey went directly to the parts cage, looking for Jenkins, but he wasn't there. She saw the QA section manager, and asked where Jerry Jenkins was.

"Jerry? He went home," the manager said.

"Why?"

"Said he wasn't feeling good."

Casey frowned. Jenkins shouldn't have left until after five. She went to the terminal to bring up the information herself.

Typing at the keyboard, she soon had called up the database of associated maintenance packages. She keyed in RT SLATS LK PIN and got the answer she was looking for:

```
RT SLATS DRV TRK   (22 / RW / 2-5455 / SLS)
RT SLATS LVR       (22 / RW / 2-5769 / SLS)
RT SLATS HYD ACT   (22 / RW / 2-7334 / SLS)
```

```
RT SLATS PSTN       (22 / RW / 2-3444 / SLS)
RT SLATS FD CPLNG (22 / RW / 2-3445 / SLC)
RT PRX SNSR         (22 / RW / 4-0212 / PRC)
RT PRX SNSR CPLNG (22 / RW / 4-0445 / PRC)
RT PRX SNSR PLT     (22 / RW / 4-0343 / PRC)
RT PRX SNSR WC      (22 / RW / 4-0102 / PRW)
```

It made sense. The associated parts package consisted of the other five elements of the slats drive track: the track, the lever, the hydraulic actuator, the piston, the forward coupling.

In addition, the list instructed mechanics to check the nearby proximity sensor, its coupling, cover plate, and wiring.

She knew Doherty had already inspected the drive track. If Amos was right, they ought to look very carefully at that proximity sensor. She didn't think anybody had done that yet.

The proximity sensor. It was located deep in the wing. Difficult to get to. Difficult to inspect.

Could that have caused a problem?

Yes, she thought. It was possible.

She shut down the terminal and crossed the plant floor, heading back to her office. She needed to call Ron Smith, to tell him to check the sensor. She walked beneath deserted aircraft toward the open doors at the north end of the building.

As she neared the doors, she saw two men enter the hangar. They were silhouetted against the midday sunlight, but she could see that one wore a red checked shirt. And the other had on a baseball cap.

Casey turned to ask the QA floor manager to call Security. But he was gone; the wire cage stood empty. Casey looked around, and suddenly realized the floor was deserted. She saw no one except an elderly black woman at the far end of the building, pushing a broom. The woman was half a mile away.

Casey looked at her watch. It would be another fifteen minutes before people started showing up.

The two men were walking toward her.

Casey turned and started to walk away from them, heading back the way she had come. She could handle this, she thought. Calmly, she opened her purse, pulled out her cell phone to call Security.

But the phone didn't work. She didn't get a signal. She realized she was in the center of the building, which was hung with copper mesh along the ceiling to block extraneous radio transmissions while the aircraft systems were being tested.

She wouldn't be able to use her cell phone until she reached the other side of the building.

Half a mile away.

She walked faster. Her shoes clicked on the concrete. The sound seemed to echo through the building. Could she really be alone here? Of course not. There were several hundred people in the building with her, right now. It was just that she couldn't see them. They were inside the airplanes, or standing behind the big tools around the planes. Hundreds of people, all around her. Any minute, she'd see some of them.

She glanced over her shoulder.

The men were gaining on her.

She picked up her pace, almost starting to jog, unsteady in her low heels. And she suddenly thought, This is ridiculous. I'm an executive of Norton Aircraft and I am running through this plant *in the middle of the day.*

She slowed to a normal walk.

She took a deep breath.

She glanced back: the men were closer now.

Should she confront them? No, she thought. Not unless other people were around.

She walked faster.

To her left was a parts staging area. Ordinarily, there would be dozens of men inside there, fetching parts kits, working the bins. But now the cage was empty.

Deserted.

She looked over her shoulder. The men were fifty yards behind, and closing.

She knew that if she started to scream, a dozen mechanics would suddenly appear. The goons would slip away, vanishing behind tools and scaffolding, and she'd look like a fool. She'd never live it down. The girl who lost it that day on the floor.

She wouldn't scream.

No.

Where the hell were the fire alarms? The medic

alert alarms? The hazardous materials alarms? She knew they were scattered all over the building. She'd spent years working in this building. She ought to be able to remember where they were located.

She could hit one and say it was an accident . . .

But she saw no alarms.

The men were now thirty yards behind. If they broke into a run, they'd reach her in a few seconds. But they were being cautious—apparently they, too, expected to see people at any moment.

But she saw nobody.

On her right, she saw a forest of blue beams—the big industrial jigs that held the fuselage barrels in place, while they were riveted together. The last place she might hide.

*I'm an executive of Norton Aircraft. And it's—*

The hell with it.

She turned right, ducking among the beams, scrambling through them. She passed staircases and hanging lamps. She heard the men behind her shout in surprise, and start to follow. But by then she was moving in near darkness through the girders. Moving fast.

Casey knew her way around here. She moved quickly, with assurance, always glancing up, hoping to see someone above. Usually there were twenty or thirty men at each position on the scaffolding overhead, joining the barrels in a glare of fluorescent light. Now she saw nobody.

Behind her, she heard the men grunt, heard them bang into the crossbeams, swearing.

She started to run, dodging low-hanging beams, jumping over cables and boxes, and then suddenly she came out into a clearing. Station fourteen: a plane stood on its landing gear, high above the floor. And higher still, all around the tail, she saw the hanging gardens, rising sixty feet into the air.

She looked up at the widebody, and she saw the silhouette of someone inside. Someone in the window.

Someone inside the plane.

Finally! Casey climbed the stairs to the plane, her feet clanging on the steel steps. She went two stories up, then paused to look. High above her, in the hanging gardens, she saw three burly mechanics in hard hats. They were only ten feet below the ceiling, working on the topmost hinge of the rudder; she heard the quick, sputtering buzz of power tools.

She looked down and saw the two men following her on the floor below. They broke clear of the forest of blue jigs, looked up, saw her, and started after her.

She continued up.

She reached the aft door of the plane, and ran inside. The unfinished widebody was huge and empty, a succession of dully gleaming curved arcs, like the belly of a metal whale. Halfway down, she saw a solitary Asian woman, attaching silver insulation blankets to the walls. The woman looked at Casey timidly.

"Is anybody else working here?" she said.

The woman shook her head, No. She looked frightened, as if she'd been caught doing something wrong.

Casey turned, ran back out the door.

Down below, she saw the men just one level beneath her.

She turned and ran up the stairs.

Into the hanging gardens.

The metal staircase had been ten feet wide when she started. Now it narrowed to two feet in width. And it was steeper, more like a ladder climbing into the air, surrounded by a dizzying crosswork of scaffolding. Power lines hung down like jungle vines on all sides; her shoulders banged into metal junction boxes as she scrambled higher. The staircase swayed beneath her feet. It turned abruptly at right angles every ten steps or so. Casey was now forty feet above the ground, looking down on the broad crown of the fuselage. And up at the tail, rising above her.

She was high up, and suddenly flooded with panic. Looking up at the men working on the rudder above, she shouted: "Hey! Hey!"

They ignored her.

Below, she saw the other two men pursuing her, their bodies intermittently visible through the scaffolding as they climbed.

"Hey! *Hey!*"

But the men still ignored her. Continuing upward, she saw why they had not responded. They were wearing audiopads, black plastic cups like earmuffs, over their ears.

They couldn't hear anything through them.

She climbed.

Fifty feet above the floor, the stairs abruptly angled right, around the black horizontal surface of the elevators, protruding from the vertical tail. The elevators obscured her view of the men above. Casey worked her way around the elevators; the surfaces were black because they were made of composite resin, and she remembered she must not touch them with her bare hands.

She wanted to grab on to them; the stairs up here were not constructed for running. They swayed wildly and her feet slipped off the steps; she clutched at the railing with sweaty hands as she slid five feet down, before coming to a stop.

She continued upward.

She could no longer see the floor below; it was obscured by the layers of scaffolding beneath her. She couldn't see if the second shift had arrived or not.

She continued up.

As she went higher, she began to feel the thick, hot air trapped beneath the roof of Building 64. She remembered what they called this high perch: the sweatbox.

Working her way upward, she finally reached the elevators. As she continued above them, the stairs angled back now, close to the broad, flat, vertical surface of the tail, blocking her view of the men working on the other side. She no longer wanted to look down; she saw the wooden beams of the ceiling above her. Only five more feet . . . one more turn of the stairs . . . coming around the rudder . . . and then she would be—

She stopped, stared.

The men were gone.

She looked down and saw the three yellow hard hats beneath her. They were on a motorized lift, descending to the factory floor.

"Hey! Hey!"

The hard hats did not look up.

Casey looked back, hearing the clang of the two men still racing up the stairs toward her. She could feel the vibration of their footsteps. She knew they were close.

And she had nowhere to go.

Directly ahead of her, the stairs ended in a metal platform, four feet square, set alongside the rudder. There was a railing around the platform, and nothing beyond.

She was sixty feet up in the air on a tiny platform astride the huge expanse of the widebody tail.

The men were coming.

And she had nowhere to go.

She should never have started to climb, she thought. She should have stayed on the ground. Now she had no choice.

Casey swung her foot over the platform railing. She reached for the scaffolding, gripped it. The metal was warm in the high air. She swung her other leg over.

And then she began to climb down the outside of the scaffolding, reaching for handholds, working her way down.

Almost immediately Casey realized her mistake. The scaffolding was constructed of X-angled girders. Wherever she grabbed, her hands slid down, jamming her fingers into the crossjoint with searing pain. Her feet slipped along the angled surfaces. The scaffolding bars were sharp edged, difficult to hold. After only a few moments of climbing, she was gasping for air. She hooked her arms through the bars, bending her elbows, and caught her breath.

She did not look down.

Looking to her left, she saw the two men on the small high platform. The man in the red shirt, and the man in the baseball cap. They were standing there, staring at her, trying to decide what to do. She was about five feet below them, on the outside of the girders, hanging on.

She saw one of the men pull on a pair of heavy work gloves.

She realized she had to get moving again. Carefully, she unhooked her arms, and started down. Five feet. Another five feet. Now she was level with the horizontal elevators, which she could see through the crisscrossed girders.

But the girders were shaking.

Looking up, she saw the man in the red shirt

climbing down after her. He was strong, and moved quickly. She knew he would reach her in just a few moments.

The second man was climbing back down the stairs, pausing now and again to peer at her through the girders.

The man in the red shirt was only about ten feet above her.

Casey went down.

Her arms burned. Her breath came in ragged gasps. The scaffolding was greasy in unexpected places; her hands kept slipping. She felt the man above her, descending toward her. Looking up she saw his big orange work boots. Heavy crepe soles.

In a few moments he would be stomping on her fingers.

As Casey continued to scramble down, something banged against her left shoulder. She looked back and saw a power cable, dangling from the ceiling. It was about two inches thick, covered in gray plastic insulation. How much weight would it support?

Above her, the man was descending.

The hell with it.

She reached out, tugged at the cable. It held firm. She looked up, saw no junction boxes above her. She pulled the cable close, wrapping her arm around it. Then her legs. Just as the man's boots came down, she released the scaffolding and swung out on the cable.

And began to slide.

She tried to go hand over hand, but her arms were too weak. She slid, hands burning.

She was going down fast.

She couldn't control it.

The pain from the friction was intense. She went ten feet, another ten feet. She lost track. Her feet slammed into a junction box and she stopped, swinging in the air. She lowered her legs around the junction box, gripped the cable between her feet, let her body weight go down—

She felt the cable pull away.

A shower of sparks flared from the box, and emergency alarms began to sound loudly throughout the building. The cable was swinging back and forth. She heard shouts from below. Looking down, she realized with a shock that she was only about seven or eight feet above the floor. Hands were reaching up to her. People shouting.

She let go, and fell.

She was surprised how quickly she recovered, getting right to her feet, embarrassed, brushing herself off. "I'm fine," she kept saying to the people around her. "I'm fine. Really." The paramedics ran over; she waved them away. "I'm fine."

By now the workers on the floor had seen her badge, seen the blue stripe, and were confused— why was an executive hanging from the gardens? They were hesitant, stepping away a little, unsure what to do.

"I'm fine. Everything is fine. Really. Just . . . go on with what you're doing."

The paramedics protested, but she pushed through the crowd, moving away, until suddenly Kenny Burne was at her side, his arm around her shoulder.

"What the hell is going on?"

"Nothing," she said.

"This is no time to be on the floor, Casey. Remember?"

"Yeah, I remember," she said.

She let Kenny walk her out of the building, into the afternoon sun. She squinted in the glare. The huge parking lot was now filled with cars for the second shift. Sunlight glinting off row after row of windshields.

Kenny turned to her. "You want to be more careful, Casey. You know what I mean?"

"Yeah," she said. "I do."

She looked down at her clothes. There was a big streak of grease running across her blouse and skirt.

Burne said, "You got a change of clothes here?"

"No. I have to go home."

"I better drive you," Burne said.

She was about to protest, but didn't. "Thanks, Kenny," she said.

# ADMINISTRATION

6:00 P.M.

John Marder looked up from behind his desk. "I heard there was a little upset in 64. What was that about?"

"Nothing. I was checking something."

He nodded. "I don't want you on the floor alone, Casey. Not after that nonsense with the crane today. If you need to go down there, have Richman or one of the engineers go with you."

"Okay."

"This is no time to take chances."

"I understand."

"Now." He shifted in his chair. "What's this about a reporter?"

"Jack Rogers is working on a story that might turn ugly," Casey said. "Union allegations we're sending the wing offshore. Leaked documents that allegedly say we're offsetting the wing. And he's relating the leaks to, ah, friction in the executive suite."

"Friction?" Marder said. "What friction?"

"He's been told that you and Edgarton are at loggerheads. He asked if I thought management conflicts would affect the sale."

"Oh, Christ," Marder said. He sounded annoyed. "That's ridiculous. I'm behind Hal one hundred percent on this. It's essential for the company. And nobody's leaked anything. What did you tell him?"

"I stalled him," Casey said. "But if we want to kill the story, we have to give him something better. An interview with Edgarton, or an exclusive on the China sale. It's the only way to do it."

"That's fine," Marder said. "But Hal won't do any press. I can ask him, but I know he won't do it."

"Well, somebody needs to," Casey said. "Maybe you should."

"That could be difficult," Marder said. "Hal has instructed me to avoid the media until the sale is finalized. I have to be careful here. Is this guy trust-worthy?"

"In my experience, yes."

"If I give him something on deep background, he'll cover me?"

"Sure. He just needs something to file."

"All right. Then I'll talk to him." Marder scribbled a note. "Was there anything else?"

"No, that's all."

She turned to leave.

"By the way, how's Richman working out?"

"Fine," she said. "He's just inexperienced."

"He seems bright," Marder said. "Use him. Give him something to do."

"All right," Casey said.

"That was the problem with Marketing. They did-n't give him anything to do."

"Okay," she said.

Marder stood. "See you tomorrow at the IRT."

After Casey had gone, a side door opened. Richman walked in.

"You dumb fuck," Marder said. "She almost got hurt in 64 this afternoon. Where the hell were you?"

"Well, I was—"

"Get this straight," Marder said. "I don't want *anything* to happen to Singleton, you understand me? We need her in one piece. She can't do this job from a hospital bed."

"Got it, John."

"You better, pal. I want you next to her at all times, until we finish this thing."

## QA

6:20 P.M.

She went back down to her fourth floor offices. Norma was still at her desk, a cigarette dangling from her lip. "You got another stack on your desk, waiting for you."

"Okay."

"Richman's gone home for the day."

"Okay."

"He seemed eager to leave, anyway. But I talked to Evelyn in Accounting."

"And?"

"Richman's travel at Marketing was billed to customer services in the program office. That's a slush fund they use for baksheesh. And the kid spent a fortune."

"How much?"

"Are you ready? Two hundred and eighty-four thousand dollars."

"Wow," Casey said. "In three months?"

"Right."

"That's a lot of ski trips," Casey said. "How were the charges billed?"

"Entertainment. Customer not specified."

"Then who approved the charges?"

"It's a production account," Norma said. "Which means it's controlled by Marder."

"Marder approved these charges?"

"Apparently. Evelyn's checking for me. I'll get more later." Norma shuffled papers on her desk. "Not much else here . . . FAA's going to be late with the transcript of the CVR. There's a lot of Chinese spoken, and their translators are fighting about the meaning. The carrier's also doing their own translation, so . . ."

Casey sighed. "What else is new," she said. In incidents like this one, the cockpit voice recorders were sent to the FAA, which generated a written transcript of the cockpit conversation, since the pilot's voices were owned by the carrier. But disputes over the translation were the rule on foreign flights. It always happened.

"Did Allison call?"

"No, honey. The only personal call you got was from Teddy Rawley."

Casey sighed. "Never mind."

"That'd be my advice," Norma said.

• • •

In her office, she thumbed through the files on her desk. Most of it was paper on TransPacific 545. The first sheet summarized the stack that followed:

FAA FORM 8020-9, ACCIDENT/INCIDENT PRELIMINARY NOTICE

FAA FORM 8020-6, REPORT OF AIRCRAFT ACCIDENT

FAA FORM 8020-6-1, REPORT OF AIRCRAFT ACCIDENT (CONTINUATION)

FAA FORM 7230-10, POSITION LOGS
        HONOLULU ARINC
        LOS ANGELES ARTCC
        SOUTHERN CALIFORNIA ATAC

AUTOMATIC SIGN-IN/SIGN-OFF LOG
        SOUTHERN CALIFORNIA ATAC

FAA FORM 7230-4, DAILY RECORD OF FACILITY OPERATION
        LOS ANGELES ARTCC
        SOUTHERN CALIFORNIA ATAC

FAA FORM 7230-8, FLIGHT PROGRESS STRIP
        LOS ANGELES ARTCC
        SOUTHERN CALIFORNIA ATAC

FLIGHT PLAN, ICAO

She saw a dozen pages of flight path charts; transcriptions of air traffic control voice recordings; and more weather reports. Next was material from Norton, including a sheaf of fault record data—so far the only hard data they had to work with.

She decided to take it home. She was tired; she could look at it at home.

# GLENDALE

### 10:45 P.M.

He sat up in bed abruptly, turned, put his feet on the floor. "So. Listen babe," he said, not looking at her.

She stared at the muscles of his bare back. The ridge of his spine. The strong lines of his shoulders.

"This was great," he said. "It's great to see you."

"Uh-huh," she said.

"But you know, big day tomorrow."

She would have preferred he stay. The truth was, she felt better having him here at night. But she knew he was going to go. He always did. She said, "I understand. It's okay, Teddy."

That made him turn back to her. He gave her his charming, crooked smile. "You're the best, Casey." He bent over and kissed her, a long kiss. She knew this was because she wasn't begging him to stay. She kissed him back, smelling the faint odor of beer. She ran her hand around his neck, caressing the fine hairs.

Almost immediately, he pulled away again. "So. Anyway. Hate to run."

"Sure, Teddy."

"By the way," Teddy said, "I hear you toured the gardens, between shifts . . ."

"Yeah, I did."

"You don't want to piss off the wrong people."

"I know."

He grinned. "I'm sure you do." He kissed her

cheek, then bent over, reaching for his socks. "So, anyway, I probably should be heading out . . ."

"Sure, Teddy," she said. "You want coffee, before you go?"

He was pulling on his cowboy boots. "Uh, no, babe. This was great. Great to see you."

Not wanting to be left alone in the bed, she got up, too. She put on a big T-shirt, walked him to the door, kissed him briefly as he left. He touched her nose, grinned. "Great," he said.

"Good night, Teddy," she said.

She locked the door, set the alarm.

Walking back through the house, she turned off the stereo, glanced around to see if he had left anything. Other men usually left something behind, because they wanted a reason to come back. Teddy never did. All trace of his presence was gone. There was only the unfinished beer on the kitchen table. She threw it in the trash, wiped away the ring of moisture.

She had been telling herself for months to end it (End what? End *what?* a voice said), but she somehow never got around to saying the words. She was so busy at work, it was such an effort to meet people. Six months earlier she had gone with Eileen, Marder's assistant, to a country-and-western bar in Studio City. The place was frequented by young movie people, Disney animators—a fun crowd, Eileen said. Casey found it agonizing. She wasn't beautiful, and she wasn't young; she didn't have the effortless glamour of the girls that glided through the room in tight jeans and crop tops.

The men were all too young for her, their smooth faces unformed. And she couldn't make small talk with them. She felt herself too serious for this setting. She had a job, a child, she was looking at forty. She never went out with Eileen again.

It wasn't that she had no interest in meeting someone. But it was just so difficult. There was never enough time, never enough energy. In the end, she didn't bother.

So when Teddy would call, say he was in the neighborhood, she'd go unlock the door for him, and get in the shower. Get ready.

That was how it had been for a year, now.

She made tea, and got back in bed. She propped herself up against the headboard, reached for the stack of papers, and began to review the records from the fault data recorders.

She started to thumb through the printout:

```
A/S PWR TEST       0 0 0 0 0 0 1 0 0 0 0
AIL SERVO COMP     0 0 0 0 1 0 0 1 0 0 0
AOA INV            1 0 2 0 0 0 1 0 0 0 1
CFDS SENS FAIL     0 0 0 0 0 0 1 0 0 0 0
CRZ CMD MON INV    1 0 0 0 0 0 2 0 1 0 0
EL SERVO COMP      0 0 0 0 0 0 0 0 0 1 0
EPR/N1 TRA-1       0 0 0 0 0 0 1 0 0 0 0
FMS SPEED INV      0 0 0 0 0 0 4 0 0 0 0
PRESS ALT INV      0 0 0 0 0 0 3 0 0 0 0
G/S SPEED ANG      0 0 0 0 0 0 1 0 0 0 0
SLAT XSIT T/O      0 0 0 0 0 0 0 0 0 0 0
G/S DEV INV        0 0 1 0 0 0 5 0 0 0 1
```

```
GND SPD INV       0 0 0 0 0 0 2 1 0 0 0
TAS INV           0 0 0 0 1 0 1 0 0 0 0
TAT INV           0 0 0 0 0 0 1 0 0 0 0
AUX 1             0 0 0 0 0 0 0 0 0 0 0
AUX 2             0 0 0 0 0 0 0 0 0 0 0
AUX 3             0 0 0 0 0 0 0 0 0 0 0
AUX COA           0 1 0 0 0 0 0 0 0 0 0
A/S ROX-P         0 0 0 0 0 0 1 0 0 0 0
RDR PROX-1        0 0 0 0 1 0 0 1 0 0 0
```

There were nine more pages of dense data. She wasn't sure what all the readings represented, particularly the AUX fault checks. One was probably the auxiliary power unit, the gas turbine in the rear of the fuselage which provided power when the plane was on the ground, and backup power in the event of electrical failure during flight. But what were the others? Auxiliary line readings? Checks of redundant systems? And what was AUX COA?

She'd have to ask Ron.

She flipped ahead to the DEU listing, which stored faults by each leg of the flight. She scanned them quickly, yawning, and then suddenly she stopped:

```
DEU FAULT REVIEW

LEG 04      FAULTS 01

R/L SIB PROX SENS MISCOMPARE
8 APR       00:36
FLT 180     FC052606H
ALT 37000
A/S 320
```

She frowned.

She could hardly believe what she was seeing.

A fault in the proximity sensor.

Exactly what her check of maintenance records told her to look for.

More than two hours into the flight, a proximity sensor error was noted on the inboard electrical bus. The wing had many proximity sensors—little electronic pads which detected the presence of metal nearby. The sensors were needed to confirm that the slats and flaps were in the proper position on the wing, since the pilots couldn't see them from the cockpit.

According to this fault, a "miscompare" had occurred between sensors on the right and left sides. If the main electrical box in the fuselage had had a problem, faults would have been generated on both wings. But the right wing alone had generated the miscompare. She looked ahead, to see if the fault repeated.

She skipped through the listing quickly, shuffling papers. She didn't see anything at once. But a single fault in the sensor meant it should be checked. Again, she would have to ask Ron . . .

It was so difficult to try and assemble a picture of the flight from these bits and pieces. She needed the continuous data from the flight recorder. She'd call Rob Wong in the morning, and see how he was coming with that.

Meanwhile . . .

Casey yawned, settled lower on the pillows, and continued to work.

# WEDNESDAY

# GLENDALE

6:12 A.M.

The telephone was ringing. She awoke, groggy, and rolled over, hearing the crunch of paper beneath her elbow. She looked down and saw the data sheets scattered all over the bed.

The phone continued to ring. She picked it up.

"Mom." Solemn, close to tears.

"Hi, Allie."

"*Mom.* Dad is making me wear the red dress, and I want to wear the blue one with the flowers."

She sighed. "What did you wear yesterday?"

"The blue one. But it's not dirty or *anything!*"

This was an ongoing battle. Allison liked to wear the clothes she had worn the day before. Some innate, seven-year-old conservatism at work. "Honey, you know I want you to wear clean clothes to school."

"But it *is* clean, Mom. And I *hate* the red dress."

Last month, the red dress had been her favorite. Allison had fought to wear it every day.

Casey sat up in bed, yawned, stared at the papers, the dense columns of data. She heard her daughter's complaining voice on the phone and thought, Do I need this? She wondered why Jim didn't handle it. Everything was so difficult, over the phone. Jim didn't hold up his end—he wasn't firm with her—and the kid's natural tendency to play one parent against the other led to an interminable string of long-distance encounters like this.

Trivial problems, childish power plays.

"Allison," she said, interrupting her daughter. "If your father says to wear the red dress, you do what he says."

"But Mom—"

"He's in charge now."

"But Mom—"

"That's it, Allison. No more discussion. The red dress."

"Oh, Mom . . ." She started to cry. "I *hate* you."

And she hung up.

Casey considered calling her daughter back, decided not to. She yawned, got out of bed, walked into the kitchen and turned on the coffeemaker. Her fax machine was buzzing in the corner of the living room. She went over to look at the paper coming out.

It was a copy of a press release issued by a public relations firm in Washington. Although the firm had a neutral name—the Institute for Aviation Research—she knew it was a PR firm representing the European consortium that made Airbus. The release was formatted to look like a breaking wire-service story, complete with headline at the top. It said:

JAA DELAYS CERTIFICATION OF N-22
WIDEBODY JET CITING CONTINUED
AIRWORTHINESS CONCERNS

She sighed.

It was going to be a hell of a day.

# WAR ROOM

### 7:00 A.M.

Casey climbed the metal stairs to the War Room. When she reached the catwalk John Marder was there, pacing back and forth, waiting for her.

"Casey."

"Morning, John."

"You've seen this JAA thing?" He held up the fax.

"Yes, I have."

"It's nonsense, of course, but Edgarton drilled a hole. He's very upset. First, two N-22 incidents in two days, and now this. He's worried we're going to get creamed in the press. And he has no confidence that Benson's Media Relations people will handle this right."

Bill Benson was one of the old Norton hands; he had handled media relations since the days when the company lived on military contracts and didn't tell the press a damned thing. Testy and blunt, Benson had never adjusted to the post-Watergate world, where journalists were celebrities who brought down governments. He was famous for feuding with reporters.

"This fax may generate press interest, Casey. Especially among reporters who don't know how screwed up the JAA is. And let's face it, they won't want to talk to press flacks. They'll want an executive in the company. So Hal wants all the inquiries on the JAA routed to you."

"To me," she said. She was thinking, Forget it. She already had a job. "Benson won't be very happy if you do that—"

"Hal's talked to him personally. Benson's on board."

"Are you sure?"

"I also think," Marder said, "we ought to prepare a decent press package on the N-22. Something besides the usual PR crap. Hal suggested you compile a comprehensive package to refute the JAA stuff—you know, service hours, safety record, dispatch reliability data, SDRs, all of that."

"Okay . . ." That was going to be a lot of work, and—

"I told Hal you were busy, and that this was an added burden," Marder said. "He's approved a two-grade bump in your IC."

Incentive compensation, the company's bonus package, was a large part of every executive's income. A two-grade increase would mean a substantial amount of money for her.

"Okay," she said.

"The point is," Marder said, "we've got a good response to this fax—a substantive response. And Hal wants to make sure we get it out. Can I count on you to help us?"

"Sure," Casey said.

"Good," Marder said. And he walked up the stairs, into the room.

Richman was already in the room, looking preppy in a sport coat and tie. Casey slipped into a chair. Marder shifted into high gear, waving the JAA fax in the air, berating the engineers. "You've probably already seen that the JAA is playing games with us. Perfectly timed to jeopardize the China sale. But if you read the memo, you know that it's all about the engine in Miami and nothing about TransPacific. At least not yet . . ."

Casey tried to pay attention, but she was distracted, calculating what the change in IC would mean. A two-grade bump was . . . she did the figures in her head . . . something like a twenty-percent raise. Jesus, she thought. Twenty percent! She could send Allison to private school. And they could vacation someplace nice, Hawaii or someplace like that. They'd stay in a nice hotel. And next year, move to a bigger house, with a big yard so Allison could run around, and—

Everyone at the table was staring at her.

Marder said, "Casey? The DFDR? When can we expect the data?"

"Sorry," she said. "I talked to Rob this morning. The calibration's going slowly. He'll know more tomorrow."

"Okay. Structure?"

Doherty began in his unhappy monotone. "John

it's very difficult very difficult indeed. We found a bad locking pin on the number-two inboard slat. It's a counterfeit part and—"

"We'll verify it at Flight Test," Marder said, interrupting him. "Hydraulics?"

"Still testing, but so far they check out. Cables rigged to spec."

"You'll finish when?"

"End of first shift today."

"Electrical?"

Ron said, "We've checked the principal wiring pathways. Nothing yet. I think we should schedule a CET on the entire aircraft."

"I agree. Can we run it overnight to save time?"

Ron shrugged. "Sure. It's expensive, but—"

"The hell with expense. Anything else?"

"Well, there's one funny thing, yes," Ron said. "The DEU faults indicate there may have been a problem with proximity sensors in the wing. If the sensors failed, we might get a slats misread in the cockpit."

This was what Casey had noticed the night before. She made a note to ask Ron about it later. And also the matter of the AUX readings on the printout.

Her mind drifted again, thinking of the raise. Allison could go to a real school, now. She saw her at a low desk, in a small classroom—

Marder said: "Powerplant?"

"We're still not sure he deployed the thrust reversers," Kenny Burne said. "It'll be another day."

"Go until you can rule it out. Avionics?"

Trung said, "Avionics check out so far."

"This autopilot thing . . ."

"Haven't gotten to autopilot yet. It's the last thing in the sequence that we confirm. We'll know by Flight Test."

"All right," Marder said. "So: new question regarding proximity sensors, check that today. Still waiting on flight recorder, powerplant, avionics. That cover it?"

Everyone nodded.

"Don't let me keep you," Marder said. "I need answers." He held up the JAA fax. "This is the tip of the iceberg, people. I don't have to remind you what happened to the DC-10. Most advanced aircraft of its time, a marvel of engineering. But it had a couple of incidents, and some bad visuals, and bang— the DC-10's history. *History.* So get me those answers!"

## NORTON AIRCRAFT

### 9:31 A.M.

Walking across the plant toward Hangar 5, Richman said, "Marder seemed pretty worked up, didn't he? Does he believe all that?"

"About the DC-10? Yes. One crash finished the aircraft."

"What crash?"

"It was an American Airlines flight from Chicago to LA," Casey said. "May, 1979. Nice day, good weather. Right after takeoff the left engine fell off the wing. The plane stalled and crashed next to the airport, killing everybody on board. Very dramatic, it was all over in thirty seconds. A couple of people taped the flight, so the networks had film at eleven. The media went crazy, called the plane a winged coffin. Travel agents were flooded with calls canceling DC-10 bookings. Douglas never sold another one of them."

"Why did the engine fall off?"

"Bad maintenance," Casey said. "American hadn't followed Douglas's instructions on how to remove the engines from the plane. Douglas told them to first remove the engine, and then the pylon that holds the engine to the wing. But to save time, American took the whole engine–pylon assembly off at once. That's seven tons of metal on a forklift. One forklift ran out of gas during the removal, and cracked the pylon. But the crack wasn't noticed, and eventually the engine fell off the wing. So it was all because of maintenance."

"Maybe so," Richman said, "but isn't an airplane still supposed to fly, even missing an engine?"

"Yes, it is," Casey said. "The DC-10 was built to survive that kind of failure. The plane was perfectly airworthy. If the pilot had maintained airspeed, he'd have been fine. He could have landed the plane."

"Why didn't he?"

"Because, as usual, there was an event cascade leading to the final accident," Casey said. "In this case, electrical power to the captain's cockpit controls came from the left engine. When the left engine fell off, the captain's instruments were shut off, including the cockpit stall warning and the backup warning, called a stick shaker. That's a device that shakes the stick to tell the pilot the plane is about to stall. The first officer still had power and instruments, so the first officer's chair didn't have a stick shaker. It's a customer option for the first officer, and American hadn't ordered it. And Douglas hadn't built any redundancy into their cockpit-stall warning system. So when the DC-10 began to stall, the first officer didn't realize he had to increase throttle."

"Okay," Richman said, "but the captain shouldn't have lost his power in the first place."

"No, that was a designed-in safety feature," Casey said. "Douglas had designed and built the aircraft to survive those failures. When the left engine tore off, the aircraft deliberately shut down the captain's power line, to prevent further shorts in the system. Remember, all aircraft systems are redundant. If one fails, the backup kicks in. And it was easy to get the captain's instrumentation back again; all the flight engineer had to do was trip a relay, or turn on emergency power. But he didn't do either one."

"Why not?"

"No one knows," Casey said. "And the first officer, lacking the necessary information on his display, intentionally reduced his airspeed, which caused the plane to stall and crash."

They were silent for a moment, walking.

"Consider all the ways this might have been avoided," Casey said. "The maintenance crews could have checked the pylons for structural damage after servicing them improperly. But they didn't. Continental had already cracked two pylons using forklifts, and they could have told American the procedure was dangerous. But they didn't. Douglas had told American about Continental's problems, but American didn't pay any attention."

Richman was shaking his head.

"And after the accident, Douglas couldn't say it was a maintenance problem, because American was a valued customer. So Douglas wasn't going to put the story out. In all these incidents, it's always the same story—the story never gets out unless the media digs it out. But the story's complicated, and that's difficult for television . . . so they just run the tape. The tape of the accident which shows the left engine falling off, the plane veering left, and crashing. The visual implies the aircraft was poorly designed, that Douglas hadn't anticipated a pylon failure and hadn't built the plane to survive it. Which was completely inaccurate. But Douglas never sold another DC-10."

"Well," Richman said. "I don't think you can blame the media for that. They don't make the news. They just report it."

"That's my point," Casey said. "They didn't report it, they just ran the film. The Chicago crash was a kind of turning point in our industry. The first time a good aircraft was destroyed by bad press. The coup de grace was the NTSB report. It came out on December 21. Nobody paid any attention.

"So now, when Boeing introduces their new 777, they arrange a complete press campaign to coincide with the launch. They allow a TV company to film the years of development, and at the end there's a six-part show on public television. There's a book to go with it. They've done everything they can think of to create a good image for the plane in advance. Because the stakes are too high."

Richman walked along beside her. "I can't believe the media has that much power," he said.

Casey shook her head. "Marder is right to be worried," she said. "If anybody in the media gets onto Flight 545, then the N-22 will have had two incidents in two days. And we're in big trouble."

## NEWSLINE/NEW YORK

### 1:54 P.M.

In midtown Manhattan, in the twenty-third-floor offices of the weekly news show *Newsline,* Jennifer Malone was in the editing bay, reviewing tape of an interview with Charles Manson. Her assistant Deborah walked in, dropped a fax on her desk, and said casually, "Pacino dumped."

Jennifer hit her pause button. "What?"

"Al Pacino just dumped."

"When?"

"Ten minutes ago. Blew Marty off, and walked."

"*What?* We shot four days of B-roll on the set in Tangier. His picture opens this weekend—and he's slated for the full twelve." A twelve minute segment on *Newsline,* the most-watched news show on television, was the kind of publicity that money couldn't buy. Every star in Hollywood wanted on the show. "What happened?"

"Marty was chatting with him during makeup, and mentioned that Pacino hadn't had a hit in four years. And I guess he got offended, and walked."

"On camera?"

"No. Before."

"Jesus," Jennifer said. "Pacino can't do that. His contract calls for him to do publicity. This was set up months ago."

"Yeah, well. He did."

"What's Marty say?"

"Marty is pissed. Marty is saying, What did he expect, this is a news show, we ask hard-hitting questions. You know, typical Marty."

Jennifer swore. "This was just what everyone was worried about."

Marty Reardon was a notoriously abrasive interviewer. Although he had left the news division to work on *Newsline*—at a much higher salary—two years before, he still viewed himself as a hard-hitting newsman, tough but fair, no-holds-barred—though in practice he liked to embarrass interviewees, putting them on the spot with intensely personal questions, even if the questions weren't relevant to the story. Nobody wanted to use Marty on the Pacino shoot, because he didn't like celebrities, and didn't like doing "puff pieces." But Frances, who usually did the celeb pieces, was in Tokyo interviewing the princess.

"Has Dick talked to Marty? Can we salvage this?" Dick Shenk was the executive producer of *Newsline.* In just three years, he had skillfully built the show from a throwaway summer replacement, into a solid prime-time success. Shenk made all the important decisions, and he was the only person with enough clout to handle a prima donna like Marty.

"Dick is still at lunch with Mr. Early." Shenk's lunches with Early, the president of the network, always lasted late into the afternoon.

"So Dick doesn't know?"

"Not yet."

"Great," Jennifer said. She glanced at her watch: it was 2 P.M. If Pacino had dumped, they had a twelve-minute hole to fill, and less than seventy-two hours to do it. "What've we got in the can?"

"Nothing. Mother Teresa's being recut. Mickey Mantle isn't in yet. All we have is that wheelchair Little League segment."

Jennifer groaned. "Dick will never go with that."

"I know," Deborah said. "It sucks."

Jennifer picked up the fax her assistant had dropped on the console. It was a press release from some PR group, one of hundreds that every news show received each day. Like all such faxes, this one was formatted to look like a breaking news story, complete with a headline at the top. It said:

JAA DELAYS CERTIFICATION OF N-22
WIDEBODY JET CITING CONTINUED
AIRWORTHINESS CONCERNS

"What's this?" she said, frowning.

"Hector said give it to you."

"Why?"

"He thought there might be something in it."

"Why? What the fuck's the JAA?" Jennifer scanned the text; it was a lot of aerospace babble, dense and impenetrable. She thought: No visuals.

"Apparently," Deborah said, "it's the same plane that caught fire in Miami."

"Oh. Hector wants to do a safety segment? Good luck. Everybody's seen the tape of the burning plane already. And it wasn't that good to begin with." Jennifer tossed the fax aside. "Ask him if he has anything else."

Deborah went away. Alone, Jennifer stared at the frozen image of Charles Manson on the screen in front of her. Then she clicked the image off, and decided to take a moment to think.

Jennifer Malone was twenty-nine years old, the youngest segment producer in the history of *Newsline.* She had advanced quickly because she was good at her job. She had shown talent early; while still an undergraduate at Brown, working as a summer intern like Deborah, she had done research

late into the night, hammering away at the Nexis ter-
minals, combing the wire services. Then, with her
heart in her mouth, she had gone in to see Dick
Shenk, to propose a story about this strange new
virus in Africa, and the brave CDC doctor on the
scene. That led to the famous Ebola segment, the
biggest *Newsline* break of the year, and another
Peabody Award for Dick Shenk's Wall of Fame.

In short order, she had followed with the Darryl
Strawberry segment, the Montana strip-mining segment, and the Iroquois gambling segment. No college intern in memory had ever gotten a segment on
air before; Jennifer had four. Shenk announced he
liked her spunk, and offered her a job. The fact that
she was bright, beautiful, and an Ivy Leaguer did
not hurt, either. The following June, when she graduated, she went to work for *Newsline.*

The show had fifteen producers doing segments.
Each was assigned to one of the on-camera talent;
each was expected to deliver a story every two weeks.
The average story took four weeks to build. After two
weeks of research, producers met with Dick, to get
the go-ahead. Then they visited the locations, shot B-
roll for background, and did the secondary interviews. The story was shaped by the producer, and
narrated by the on-air star, who flew in for a single
day, did the stand-ups and the major interviews, and
then flew on to the next shoot, leaving the producer
to cut the tape. Sometime before air, the star would
come into the studio, read the script the producer had
prepared, and do the voice-overs for visuals.

When the segment finally aired, the on-camera star would come off as a real reporter: *Newsline* jealously protected the reputations of its stars. But in fact the producers were the real reporters. The producers picked the stories, researched and shaped them, wrote the scripts and cut the tape. The on-camera talent just did as they were told.

It was a system Jennifer liked. She had considerable power, and she liked working behind the scenes, her name unknown. She found the anonymity useful. Often, when she conducted interviews, she would be treated as a flunky, the interviewees speaking freely, even though tape was rolling. At some point, the interviewee would say, "When will I get to meet Marty Reardon?" She would solemnly answer that that hadn't been decided yet, and continue with her questions. And in the process, nail the stupid bozo who thought she was just a dress rehearsal.

The fact was, she made the story. She didn't care if the stars got the credit. "We never say they do the reporting," Shenk would intone. "We never imply they are interviewing someone they didn't actually interview. On this show, the talent is not the star. The star is the story. The talent is just a guide—leading the audience through the story. The talent is someone they trust, someone they're comfortable inviting into their home."

That was true, she thought. And anyway, there wasn't time to do it any other way. A media star like Marty Reardon was more heavily booked than the president, and arguably more famous, more recognizable on the street. You couldn't expect a person like Marty to waste his valuable time doing spadework, stumbling over false leads, putting together a story.

There just wasn't time.

This was television: there was never enough time.

She looked again at her watch. Dick wouldn't return from lunch until three or three-thirty. Marty Reardon was not going to apologize to Al Pacino. So when Dick came back from lunch, he was going to blow his top, rip Reardon a new one—and then be desperate for a package to fill the hole.

Jennifer had an hour to find him one.

She turned on her TV, and started idly flipping channels. And she looked again at the fax on her desk.

JAA DELAYS CERTIFICATION OF N-22
WIDEBODY JET CITING CONTINUED
AIRWORTHINESS CONCERNS

Wait a minute, she thought. *Continued* airworthiness concerns? Did that mean an ongoing safety problem? If so, there might be a story here. Not air safety—that had been done a million times. Those endless stories about air traffic control, how they were using 1960s computers, how outdated and risky the system was. Stories like that just made people anxious. The audience couldn't relate because there was nothing they could do about it.

But a specific aircraft with a problem? That was a product safety story. Don't buy this product. Don't fly this airplane.

That might be very, *very* effective, she thought.

She picked up the phone and dialed.

# HANGAR 5

11:15 A.M.

Casey found Ron Smith with his head in the forward accessory compartment, just back of the nose wheel. All around him, his electrical team was hard at work.

"Ron," she said, "tell me about this fault list." She had brought the list with her, all ten pages.

"What about it?"

"There's four AUX readings here. Lines one, two, three, and COA. What do they service?"

"Is this important?"

"That's what I'm trying to determine."

"Well." Ron sighed. "AUX 1 is the auxiliary power generator, the turbine in the tail. AUX 2 and AUX 3 are redundant lines, in case the system gets an upgrade and needs them later. AUX COA is an auxiliary line for Customer Optional Additions. That's the line for customer add-ons, like a QAR. Which this plane doesn't have."

Casey said, "These lines are registering a zero value. Does that mean they're being used?"

"Not necessarily. The default is zero, so you'd have to check them."

"Okay." She folded up the data sheets. "And what about the proximity sensor faults?"

"We're doing that now. We may turn up something. But look. The fault readings are snapshots of a moment in time. We'll never figure out what happened to this flight with snapshots. We need the DFDR data. You've got to get it for us, Casey."

"I've been pushing Rob Wong . . ."

"Push him harder," Smith said. "The flight recorder is the key."

From the back of the airplane, she heard a pained shout: "Fuck a hairy duck! I don't *believe* this!"

It had come from Kenny Burne.

He was standing on a platform behind the left engine, waving his arms angrily. The other engineers around him were shaking their heads.

Casey went over. "You found something?"

"Let me count the ways," Burne said, pointing to the engine. "First off, the coolant seals are installed wrong. Some maintenance idiot put them in backward."

"Affecting flight?"

"Sooner or later, yeah. But that's not all. Take a look at this inboard cowl on the reversers."

Casey climbed the scaffolding to the back of the engine, where the engineers were peering inside the open cowls of the thrust reversers.

"Show her, guys," Burne said.

They shone a work light on the interior surface of one cowl. Casey saw a solid steel surface, precisely curved, covered with fine soot from the engine. They held the light close to the Pratt and Whitney logo, which was embossed near the leading edge of the metal sleeve.

"See it?" Kenny said.

"What? You mean the parts stamp?" Casey said. The Pratt and Whitney logo was a circle with an eagle inside it, and the letters *P* and *W.*

"That's right. The stamp."

"What about it?"

Burne shook his head. "Casey," he said. "The eagle is *backward.* It's facing the wrong way."

"Oh." She hadn't noticed that.

"Now, do you think Pratt and Whitney put their eagle on backward? No way. This is a goddamn counterfeit part, Casey."

"Okay," she said. "But did it affect flight?"

That was the critical point. They'd already found counterfeit parts on the plane. Amos had said there would be more, and he was undoubtedly right. But the question was, Did any of them affect the behavior of the plane during the accident?

"Could have," Kenny said, stomping around. "But I can't tear down this engine, for Chrissakes. That'd be two weeks right there."

"Then how will we find out?"

"We need that flight recorder, Casey. We've got to have that data."

Richman said, "You want me to go over to Digital? See how Wong is coming?"

"No," Casey said. "It won't do any good." Rob Wong could be temperamental. Putting more pressure on him wouldn't accomplish anything; he was likely to walk out, and not return for two days.

Her cell phone rang. It was Norma.

"It's starting," she said. "You got calls from Jack Rogers, from Barry Jordan at the LA *Times,* from somebody named Winslow at the Washington *Post.* And a request for background material on the N-22, from *Newsline.*"

"*Newsline?* That TV show?"

"Yeah."

"They doing a story?"

"I don't think so," Norma said. "It sounded like a fishing expedition."

"Okay," Casey said. "I'll call you back." She sat down in a corner of the hangar and took out her notepad. She began to write out a list of documents to be included in a press package. Summary of FAA certification procedures for new aircraft. Announcement of FAA certification of the N-22; Norma would have to dig that up from five years ago. Last year's FAA report on aircraft safety. The company's internal report on N-22 safety in flight from 1991 to present—the record was outstanding. The annual updated history of the N-22. The list of ADs issued for the aircraft to date—there were very few. The one-sheet features summary on the plane, basic stats on speed and range, size and weight. She didn't want to send too much. But that would cover the bases.

Richman was watching her. "What now?" he said.

She tore off the sheet, gave it to him. "Give this to Norma. Tell her to prepare a press packet, and send it to whoever asks for it."

"Okay." He stared at the list. "I'm not sure I can read—"

"Norma will know. Just give it to her."

"Okay."

Richman walked away, humming cheerfully.

Her phone rang. It was Jack Rogers, calling her directly. "I keep hearing the wing's being offset. I'm told Norton is shipping the tools to Korea, but they're going to be transshipped from there to Shanghai."

"Did Marder talk to you?"

"No. We've traded calls."

"Talk to him," Casey said, "before you do anything."

"Will Marder go on the record?"

"Just talk to him."

"Okay," Rogers said. "But he'll deny it, right?"

"Talk to him."

Rogers sighed. "Look, Casey. I don't want to sit on a story that I've got right—and then read it two days from now in the LA *Times*. Help me out, here. Is there anything to the wing tooling story, or not?"

"I can't say anything."

"Tell you what," Rogers said. "If I were to write that several high-level Norton sources deny the wing is going to China, I assume you wouldn't have a problem with that?"

"I wouldn't, no." A careful answer, but then it was a careful question.

"Okay, Casey. Thanks. I'll call Marder."

He hung up.

## *NEWSLINE*

### 2:25 P.M.

Jennifer Malone dialed the number on the fax, and asked for the contact: Alan Price. Mr. Price was still at lunch, and she spoke to his assistant, Ms. Weld.

"I understand there's a delay in European certification of the Norton aircraft. What's the problem?"

"You mean the N-22?"

"That's right."

"Well, this is a contentious issue, so I'd prefer to go off the record."

"How far off?"

"Background."

"Okay."

"In the past, the Europeans accepted FAA certification of a new aircraft, because that certification was thought to be very rigorous. But lately JAA has been questioning the U.S. certification process. They feel that the American agency, the FAA, is in bed with the American manufacturers, and may have relaxed its standards."

"Really?" Perfect, Jennifer thought. Inept American bureaucracy. Dick Shenk loved those stories. And the FAA had been under attack for years; there must be plenty of skeletons there. "What's the evidence?" she asked.

"Well, the Europeans find the whole system unsatisfactory. For example, the FAA doesn't even store certification documents. They allow the aircraft companies to do that. It seems entirely too cozy."

"Uh-huh." She wrote:

*—FAA in bed with mfrs. Corrupt!*

"Anyway," the woman said, "if you want more information, I suggest you call the JAA directly, or maybe Airbus. I can give you the numbers."

She called the FAA instead. She got put through to their public affairs office, a man named Wilson.

"I understand the JAA is refusing to validate certification of the Norton N-22."

"Yes," Wilson said. "They've been dragging their feet for a while now."

"The FAA has already certified the N-22?"

"Oh sure. You can't build an airplane in this country without FAA approval and certification of the design and manufacturing process from start to finish."

"And do you have the certification documents?"

"No. They're kept by the manufacturer. Norton has them."

Ah-ha, she thought. So it was true.

*—Norton keeps certification, not FAA.*

*—Fox guarding chicken coop?*

"Does it bother you that Norton holds the documentation?"

"No, not at all."

"And you're satisfied that the certification process was proper?"

"Oh sure. And like I said, the plane was certified five years ago."

"I've been hearing that the Europeans are dissatisfied with the entire process of certification."

"Well, you know," Wilson said, adopting a diplomatic tone, "the JAA's a relatively new organization. Unlike the FAA, they have no statutory authority. So, I think they're still trying to decide how they want to proceed."

She called the information office for Airbus Industrie in Washington, and got put through to a marketing guy named Samuelson. He reluctantly confirmed that he had heard of the JAA confirmation delays, though he didn't have any details.

"But Norton's having a lot of problems these days," he said. "For example, I think the China sale is not as firm as they pretend it is."

This was the first she had heard of a China sale. She wrote:

*—China sale N-22?*

She said, "Uh-huh . . ."

"I mean, let's face it," Samuelson continued, "the Airbus A-340 is a superior plane in every way. It's newer than the Norton widebody. Better range. It's better in every way. We've been trying to explain this to the Chinese, and they are starting to understand our perspective. Anyway, if I had to guess, I'd guess the Norton sale to the People's Republic is going to fall apart. And of course safety concerns are part of that decision. Off the record, I think the Chinese are very concerned the plane is unsafe."

—*C thinks airplane unsafe.*

"Who would I talk to about that?" she said.

"Well, as you know, the Chinese are generally reluctant to discuss negotiations in progress," Samuelson said. "But I know a guy over at Commerce who may be able to help you. He's with the Ex-Im Bank, which provides long-term financing for overseas sales."

"What's his name?" she said.

His name was Robert Gordon. It took fifteen minutes for the operator at the Commerce Department to find him. Jennifer doodled. Finally the secretary said, "I'm sorry, Mr. Gordon is in a meeting."

"I'm calling from *Newsline*," she said.

"Oh." A pause. "Just a minute, please."

She smiled. It never failed.

Gordon came on, and she asked him about the JAA certification, and the Norton sale to the People's Republic. "Is it true the sale is in jeopardy?"

"Every airplane sale is in jeopardy until it's concluded, Ms. Malone," Gordon said. "But as far as I know, the China sale is in good standing. I did hear a rumor that Norton is having trouble with JAA certification for Europe."

"What's the trouble there?"

"Well," Gordon said, "I'm not really an aircraft expert, but the company's had an awful lot of problems."

*—Norton has problems.*

Gordon said, "There was that thing in Miami yesterday. And of course you heard about that incident in Dallas."

"What's that?"

"Last year, they had an engine flameout on the runway. And everybody jumped off the plane. A bunch of people broke their legs jumping off the wings."

*—Dallas incident—engine/broken legs. Tape?*

She said, "Uh-huh . . ."

"I don't know about you," Gordon said, "but I don't like to fly very much, and uh, Jesus Christ, people are jumping off the airplane, that's not a plane I'd want to be on."

She wrote:

*—jumping off plane YOW!*

*—unsafe aircraft.*

And beneath it, in large block letters, she wrote: *DEATHTRAP.*

She called Norton Aircraft for their version of the story. She got a PR guy named Benson. He sounded like one of those drawling, half-asleep corporate guys. She decided to hit him right between the eyes. "I want to ask you about the Dallas incident."

"Dallas?" His voice sounded startled.

Good.

"Last year," she said. "You had a flameout of the engine, and people jumped off the plane. Broke their legs."

"Oh, right. That incident involved a 737," Benson said.

—*incident w/737.*

"Uh-huh. Well, what can you tell me about it?"

"Nothing," Benson said. "That wasn't our plane."

"Oh, come on," she said. "Look, I already know about the incident."

"That's a Boeing plane."

She sighed. "Jesus. Give me a break." It was so tedious, the way these PR types stonewalled. As if a good investigative reporter would never find out the truth. They seemed to think if they didn't tell her, no one would.

"I'm sorry, Ms. Malone, but we don't make that plane."

"Well, if that's really true," she said, her tone openly sarcastic, "I suppose you can tell me how I can confirm it?"

"Yes ma'am," Benson said. "You dial area code 206 and ask for Boeing. They'll help you."

*Click.*

Jesus! What a prick! How could these companies treat the media this way? You piss off a reporter,

you'll always get paid back. Didn't they understand that?

She called Boeing, asked for the PR department.
She got an answering machine, some bitch reciting
a fax number and saying questions should be faxed,
and they would get back to her. Unbelievable,
Jennifer thought. A major American corporation,
and they didn't even answer the phone.

Irritably, she hung up. There was no point in waiting. If the Dallas incident involved a Boeing plane,
she had no story.

No damn story.

She drummed her fingers on the desk, trying to
decide what to do.

She called Norton back, saying she wanted to talk to
someone in management, not PR. She was put
through to the president's office, then was transferred to some woman named Singleton. "How can
I help you?" the woman said.

"I understand there's been a delay in European
certification of the N-22. What's the problem with
the plane?" Jennifer asked.

"No problem at all," Singleton said. "We've been
flying the N-22 in this country for five years."

"Well, I've been hearing from sources that this is
an unsafe aircraft," Jennifer said. "You had an engine
flameout on the runway at Miami yesterday . . ."

"Actually, we had a rotor burst. That's being

investigated now." The woman was speaking smoothly, calmly, as if it was the most normal thing in the world for an engine to blow up.

—*"rotor burst"!*

"Uh-huh," Jennifer said. "I see. But if it's true your plane has no problems, why is the JAA withholding certification?"

The woman at the other end paused. "I can only give you background on this," she said. "Off the record."

She sounded unsettled, tense.

Good. Getting somewhere.

"There is no problem with the aircraft, Ms. Malone. The issue concerns powerplant. In this country, the plane flies with Pratt and Whitney engines. But the JAA is telling us that if we want to sell the plane in Europe, we're going to have to equip it with IAE engines."

"IAE?"

"A European consortium that makes engines. Like Airbus. A consortium."

"Uh-huh," Jennifer said.

—*IAE = consortium Europe*

"Now allegedly," Singleton continued, "the JAA wants us to equip the aircraft with the IAE engine to meet European noise and emission standards, which are more stringent than those in the U.S. But the reality is we make airframes, not engines, and we believe the engine decision should be left up to the customer. We install the engine the customer asks for. If they want an IAE, we put an IAE on. If they want a Pratt and Whitney, we put Pratt and Whitney on. They want GE, we put GE on. That's the way it's always been in this business. The customer picks the engine. So we consider this an unwarranted regulatory intrusion by the JAA. We're happy to put on IAE engines, if Lufthansa or Sabena tells us to do it. But we don't think JAA should dictate the terms of market entry. In other words, the issue has nothing to do with airworthiness."

Listening, Jennifer frowned. "You're saying it's a regulatory dispute?"

"Exactly. This is a trading bloc issue. The JAA is trying to force us to use European engines. But if that's their goal, we think they should force it on the European airlines, not us."

—*regulatory dispute!!!*

"And why haven't they forced it on the Europeans?"

"You'd have to ask JAA. But frankly, I imagine they've already tried, and been told to go to hell. Aircraft are custom built to the carrier's specs. The operators choose the engines, the electronics packages, the interior configuration. It's their choice."

Jennifer was now doodling. She was listening to the tone of the woman's voice at the other end of the line, trying to sense the emotion. This woman sounded slightly bored, like a schoolteacher at the end of the day. Jennifer detected no tension, no hesitation, no hidden secrets.

Fuck, she thought. No story.

She made one last try: she called the National Transportation Safety Board in Washington. She got put through to a man named Kenner in public affairs.

"I'm calling about the JAA certification of the N-22."

Kenner sounded surprised. "Well, you know, that's really not our area. You probably want to talk to someone at the FAA."

"Can you give me anything on background?"

"Well, FAA aircraft certification is extremely rigorous and has served as the model for foreign regulatory bureaucracies. As long as I can remember, foreign agencies around the world have accepted FAA certification as sufficient. Now the JAA has broken that tradition, and I don't think it's any secret why. It's politics, Ms. Malone. The JAA wants the Americans to use European engines, so they're threatening to withhold certification. And, of course, Norton's about to make a sale of N-22s to China, and Airbus wants that sale."

"So the JAA is trashing the plane?"

"Well. They're certainly raising doubts."

"Legitimate doubts?"

"Not as far as I'm concerned. The N-22's a good plane. A proven plane. Airbus says they have a brand-new plane; Norton says they have a proven plane. The Chinese are probably going to take the proven product. It's also somewhat less expensive."

"But is the plane safe?"

"Oh, absolutely."

—*NTSB says plane is safe.*

Jennifer thanked him, and hung up. She sat back in her chair, and sighed. No story.

Nothing.

Period.

The end.

"Shit," she said.

She punched the intercom. "Deborah," she said. "About this aircraft thing—"

"*Are you watching?*" Deborah said, squealing.

"Watching what?"

"CNN. It's un-*fucking*-believable."

Jennifer grabbed her remote.

## EL TORITO RESTAURANT

### 12:05 P.M.

The El Torito offered acceptable food at a reasonable price, and fifty-two kinds of beer; it was a local favorite of the engineers. The IRT members were all sitting at a center table in the main room, right off the bar. The waitress had taken their order and was leaving, when Kenny Burne said, "So, I hear Edgarton's got a few problems."

"Don't we all," Doug Doherty said, reaching for the chips and salsa.

"Marder hates him."

"So what?" Ron Smith said. "Marder hates everybody."

"Yeah but the thing is," Kenny said, "I keep hearing Marder is not going to—"

"Oh Jesus! *Look!*" Doug Doherty pointed across the room, toward the bar.

They all turned to stare at the television set mounted above the bar. The sound was down, but the image was unmistakable: the interior of a Norton widebody jet, as seen by a badly shaking video camera. Passengers were literally flying through the air, bouncing off luggage racks and wall panels, tumbling over the seats.

"Holy *shit,*" Kenny said.

They got up from the table, ran into the bar shouting, "Sound! Turn up the sound!" The horrifying images continued.

By the time Casey got into the bar, the video segment had ended. The television now showed a thin man with a moustache, wearing a carefully cut blue suit which somehow suggested a uniform. She recognized Bradley King, an attorney who specialized in airline accidents.

"Well that figures," Burne said, "it's Sky King."

"I think this footage speaks for itself," Bradley King was saying. "My client, Mr. Song, provided it to us, and it vividly portrays the terrible ordeal passengers were subjected to on this doomed flight. This aircraft went into an unprovoked and uncontrolled dive—it came within five hundred feet of crashing in the Pacific Ocean!"

"*What?*" Kenny Burne said. "It did *what?*"

"As you know, I'm a pilot myself, and I can say with absolute conviction that what occurred is a result of well-known design flaws on the N-22 jet. Norton has known about these design flaws for years and has done nothing. Pilots, operators, and FAA specialists have all complained bitterly about the aircraft. I personally know pilots who refuse to fly the N-22 because it is so unsafe."

"Especially the ones on your payroll," Burne said.

On the television, King was saying, "Yet the Norton Aircraft Company has done nothing substantive to address these safety concerns. It's inexplicable, really, that they could know about these problems and do nothing. Given their criminal negligence, it was only a matter of time until a tragedy like this occurred. Now three people are dead, two passengers paralyzed, the copilot in a coma as we speak. All together, fifty-seven passengers required hospitalization. That's a disgrace to aviation."

"That sleazebag," Kenny Burne said. "He *knows* it's not true!"

But the television was showing the CNN tape again, this time in slow motion, the bodies spiraling through the air, alternately blurred and sharp. Watching it, Casey started to sweat. She felt dizzy and cold, her chest tight. The restaurant around her became dim, pale green. She dropped quickly to a bar stool, took a deep breath.

Now the television showed a bearded man with a scholarly air, standing near one of the runways at LAX. Aircraft were taxiing in the background. She couldn't hear what the man was saying because the engineers around her were screaming at the image.

"You asshole!"

"Fuckface!"

"Weenyprick!"

"Lying dipshit!"

"Will you guys shut up?" she said. The bearded man on the screen was Frederick Barker, a former FAA official, no longer with the agency. Barker had testified in court against the company several times in recent years. The engineers all hated him.

Barker was saying, "Oh yes, I'm afraid there's no question about the problem." About what problem? she thought, but now the television cut back to the CNN studio in Atlanta, the female anchor in front of a photograph of the N-22. Beneath the photograph it said, UNSAFE? in huge red letters.

"Christ, do you believe that shit," Burne said. "Sky King and then that scumbag Barker. Don't they know Barker *works* for King?"

The television now showed a bombed-out building in the Middle East. Casey turned away, got off the bar stool, took a deep breath.

"Goddamn, I want a beer," Kenny Burne said. He headed back to the table. The others followed him, muttering about Fred Barker.

Casey picked up her purse, got her cell phone out and called the office. "Norma," she said, "call CNN and get a copy of the tape they just ran on the N-22."

"I was just going out to—"

"Now," Casey said. "Do it right now."

# NEWSLINE

### 3:06 P.M.

"Deborah!" Jennifer screamed, watching the tape. "Call CNN and get a copy of that Norton tape!" Jennifer watched, transfixed. Now they were running it again, this time in slow motion, six frames a second. And it held up! Fantastic!

She saw one poor bastard tumble through the air like a diver out of control, arms and legs flailing in all directions. The guy smashed into a seat, and his neck *snapped,* the body twisting, before he bounced up in the air again and hit the ceiling . . . Incredible! His neck being broken, *right on tape!*

It was the greatest piece of tape she'd ever seen. And the sound! Fabulous! People screaming in pure terror—sounds you couldn't fake—people shouting in Chinese, which made it *very exotic,* and all these incredible *crashing noises* as people and bags and shit smashed into the walls and ceilings—Jesus!

It was fabulous tape! Unbelievable! And it *went on* for an eternity, forty-five seconds—and all of it good! Because even when the camera wobbled, when it streaked and blurred, that just added to it! You couldn't *pay* a cameraman to do that!

"Deborah!" she screamed. "Deborah!"

She was so excited her heart was pounding. She felt like she was going to jump out of her skin. She was dimly aware of the guy on camera now, some weasel lawyer, feeding the segment his opening arguments; it must be his tape. But she knew he would give it to *Newsline,* he'd want the exposure, which meant—they had a story! Fantastic! A little frill and build, and they were there!

Deborah came in, flushed, excited. Jennifer said, "Get me the clips on Norton Aircraft for the last five years. Do a Nexis search on the N-22, on a guy named Bradley King, and a guy named"—she looked back at the screen—"Frederick Barker. Download it all. I want it now!"

Twenty minutes later, she had the outlines of the story, and the background on the key figures. LA *Times* story from five years ago on the roll-out, certification, and maiden flight for the launch customer of the Norton N-22. Advanced avionics, advanced electronic control systems and autopilot, blah blah blah.

*New York Times* story on Bradley King, the controversial plaintiff's attorney, under fire for approaching the families of crash victims before they had been officially informed of their relative's death by the airlines. Another LA *Times* story on Bradley King, settling a class-action suit after the

Atlanta crash. Long Beach *Independent Press-Telegram,* Bradley King, "the King of Aviation Torts," censured by the Ohio bar for misconduct in contacting victims' families; King denies wrongdoing. *New York Times* story, has Bradley King gone too far?

LA *Times* story on "whistle-blower" Frederick Barker's controversial departure from the FAA. Barker, an outspoken critic, says he quit in dispute over the N-22. Supervisor says Barker was fired for leaking reports to media. Barker sets up private practice as "aviation consultant."

Long Beach *Independent Press-Telegram,* Fred Barker launches crusade against Norton N-22, which he claims has a "history of unacceptable safety incidents." Orange County *Telegraph-Star,* Fred Barker's campaign to make airlines safe. Orange County *Telegraph-Star,* Barker accuses FAA of failing to clamp down on "unsafe Norton aircraft." Orange County *Telegraph-Star,* Barker key witness for Bradley King lawsuit, settled out of court.

Jennifer was beginning to see the shape that the story would take. Clearly they should stay away from the ambulance chaser, Bradley King. But Barker, a former FAA official, would be useful. He would probably also be able to criticize certification practices by the FAA.

And she noticed that Jack Rogers, the reporter for the Orange County *Telegraph-Star,* took a particularly critical view of Norton Aircraft. She noted several recent stories under Rogers's byline:

Orange County *Telegraph-Star,* Edgarton under pressure to make new sales for troubled company. Dissension among directors, top management. Doubts he will succeed.

Orange County *Telegraph-Star,* drug and gang activity on Norton twinjet assembly line.

Orange County *Telegraph-Star,* rumors of union trouble. Workers oppose the China sale, which they say will ruin the company.

Jennifer smiled.

Things were definitely looking up.

She called Jack Rogers at his newspaper. "I've been reading your pieces on Norton. They're excellent. I gather you think the company's got some problems."

"A lot of problems," Rogers said.

"You mean with the airplanes?"

"Well, yes, but they're also having union problems."

"What's that about?"

"It's not clear. But the plant's in turmoil, and management's not leading. The union's angry about the China sale. Thinks it shouldn't happen."

"Will you talk about this on camera?"

"Sure. I can't give you my sources, but I'll tell you what I know."

Of course he would, Jennifer thought. It was the dream of every print reporter to somehow get on television. The print guys all understood the real money came from appearing on the box. No matter how successful you were in print, you were nothing unless you could get on TV. Once you had name recognition from TV, you could migrate to the lucrative lecture circuit, getting five, ten thousand dollars just to speak at a lunch.

"I'll probably be out later in the week . . . My office will contact you."

"Just tell me when," Rogers said.

She called Fred Barker in Los Angeles. He almost seemed to be expecting her call. "That's pretty dramatic videotape," she said.

"It's frightening," Barker said, "when an aircraft's slats deploy at nearly the speed of sound. That's what happened on the TransPacific flight. It's the ninth such incident since the aircraft entered service."

"The *ninth?*"

"Oh yes. This is nothing new, Ms. Malone. At least three other deaths are attributable to Norton's shoddy design, and yet the company has done nothing."

"You have a list?"

"Give me your fax number."

She stared at the list. It was a little too detailed for her taste, but still compelling:

### Norton N-22 Slats Deployment Incidents

**1. January 4, 1992.** Slats deployed at FL350, at .84 Mach. The flap/slat handle moved inadvertently.

**2. April 2, 1992.** Slats deployed while the airplane was in cruise at .81 Mach. A clipboard reportedly fell on the flap/slat handle.

**3. July 17, 1992.** Initially reported as severe turbulence; however it was later learned that the slats had extended as a result of inadvertent flap/slat handle movement. Five passenger injuries, three serious.

**4. December 20, 1992.** Slats extended in cruise flight without movement of the flap/slat handle in cockpit. Two passenger injuries.

**5. March 12, 1993.** Airplane entered a prestall buffet at .82 Mach. The slats were found to be extended and the handle was not in the up and locked position.

**6. April 4, 1993.** First officer rested his arm on the flap/slat handle, moved the handle down, extending the slats. Several passenger injuries.

**7. July 4, 1993.** Pilot reported the flap/slat handle moved and slats extended. Aircraft was in cruise flight at .81 Mach.

**8. June 10, 1994.** The slats extended while the airplane was in cruise flight without movement of the flap/slat handle.

She picked up the phone and called Barker back. "Will you talk about these incidents on camera?"

"I've testified in court about this on numerous occasions," Barker said. "I'll be happy to speak to you on the record. The fact is, I want this airplane fixed before more people die. And nobody has been willing to do it—not the company, and not the FAA. It's a disgrace."

"But how can you be so sure this flight was a slats accident?"

"I have a source inside Norton," Barker said. "A disgruntled employee who is tired of all the lying. My source tells me it is slats, and the company is covering up."

Jennifer got off the phone with Barker, and pushed the intercom button. "Deborah!" she screamed. "Get me travel!"

Jennifer closed the door to her office, and sat quietly. She knew she had a story.

A fabulous story.

The question now was: What's the angle? How do you frame it?

On a show like *Newsline,* the frame was all-important. Older producers on the show talked about "context," which to them meant putting the story in a larger setting. Indicating what the story meant, by reporting what had happened before, or reporting similar things that had occurred. The older guys thought context so important, they seemed to regard it as a kind of moral or ethical obligation.

Jennifer disagreed. Because when you cut out all the sanctimonious bullshit, context was just spin, a way of pumping the story—and not a very useful way, because context meant referring to the past.

Jennifer had no interest in the past; she was one of the new generation that understood that gripping television was *now,* events happening *now,* a flow of images in a perpetual unending electronic present. Context by its very nature required something more than *now,* and her interest did not go beyond *now.* Nor, she thought, did anyone else's. The past was dead and gone. Who cared what you ate yesterday? What you did yesterday? What was immediate and compelling was *now.*

And television at its best was *now.*

So a good frame had nothing to do with the past. Fred Barker's damning list of prior incidents was actually a problem, because it drew attention to the fading, boring past. She'd have to find a way around it—give it a mention and go on.

What she was looking for was a way to shape the story so that it unfolded *now,* in a pattern that the viewer could follow. The best frames engaged the viewer by presenting the story as conflict between good and bad, a morality story. Because the audience got that. If you framed a story that way, you got instant acceptance. You were speaking their language.

But because the story also had to unfold quickly, this morality tale had to hang from a series of hooks that did not need to be explained. Things the audience already knew to be true. They already knew big corporations were corrupt, their leaders greedy sexist pigs. You didn't have to prove that; you just had to mention it. They already knew that government bureaucracies were inept and lazy. You didn't have to prove that, either. And they already knew that products were cynically manufactured with no concern for consumer safety.

From such agreed-upon elements, she must construct her morality story.

A fast-moving morality story, happening now.

Of course, there was still another requirement for the frame. Before anything else, she must sell the segment to Dick Shenk. She had to come up with an angle that would appeal to Shenk, that would fit his view of the world. And that was no easy matter: Shenk was more sophisticated than the audience. More difficult to please.

Within the *Newsline* offices Shenk was known as the Critic, for the harsh way he shot down proposed segments. Walking around the office, Shenk adopted an affable air, playing the grand old man. But all that changed when he listened to a proposal. Then he became dangerous. Dick Shenk was well educated and smart—very smart—and he could be charming when he wanted to. But at bottom he was mean. He had grown meaner with age, cultivating his nasty streak, regarding it as a key to his success.

Now she was going to take a proposal in to him. She knew Shenk would want a story badly. But he would also be angry about Pacino, angry about Marty, and his anger could quickly turn against Jennifer, and her proposed segment.

To avoid his anger, to sell him this segment, she

would have to proceed carefully. She would have to fashion the story into a shape that, more than anything else, gave vent to Dick Shenk's hostility and anger, and turned it in a useful direction.

She reached for a notepad, and began to sketch the outlines of what she would say.

# ADMINISTRATION

### 1:04 P.M.

Casey got into the elevator in Administration, Richman following her. "I don't understand," he said. "Why is everybody so angry with King?"

"Because he's lying," Casey said. "He knows the aircraft didn't come within five hundred feet of the Pacific Ocean. Everybody'd be dead if it did. The incident happened at thirty-seven thousand feet. At most the aircraft dropped three or four thousand feet. That's bad enough."

"So? He's getting attention. Making the case for his client. He knows what he's doing."

"Yes, he does."

"Hasn't Norton settled out of court with him in the past?"

"Three times," she said.

Richman shrugged. "If you have a strong case, take him to trial."

"Yes," Casey said. "But trials are very expensive, and the publicity doesn't do us any good. It's cheaper to settle, and just add the cost of his greenmail to the price of our aircraft. The carriers pay that price, and pass it on to the customer. So in the end, every airline passenger pays a few dollars extra for their ticket, in a hidden tax. The litigation tax. The Bradley King tax. That's how it works in the real world."

The doors opened, and they came out on the fourth floor. She hurried down the corridor toward her department.

"Where are we going now?" Richman said.

"To get something important that I forgot all about." She looked at him. "And you did, too."

## NEWSLINE

### 4:45 P.M.

Jennifer Malone headed toward Dick Shenk's office. On the way, she passed his Wall of Fame, a tight arrangement of photographs, plaques, and awards. The photographs showed intimate moments with the rich and famous: Shenk riding horses with Reagan; Shenk on a yacht with Cronkite; Shenk in a Southampton softball game with Tisch; Shenk with Clinton; Shenk with Ben Bradlee. And in the far corner, a photograph of an absurdly young Shenk with shoulder-length hair, an Arriflex mounted on his shoulder, filming John Kennedy in the Oval Office.

Dick Shenk had begun his career in the sixties as a scrappy documentary producer, back in the days when the news divisions were prestige loss leaders for the networks—autonomous, handsomely budgeted, and lavishly staffed. Those were the great days of the CBS *White Papers* and NBC *Reports*. Back then, when Shenk was a kid running around with an Arri, he was in the world, getting real stuff that mattered. With age and success, Shenk's horizons had narrowed. His world was now limited to his weekend house in Connecticut and his brownstone in New York. If he went anywhere else, it was in a limousine. But despite his privileged upbringing, his Yale education, his beautiful ex-wives, his comfortable existence, and his worldly success, Shenk at sixty was dissatisfied with his life. Riding around in his limousine, he felt unappreciated: not enough recognition, not enough respect for his accomplishments. The questing kid with the camera had aged into a querulous and bitter adult. Feeling he had been denied respect himself, Shenk in turn denied it to others—adopting a pervasive cynicism toward everything around him. And that was why, she felt certain, he would buy her frame on the Norton story.

Jennifer entered the outer office, stopped by Marian's desk. "Going to see Dick?" Marian said.

"Is he in?"

She nodded. "You want company?"

"Do I need it?" Jennifer said, raising an eyebrow.

"Well," Marian said. "He's been drinking."

"It's okay," Jennifer said. "I can handle him."

. . .

Dick Shenk listened to her, eyes closed, fingers pressed together to make a steeple. From time to time, he nodded slightly as she spoke.

She ran through the proposed segment, hitting all the beats: the Miami incident, the JAA certification story, the TransPacific flight, the jeopardized China sale. The former FAA expert who says the plane has a long history of uncorrected design problems. The aviation reporter who says the company is mismanaged, drugs and gang activity on the factory floor; a controversial new president, trying to boost flagging sales. Portrait of a once-proud company in trouble.

The way to frame the piece, she said, was Rot Beneath the Surface. She laid it out: badly run company makes a shoddy product for years. Knowledgeable people complain, but the company never responds. FAA is in bed with the company and won't force the issue. Now, at last, the truth comes out. The Europeans balk at certification; the Chinese have cold feet; the plane continues to kill passengers, just as critics said it would. And there's tape, riveting tape, showing the agonies passengers went through as several died. At the close, it's obvious to all: the N-22 is a deathtrap.

She finished. There was a long moment of silence. Then Shenk opened his eyes.

"Not bad," he said.

She smiled.

"What's the company's response?" he asked, in a lazy voice.

"Stonewall. The plane's safe; the critics are lying."

"Just what you'd expect," Shenk said, shaking his head. "American stuff is so shitty." Dick drove a BMW; his tastes ran to Swiss watches, French wines, English shoes. "Everything this country makes is crap," he said. He slumped back in his chair, as if fatigued by the thought. Then his voice became lazy again, thoughtful: "But what can they offer as proof?"

"Not much," Jennifer said. "The Miami and TransPacific incidents are still under investigation."

"Reports due when?"

"Not for weeks."

"Ah." He nodded slowly. "I like it. I like it very much. It's compelling journalism—and it beats the shit out of *60 Minutes*. They did unsafe airplane parts last month. But we're talking about a whole unsafe aircraft! A deathtrap. *Perfect!* Scare the hell out of everybody."

"I think so, too," she said. She was smiling broadly now. He had bought it!

"And I'd love to stick it to Hewitt," Dick said. Don Hewitt, the legendary producer of *60 Minutes,* was Shenk's nemesis. Hewitt consistently got better press than Shenk, which rankled. "Those jerkoffs," he said. "Remember when they did their hard-hitting segment on off-season golf pros?"

She shook her head. "Actually, no . . ."

"It was a while back," Dick said. He got fuzzy for

a moment, staring into space, and it was clear to her that he had been drinking heavily at lunch. "Never mind. Okay, where are we? You got the FAA guy, you got the reporter, you got tape of Miami. The peg is the home video, we lead with that."

"Right," she said, nodding.

"But CNN is going to run it day and night," he said. "By next week, it'll be ancient history. We have to go with this story Saturday."

"Right," she said.

"You got twelve minutes," he said. He spun in his chair, looked at the colored strips on the wall, representing the segments in production, where the talent was going to be. "And you got uh, Marty. He's doing Bill Gates in Seattle on Thursday; we'll shuttle him to LA Friday. You'll have him six, seven hours."

"Okay."

He spun back. "Go do it."

"Okay," she said. "Thanks, Dick."

"You sure you can put it together in time?"

She started collecting her notes. "Trust me."

As she headed out through Marian's office, she heard him shout, "Just remember, Jennifer—don't come back with a *parts* story! I don't want a fucking *parts* story!"

# QA/NORTON

2:21 P.M.

Casey came into the QA office with Richman. Norma was back from lunch, lighting another cigarette. "Norma," she said, "have you seen a videotape around here? One of those little eight-millimeter things?"

"Yeah," Norma said, "you left it on your desk the other night. I put it away." She rummaged in her drawer, brought it out. She turned to Richman. "And you got two calls from Marder. He wants you to call him right away."

"Okay," Richman said. He walked down the hall to his office. When he was gone, Norma said, "You know, he talks to Marder a lot. I heard it from Eileen."

"Marder's getting in with the Norton relatives?"

Norma was shaking her head. "He's already married Charley's only daughter, for Christ's sake."

"What're you saying?" Casey said. "Richman's reporting to Marder?"

"About three times a day."

Casey frowned. "Why?"

"Good question, honey. I think you're being set up."

"For what?"

"I have no idea," Norma said.

"Something about the China sale?"

Norma shrugged. "I don't know. But Marder is the best corporate infighter in the history of the company. And he's good at covering his tracks. I'd be real careful around this kid." She leaned across her desk, lowered her voice. "When I got back from lunch," she said, "nobody was around. The kid keeps his briefcase in his office. So I had a look."

"And?"

"Richman's copying everything in sight. He's got a copy of every memo on your desk. And he's Xeroxed your phone logs."

"My phone logs? What's the point of that?"

"I couldn't begin to imagine," Norma said. "But there's more. I also found his passport. He's been to Korea five times in the last two months."

"Korea?" Casey said.

"That's right, honey. Seoul. Went almost every week. Short trips. One, two days only. Never more than that."

"But—"

"There's more," Norma said. "The Koreans mark entry visas with a flight number. But the numbers on Richman's passport weren't commercial flight numbers. They were tail numbers."

"He went on a private jet?"

"That's what it looks like."

"A Norton jet?"

Norma shook her head. "No. I talked to Alice in Flight Ops. None of the company jets has been to Korea in the last year. They've been shuttling back and forth from Beijing for months. But none to Korea."

Casey frowned.

"There's more," Norma said. "I talked to the Fizer

in Seoul. He's an old beau of mine. Remember when Marder had that dental emergency last month, and took three days off?"

"Yeah . . ."

"He and Richman were together in Seoul. Fizer heard about it after they'd gone, and was annoyed to be kept out of the loop. Wasn't invited to any of the meetings they attended. Took it as a personal insult."

"What meetings?" Casey said.

"Nobody knows." Norma looked at her. "But be careful around that kid."

She was in her office, going through the most recent pile of telexes, when Richman poked his head in. "What's next?" he said cheerfully.

"Something's come up," Casey said. "I need you to go to the Flight Standards District Office. See Dan Greene over there, and get copies of the flight plan and the crew list for TPA 545."

"Don't we already have that?"

"No, we just have the preliminaries. By now Dan will have the finals. I want them in time for the meeting tomorrow. The office is in El Segundo."

"El Segundo? That'll take me the rest of the day."

"I know, but it's important."

He hesitated. "I think I could be more help to you if I stayed here—"

"Get going," she said. "And call me when you have them."

# VIDEO IMAGING SYSTEMS

4:30 P.M.

The back room of Video Imaging Systems in Glendale was packed with row after row of humming computers, the squat purple-striped boxes of Silicon Graphics Indigo machines. Scott Harmon, his leg in a cast, hobbled over the cables that snaked across the floor.

"Okay," he said, "we should have it up in a second."

He led Casey into one of the editing bays. It was a medium-size room with a comfortable couch along the back wall, beneath movie posters. The editing console wrapped around the other three walls of the room; three monitors, two oscilloscopes, and several keyboards. Scott began punching the keys. He waved her to a seat alongside him.

"What's the material?" he said.

"Home video."

"Plain vanilla high eight?" He was looking at an oscilloscope as he spoke. "That's what it looks like. Dolby encoded. Standard stuff."

"I guess so . . ."

"Okay. According to this, we got nine-forty on a sixty-minute cassette."

The screen flickered, and she saw mountain peaks shrouded in fog. The camera panned to a young American man in his early thirties, walking up a road, carrying a small baby on his shoulder. In the background was a village, beige roofs. Bamboo on both sides of the road.

"Where's this?" Harmon said.

Casey shrugged. "Looks like China. Can you fast-forward?"

"Sure."

The images flicked quickly past, streaked with static. Casey glimpsed a small house, the front door open; a kitchen, black pots and pans; an open suitcase on a bed; a train station, a woman climbing on the train; busy traffic in what looked like Hong Kong; an airport lounge at night, the young man holding the baby on his knees, the baby crying, writhing. Then a gate, tickets being taken by a flight attendant—

"Stop," she said.

He punched buttons, ran at normal speed. "This what you want?"

"Yes."

She watched as the woman, holding the baby, walked down the ramp to the aircraft. Then there was a cut, and the image showed the baby in the woman's lap. The camera panned up and showed the woman, giving a theatrical yawn. They were on the aircraft, during the flight; the cabin was lit by night lights; windows in the background were black. The steady whine of the jet engines.

"No kidding," Casey said. She recognized the woman she had interviewed in the hospital. What was her name? She had it in her notes.

Beside her at the console, Harmon shifted his leg, grunted. "That'll teach me," he said.

"What's that?"

"Not to ski black-diamond runs in chowder."

Casey nodded, kept her eyes on the video monitor. The camera panned back to the sleeping baby again, then blurred, before turning black. Harmon said, "Guy couldn't turn off the camera."

The next image showed glaring daylight. The baby was sitting up, smiling. A hand came into the frame, wiggling to get the baby's attention. The man's voice said, "Sarah . . . Sar-ah . . . Smile for Daddy. Smi-le . . ."

The baby smiled and made a gurgling sound.

"Cute kid," Harmon said.

On the monitor, the man's voice said, "How does it feel to be going to America, Sarah? Ready to see where your parents are from?"

The baby gurgled and waved her hands in the air, reaching for the camera.

The woman said something about everybody looking weird, and the lens panned up to her. The man said, "And what about you, Mom? Are you glad to be going home?"

"Oh, Tim," she said, turning her head away. "Please."

"Come on, Em. What are you thinking?"

The woman said, "Well, what I really want—what I have dreamed about for months—is a cheeseburger."

"With Xu-xiang hot bean sauce?"

"God *no*. A cheeseburger," she said, "with onions and tomatoes and lettuce and pickles and mayonnaise."

Now the camera panned back down to the kid, who was tugging her foot into her mouth, slobbering over her toes.

"Taste good?" the man said, laughing. "Is that breakfast for you, Sarah? Not waiting for the stewardess on this flight?"

Abruptly, the wife jerked her head around, looking past the camera. "What was that?" she said in a worried tone.

"Take it easy, Em," the man answered, still laughing.

Casey said, "Stop the tape."

Harmon hit a key. The image froze on the wife's anxious expression.

"Run it back five seconds," Casey said.

The white frame counter appeared at the bottom of the screen. The tape ran backward, streaking jags again.

"Okay," Casey said. "Now turn the sound up."

The baby sucked its toes, the slobbering so loud, it almost sounded like a waterfall. The hum inside the cabin became a steady roar. "Taste good?" the man said, laughing very loudly, his voice distorted. "Is that breakfast for you, Sarah? Not waiting for the stewardess on this flight?"

Casey tried to listen between the man's sentences. To hear the sounds of the cabin, the soft murmur of other voices, rustle of fabric moving, the intermittent clink of knives and forks from the forward galley . . .

And now something else.

Another sound?

The wife's head jerked around. "What was that?"

"Damn," Casey said.

She couldn't be sure. The roar of ambient cabin sound drowned out anything else. She leaned forward, straining to hear.

The man's voice broke in, his laugh booming: "Take it easy, Em."

The baby giggled again, a sharp earsplitting noise.

Casey was shaking her head in frustration. Was there a low-pitched rumble or not? Perhaps they should go back, and try to hear it again. She said, "Can you put this through an audio filter?"

The husband said, "We're almost home, honey."

"Oh my God," Harmon said, staring at the tape.

On the monitor, everything seemed to be crazy angles. The baby slid forward on the mother's lap; she grabbed at the kid, clutched it to her chest. The camera was shaking and twisting. Passengers in the background were yelling, grabbing the armrests, as the plane went into a steep descent.

Then the camera twisted again, and everybody seemed to sink in the seats, the mother slumping down under the G-force, her cheeks sagging, shoulders falling, baby crying. Then the man shouted, "What the hell?" and the wife rose into the air, restrained only by the seat belt.

Then the camera flew up in the air, and there was an abrupt, crunching sound, after which the image began to spiral rapidly. When the image became steady again, it showed something white, with lines. Before she could register what it was, the camera moved and she saw an armrest from below, fingers gripping the pad. The camera had fallen in the aisle and was shooting straight up. The screams continued.

"My God," Harmon said again.

The video image began to slide, gaining speed, moving past seat after seat. But it was going aft, she realized: the plane must be climbing again. Before she could get her bearings, the camera lifted into the air.

*Weightless,* she thought. The plane must have reached the end of the climb, and now it was nosing over again, for a moment of weightlessness before—

The image crashed down, twisting and tumbling rapidly. There was a *thunk!* and she glimpsed a blurred gaping mouth, teeth. Then it was moving again, and apparently landed on a seat. A large shoe swung toward the lens, kicked it.

The image spun rapidly, settled again. It was back in the aisle, facing the rear of the plane. The briefly steady image was horrifying: arms and legs stuck out into the aisle from the rows of seats. People were screaming, clutching anything they could. The camera immediately began to slide again, this time forward.

The plane was in a dive.

The camera slid faster and faster, banging into a midships bulkhead, spinning so it was now facing forward. It raced toward a body lying in the aisle.

An elderly Chinese woman looked up in time for the camera to strike her in the forehead, and then the camera flew into the air, tumbling crazily, and came down again.

There was a close view of something shiny, like a belt buckle, and then it was sliding forward once more, into the forward compartment, still going, banging into a woman's shoe in the aisle, twisting, racing forward.

It went into the forward galley, where it lodged for a moment. A wine bottle rolled across the floor, banged into it, and the camera spun several times, then began to fall end over end, the image flipping as the camera went all the way past the forward galley to the cockpit.

The cockpit door was open; she had a brief glimpse of sky through the flight deck windows, blue shoulders and a cap, and then with a crash the camera came to rest, giving a steady view of a uniform gray field. After a moment, she realized the camera had at this point lodged beneath the cockpit door, right where Casey had found it, and it was taping the carpet. There was nothing more to see, just the gray blur of carpet, but she could hear the alarms in the cockpit, the electronic warnings, and the voice reminders coming one after another, "Airspeed . . . Airspeed," and "Stall . . . Stall." More electronic warnings, excited voices shouting in Chinese.

"Stop the tape," she said.

Harmon stopped it.

"Jesus Christ," he said.

She ran through the tape once more, and then did it in slow motion. But even in slow motion, she realized, much of the movement was an indistinguishable blur. She kept saying, "I can't see, I can't see what's happening."

Harmon, who had by now become accustomed to the sequence, said, "I can do an enhanced frame analysis for you."

"What's that?"

"I can use the computers to go in and interpolate frames where the movement is too fast."

"Interpolate?"

"The computer looks at the first frame, and the frame following, and generates an intermediate frame between the two. It's a point-mapping decision, basically. But it will slow down—"

"No," she said. "I don't want anything added by the computers. What else can you do?"

"I can double or triple the frames. In fast segments, it would give you a little jerkiness, but at least you'd be able to see. Here, look." He went to one segment, where the camera was tumbling through the air, then slowed it down. "Now here, all these frames are just a blur—it's camera movement, not subject movement—but here. See this one frame here? You get a readable image."

It showed a view looking back down the aircraft. Passengers falling over the seats, their arms and legs streaks from swift movement.

"So that's a usable frame," Harmon said. She saw

what he was driving at. Even in rapid movement the camera was steady enough to create a useful image, every dozen frames or so.

"Okay," she said, "do it."

"We can do more," he said. "We can send it out, and—"

She shook her head. "Under no circumstances does this tape leave this building," she said.

"Okay."

"I need you to run me two copies of this video-tape," she said. "And make sure you run it all the way to the end."

# IAA/HANGAR 4

### 5:25 P.M.

The RAMS team was still swarming over the TransPacific aircraft in Hangar 5. Casey walked past to the next hangar in the line, and went inside. There, working in near silence in the cavernous space, Mary Ringer's team was doing Interior Artifact Analysis.

Across the concrete floor, strips of orange tape nearly three hundred feet long marked the interior walls of the TransPacific N-22. Crosswise strips indicated the principal bulkheads; parallel strips were placed for each row of seats. Here and there, white flags stood in wooden blocks, indicating various critical points.

Six feet overhead, still more strips had been

pulled taut, demarcating the ceiling and upper luggage compartments of the aircraft. The total effect was a ghostly orange outline of the dimensions of the passenger cabin.

Within this outline, five women, all psychologists and engineers, moved carefully and quietly. The women were placing articles of clothing, carry-on bags, cameras, children's toys, and other personal objects on the floor. In some cases, thin blue tape ran from the object to some other location, indicating how the object had moved during the accident.

All around them on the hangar walls hung large, blowup photographs of the interior, taken on Monday. The IAA team worked in near silence, thoughtfully, referring to the photos and notes.

Interior Artifact Analysis was rarely done. It was a desperation effort, seldom yielding useful information. In the case of TPA 545, Ringer's team had been brought in from the start, because the large number of injuries carried with it the threat of litigation. Passengers literally would not know what happened to them; assertions were often wild. IAA attempted to make sense of the movement of people and objects within the cabin. But it was a slow and difficult undertaking.

She saw Mary Ringer, a heavyset, gray-haired woman of fifty, near the aft section of the plane. "Mary," she said. "Where are we on cameras?"

"I figured you'd want to know." Mary consulted her notes. "We found nineteen cameras. Thirteen still and six video. Of the thirteen still cameras, five were broken, the film exposed. Two others had no film. The remaining six were developed, and three had shots, all taken before the incident. But we're using the pictures to try and place passengers, because TransPacific still hasn't provided a seating chart."

"And videos?"

"Uh, let's see . . ." She consulted her notes, sighing again. "Six video cameras, two with footage on board the aircraft, none during the incident. I heard about the video on television. I don't know where that came from. Passenger must have carried it off at LAX."

"Probably."

"What about the flight data recorder? We really need it to—"

"You and everybody else," Casey said. "I'm working on it." She glanced around the aft compartment, laid out by tape. She saw the pilot's cap lying on the concrete, in the corner. "Wasn't there a name in that cap?"

"Yeah, on the inside," Mary said. "It's Zen Ching, or something like that. We got the label translated."

"Who translated it?"

"Eileen Han, in Marder's office. She reads and writes Mandarin, helps us out. Why?"

"I just had a question. Not important." Casey headed for the door.

"Casey," Mary said. "We need that flight recorder."

"I know," Casey said. "I know."

She called Norma. "Who can translate Chinese for me?"

"You mean, besides Eileen?"

"Right. Besides her." She felt she should keep this away from Marder's office.

"Let me see," Norma said. "How about Ellen Fong, in Accounting? She used to work for the FAA, as a translator."

"Isn't her husband in Structure with Doherty?"

"Yeah, but Ellen's discreet."

"You sure?"

"I *know*," Norma said, in a certain tone.

## BLDG 102/ACCOUNTING

### 5:50 P.M.

She went to the accounting department, in the basement of Building 102, arriving just before six. She found Ellen Fong getting ready to go home.

"Ellen," she said, "I need a favor."

"Sure." Ellen was a perpetually cheerful woman of forty, a mother of three.

"Didn't you used to work for the FAA as a translator?"

"A long time ago," Ellen said.

"I need something translated."

"Casey, you can get a much better translator—"

"I'd rather you do it," she said. "This is confidential."

She handed Ellen the tape. "I need the voices in the last nine minutes."

"Okay . . ."

"And I'd prefer you not mention this to anybody."

"Including Bill?" That was her husband.

Casey nodded. "Is that a problem?"

"Not at all." She looked at the tape in her hand. "When?"

"Tomorrow? Friday at the latest?"

"Done," Ellen Fong said.

# NAIL

5:55 P.M.

Casey took the second copy of the tape to the Norton Audio Interpretation Lab, in the back of Building 24. NAIL was run by a former CIA guy from Omaha, a paranoid electronics genius named Jay Ziegler, who built his own audio filter boards and playback equipment because, he said, he didn't trust anyone to do it for him.

Norton had constructed NAIL to help the government agencies interpret cockpit voice recorder tapes. After an accident, the government took CVRs and analyzed them in Washington. This was done to prevent them from being leaked to the press before an investigation was completed. But although the agencies had experienced staff to transcribe the tapes, they were less skilled at interpreting sounds inside the cockpit—the alarms and audio reminders that often went off. These sounds represented proprietary Norton systems, so Norton had built a facility to analyze them.

The heavy soundproof door, as always, was locked. Casey pounded on it, and after a while a voice on the speaker said, "Give the password."

"It's Casey Singleton, Jay."

"Give the password."

"Jay, for Christ's sake. Open the door."

There was a click, and silence. She waited. The thick door pushed open a crack. She saw Jay Ziegler, hair down to his shoulders, wearing dark sunglasses. He said, "Oh. All right. Come ahead, Singleton. You're cleared for this station."

He opened the door a fraction wider, and she squeezed past him into a darkened room. Ziegler immediately slammed the door shut, threw three bolts in succession.

"Better if you call first, Singleton. We have a secure line in. Four-level scramble encoded."

"I'm sorry, Jay, but something's come up."

"Security's everybody's business."

She handed him the spool of magnetic tape. He glanced at it. "This is one-inch mag, Singleton. We don't often see this, at this station."

"Can you read it?"

Ziegler nodded. "Can read anything, Singleton. Anything you throw at us." He put the tape on a horizontal drum and threaded it. Then he glanced over his shoulder. "Are you cleared for the contents of this?"

"It's my tape, Jay."

"Just asking."

She said, "I should tell you that this tape is—"

"Don't tell me anything, Singleton. Better that way."

On all the monitors in the room, she saw oscilloscope squiggles, green lines jumping against black, as the tape began to play. "Uh . . . okay," Ziegler said. "We got high-eight audio track, Dolby D encoded, got to be a home video camera . . ." Over the speaker, she heard a rhythmic crunching sound.

Ziegler stared at his monitors. Some of them were now generating fancy data, building three-dimensional models of the sound, which looked like shimmering multicolored beads on a string. The programs were also generating slices at various hertz.

"Footsteps," Ziegler announced. "Rubber-soled feet on grass or dirt. Countryside, no urban signature. Footsteps probably male. And, uh, slight dysrhythmic, he's probably carrying something. Not too heavy. But consistently off-balance."

Casey remembered the first image on the videotape: a man walking up the path, away from a Chinese village, with the child on his shoulder.

"You're right," she said, impressed.

Now there was a tweeting sound—some sort of birdcall. "Hold on, hold on," Ziegler said, punching buttons. The tweet replayed, again and again, the beads jumping on the string. "Huh," Ziegler said finally. "Not in the database. Foreign locale?"

"China."

"Oh well. I can't do everything."

The footsteps continued. There was the sound of wind. On the tape, a male voice said, "She's fallen asleep . . ."

Ziegler said, "American, height five-nine to six-two, mid thirties."

She nodded, impressed again.

He pushed a button, and one of the monitors showed the video image, the man walking up the path. The tape froze. "Okay," Ziegler said. "So what am I doing here?"

Casey said, "The last nine minutes of tape were shot on Flight 545. This camera recorded the whole incident."

"Really," Ziegler said, rubbing his hands together. "That should be interesting."

"I want to know what you can tell me about unusual sounds in the moments just prior to the event. I have a question about—"

"Don't tell me," he said, holding up his hand. "I don't want to know. I want to take a clean look."

"When can you have something?"

"Twenty hours." Ziegler looked at his watch. "Tomorrow afternoon."

"Okay. And Jay? I'd appreciate if you'd keep this tape to yourself."

Ziegler looked at her blankly. "What tape?" he said.

# QA

6:10 P.M.

Casey was back at her desk a little after 6 P.M. There were more telexes waiting for her.

```
FROM: S. NIETO, FSR VANC
TO: C. SINGLETON, QA/IRT

F/O ZAN PING AT VANC GEN HOSPITAL
FOLLOWING COMPLICATIONS FROM SURGERY
REPORTED UNCONSCIOUS BUT STABLE.
CARRIER REP MIKE LEE WAS AT THE
HOSPITAL TODAY. I WILL TRY TO SEE
F/O TOMORROW TO VERIFY HIS CONDI-
TION AND INTERVIEW HIM IF POSSIBLE.
```

"Norma," she called, "remind me to call Vancouver tomorrow morning."

"I'll make a note," she said. "By the way, you got this." She handed Casey a fax.

The single sheet appeared to be a page from an in-flight magazine. The top read: "Employee of the Month," followed by an inky, unreadable photograph.

Underneath the photo was a caption: "Captain John Zhen Chang, Senior Pilot for TransPacific Airlines, is our employee of the month. Captain Chang's father was a pilot, and John himself has flown for twenty years, seven of those with TransPacific. When not in the cockpit, Captain Chang enjoys biking and golf. Here he relaxes on the beach at Lantan Island with his wife, Soon, and his children, Erica and Tom."

Casey frowned. "What's this?"

"Beats me," Norma said.

"Where'd it come from?" There was a phone number at the top of the page, but no name.

"A copy shop on La Tijera," Norma said.

"Near the airport," Casey said.

"Yes. It's a busy place, they had no idea who sent it."

Casey stared at the photo. "It's from an in-flight magazine?"

"TransPacific's. But not this month. They pulled the contents of the seat pockets—you know, passenger announcements, safety cards, barf bags, monthly magazine—and sent it over. But that page isn't in the magazine."

"Can we get back copies?"

"I'm working on it," she said.

"I'd like to get a better look at this picture," Casey said.

"I figured," Norma said.

She went back to the other papers on her desk.

FROM: T. Korman, PROD SUPPORT
TO: C. Singleton, QA/IRT

We have finalized the design parameters of the N-22 Virtual Heads-Up Display (VHUD) for use by ground personnel at domestic and foreign repair stations. The CD-ROM player now clips to the belt, and the goggles have been reduced in weight. The VHUD allows maintenance personnel to scroll Maintenance Manuals 12A/102-12A/406, including diagrams and parts cutaways. Preliminary articles will be distributed for comments tomorrow. Production will begin 5/1.

This Virtual Heads-Up Display was part of Norton's ongoing effort to help the customers improve maintenance. Airframe manufacturers had long recognized that the majority of operational problems were caused by bad maintenance. In general, a properly maintained commercial aircraft would run for decades; some of the old Norton N-5s were sixty years old and still in service. On the other hand, an improperly maintained aircraft could get in trouble—or crash—within minutes.

Under financial pressure from deregulation, the airlines were cutting personnel, including maintenance personnel. And they were shortening the turnaround time between cycles; time on the ground had in some cases gone from two hours to less than twenty minutes. All this put intense pressure on maintenance crews. Norton, like Boeing and Douglas, saw it as in their interest to help crews work more effectively. That was why the Virtual Heads-Up Display, which projected the repair manuals on the inside of a set of glasses for maintenance people, was so important.

She went on.

Next she saw the weekly summary of parts failures, compiled to enable the FAA to track parts problems more carefully. None of the failures in the previous week was serious. An engine compressor stalled; an engine EGT indicator failed; an oil filter clog light illuminated incorrectly; a fuel heat indicator went on erroneously.

Then there were more IRT follow-up reports from past incidents. Product Support checked all incident aircraft every two weeks for the next six months, to make sure that the assessment of the Incident Review Team had been accurate, and that the aircraft was not experiencing further trouble. Then they issued a summary report, like the one she now saw on her desk:

## AIRCRAFT INCIDENT REPORT

PRIVILEGED INFORMATION—FOR INTERNAL USE ONLY

| | |
|---|---|
| REPORT NO: | IRT-8-2776 |
| TODAY'S DATE: | 08 April |
| MODEL: | N-20 |
| INCIDENT DATE: | 04 March |
| OPERATOR: | Air Portugal |
| FUSELAGE NO: | 1280 |
| REPORTED BY: | J. Ramones FSR |
| LOCATION: | PS Portugal |
| REFERENCE: | a) AVN-SVC-08774/ADH |
| SUBJECT: | Main Landing Gear Wheel Failure During Takeoff |

DESCRIPTION OF EVENT:

It was reported that during takeoff roll the "Wheel Not Turning" alert came on and the flight crew aborted the takeoff. The nose landing gear (NLG) tires blew and there was a fire in the wheel well which was extinguished by fire trucks on the ground. Passengers and flight crew exited via evacuation slides. No reported injuries.

ACTION TAKEN:

Inspection of the aircraft revealed the following damage:

1. Both flaps sustained significant damage.
2. The Number 1 engine sustained heavy soot damage.
3. The inboard flap hinge fairing sustained minor damage.
4. The Number 2 wheel was flat spotted with approximately 30 percent missing. There was no damage to NLG axle or piston.

Review of human factors revealed the following:

1. Flight deck procedures require added carrier scrutiny.
2. Foreign repair procedures require added carrier scrutiny.

The aircraft is in the process of being repaired. Internal procedures are being reviewed by the carrier.

> David Levine
> Technical Integration
> Product Support
> Norton Aircraft Company
> Burbank, CA

Summary reports were always diplomatic; in this incident, she knew, ground maintenance had been so inept that the nose wheel locked on takeoff, blowing the tires, causing what was very nearly a serious incident. But the report didn't say that; you had to read between the lines. The problem lay with the carrier, but the carrier was also the customer—and it was bad form to knock the customer.

Eventually, Casey knew, TransPacific Flight 545 would end up summarized in an equally diplomatic report. But there was much to do before then.

Norma came back. "TransPacific's office is closed. I'll have to find that magazine tomorrow."

"Okay."

"Hon?"

"What."

"Go home."

She sighed. "You're right, Norma."

"And get some rest, will you?"

## GLENDALE

### 9:15 P.M.

Her daughter had left a message saying she was having a sleep-over at Amy's house, and that Dad said it was all right. Casey wasn't happy about it, she thought her daughter shouldn't have sleep-overs on school nights, but there was nothing she could do now. She got into bed, pulled her daughter's photograph on the bedside table over to look at it, and then turned to her work. She was going through the flight tapes of TPA 545, checking the waypoint coordinates for each leg against the written radio transcripts from Honolulu ARINC and Oakland Center, when the phone rang.

"Casey Singleton."

"Hello, Casey. John Marder here."

She sat up in bed. Marder never called her at home. She looked at the clock; it was after nine P.M.

Marder cleared his throat. "I just got a call from Benson in PR. He's had a request from a network news crew to film inside the plant. He turned them down."

"Uh-huh . . ." That was standard; news crews were never allowed inside the plant.

"Then he got a call from a producer on that program *Newsline* named Malone. She said *Newsline* was making the request for plant access, and insisted they be allowed in. Very pushy and full of herself. He told her to forget it."

"Uh-huh."

"He said he was nice about it."

"Uh-huh." She was waiting.

"This Malone said *Newsline* was doing a story on the N-22, and she wanted to interview the president. He told her Hal was overseas, and unavailable."

"Uh-huh."

"Then she suggested we reconsider her request, because the *Newsline* story was going to focus on flight safety concerns, two problems in two days, an engine problem and slats deployment, several passengers killed. She said she'd spoken to critics—no names, but I can guess—and she wanted to give the president an opportunity to respond."

Casey sighed.

Marder said, "Benson said he might be able to get her an interview with the president next week, and she said no, that wouldn't work, *Newsline* was running the story this weekend."

"This weekend?"

"That's right," Marder said. "Timing couldn't be worse. The day before I leave for China. It's a very popular show. The whole damned country will see it."

"Yes," she said.

"Then the woman said she wanted to be fair, that it always looked bad if the company didn't respond to allegations. So if the president wasn't available to talk to *Newsline,* maybe some other highly placed spokesman would."

"Uh-huh . . ."

"So I'm seeing this twit in my office tomorrow at noon," Marder said.

"On camera?" Casey said.

"No, no. Background only, no cameras. But we'll cover the IRT investigation, so I think you'd better be there."

"Of course."

"Apparently they're going to do some terrible story on the N-22," Marder said. "It's that damn CNN tape. That's what's started it all. But we're in it now, Casey. We have to handle this as best we can."

"I'll be there," she said.

# THURSDAY

# AIRPORT MARINA

6:30 A.M.

Jennifer Malone awoke to the soft, insistent buzz of the bedside alarm. She turned it off, and looked over at the tanned shoulder of the man next to her, and felt a burst of annoyance. He was a stuntman on a TV series, she'd met him a few months back. He had a craggy face and a nice muscular body and he knew how to perform . . . but Jeez, she hated it when guys stayed over. She had hinted politely, after the second time. But he'd just rolled over and gone to sleep. And now here he was, snoring away.

Jennifer hated to wake up with some guy in the room. She hated everything about it, the sounds they made breathing, the smell coming off their skin, their greasy hair on the pillow. Even the catches, the celebrities who made her heart skip over candlelight, looked like soggy beached whales the next day.

It was like the guys didn't know their place. They came over; they got what they wanted; she got what she wanted; everyone was happy. So why didn't they go the fuck home?

She'd called him from the plane: Hi, I'm coming into town, what are you doing tonight? And he said, without hesitation, Doing you. Which was fine with her. It was sort of funny, sitting in an airplane seat next to some accountant bent over his laptop, the voice in her ear saying, I'm doing you tonight, in every room of your suite.

Which, to his credit, he did. Not subtle, this guy, but he had lots of energy, that pure California body energy that you never found in New York. No reason to talk about anything. Just fuck.

But now, sunlight streaming through the windows . . .

Damn.

She got up from the bed, feeling the cold air-conditioned air on her naked skin, and went to the closet to choose the clothes she would wear. She was doing pretty straight types, so she picked jeans, a white Agnes B. T-shirt, and a navy Jil Sander jacket. She carried them into the bathroom, ran a shower. While the water was getting warm, she called the cameraman and told him to have the crew ready in the lobby in an hour.

While she took her shower, she reviewed the coming day. Barker first at nine, she'd film him briefly with some aviation background to warm him up, then break to do the rest at his office.

Next the reporter, Rogers. No time to do him at his newsroom in Orange County; she'd start him at Burbank, another airport, different look. He'd talk about Norton with the Norton buildings behind him.

Then at noon, she'd talk to the Norton guy. By then she'd already know the arguments from the other two guys, and she'd try to scare Norton enough that they'd give her access to the president.

And then . . . let's see. The ambulance chaser later in the day, briefly. Someone from the FAA on

Friday, for balance. Someone from Norton on Friday, as well. Marty would do a stand-up outside Norton, the script wasn't prepared but all she needed was the intro and the rest was voice-over. B-roll of passengers boarding, going to their doom. Takeoffs and landings, then some good crash shots.

And she was done.

This segment was going to work, she thought, as she stepped out of the shower. There was only one thing that troubled her.

That damned guy in the bed.

Why didn't he go home?

## QA

### 6:40 A.M.

As Casey came into the QA offices, Norma glanced up at her, then pointed down the hall.

Casey frowned.

Norma jerked her thumb. "He was here when I came in this morning," she said. "Been on the phone for an hour solid. Mr. Sleepyhead's suddenly not so sleepy."

Casey went down the hall. As she came to Richman's office, she heard him say, "Absolutely not. We are very confident of how this will turn out. No. No. I'm sure. Hasn't a clue. No idea."

Casey stuck her head in.

Richman was leaning back in his chair, with his feet up on the desk, while he spoke on the phone. He appeared startled when he saw her. He put his hand over the phone. "I'll just be a minute here."

"Fine." She went back to her office, shuffled through papers. She didn't want him around. It was time for another errand, she thought.

"Good morning," he said as he came in. He was very cheerful, big smile. "I got those FAA documents you wanted. I left them on your desk."

"Thank you," she said. "Today I need you to go to TransPacific's main office."

"TransPacific? Isn't that at the airport?"

"Actually, I think they're in downtown LA. Norma will get you the address. I need you to pick up back issues of their in-flight magazine. As far back as they go. At least a year."

"Gee," Richman said. "Couldn't we have a messenger do that?"

"This is urgent," Casey said.

"But I'll miss the IRT."

"You're not needed at the IRT. And I want these magazines as soon as possible."

"In-flight magazines? What are they for?" he said.

"Bob," she said. "Just get them."

He gave a crooked smile. "You're not trying to get rid of me, are you?"

"Pick up the magazines, get them to Norma, and call me."

# WAR ROOM

### 7:30 A.M.

John Marder was late. He came striding into the room with an irritable, distracted look, and dropped into a seat. "All right," he said. "Let's have it. Where are we on Flight 545? Flight recorder?"

"Nothing yet," Casey said.

"We need that data—make it happen, Casey. Structure?"

"Well it's very difficult very difficult indeed," Doherty said, dolefully. "I still worry about that bad locking pin. I think we ought to be more cautious—"

"Doug," Marder said. "I already told you. We'll check it at Flight Test. Now what about hydraulics?"

"Hydraulics are fine."

"Cable rigging?"

"Fine. Of course we're at ambient. Have to cold soak to be sure."

"Okay. We'll do that at Flight Test. Electrical?"

Ron said, "We've scheduled the Cycle Electrical Test beginning at 6 P.M., running through the night. If there's a problem we'll know in the morning."

"Any suspicions now?"

"Just those proximity sensors, in the right wing."

"Have we functioned them?"

"Yes, and they appear normal. Of course, to really check them we'd have to remove the sensors from the housings, take them out of the wing, and that means—"

"Delaying everything," Marder said. "Forget it. Powerplant?"

"Zip," Kenny Burne said. "Engines are fine. Some seals on the cooling system were installed backward. And we got a counterfeit reverser cowl. But it's nothing that would cause the accident."

"Okay. Powerplant is eliminated. Avionics?"

Trung said, "Avionics check out within normal limits."

"What about the autopilot? The pilot fighting to override?"

"Autopilot is fine."

"I see." Marder looked around the room. "So we have nothing, is that right? Seventy-two hours into this investigation and we have no damned idea what happened to Flight 545? Is that what you're telling me?"

There was silence around the table.

"Christ," Marder said, disgusted. He pounded the table. "Don't you people understand? I want this fucking thing *solved!*"

## SEPULVEDA BLVD

### 10:10 A.M.

Fred Barker was solving all her problems.

To start, Jennifer needed a walk-to-work shot for Marty's voice-over intro ("We talked to Frederick Barker, a former FAA official, now a controversial crusader for aircraft safety"). Barker suggested a location on Sepulveda, with a sweeping view of the south runways of Los Angeles International Airport. It was perfect, and he was careful to mention that no other film crew had used it before.

Next she needed an at-work shot, again for voice-over ("Since leaving the FAA, Barker has worked tirelessly to bring defective aircraft designs to the public's attention—particularly the design of the Norton N-22"). Barker suggested a corner of his office, where he placed himself in front of a book-shelf of thick FAA documents, at a desk heaped high with technical-looking pamphlets, which he thumbed through for camera.

Next she needed his basic spiel, in the kind of detail that Reardon wouldn't have time to bother with during the interview. Barker was ready for this, too. He knew where the switches were for the air-conditioning, the refrigerator, the telephones, and all the other noise sources they'd need to turn off for filming. Barker also had a video monitor ready, to replay the CNN tape from Flight 545 while he commented on it. The monitor was a studio-grade Trinitron, placed in a dark corner of the room, so they could get an image off it. There was a V-plug so they could take the feed directly, to sync his audio comments. And Barker was running one-inch tape, so image quality was excellent. He even had a large model of the N-22 aircraft, with moving parts on the wing and tail that he could use to demonstrate what had gone wrong in flight. The model sat on a stand on his desk, so it didn't look like a prop. And

Barker was dressed for the part: informal shirt-sleeves and tie, reminiscent of an engineer, an authoritative look.

Barker was good on camera, too. He appeared relaxed. He didn't use jargon; his answers were short. He seemed to understand how she would cut the tape together, so he didn't lock her into any-thing. For example, he didn't reach for the model airplane in the middle of an answer. Instead, he gave his answer, then said, "At this point, I'd like to refer to the model." When she agreed, he repeated the previous answer, picking up the model at the same time. Everything he did was smooth, with no fumbling or awkwardness.

Of course Barker was experienced, not only on television but in the courtroom. The only problem was that he didn't give her strong emotion—no shock, no outrage. On the contrary, his tone, his manner, his body language, suggested profound regret. It was unfortunate that this situation arose. It was unfortunate that steps hadn't been taken to correct the problem. It was unfortunate that authorities hadn't listened to him for all these years.

"There have been eight previous problems with slats on the airplane," he said. He held the model up, near his face, turned it so that it didn't gleam in the crew lights. "These are the slats," he said, pulling out a sliding panel from the front of the wing. He took his hand away, and said, "You get that in close-up?"

"I was late," the cameraman said. "Could you do it again?"

"Sure. Are you starting wide?"

"Two Ts," the cameraman said.

Barker nodded. He paused, then began again. "There have been eight previous problems with slats on this airplane." Again he held the model up, this time already correctly turned so it didn't reflect in the light. "These are the slats," he said, and pulled out the panel in front of the wing. Then he paused again.

"Got it that time," the cameraman said.

Barker continued. "The slats are only deployed for takeoff and landing. During flight, they are tucked back in the wing. But on the Norton N-22, the slats have been known to extend by themselves during flight. It's a design error." Another pause. "I'm going to demonstrate what happens now, so you may want to be wide enough to see the whole plane."

"Widening," the cameraman said.

Barker waited patiently for a moment, then said, "The consequence of this design error is that when the slats extend, the airplane noses upward, like this, threatening to stall." He tilted the model up slightly. "At this point, it is almost impossible to control. If the pilot tries to restore the plane to level flight, the plane overcompensates, and goes into a dive. Again, the pilot corrects, to come out of the dive. The plane climbs. Then dives. Then climbs again. That is what happened to Flight 545. That is why people died."

Barker paused.

"Now we're through with the model," he said. "So I'm going to put it down."

"Okay," Jennifer said. She had been watching Barker on the monitor on the floor, and now she was thinking that she might have difficulty cutting from the wider shot to a shot of putting the model down. What she really needed was a repetition of—

Barker said, "The plane dives. Then climbs. Then dives again. That is what happened to Flight 545. That is why people died." With a regretful look, he put the model down. Although he did it gently, his very gesture seemed to suggest a crash.

Jennifer had no illusions about what she was watching. This wasn't an interview; it was a performance. But a skilled approach was not rare these days. More and more interview subjects seemed to understand camera angles and editing sequences. She had seen executives show up in full makeup for an interview. At first, television people had been alarmed by this new sophistication. But lately, they'd become used to it. There was never enough time; they were always rushing from one location to the next. A prepared subject made their work so much easier.

But just because Barker was smooth and camera savvy, she wasn't going to let him get away without a little probing. The final part of her job today was to cover the basic questions, in case Marty ran out of time, or forgot to ask them.

She said, "Mr. Barker?"

"Yes?" He turned toward her.

"Check the look," she said to the cameraman.

"His look is wide. Move a little closer to camera."

Jennifer slid her chair over so she was right beside the lens. Barker turned slightly to face her, at her new position.

"His look is fine, now."

"Mr. Barker," Jennifer said, "you are a former FAA employee . . ."

"I used to work for the FAA," Barker said, "but I left the agency because I disagreed with their hands-off attitude toward manufacturers. The Norton plane is a result of those lax policies."

Barker was again demonstrating his skill: his answer was a complete statement. He knew that he was more likely to get his comments on camera if they were not responses to a question.

Jennifer said, "There is some controversy sur-rounding your departure."

"I am familiar with some of the allegations about why I left the FAA," Barker said, again making a statement. "But the fact is my departure was an embarrassment to the agency. I criticized the way they worked, and when they refused to respond, I left. So I'm not surprised they are still trying to dis-credit me."

She said, "The FAA claims you leaked materials to the press. They say they fired you for that."

"There's never been any proof of the allegations the FAA has made about me. I have never seen any FAA official produce one shred of evidence to back their criticisms of me."

"You work for Bradley King, the attorney?"

"I have served as an expert aviation witness on a

number of legal cases. I think it's important that somebody with knowledge speak out."

"You are paid by Bradley King?"

"Any expert witness is reimbursed for time and expenses. That's standard procedure."

"Isn't it true that you're a full-time employee of Bradley King? That your office, everything in this room, everything we see here, is paid for by King?"

"I am funded by the non-profit Institute for Aviation Research in Washington. My job is to promote safety in civil aviation. I do whatever I can to make the skies safe for travelers."

"Mr. Barker, come on: Aren't you an expert for hire?"

"I certainly have strong opinions about air safety. It's only natural that I would be hired by employers who share my concerns."

"What is your opinion of the FAA?"

"The FAA is well intentioned, but it has a dual mandate, both to regulate air travel and to promote it. The agency needs complete reform. It is much too cozy with the manufacturers."

"Can you give me an example?" It was a feed; she knew from previous conversations what he would say.

Again, Barker made a statement. "One good example of this cozy relationship is the way the FAA treats certification. The documents required to certify a new airplane are not maintained by the FAA, but by the manufacturers themselves. This hardly seems proper. The fox is guarding the chicken coop."

"Is the FAA doing a good job?"

"I'm afraid the FAA is doing a very poor job. American lives are needlessly put at risk. Frankly it's time for a thorough overhaul. Otherwise I am afraid passengers will continue to die, as they did on this Norton aircraft." He gestured—slowly, so the camera could follow—to the model on his desk. "In my opinion," he said, "what happened on that airplane . . . is a disgrace."

The interview ended. While her crew was packing up, Barker came over to her. "Who else are you seeing?"

"Jack Rogers is next."

"He's a good man."

"And someone from Norton." She consulted her notes. "A John Marder."

"Ah."

"What does that mean?"

"Well, Marder is a fast-talker. He'll give you a lot of double-talk about Airworthiness Directives. A lot of FAA jargon. But the fact is that he was the program manager on the N-22. He supervised the development of that aircraft. He knows there's a problem—he's part of it."

# OUTSIDE NORTON

11:10 A.M.

After the practiced smoothness of Barker, the reporter, Jack Rogers, was a bit of a shock. He showed up wearing a lime-green sport coat that screamed Orange County, and his check-patterned tie jumped on the monitor. He looked like a golf pro, spruced up for a job interview.

Jennifer said nothing at first; she just thanked the reporter for coming, and positioned him in front of the chain-link fence, with Norton Aircraft in the background. She went over her questions with him; he gave tentative little answers, excited, eager to please.

"Gee, it's hot," she said. She turned to the cameraman. "How we coming, George?"

"Almost there."

She turned back to Rogers. The sound guy unbuttoned Rogers's shirt, threaded the microphone up to his collar. As preparations continued, Rogers began to sweat. Jennifer called for the makeup girl to wipe him down. He seemed relieved. Then, pleading the heat, she convinced Rogers to remove his sport coat and sling it over his shoulder. She said it would give him a working-journalist look. He gratefully agreed. She suggested he loosen his tie, which he did.

She went back to the cameraman. "How is it?"

"Better without the jacket. But that tie is a nightmare."

She returned to Rogers, smiled. "This is working so well," she said. "How would it be if you take off the tie, and roll up your sleeves?"

"Oh, I never do that," Rogers said. "I never roll up my sleeves."

"It would give you that strong but casual look. You know, rolled-up shirtsleeves, ready to fight. Hard-hitting journalist. That idea."

"I never roll up my sleeves."

She frowned. "Never?"

"No. I never do."

"Well, it's just a look we're talking about here. You'd come off stronger on camera. More emphatic, more forceful."

"I'm sorry."

She thought: What is this? Most people would do anything to get on *Newsline*. They'd do the interview in their underwear, if she asked them to. Several had. And here was this fucking print journalist, what did he make, anyway? Thirty grand a year? Less than Jennifer's monthly expense account.

"I, uh, can't," Rogers said, "because, uh, I have psoriasis."

"No problem. *Makeup!*"

Standing with his jacket slung over his shoulder, his tie removed, shirt sleeves rolled up, Jack Rogers answered her questions. He rambled, speaking thirty, forty seconds at a time. If she asked him the same question twice, hoping for a shorter answer, he just started to sweat, and gave a longer answer.

They had to keep breaking for makeup to wipe him down. She had to reassure him again and again that he was doing great, just *great*. That he was giving her really good stuff.

And he was, but he couldn't punch it. He didn't seem to understand she was making an assembled piece, that the average shot would be less than three seconds, and they would cut to him for a sentence, or a fragment of a sentence, before they cut to something else. Rogers was earnest, trying to be helpful, but he was burying her in detail she couldn't use, and background she didn't care about.

Finally she began to worry that she couldn't use any of the interview, that she was wasting her time with this guy. So she followed her usual procedure in a situation like this.

"That's all perfect," she said. "Now we're coming to the conclusion of the piece. We need something punchy"—she made a fist—"to close. So I'll ask you a series of questions, and you answer them with one punchy sentence."

"Okay," Rogers said.

"Mr. Rogers, could the N-22 cost Norton the China sale?"

"Given the frequency of incidents involving—"

"I'm sorry," she said. "I just need a simple sentence. Could the N-22 cost Norton the China sale?"

"Yes, it certainly could."

"I'm sorry," she said again. "Jack, I need a sentence like, 'The N-22 might very well cost Norton the China sale.'"

"Oh. Okay." He swallowed.

"Could the N-22 cost Norton the China sale?"

"Yes, I'm afraid I have to say that it might cost the China sale."

*Jesus,* she thought.

"Jack, I need you to say 'Norton' in the sentence. Otherwise we won't know what you're referring to."

"Oh."

"Go ahead."

"The N-22 might very well cost Norton the China sale, in my opinion."

She sighed. It was dry. No emotional force. He might as well be talking about his phone bill. But she was running out of time. "Excellent," Jennifer said. "Very good. Let's go on. Tell me: Is Norton a troubled company?"

"Absolutely," he said, nodding and swallowing.

She sighed. "Jack."

"Oh. Sorry." He took a breath. Then, standing there, he said, "I think that—"

"Wait a minute," she said. "Put your weight on your forward foot. So you're leaning in toward camera."

"Like this?" He shifted his body weight, turned slightly.

"Yeah, that's it. Perfect. Now go ahead."

Standing there, in front of the fence outside Norton Aircraft, with his jacket slung over his shoulder, and his shirtsleeves rolled up, reporter Jack Rogers said, "I think there's no doubt that Norton Aircraft is a company in serious trouble."

Then he paused. He looked at her.

Jennifer smiled. "Thank you very much," she said. "You were great."

# NORTON ADMINISTRATION

### 11:55 A.M.

Casey came into John Marder's office a few minutes before noon, and found him smoothing his tie, shooting his cuffs. "I thought we would sit here," he said, pointing to a coffee table with chairs in the corner of his office. "You all set for this?"

"I think so," Casey said.

"Just let me take it, at the beginning," Marder said. "I'll turn to you for assistance if I need it."

"Okay."

Marder continued to pace. "Security says there was a film crew out by the south fence," he said. "They were doing an interview with Jack Rogers."

"Uh-huh," Casey said.

"That idiot. Christ. I can imagine what *he* had to say."

"Did you ever talk to Rogers?" Casey said.

The intercom buzzed. Eileen said, "Ms. Malone is here, Mr. Marder."

"Send her in," Marder said.

And he strode to the door, to greet her.

Casey was shocked by the woman who walked in. Jennifer Malone was a *kid,* hardly older than Richman. She couldn't be more than twenty-eight or -nine, Casey thought. Malone was blond, and quite pretty—in an uptight, New York sort of way. She had short bobbed hair that downplayed her sexuality, and she was dressed very casually: jeans and a white T-shirt, and a blue blazer with a weird collar. The trendy Hollywood look.

Casey felt uncomfortable, just looking at her. But now Marder had turned, and was saying "Ms. Malone, I'd like to introduce Casey Singleton, our Quality Assurance specialist on the Incident Review Team."

The blond kid smirked.

Casey shook her hand.

You got to be kidding, Jennifer Malone thought. This is a captain of industry? This jumpy guy with slicked back hair and a bad suit? And who was this woman out of a Talbot's catalog? Singleton was taller than Jennifer—which Jennifer resented—and good-looking in a wholesome, midwestern way. She looked like an athlete, and she seemed to be in pretty good shape—although she was long past the age where she could get by with the minimal makeup she wore. And her features were strained, tense. Under pressure.

Jennifer felt disappointed. She had been preparing for this meeting all day, honing her arguments. But she had imagined a much more commanding adversary. Instead, she was back in high school—with the assistant principal and the timid librarian. Little people with no style.

And this office! Small, with gray walls and cheap,

utilitarian furniture. It had no character. It was just as well she wasn't filming here, because this room wouldn't photograph. Did the president's office look like this, too? If so, they would have to tape his interview somewhere else. Outside, or on the assembly line. Because these shabby little offices just didn't work for the show. Airplanes were big and powerful. The audience wouldn't believe that they were made by crummy little people in drab offices.

Marder led her to a seating arrangement, to one side. He gestured grandly, as if he were taking her to a banquet. Since he gave her a choice of where to sit, she took a chair with her back to the window, so the sun would be in their eyes.

She got out her notes, shuffled through them. Marder said, "Would you like something to drink? Coffee?"

"Coffee would be great."

"How do you take it?"

"Black," Jennifer said.

Casey watched as Jennifer Malone set out her notes. "I'll be frank," Malone said. "We've gotten some damning material on the N-22 from critics. And on the way this company operates. But there are two sides to every story. We want to make sure we include your response to the criticism."

Marder said nothing, just nodded. He was sitting with his legs crossed, a notepad on his lap.

"To begin," Malone said, "we know what happened on the TransPacific flight."

Really? Casey thought. Because we don't.

Malone said, "The slats came out—deployed?— in midair, and the airplane became unstable, went up and down, killing passengers. Everyone has seen the film of that tragic accident. We know passengers have filed lawsuits against the company. We also know the N-22 has a long history of slats problems, which neither the FAA nor the company has been willing to deal with. This, despite nine separate incidents in recent years."

Malone paused for a moment, then went on. "We know that FAA is so lax in its regulatory policies that it doesn't even require certification documents to be submitted. The FAA has allowed Norton to keep the certification documents here."

Jesus, Casey thought. She doesn't understand *anything*.

"Let me dispose of your last point first," Marder said. "The FAA doesn't have physical possession of certification documents from any manufacturer. Not Boeing, not Douglas, not Airbus, not us. Frankly, we'd prefer the FAA do the warehousing. But the FAA can't store them, because the documents contain proprietary information. If they were in possession of the FAA, our competitors could obtain this information under the Freedom of Information Act. Some of our competitors would like nothing better. Airbus in particular has been lobbying for a change in FAA policy—for the reasons I've just explained. So I presume you got this idea about the FAA from someone at Airbus."

Casey saw Malone hesitate, glance down at her papers. It was true, she thought. Marder had nailed her source. Airbus had fed her that tidbit, probably through its publicity arm, the Institute for Aviation Research. Did Malone realize the Institute was an Airbus front?

"But don't you agree," Malone said coolly, "that the arrangement is a little too cozy if the FAA lets Norton store its own documents?"

"Ms. Malone," Marder said, "I've already told you we'd prefer the FAA do the storage. But we didn't write the Freedom of Information Act. We don't make the laws. We *do* think that if we spend billions of dollars developing a proprietary design, it should not be made available free of charge to our competitors. As I understand it, FOIA wasn't enacted to enable foreign competitors to pillage American technology."

"So you oppose the Freedom of Information Act?"

"Not at all. I'm simply saying that it was never designed to facilitate industrial espionage." Marder shifted in his chair. "Now, you mentioned Flight 545."

"Yes."

"First of all, we don't agree that the accident was the result of slats deployment."

Uh-oh, Casey thought. Marder was going out on a limb. What he was saying wasn't true, and it might very well—

Marder said, "We're currently investigating this situation, and although it's premature for me to discuss the findings of our inquiry, I believe you have been misinformed on the situation. I presume you've gotten this slats information from Fred Barker."

"We are talking to Mr. Barker, among others . . ."

"Have you spoken to the FAA about Mr. Barker?" Marder said.

"We know he's controversial . . ."

"To put it mildly. Let's just say he adopts an advocacy position that is factually incorrect."

"You *believe* it is incorrect."

"No, Ms. Malone. It *is* factually incorrect," Marder said, testily. He pointed to the papers Malone had spread out on the table. "I couldn't help noticing your list of slats incidents. Did you get that from Barker?"

Malone hesitated a fraction. "Yes."

"May I see it?"

"Sure."

She handed the paper to Marder. He glanced at it.

Malone said, "Is it factually incorrect, Mr. Marder?"

"No, but it's incomplete and misleading. This list is based on our own documents, but it is incomplete. Do you know about Airworthiness Directives, Ms. Malone?"

"Airworthiness Directives?"

Marder got up, went to his desk. "Every time there is an in-flight incident involving our aircraft, we review the incident thoroughly, to find out what happened and why. If there's a problem with the aircraft, we issue a Service Bulletin; if the FAA feels compliance with our bulletin should be mandatory, it then issues an Airworthiness Directive. After the N-22 went into active service, we discovered a slats problem, and an Airworthiness Directive was issued to correct the problem. Domestic carriers are required by law to fix the airplanes, to prevent further occurrences."

He came back with another sheet of paper, which he handed to Malone. "This is a complete list of incidents."

### Slats Events of Norton N-22

**1. January 4, 1992. (DO)** Slats deployed at FL350, at .84 Mach. The flap/slat handle moved inadvertently. <u>A/D 44-8 was issued as a result of this incident.</u>

**2. April 2, 1992. (DO)** Slats deployed while the airplane was in cruise at .81 Mach. A clipboard reportedly fell on the flap/slat handle. <u>A/D 44-8 was not accomplished but would have prevented this occurrence.</u>

**3. July 17, 1992. (DO)** Initially reported as severe turbulence, it was later learned that the slats had extended as a result of inadvertent flap/slat handle movement. <u>A/D 44-8 was not incorporated and would have prevented this occurrence.</u>

**4. December 20, 1992. (DO)** Slats extended in cruise flight without movement of the flap/slat handle in cockpit. Confirmed slat cable rigging was out of tolerance in three places. <u>A/D 51-29 was issued as a result of this incident</u>.

**5. March 12, 1993. (FO)** Airplane entered a prestall buffet at .82 Mach. The slats were found to be extended and the handle was not in the up and locked position. <u>A/D 51-29 was not incorporated and would have prevented this occurrence</u>.

**6. April 4, 1993. (FO)** First officer rested his arm on the flap/slat handle as he was operating the autopilot and the action moved the handle down, extending the slats. <u>A/D 44-8 was not incorporated and would have prevented this occurrence</u>.

**7. July 4, 1993. (FO)** Pilot reported the flap/slat handle moved and slats extended. Aircraft was in cruise flight at .81 Mach. <u>A/D 44-8 was not incorporated and would have prevented this occurrence</u>.

**8. June 10, 1994. (FO)** The slats extended while the airplane was in cruise flight without movement of the flap/slat handle. Confirmed slat cable rigging was out of tolerance. <u>A/D 51-29 was not incorporated and would have prevented this occurrence</u>.

"The underlined sentences," Marder said, "are what Mr. Barker omitted from the document he gave you. After the first slats incident, the FAA issued an Airworthiness Directive to change cockpit controls.

The airlines had a year to comply. Some did it immediately, others didn't. As you can see, the subsequent incidents all occurred in aircraft which had not yet made the change."

"Well, not quite . . ."

"Please let me finish. In December of 1992, we discovered a second issue. The cables running to the slats sometimes became slack. Maintenance crews weren't catching the problem. So we issued a second Service Bulletin, and added a tension measurement device, so ground crews could check more easily whether cable rigging was within spec. That solved it. By December, everything was resolved."

"Clearly not, Mr. Marder," Malone said, pointing to the list. "You have more incidents in 1993 and in 1994."

"Only on foreign carriers," Marder said. "You see that notation, DO and FO? That stands for "domestic operator" or "foreign operator." The domestic operators must make the changes called for in the FAA Airworthiness Directives. But foreign operators aren't under FAA jurisdiction. And they don't always make the changes. Since 1992, all incidents have involved foreign carriers that hadn't made the retrofits."

Malone scanned the list. "So you knowingly allow carriers to fly unsafe airplanes? You just sit back and let it happen, is that what you're telling me?"

Marder sucked in his breath. Casey thought he was going to blow, but he didn't. "Ms. Malone, we build airplanes, we don't operate them. If Air

Indonesia or Pakistani Air won't follow the Airworthiness Directives, we can't force them to."

"All right. If all you do is build airplanes, let's talk about how well you do that," Malone said. "Looking at this list here, you had how many design changes on the slats? Eight?"

Casey thought, She doesn't understand. She's not listening. She doesn't get what she's being told.

"No. Two retrofits," Marder said.

"But there are eight incidents here. You'd agree to that . . ."

"Yes," Marder said irritably, "but we're not talking about incidents, we're talking about ADs, and there are only two ADs." He was getting angry, his face flushed.

"I see," Malone said. "So. Norton had two design problems on the slats for this aircraft."

"There were two corrections."

"Two corrections of your original erroneous design," Malone said. "And that's just for slats. We haven't gotten to the flaps or the rudder or the fuel tanks and the rest of the airplane. Just in this one tiny system, two corrections. Didn't you test this aircraft, before you sold it to unsuspecting customers?"

"Of course we tested it," Marder said, through clenched teeth. "But you have to realize—"

"What I realize," Malone said, "is that people have died because of your design errors, Mr. Marder. That plane is a deathtrap. And you don't seem to care about that at all."

"*Oh for Christ's fucking sake!*" Marder threw up his hands and jumped out of his seat. He stomped around the room. "I can't fucking believe this!"

It was almost too easy, Jennifer thought. In fact, it *was* too easy. She was suspicious of Marder's histrionic outburst. During the interview, she'd formed a different impression of this man. He wasn't the assistant principal. He was much smarter than that. She realized it from watching his eyes. Most people made an involuntary eye movement when asked a question. They looked up, down, or sideways. But Marder's gaze was steady, calm. He was completely in control.

And she suspected he was in control now, deliberately losing his temper. Why?

She didn't really care. Her goal from the beginning had been to blow these people out. To make them worried enough to pass her on to the president. Jennifer wanted Marty Reardon to interview the president.

This was vital to her story. It would undermine the segment if *Newsline* made serious charges against the N-22, and the company fielded a middle-level flunky or a press nerd to respond. But if she could get the president on camera, her whole segment attained a new level of credibility.

She wanted the president.

Things were going well.

Marder said, "You explain it, Casey."

·  ·  ·

Casey had been appalled by Marder's explosion. Marder was famously bad tempered, but it was a major tactical error to blow up in front of a reporter. And now, still red faced and huffing behind his desk, Marder said, "You explain it, Casey."

She turned to face Malone.

"Ms. Malone," Casey said, "I think everyone here is deeply committed to flight safety." She hoped that would explain Marder's outburst. "We're committed to product safety, and the N-22 has an excellent safety record. And if something does go wrong with one of our planes—"

"Something *did* go wrong," Malone said, looking evenly at Casey.

"Yes," Casey said. "And we're investigating that incident now. I'm on the team conducting that investigation, and we are working around the clock to understand what happened."

"You mean why the slats extended? But you must know. It's happened so many times before."

Casey said, "At this point—"

"Listen," Marder said, breaking in, "it wasn't the damn slats. Frederick Barker is a hopeless alcoholic and a paid liar who works for a sleazebag lawyer. No one in his right mind would listen to him."

Casey bit her lip. She couldn't contradict Marder in front of the reporter, but—

Malone said, "If it wasn't the slats—"

"It wasn't the slats," Marder said firmly. "We'll issue a preliminary report in the next twenty-four hours that will conclusively demonstrate that."

Casey thought: *What?* What was he saying? There was no such thing as a preliminary report.

"Really," Malone said, softly.

"That's right," Marder said. "Casey Singleton's the press liaison on the IRT. We'll be getting back to you, Ms. Malone."

Malone seemed to realize that Marder was terminating the interview. She said, "But there's much more we need to go over, Mr. Marder. There is also the Miami rotor burst. And union opposition to the China sale—"

"Oh, *come on,*" Marder said.

"Given the seriousness of these charges," she continued, "I think that you may want to consider our offer to give your president, Mr. Edgarton, an opportunity to respond."

"That's not going to happen," Marder said.

"It's for your own benefit," Malone said. "If we have to say that the president refused to talk to us, that sounds—"

"Look," Marder said. "Let's cut the crap. Without TransPacific, you have no story. And we are going to issue a preliminary report on TransPacific tomorrow. You'll be informed when. That's all we have for the moment, Ms. Malone. Thank you for coming by."

The interview was over.

# NORTON ADMINISTRATION

"I can't believe that woman," Marder said, after Malone had gone. "She isn't interested in the facts. She isn't interested in the FAA. She isn't interested in how we build airplanes. She's just doing a hatchet job. Is she working for Airbus? That's what I want to know."

"John," Casey said, "about the preliminary finding—"

"Forget it," Marder snapped. "I'll deal with it. You go back to work. I'll talk to the tenth floor, get some input, arrange a few things. We'll talk later today."

"But John," Casey said, "you told her it wasn't the slats."

"It's my problem," Marder said. "You go back to work."

When Casey was gone, Marder called Edgarton.

"My flight's in an hour," Edgarton said. "I'm going to Hong Kong to show my concern for the families of the deceased by personally visiting them. Talk to the carrier, express my sympathies to the relatives."

"Good idea, Hal," Marder said.

"Where are we on this press thing?"

"Well, it's as I suspected," Marder said. "*Newsline* is putting together a story that's extremely critical of the N-22."

"Can you stop it?"

"Absolutely. No question," Marder said.

"How?" Edgarton said.

"We'll issue a preliminary report that it wasn't slats. Our preliminary will say the accident was caused by a counterfeit cowl on the thrust reversers."

"Is there a bad cowl on the plane?"

"Yes. But it didn't cause the accident."

"That's fine," Edgarton said. "A bad part is fine. Just so it's not a Norton problem."

"Right," Marder said.

"And the girl's going to say that?"

"Yes," Marder said.

"She better," Edgarton said. "Because it can be tricky talking to these pricks."

"Reardon," Marder said. "It's Marty Reardon."

"Whatever. She knows what to say?"

"Yes."

"You've briefed her?"

"Yes. And I'll go over it with her again later."

"Okay," Edgarton said. "I also want her to see that media training woman."

"I don't know, Hal, do you really think—"

"Yes, I do," Edgarton said, cutting in. "And so do you. Singleton should be fully prepared for the interview."

"Okay," Marder said.

"Just remember," Edgarton said. "You fuck this up, you're dead."

He hung up.

# OUTSIDE NORTON ADMINISTRATION

1:04 P.M.

Outside the Administration building, Jennifer Malone got into her car, more distressed than she cared to admit. She now felt it was unlikely the company would produce the president. And she was worried—she had the feeling—that they might make Singleton their spokesperson.

That could alter the emotional tenor of the segment. The audience wanted to see beefy, arrogant captains of industry get their just deserts. An intelligent, earnest, attractive woman wouldn't play nearly as well. Were they smart enough to know that?

And, of course, Marty would attack her.

That wouldn't look so good, either.

Just imagining the two of them together gave Jennifer the shivers. Singleton was bright, with an appealing, open quality. Marty'd be attacking motherhood and apple pie. And you couldn't hold Marty back. He'd go for the throat.

But beyond that, Jennifer was starting to worry that the entire segment was weak. Barker had been so convincing when she interviewed him; she had felt elated afterward. But if these ADs were for real, then the company was on solid ground. And she worried about Barker's record. If the FAA had the goods on him, then his credibility was shot. They'd look foolish giving him airtime.

The reporter, Jack Whatshisname, was disappointing. He didn't play well on camera, and his material was thin. Because in the end, nobody gave a damn about drugs on the factory floor. Every company in America had drug problems. That wasn't news. And it didn't prove the airplane was bad—which was what she needed. She needed vivid, persuasive visuals to demonstrate that airplane was a deathtrap.

She didn't have them.

So far, all she had was the CNN tape, which was old news, and the Miami rotor burst, which was not very compelling visually. Smoke coming out from a wing.

Big deal.

Worst of all, if the company really was going to issue a preliminary finding that contradicted Barker—

Her cell phone rang.

"Speak to me," Dick Shenk said.

"Hi, Dick," she said.

"So? Where are we?" Shenk said. "I'm looking at the board right now. Marty finishes with Bill Gates in two hours."

Some part of her wanted to say, Forget it. The story's flaky. It isn't coming together. I was dumb to think I could nail it in two days.

"Jennifer? Do I send him, or not?"

But she couldn't say no. She couldn't admit she had been wrong. He'd kill her if she backed off the story now. Everything about the way she had made her proposal, and the cool way she had walked out of his office, forced her hand now. There was only one possible answer.

"Yes, Dick. I want him."

"You'll have the piece for Saturday?"

"Yes, Dick."

"And it's not a parts story?"

"No, Dick."

"Because I don't want sloppy seconds on *60 Minutes,* Jennifer. It better not be a parts story."

"It's not, Dick."

"I don't hear confidence," he said.

"I'm confident, Dick. I'm just tired."

"Okay. Marty leaves Seattle at four. He'll be at the hotel about eight. Have the shoot schedule ready when he arrives and fax me a copy at home. You've got him all tomorrow."

"Okay, Dick."

"Nail it, babe," he said, and hung up.

She flipped the phone shut, and sighed.

She turned on the ignition, and put the car in reverse.


Casey saw Malone backing out of the parking lot. She was driving a black Lexus, the same car Jim drove. Malone didn't see her, which was just as well. Casey had a lot on her mind.

She was still trying to figure out what Marder was doing. He had blown up at the reporter, told her it wasn't a slats incident, and told her there was going to be a preliminary finding from the IRT. How could he say that? Marder had bravado to spare, but this time he was digging a hole. She didn't understand how his behavior could do anything but damage the company—and himself.

And John Marder, she knew, never damaged himself.

## QA

2:10 P.M.

Norma listened to Casey for several minutes without interruption. Finally she said, "And what's your question?"

"I think Marder's going to make me the spokesman for the company."

"Par for the course," Norma said. "The big guys always run for cover. Edgarton will never do it. And Marder won't, either. You're the press liaison for the IRT. And you're a vice-president of Norton Aircraft. That's what it will say at the bottom of the screen."

Casey was silent.

Norma looked at her. "What's your question?" she said again.

"Marder told the reporter that TPA 545 wasn't a slats problem," she said, "and that we were going to have a preliminary report by tomorrow."

"Hmmm."

"It's not true."

"Hmmm."

"Why is Marder doing this?" Casey said. "Why did he set me up for this?"

"Saving his skin," Norma said. "Probably avoiding a problem he knows about, and you don't."

"What problem?"

Norma shook her head. "My guess is something about the plane. Marder was program manager on the N-22. He knows more about that aircraft than any other person in the company. There may be something he doesn't want to come out."

"So he announces a phony finding?"

"That's my guess."

"And I'm the one carrying the water?"

"Looks like it," Norma said.

Casey was silent. "What should I do?"

"Figure it out," Norma said, squinting through the smoke of her cigarette.

"There's no *time* . . . "

Norma shrugged. "Find out what happened to that flight. Because your tail is on the line, honey. That's how Marder's set it up."

Walking down the hall, she saw Richman.

"Well, hi—"

"Later," she said.

She went into her office and shut the door. She picked up a photograph of her daughter and stared at it. In the picture, Allison had just emerged from a neighbor's swimming pool. She stood with another girl her age, both of them in swimming suits, dripping water. Sleek young bodies, smiling gap-toothed faces, carefree and innocent.

Casey pushed the picture aside, turned to a large box on her desk; opening it, she removed a black portable CD player, with a neoprene sling. There were wires that ran to a strange pair of goggles. They were oversize, and looked like safety goggles, except they didn't wrap around. And there was a funny coating on the inside of the lenses, sort of shimmery in the light. This, she knew, was the maintenance Heads-Up Display. A card from Tom Korman fell out of the box. It said, "First test of VHUD. Enjoy!"

Enjoy.

She pushed the goggles aside, looked at the other papers on her desk. The CVR transcript of cockpit communications had finally come in. She also saw a copy of *TransPacific Flightlines*. There was a Post-it on one page.

She flipped it open to the picture of John Chang, employee of the month. The picture was not what she had imagined from the fax. John Chang was a very fit man in his forties. His wife stood beside him, heavier, smiling. And the children, crouched at the parents' feet, were fully grown: a girl in her late teens, and a boy in his early twenties. The son resembled his father, except he was a little more contemporary; he had extremely closely cropped hair, a tiny gold stud in his ear.

She looked at the caption: "Here he relaxes on the

beach at Lantan Island with his wife, Soon, and his children, Erica and Tom."

In front of the family a blue towel was spread across the sand; nearby, a wicker picnic basket, with blue-checked cloth peeking out. The scene was mundane and uninteresting.

Why would anyone fax this to her?

She looked at the date on the magazine. January, three months ago.

But someone had had a copy of that magazine, and had faxed it to Casey. Who? An employee of the airline? A passenger? Who?

And *why?*

What was it supposed to tell her?

As Casey looked at the magazine picture, she was reminded of the unresolved threads of the investigation. There was a great deal of checking still to do, and she might as well get started.

Norma was right.

Casey didn't know what Marder was up to. But maybe it didn't matter. Because her job was still the same as it had always been: to find out what happened to Flight 545.

She came out of the office.

"Where's Richman?"

Norma smiled. "I sent him over to Media Relations to see Benson. Pick up some standard press packets, in case we need them."

"Benson's got to be pissed off about this," Casey said.

"Uh-huh," Norma said. "Might even give Mr. Richman a hard time." She smiled, looked at her watch. "But I'd say you've got an hour or so, to do what you want. So get going."

## NAIL

### 3:05 P.M.

"So. Singleton," Ziegler said, waving her to a seat. After five minutes of pounding on the soundproof door, she had been admitted to the Audio Lab. "I believe we found what you were looking for," Ziegler said.

On the monitor in front of her she saw a freeze-frame of the smiling baby, sitting on the mother's lap.

"You wanted the period just prior to the incident," Ziegler said. "Here we're approximately eighteen seconds prior. I'll start with full audio, and then cut in the filters. Ready?"

"Yes," she said.

Ziegler ran the tape. At high volume, the baby's slobbering was like a bubbling brook. The hum inside the cabin was a constant roar. "Taste good?" the man's voice said to the baby, very loudly.

"Cutting in," Ziegler said. "High-end bypass."

The sound got duller.

"Cabin ambient bypass."

The slobbering was suddenly loud against a silent background, the cabin roar gone.

"High delta-V bypass."

The slobbering was diminished. What she heard now were mostly background sounds—silverware clinking, fabric movement.

The man said, "Is—at—akfast—or you—arah?" His voice cut in and out.

"Delta-V bypass is no good for human speech," Ziegler said. "But you don't care, right?"

"No," Casey said.

The man said, "Not—aiting—or—ewardess—on—is—ight?"

When the man finished, the screen became almost silent again, just a few distant noises.

"Now," Ziegler said. "It starts."

A counter appeared on the screen. The timer ran forward, red numerals flickering fast, counting tenths and hundredths of a second.

The wife jerked her head around. "What—wa—at?"

"Damn," Casey said.

She could hear it now. A low rumble, a definite shuddering bass sound.

"It's been thinned by the bypass," Ziegler said. "Deep, low rumble. Down in the two to five hertz range. Almost a vibration."

No question, Casey thought. With the filters in place, she could hear it. It was there.

The man's voice broke in, a booming laugh: "Ake it—easy—Em."

The baby giggled again, a sharp earsplitting crackle.

The husband said, "—ost—ome—oney."

The low-pitched rumbling ended.

"Stop!" Casey said.

The red numerals froze. The numbers were big on the screen—11:59:32.

Nearly twelve seconds, she thought. And twelve seconds was the time it took for the slats to fully deploy.

*The slats had deployed on Flight 545.*

By now, the tape was showing the steep descent, the baby sliding on the mother's lap, the mother clutching it, her panicked face. The passengers anxious in the background. With the filters in place, all their shouts produced unusual clipped-off noise, almost like static.

Ziegler stopped the tape.

"There's your data, Singleton. Unequivocal, I'd say."

"The slats deployed."

"Sure sounds like it. It's a fairly unique signature."

"Why?" The aircraft was in cruise flight. Why would they deploy? Was it uncommanded, or had the pilot done it? Casey wished again for the flight data recorder. All these questions could be answered in a few minutes, if they just had the data from the FDR. But it was going very slowly.

"Did you look at the rest of the tape?"

"Well, the next point of interest is the cockpit alarms," Ziegler said. "Once the camera jams in the door, I can listen to the audio, and assemble a sequence of what the aircraft was telling the pilot. But that'll take me another day."

"Stay with it," she said. "I want everything you can give me."

Then her beeper went off. She pulled it off her belt, looked at it.

***JM ADMIN ASAP BTOYA

John Marder wanted to see her. In his office. Now.

## NORTON ADMINISTRATION

### 5:00 P.M.

John Marder was in his calm mood—the dangerous one.

"Just a short interview," he said. "Ten, fifteen minutes at most. You won't have time to go into specifics. But as the head of the IRT, you're in the perfect position to explain the company's commitment to safety. How carefully we review accidents. Our commitment to product support. Then you can explain that our preliminary report shows the accident was caused by a counterfeit thruster cowl, installed at a foreign repair station, so it could not have been a slats event. And blow Barker out of the water. Blow *Newsline* out of the water."

"John," she said. "I just came from Audio. There's no question—the slats deployed."

"Well, audio's circumstantial at best," Marder said. "Ziegler's a nut. We have to wait for the flight data recorder to know precisely what happened. Meanwhile, the IRT has made a preliminary finding which excludes slats."

As if hearing her own voice from a distance, she said, "John, I'm uncomfortable with this."

"We're talking about the future, Casey."

"I understand, but—"

"The China sale will save the company. Cash flow, stretch development, new aircraft, bright future. That's what we're talking about here, Casey. Thousands of jobs."

"I understand, John, but—"

"Let me ask you something, Casey. Do *you* think there's anything wrong with the N-22?"

"Absolutely not."

"You think it's a deathtrap?"

"No."

"What about the company? Think it's a good company?"

"Of course."

He stared at her, shaking his head. Finally he said, "There's someone I want you to talk to."

Edward Fuller was the head of Norton Legal. He was a thin, ungainly man of forty. He sat uneasily in the chair in Marder's office.

"Edward," Marder said, "we have a problem.

*Newsline* is going to run a story on the N-22 this weekend on prime-time television, and it is going to be highly unfavorable."

"How unfavorable?"

"They're calling the N-22 a deathtrap."

"Oh dear," Fuller said. "That's very unfortunate."

"Yes, it is," Marder said. "I brought you in because I want to know what I can do about it."

"Do about it?" Fuller said, frowning.

"Yes," Marder said. "We feel *Newsline* is being crudely sensationalistic. We regard their story as uninformed, and prejudicial to our product. We believe they are deliberately and recklessly defaming us."

"I see."

"So," Marder said. "What can we do? Can we prevent them from running the story?"

"No."

"Can we get a court injunction barring them?"

"No. That's prior restraint. And from a publicity standpoint, it's ill advised."

"You mean it'd look bad."

"An attempt to muzzle the press? Violate the First Amendment? That would suggest you have something to hide."

"In other words," Marder said, "they can run the story, and we are powerless to stop them."

"Yes."

"Okay. But I think *Newsline*'s information is inaccurate and biased. Can we demand they give equal time to our evidence?"

"No," Fuller said. "The fairness doctrine, which

included the equal-time provision, was scrapped under Reagan. Television news programs are under no obligation to present all sides of an issue."

"So they can say anything they want? No matter how unbalanced?"

"That's right."

"That doesn't seem proper."

"It's the law," Fuller said, with a shrug.

"Okay," Marder said. "Now, this program is going to air at a very sensitive moment for our company. Adverse publicity may very well cost us the China sale."

"Yes, it might."

"Suppose we lost business as a result of their show. If we can demonstrate that *Newsline* presented an erroneous view—and we told them it was erroneous—can we sue them for damages?"

"As a practical matter, no. We would probably have to show they proceeded with 'reckless disregard' for the facts known to them. Historically, that has been extremely difficult to prove."

"So *Newsline* is not liable for damages?"

"No."

"They can say whatever they want, and if they put us out of business, it's our tough luck?"

"That's correct."

"Is there any restraint *at all* on what they say?"

"Well." Fuller shifted in the chair. "If they falsely portrayed the company, they might be liable. But in this instance, we have a lawsuit brought by an attorney for a passenger on 545. So *Newsline* is able to say they're just reporting the facts: that an attorney has made the following accusations about us."

"I understand," Marder said. "But a claim filed in a court has limited publicity. *Newsline* is going to present these crazy claims to forty million viewers. And at the same time, they'll automatically validate the claims, simply by repeating them on television. The damage to us comes from their exposure, not from the original claims."

"I take your point," Fuller said. "But the law doesn't see it that way. *Newsline* has the right to report a lawsuit."

"*Newsline* has no responsibility to independently assess the legal claims being made, no matter how outrageous? If the lawyer said, for example, that we employed child molesters, *Newsline* could still report that, with no liability to themselves?"

"Correct."

"Let's say we go to trial and win. It's clear that *Newsline* presented an erroneous view of our product, based on the attorney's allegations, which have been thrown out of court. Is *Newsline* obligated to retract the statements they made to forty million viewers?"

"No. They have no such obligation."

"Why not?"

"*Newsline* can decide what's newsworthy. If they think the outcome of the trial is not newsworthy, they don't have to report it. It's their call."

"And meanwhile, the company is bankrupt," Marder said. "Thirty thousand employees lose their jobs, houses, health benefits, and start new careers at Burger King. And another fifty thousand lost their jobs, when our suppliers go belly up in Georgia, Ohio, Texas, and Connecticut. All those fine people who've devoted their lives working to design, build, and support the best airframe in the business get a firm handshake and a swift kick in the butt. Is that how it works?"

Fuller shrugged. "That's how the system works. Yes."

"I'd say the system sucks."

"The system is the system," Fuller said.

Marder glanced at Casey, then turned back to Fuller. "Now Ed," he said. "This situation sounds very lopsided. We make a superb product, and all the objective measures of its performance demonstrate that it's safe and reliable. We've spent years developing and testing it. We've got an irrefutable track record. But you're saying a television crew can come in, hang around a day or two, and trash our product on national TV. And when they do, they have no responsibility for their acts, and we have no way to recover damages."

Fuller nodded.

"Pretty lopsided," Marder said.

Fuller cleared his throat. "Well, it wasn't always that way. But for the last thirty years, since Sullivan in 1964, the First Amendment has been invoked in defamation cases. Now the press has a lot more breathing room."

"Including room for abuse," Marder said.

Fuller shrugged. "Press abuse is an old complaint," he said. "Just a few years after the First Amendment was passed, Thomas Jefferson complained about how inaccurate the press was, how unfair—"

"But Ed," Marder said. "We're not talking about two hundred years ago. And we're not talking about a few nasty editorials in colonial newspapers. We're talking about a television show with compelling images that goes instantaneously to forty, fifty million people—a sizable percentage of the whole country— and *murders* our reputation. Murders it. Unjustifiably. That's the situation we're talking about here. So," Marder said, "what do you advise us to do, Ed?"

"Well." Fuller cleared his throat again. "I always advise my clients to tell the truth."

"That's fine, Ed. That's sound counsel. But what do we *do?*"

"It would be best," he said, "if you were prepared to explain what occurred on Flight 545."

"It happened four days ago. We don't have a finding yet."

Fuller said, "It would be best if you did."

After Fuller had left, Marder turned to Casey. He didn't say anything. He just looked at her.

Casey stood there for a moment. She understood what Marder and the lawyer were doing. It had been a very effective performance. But the lawyer was also right, she thought. It would be best if they could tell the truth, and explain the flight. As she listened to him, she had begun to think that somehow she might find a way to tell the truth—or enough of the truth—to make this work. There were enough loose ends, enough uncertainties, that she might pull them together to form a coherent story.

"All right, John," she said. "I'll do the interview."

"Excellent," Marder said, smiling and rubbing his hands together. "I knew you'd do the right thing, Casey. *Newsline* has scheduled a slot at four P.M. tomorrow. Meantime I want you to work briefly with a media consultant, someone from outside the company—"

"John," she said. "I'll do it my way."

"She's a very nice woman, and—"

"I'm sorry," Casey said. "I don't have time."

"She can help you, Casey. Give you a few pointers."

"John," she said. "I have work to do."

And she left the room.

## DIGITAL DATA CENTER

6:15 P.M.

She had not promised to say what Marder wanted her to say; she had only promised to do the interview. She had less than twenty-four hours to make significant progress in the investigation. She was not so foolish as to imagine she could determine what had happened in that time. But she could find something to tell the reporter.

There were still many dangling leads: the possible

problem with the locking pin. The possible problem with the proximity sensor. The possible interview with the first officer in Vancouver. The videotape at Video Imaging. The translation Ellen Fong was doing. The fact that the slats had deployed, but had been stowed immediately afterward—what exactly did that mean?

Still so much to check.

"I know you need the data," Rob Wong said, spinning in his chair. "I know, believe me." He was in the Digital Display Room, in front of the screens filled with data. "But what do you expect me to do?"

"Rob," Casey said. "The slats deployed. I have to know why—and what else happened on the flight. I can't figure it out without the flight recorder data."

"In that case," Wong said, "you better face the facts. We've been recalibrating all the one hundred and twenty hours of data. The first ninety-seven hours are okay. The last twenty-three hours are anomalous."

"I'm only interested in the last three hours."

"I understand," Wong said. "But to recalibrate those three hours, we have to go back to where the bus blew, and work forward. We have to calibrate twenty-three hours of data. And it's taking us about two minutes a frame to recalibrate."

She frowned. "What are you telling me?" But she was already calculating it in her head.

"Two minutes a frame means it'll take us sixty-five weeks."

"That's more than a year!"

"Working twenty-four hours a day. Real world, it'd take us three years to generate the data."

"Rob, we need this *now.*"

"It just can't be done, Casey. You're going to have to work this without the FDR. I'm sorry, Casey. That's the way it is."

She called Accounting. "Is Ellen Fong there?"

"She didn't come in today. She said she was working at home."

"Do you have her number?"

"Sure," the woman said. "But she won't be there. She had to go to a formal dinner. Some charity thing with her husband."

"Tell her I called," Casey said.

She called Video Imaging in Glendale, the company that was working on the videotape for her. She asked for Scott Harmon. "Scott's gone for the day. He'll be in at nine tomorrow morning."

She called Steve Nieto, the Fizer in Vancouver, and got his secretary. "Steve's not here," she said. "He had to leave early. But I know he wanted to talk to you. He said he had bad news."

Casey sighed. That seemed to be the only kind of news she was getting. "Can you reach him?"

"Not until tomorrow."

"Tell him I called."

·  ·  ·

Her cell phone rang.

"Jesus, that Benson is unpleasant," Richman said. "What's his problem? I thought he was going to hit me."

"Where are you?"

"At the office. Want me to come to you?"

"No," Casey said. "It's after six. You're done for today."

"But—"

"See you tomorrow, Bob."

She hung up.

On the way out of Hangar 5, she saw the electrical crews rigging TPA 545 for the CET that night. The entire aircraft had been raised ten feet into the air, and now rested on heavy blue metal fixtures beneath each wing, and fore and aft on the fuselage. The crews had then slung black safety webbing beneath the underside of the aircraft, some twenty feet above the ground. All along the fuselage, doors and accessory panels were open, and electricians standing on the webbing were running cables from the junction boxes back to the main CET test console, a six-foot square box that was placed in the center of the floor to one side of the aircraft.

The Cycle Electrical Test, as it was known, consisted of sending electrical impulses to all parts of the aircraft's electrical system. In rapid succession, every component was tested—everything from cabin lights to reading lights, cockpit display panels, engine ignition, and landing-gear wheels. The full test cycle ran two hours. It would be repeated a dozen times, throughout the night.

As she passed the console, she saw Teddy Rawley. He gave her a wave, but didn't approach her. He was busy; undoubtedly he'd heard that Flight Test was scheduled three days from now, and he would want to be sure the electrical test was performed correctly.

She waved to Teddy, but he had already turned away.

Casey headed back to her office.

Outside, it was growing dark, the sky a deep blue. She walked back toward Administration, hearing the distant rush of takeoffs from Burbank airport. On the way, she saw Amos Peters, shuffling toward his car, carrying a stack of papers under his arm. He looked back and saw her.

"Hey, Casey."

"Hi, Amos."

He dropped his papers with a thud on the roof of his car, bent to unlock the door. "I hear they're putting the screws to you."

"Yeah." She was not surprised he knew. The whole plant probably knew by now. It was one of the first things she had learned at Norton. Everyone knew everything, minutes after it happened.

"You going to do the interview?"

"I said I would."

"You going to say what they want you to say?"

She shrugged.

"Don't get high and mighty," he said. "These are television people. They're beneath pond scum on the evolutionary scale. Just lie. Hell with it."

"We'll see."

He sighed. "You're old enough to know how it works," he said. "You going home now?"

"Not for a while."

"I wouldn't be hanging around the plant at night, Casey."

"Why not?"

"People are upset," Amos said. "Next few days, it'd be better to go home early. You know what I mean?"

"I'll bear it in mind."

"Do that, Casey. I mean it."

He got in his car, and drove off.


# QA

### 7:20 P.M.

Norma was gone. The QA office was deserted. The cleaning crews had already started in the back offices; she heard a tinny portable radio playing "Run Baby Run."

Casey went to the coffeemaker, poured a cup of cold coffee, and took it into her own office. She flicked on the lights, stared at the stack of papers waiting on her desk.

She sat down and tried not to be discouraged by the way things were going. She had twenty hours until the interview, and her leads were falling apart.

*Just lie. Hell with it.*

She sighed. Maybe Amos was right.

She stared at the papers, pushing aside the picture of John Chang and his smiling family. She didn't know what to do, except go through the papers. And check.

She again came to the charts of the flight plan. Again, they teased her. She remembered she had had an idea, just before Marder called her the night before. She had a feeling . . . but what was it?

Whatever it was, it was gone now. She set the flight plan aside, including the General Declaration (Outward/Inward) that had been filed with it, which listed the crew:

```
John Zhen Chang, Captain           5/7/51  M
Leu Zan Ping, First Officer        3/11/59 M
Richard Yong, First Officer        9/9/61  M
Gerhard Reimann, First Officer   7/23/49 M
Thomas Chang, First Officer        6/29/70 M
Henri Marchand, Engineer           4/25/69 M
Robert Sheng, Engineer             6/13/62 M
```

She paused, sipped the cold coffee. There was something odd about this list, she thought. Something obvious, right in front of her face. But she couldn't put her finger on it.

She set the list aside.

Next, a transcript of communications from Southern California Air Traffic Approach Control.

As usual it was printed without punctuation, the transmission to 545 intermixed with transmissions to several other aircraft:

| | | |
|---|---|---|
| 0543:12 | UAH198 | three six five ground thirty five thousand |
| 0543:17 | USA2585 | on frequency again changed radios sorry about that |
| 0543:15 | ATAC | one nine eight copy |
| 0543:19 | AAL001 | fuel remaining four two zero one |
| 0543:22 | ATAC | copy that two five eight five no problem we have you now |
| 0543:23 | TPA545 | this is transpacific five four five we have an emergency |
| 0543:26 | ATAC | affirmative zero zero one |
| 0543:29 | ATAC | go ahead five four five |
| 0543:31 | TPA545 | request priority clearance for emergency landing in los angeles |
| 0543:32 | AAL001 | down to twenty nine thousand |

| | | |
|---|---|---|
| 0543:35 | ATAC | okay five four five understand you request priority clearance to land |
| 0543:40 | TPA545 | affirmative |
| 0543:41 | ATAC | say the nature of your emergency |
| 0543:42 | UAH198 | three two one ground thirty two thousand |
| 0543:55 | AAL001 | holding two six nine |
| 0544:05 | TPA545 | we have a passenger emergency we need ambulances on the ground i would say thirty or forty ambulances maybe more |
| 0544:10 | ATAC | tpa five four five say again are you asking for forty ambulances |
| 0544:27 | UAH198 | turn one two four point niner |
| 0544:35 | TPA545 | affirmative we encountered severe turbulence during flight we have injuries of passengers and flight crew |
| 0544:48 | ATAC | copy one nine eight good day |

0544:50   ATAC        transpacific i copy your ground request for forty ambulances

0544:52   UAH198    thank you

Casey puzzled over the exchanges. Because they suggested very erratic behavior by the pilot.

For example, the TransPacific incident had occurred shortly after five in the morning. At that time, the plane was still in radio contact with Honolulu ARINC. With so many injuries, the captain could have reported an emergency to Honolulu.

But he hadn't done that.

Why not?

Instead, the pilot continued to Los Angeles. And he had waited until he was about to land before reporting an emergency.

Why had he waited so long?

And why would he say the incident had been caused by turbulence? He knew that wasn't true. The captain had told the stewardess the slats deployed. And she knew, from Ziegler's audio, that the slats *had* deployed. So why hadn't the pilot announced it? Why lie to approach control?

Everyone agreed John Chang was a good pilot. So what was the explanation for his behavior? Was he in shock? Even the best pilots sometimes behaved oddly in a crisis. But there seemed to be a pattern here—almost a plan. She looked ahead:

| 0544:59 | ATAC | do you need medical personnel too what is the nature of the injuries you are bringing in |
|---|---|---|
| 0545:10 | TPA545 | i am not sure |
| 0545:20 | ATAC | can you give us an estimate |
| 0545:30 | TPA545 | i am sorry no an estimate is not possible |
| 0543:32 | AAL001 | two one two niner clear |
| 0545:35 | ATAC | is anyone unconscious |
| 0545:40 | TPA545 | no i do not think so but two are dead |

The captain seemed to report the fatalities as an afterthought. What was really going on?

| 0545:43 | ATAC | copy zero zero one |
| 0545:51 | ATAC | tpa five four five what is the condition of your aircraft |
| 0545:58 | TPA545 | we have damage to the passenger cabin minor damage only |

Casey thought, *Minor damage only?* That cabin

had sustained millions of dollars of damage. Hadn't the captain gone back to look for himself? Did he not know the extent of the damage? Why would he say what he did?

| | | |
|---|---|---|
| 0546:12 | ATAC | what is the condition of the flight deck |
| 0546:22 | TPA545 | flight deck is operational fdau is nominal |
| 0546:31 | ATAC | copy that four five four what is the condition of your flight crew |
| 0546:38 | TPA545 | captain and first officer in good condition |

At that moment one of the first officers had been covered in blood. Again, did the pilot not know? She glanced at the rest of the transcript, then pushed it aside. She'd show it to Felix tomorrow, and get his opinion.

She went on, looking through the Structure Reports, the Interior Cabin Reports, the relevant PMA records for the counterfeit slats locking pin and the counterfeit thruster cowl. Steadily, patiently, she worked on into the night.

It was after ten o'clock when she again turned to the faults printout from Flight 545. She had been hoping she could skip this, and use the flight recorder data instead. But now there was nothing to do but slog through it.

Yawning, tired, she stared at the columns of numbers on the first page:

```
A/S PWR TEST      0 0 0 0 0 0 1 0 0 0 0
AIL SERVO COMP    0 0 0 0 1 0 0 1 0 0 0
AOA INV           1 0 2 0 0 0 1 0 0 0 1
CFDS SENS FAIL    0 0 0 0 0 0 1 0 0 0 0
CRZ CMD MON INV   1 0 0 0 0 0 2 0 1 0 0
EL SERVO COMP     0 0 0 0 0 0 0 0 0 1 0
EPR/N1 TRA-1      0 0 0 0 0 0 1 0 0 0 0
FMS SPEED INV     0 0 0 0 0 0 4 0 0 0 0
PRESS ALT INV     0 0 0 0 0 0 3 0 0 0 0
G/S SPEED ANG     0 0 0 0 0 0 1 0 0 0 0
SLAT XSIT T/O     0 0 0 0 0 0 0 0 0 0 0
G/S DEV INV       0 0 1 0 0 0 5 0 0 0 1
GND SPD INV       0 0 0 0 0 0 2 1 0 0 0
TAS INV           0 0 0 0 1 0 1 0 0 0 0
TAT INV           0 0 0 0 0 0 1 0 0 0 0
AUX 1             0 0 0 0 0 0 0 0 0 0 0
AUX 2             0 0 0 0 0 0 0 0 0 0 0
AUX 3             0 0 0 0 0 0 0 0 0 0 0
AUX COA           0 1 0 0 0 0 0 0 0 0 0
A/S ROX-P         0 0 0 0 0 0 1 0 0 0 0
RDR PROX-1        0 0 0 0 1 0 0 1 0 0 0
AOA BTA           1 0 2 0 0 0 0 0 0 0 1
FDS RG            0 0 0 0 0 0 1 0 0 0 0
F-CMD MON         1 0 0 0 0 0 2 0 1 0 0
```

She didn't want to do this. She hadn't eaten dinner yet, and she knew she should eat. Anyway, the only questions she had about these fault listings were the AUX readings. She had asked Ron, and he had said the first was the auxiliary power unit, the second and third were unused, and the fourth, AUX COA, was a customer installed line. But there wasn't anything on those lines, Ron said, because a zero reading was normal. It was the default reading.

So she was really finished with this listing.

She was done.

Casey stood up at her desk, stretched, looked at her watch. It was ten-fifteen. She'd better get some sleep, she thought. After all, she was going to appear on television tomorrow. She didn't want her mother to call afterward saying, "Dear, you looked so *tired . . .*"

Casey folded up the printout, and put it away.

Zero, she thought, was the perfect default value. Because that was what she was coming up with, on this particular night's work.

A big zero.

Nothing.

"A big fat zero," she said aloud. "Means nothing on the line."

She didn't want to think what it meant—that time was running out, that her plan to push the investigation had failed, and that she was going to end up in front of a television camera tomorrow afternoon, with the famous Marty Reardon asking her questions, and she would have no good answers to give him. Except the answers that John Marder wanted her to give.

*Just lie. Hell with it.*

Maybe that was how it was going to turn out.

*You're old enough to know how it works.*

Casey turned out her desk light, and started for the door.

She said good night to Esther, the cleaning woman, and went out into the hallway. She got into the elevator, and pushed the button to go down to the ground floor.

The button lit up when she touched it.

Glowing "1."

She yawned as the doors started to close. She was really very tired. It was silly to work this late. She'd make foolish mistakes, overlook things.

She looked at the glowing button.

And then it hit her.

"Forget something?" Esther said, as Casey came back into the office.

"No," Casey said.

She rifled through the sheets on her desk. Fast, searching. Tossing papers in all directions. Letting them flutter to the floor.

Ron had said the default was zero, and therefore when you got a zero you didn't know if the line was used or not. But if there was a 1 . . . then that would mean . . . She found the listing, ran her finger down the columns of numbers:

```
AUX  1        0 0 0 0 0 0 0 0 0 0 0
AUX  2        0 0 0 0 0 0 0 0 0 0 0
AUX  3        0 0 0 0 0 0 0 0 0 0 0
AUX  COA      0 1 0 0 0 0 0 0 0 0 0
```

There was a numeral 1! AUX COA had registered a fault, on the second leg of the flight. That meant the AUX COA line *was* being used by the aircraft.

But what was it used for?

She sucked in her breath.

She hardly dared to hope.

Ron said that AUX COA was a line for Customer Optional Additions. The customer used it for add-ons, like a QAR.

The QAR was the Quick Access Recorder, another flight data recorder installed to help the maintenance crews. It recorded many of the same parameters as a regular DFDR. If a QAR was on this aircraft, it could solve all her problems.

But Ron insisted this plane didn't have a QAR.

He said he'd looked in the tail, which was where it was usually installed on an N-22. And it wasn't there.

Had he ever looked anywhere else?

Had he really searched the plane?

Because Casey knew an optional item like the QAR was not subject to FAA regulation. It could be anyplace in the aircraft the operator wanted it—in the aft accessory compartment, or the cargo hold, or the radio rack beneath the cockpit . . . It could be just about anywhere.

Had Ron really looked?

She decided to check for herself.

She spent the next ten minutes thumbing through thick Service Repair Manuals for the N-22, without any success. The manuals didn't mention the QAR at all, or at least she couldn't find any reference. But the manuals she kept in her office were her personal copies; Casey wasn't directly involved in maintenance, and she didn't have the latest versions. Most of the manuals dated back to her own arrival at the company; they were five years old.

That was when she noticed the Heads-Up Display, sitting on her desk.

Wait a minute, she thought. She grabbed the goggles, slipped them on. She plugged them into the CD player. She pressed the power switch.

Nothing happened.

She fiddled with the equipment for a few moments, until she realized there was no CD-ROM in the machine. She looked in the cardboard box, found a silver platter, and slid it into the player. She pressed the power button again.

The goggles glowed. She was staring at a page from the first maintenance manual, projected onto the inside of the goggles. She wasn't quite sure how the system worked, because the goggles were just an inch from her eyes, but the projected page appeared to float in space, two feet in front of her. The page was almost transparent; she could see right through it.

Korman liked to say that virtual reality was virtually useless, except for a few specialized applications. One was maintenance. Busy people working in technical environments, people who had their hands full, or covered in grease, didn't have the time or inclination to look through a thick manual. If you were thirty feet up in the air trying to repair a jet engine, you couldn't carry a stack of five-pound manuals around with you. So virtual displays were perfect for those situations. And Korman had built one.

By pressing buttons on the CD player, Casey found that she could scroll through the manuals. There was also a search function, that flashed up a keyboard hanging in space; she had to repeatedly press another button to move a pointer to the letter *Q,* then *A,* then *R.* It was clumsy.

But it worked.

After a moment of whirring, a page hung in the air before her:

```
N-22
QUICK ACCESS RECORDER (QAR)
RECOMMENDED LOCATIONS
```

Pressing more buttons, she scrolled through a sequence of diagrams, showing in detail all the places where the QAR could be located on the N-22 aircraft.

There were about thirty places in all.

Casey clipped the player onto her belt, and headed for the door.

## AIRPORT MARINA

10:20 P.M.

Marty Reardon was still in Seattle.

His interview with Gates had run long, and he'd missed his plane. Now he was coming down in the morning. Jennifer had to revise the schedule.

It was going to be a difficult day, she realized. She'd hoped to start at nine. Now she couldn't begin until ten at the earliest. She sat in the hotel room with her laptop, figuring it out.

| | |
|---|---|
| 9:00-10:00 | Transfer from LAX |
| 10:00-10:45 | Barker at ofc |
| 11:00-11:30 | King at airport |
| 11:30-12:00 | FAA at airport |
| 12:15-1:45 | Transfer to Burbank |
| 2:00-2:30 | Rogers at Burbank |
| 2:30-3:30 | Stand-up outside Norton |
| 4:00-4:30 | Singleton at Norton |
| 4:30-6:00 | Transfer to LAX |

Too tight. No time for lunch, for traffic delays, for normal production screwups. And tomorrow was Friday; Marty would want to make the six o'clock plane back to New York. Marty had a new girlfriend, and he liked to spend the weekend with her. Marty would be very pissy if he missed the flight.

And he was definitely going to miss it.

The problem was that by the time Marty finished

with Singleton in Burbank, it would be rush hour. He'd never make his plane. He really should leave Burbank by two-thirty. Which meant pushing Singleton up, and holding off the lawyer. She was afraid she'd lose the FAA guy if she changed him at the last minute. But the lawyer would be flexible. He'd wait until midnight if they asked him to.

She'd talked with the lawyer earlier. King was a blowhard, but he was plausible in short bites. Five, ten seconds. Punchy. Worth doing.

| | |
|---|---|
| 9:00-10:00 | Transfer from LAX |
| 10:00-10:45 | Barker at ofc |
| 11:00-11:30 | FAA at airport |
| 11:30-12:30 | Transfer to Burbank |
| 12:30-1:00 | Rogers at Burbank |
| 1:00-2:00 | Stand-up outside Norton |
| 2:00-2:30 | Singleton at Norton |
| 2:30-4:00 | Transfer to LAX |
| 4:00-4:30 | King at airport |
| 5:00-6:00 | Pad |

That would work. In her mind, she reviewed her pullouts. If the FAA guy was good (Jennifer hadn't met him yet, just talked on the phone), then Marty might run over with him. If it took too long to transfer to Burbank, she'd blow off Rogers, who was weak anyway, and go right to Marty's stand-up. Singleton would be fast—Jennifer wanted to keep Marty moving there, so he didn't attack the woman too much. A tight schedule would help.

Back to LAX, finish with King, Marty'd leave at six, and Jennifer would have her tape. She'd go to an editing bay at the O and O, cut the segment, and uplink to New York that night. She'd call in and get Dick's comments Saturday morning, revise it, and uplink it again about noon. That was plenty of time to make air.

She made a note to call Norton in the morning and tell them she needed to move Singleton up two hours.

Finally she turned to the stack of faxed background documents Norton had sent her office, for Deborah's research. Jennifer had never bothered to look at these, and she wouldn't bother now, except she had nothing better to do. She thumbed through them quickly. It was what she expected—self-justifying papers that said the N-22 was safe, that it had an excellent record . . .

Flipping from page to page, she suddenly stopped. She stared.

"They've got to be kidding," she said.

And she closed the file.

# HANGAR 5

## 10:30 P.M.

At night, the Norton plant appeared deserted, the parking lots nearly empty, the perimeter buildings silent. But it was brightly lit. Security kept floodlights on all night. And there were video monitors mounted on the corners of all the buildings. As she crossed from Administration to Hangar 5, she heard her footsteps clicking on the asphalt.

The big doors to Hangar 5 were pulled down and locked. She saw Teddy Rawley, standing outside, talking to one of the electrical team. A wisp of cigarette smoke rose up toward the floodlights. She went over to the side door.

"Hey, babe," Teddy said. "Still here, huh?"

"Yeah," she said.

She started through the door. The electrical guy said, "The building's closed. Nobody's allowed in. We're doing the CET now."

"It's okay," she said.

"I'm sorry, you can't," the guy said. "Ron Smith gave strict orders. Nobody's to go inside. If you touch anything on the airplane—"

"I'll be careful," she said.

Teddy looked at her, walked over. "I know you will," he said, "but you're going to need this." He handed her a heavy flashlight, three feet long. "It's dark in there, remember?"

The electrical guy said, "And you can't turn the lights on, we can't have change in the ambient flux—"

"I understand," she said. The test equipment was sensitive; turning on the overhead fluorescents might change readings.

The electrician was still fretting. "Maybe I better call Ron and tell him you're going in."

"Call whoever you want," Casey said.

"And don't touch the handrails, because—"

"I won't," she said. "For Christ's sake, I know what I'm doing."

She went into the hangar.

Teddy was right; it was dark inside. She felt, rather than saw, the large space around her. She could barely discern the outlines of the plane, looming above her; all its doors and compartments were open, cabling hanging down everywhere. Beneath the tail, the test box sat in a pool of faint blue light. The CRT screen flickered, as systems were activated in sequence. She saw the cockpit lights go on, then off. Then the forward cabin lights, brightly lit, thirty feet above her. Then darkness again. A moment later, the beacon lights on the wing tips and the tail came on, sending hot white strobe flashes through the room. Then darkness again.

The front headlights suddenly glared brightly from the wing, and the landing gear began to retract. Because the plane was mounted above the ground, the landing gear was free to retract and extend. It would happen a dozen times that night.

Outside the hangar, she heard the electrician, still talking in a worried tone. Teddy laughed, and the electrician said something else.

Casey turned on her flashlight and moved forward. The flashlight cast a powerful glow. She twisted the rim, spreading the beam wider.

Now the landing gear was fully raised. Then the gear doors opened, and the landing gear began to extend, the big rubber wheels coming down flat, then turning with a hydraulic whine. A moment later, the insignia light shone up at the rudder, illuminating the tail. Then it went off again.

She headed for the aft accessory compartment in the tail. She knew Ron had said the QAR wasn't there, but she felt she had to check again. She climbed the broad stairs rolled up to the back of the plane, being careful not to touch the handrails. Electrical test cables were taped to the handrails; she didn't want to disturb them, or to cause field fluctuation from the presence of her hand.

The aft accessory compartment, built into the upward slope of the tail, was directly above her head. The compartment doors were open. She shone her light in. The upper surface of the compartment was taken up by the underside of the APU, the turbine generator that served as the auxiliary power unit: a maze of semicircular pipes and white couplings wrapped around the main unit. Below was a cramped series of readout meters, rack slots, and black FCS boxes, each with the milled vanes for heat transfer. If there was a QAR in here as well, she might easily miss it; the QARs were only about eight inches square.

She paused to put on her goggles, and turned on the CD player. Immediately a diagram of the aft accessory compartment hung in space before her eyes. She could see through the diagram to the actual compartment behind. The rectangular block marking the QAR was outlined in red on the diagram. In the actual compartment, the space was taken up by an extra readout meter: hydraulic pressure for a flight control system.

Ron was right.

There was no QAR here.

Casey climbed back down the stairs to the floor, and walked beneath the plane to the forward accessory compartment, just behind the nose wheel. It, too, was open. Standing on the ground, she shone her flashlight up into the compartment, and flicked to the correct manual page. A new image hung in the air. It showed the QAR located in the right anterior electrical rack, next to the hydraulic activator buses.

It wasn't there. The slot was empty, the round connector plug exposed at the back, the shiny metal contact points glinting.

It had to be somewhere inside the plane.

She headed off to the right, where a roll-up staircase led up thirty feet to the passenger door, just behind the cockpit. She heard her feet ring on the metal as she entered the aircraft.

It was dark; she shone her flashlight aft, the beam moving over the cabin. The passenger cabin looked worse than before; in many places her beam caught the dull silver of the insulation pads. The electrical crews had pulled the interior panels around the windows, to get at junction boxes along the walls. She noticed a lingering faint odor of vomit; someone had tried to mask it with a sweet floral spray.

Behind her, the cockpit suddenly glowed. The overhead map lights came on, softly illuminating the two seats; then the row of video display screens, the twinkling lights of the overhead panels. The FDAU printer on the pedestal buzzed, printing out a couple of test lines, then was silent. All the cockpit lights went out.

Dark again.

Cycling.

Immediately, the forward galley lights just ahead of her came on; the illuminators for heating and microwaves flashed; the overheat and timer warnings beeped. Then everything went off. Silence.

Dark again.

Casey was still standing just inside the door, fiddling with the CD player at her waist, when she thought she heard footsteps. She paused, listening.

It was difficult to tell; as the electrical systems cycled through, there was a continuous succession of soft buzzes and clicks from relays and solenoids in the avionics racks around her. She listened hard.

Yes, she was sure of it now.

Footsteps.

Someone was walking slowly, steadily, through the hangar.

Frightened, she leaned out the door and called loudly, "Teddy? Is that you?"

She listened.

No more footsteps.

Silence.

The clicking of the relays.

The hell with it, she decided. She was up here, alone inside this torn-up airplane, and it was getting on her nerves. She was tired. She was imagining things.

She walked around the galley to the left side, where the display showed an additional electrical storage panel, down near the floor. The panel cover had already been removed. She looked at it through the transparent diagram. This was mostly taken up with secondary avionics boxes, and there was little room . . .

No QAR.

She moved down the cabin, to the midships bulkhead. There was a small storage compartment here, built into the bulkhead frame, just below a slot for magazines. It was a foolish place to install a QAR, she thought, and she was not surprised when she didn't find one there, either.

Four down. Twenty-six to go.

Now she moved toward the tail, to the aft interior storage compartment. This was a more likely place: a square service panel that was just to the left of the rear exit door, on the side of the aircraft. The panel didn't screw down; it flipped up on a hinge, which made it more accessible for crews in a hurry.

She came to the door, which was open. She felt a cool breeze. Darkness outside: she couldn't see the ground, forty feet below. The panel was just to the left of the door, and it was already open. She looked, seeing it through the diagram. If the QAR was there, it would be in the lower-right corner, next to the breaker switches for the cabin lights and the crew intercom.

It wasn't there.

The wing tip lights came on, brilliant strobes flashing repeatedly. They cast harsh shadows in the interior, through the open door and the row of windows. Then off again.

*Clink.*

She froze.

The sound had come from somewhere near the cockpit. It was a metallic sound, like a foot kicking a tool.

She listened again. She heard a soft tread, a creak. *Someone was in the cabin.*

She pulled the goggles off her head, leaving them hanging around her neck. Silently, she slid to her right, crouching behind a row of seats at the rear of the plane.

She heard footsteps coming closer. A complicated pattern of sound. A murmur. Was there more than one?

She held her breath.

The cabin lights came on, first in front, then midships, then aft. But most of the ceiling lights were hanging, so they cast odd shadows, then went off again.

She gripped the flashlight. The weight felt comforting in her hand. She moved her head to the right, so she could peer between the seats.

She heard the footsteps again, but could see nothing.

Then the landing lights came on, and in their reflected glare, a row of hot ovals appeared on the ceiling, from the windows along both sides. And a shadow, blotting out the ovals, one after another.

Someone walking down the aisle.

Not good, she thought.

What could she do? She had the flashlight in her hand, but she had no illusions about her ability to defend herself. She had her cell phone. Her beeper. Her—

She reached down, and silently flicked the beeper off.

The man was close now. She edged forward, her neck aching, and she saw him. He was almost to the rear of the plane, looking in every direction. She could not see his face, but in the reflected landing lights, she could see his red-checked shirt.

The landing lights went out.

Darkness in the cabin.

She held her breath.

She heard the faint *thunk* of a relay, coming from somewhere in the forward compartment. She knew it was electrical, but apparently the man in the red shirt did not. He grunted softly, as if surprised, and moved forward quickly.

She waited.

After a while, she thought she heard the sound of footsteps on the metal stairs, going down. She wasn't sure, but she thought so.

The airplane was silent around her.

Cautiously, she came out from behind the seat. It was time to get out of here, she thought. She moved to the open door, listening. There was no question, the footsteps walking away, the sound diminishing. The nose lights came on, and she saw a long streak of shadow. A man.

Walking away.

A voice inside said, *Get out of here,* but she felt the goggles around her neck, and hesitated. She ought to give the man plenty of time to leave the hangar—she didn't want to go down and find him on the floor. So she decided to look in another compartment.

She pulled on the goggles, pressed the button on the unit. She saw the next page.

The next compartment was nearby, located just outside the rear door, where she was standing. She leaned out the door and, holding on with her right hand, found she could easily look into the panel box. The cover was already open. There were three vertical rows of electrical buses, which probably controlled the two rear doors; they were overrides. And at the bottom . . .

Yes.

The Quick Access Recorder.

It was green, with a white stripe around the top. Stenciled lettering: MAINT QAR 041/B MAINT. A metal box about eight inches square, with a plug facing outward. Casey reached in, gripped the box, and pulled gently. With a metallic click it came free of the inner coupling. And she had it in her hand.

All right!

She stepped back inside the doorway, holding the

box in both hands now. She was so excited she was trembling. This changed everything!

She was so excited, she did not hear the rush of footsteps behind her until it was too late. Strong hands shoved against her, she grunted, and her hands slipped away, and then her body fell through the door, into space.

Falling.

To the floor thirty feet below.

Too soon—much too soon—she felt a sharp pain on her cheek—and then her body landed, but something was wrong. There were strange pressure points all over her body. She was no longer falling, but rising. Then falling again. It was like a giant hammock.

The webbing.

She'd hit the safety webbing.

She couldn't see it in the darkness, but the black safety webbing was hung beneath the plane, and she had fallen into it. Casey rolled over onto her back, saw a silhouette at the door. The figure turned and ran through the airplane. She scrambled to her feet, but it was difficult to balance. The webbing was slowly undulating.

She moved forward, toward the dull metal expanse of the wing. She heard footsteps clattering on the metal stairs, somewhere forward. The man was coming.

She had to get out.

She had to get off the webbing before he caught

her. She moved closer to the wing, and then she
heard a cough. It had come from the far edge of the
wing, somewhere off to her left.

Someone else was here.

Down on the floor.

Waiting.

She paused, feeling the gentle swaying of the
webbing beneath her. In a moment, she knew, more
lights would come on. Then she could see where the
man was.

Suddenly, the hot strobe lights above the tail
flickered rapidly. They were so bright, they illuminated the entire hangar.

Now she could see who had coughed.

It was Richman.

He wore a dark blue windbreaker and dark slacks.
The lazy, collegiate manner was gone. Richman
stood near the wing, tense, alert. He looked left and
right carefully, scanning the floor.

Abruptly, the strobe lights went out, plunging the
hangar into darkness. Casey moved forward, hearing the webbing creak beneath her feet. Would
Richman hear? Could he figure out where she was?

She came to the wing, stretching forward in
darkness.

She grabbed it with her hand, moved outward to
the edge. Sooner or later, she knew, the webbing
would end. Her foot struck a thick cord; she bent
down, felt knots.

Casey lay down on the webbing, gripped the edge

in both hands, and rolled over the side, falling. For a moment she hung by one arm, the webbing stretching downward. She was surrounded by blackness. She did not know how far it was to the floor: Six feet? Ten feet?

Running footsteps.

She released the webbing, and fell.

She hit the ground standing, dropped to her knees. Sharp pain in her kneecap as she banged into concrete. She heard Richman cough again. He was very close, off to her left. She got up and began to run toward the exit door. The landing lights came on again, harsh and strong. In their glare she saw Richman throw up his hands to cover his eyes.

She knew he would be blinded for a few seconds. Not long.

But perhaps enough.

Where was the other man?

She ran.

She hit the wall of the hangar with a dull metallic thud. Someone behind her said, "Hey!" She moved along the wall feeling for the door. She heard running footsteps.

Where? Where?

Behind her, running footsteps.

Her hand touched wood, vertical runners, more wood, then the metal bar. The door latch. She pushed.

Cool air.

She was outside.

Teddy turned. "Hey, babe," he said, smiling. "How's it going?"

She fell to her knees, gasping for breath. Teddy and the electrical guy came running over. "What is it? What's the matter?"

They were standing over her, touching her, solicitous. She tried to catch her breath. She managed to gasp, "Call Security."

"What?"

"Call Security! Someone's inside!"

The electrical guy ran to the phone. Teddy stayed with her. Then she remembered the QAR. She had a moment of sudden panic. Where was it?

She stood. "Oh no," she said. "I dropped it."

"Dropped what, babe?"

"That box . . ." She turned, looking back at the hangar. She'd have to get them to go back inside, to—

"You mean the one in your hand?" Teddy said.

She looked at her left hand.

The QAR was there, clutched so tightly her fingers were white.

## GLENDALE

### 11:30 P.M.

"Come on, now," Teddy said, arm around her, walking her into the bedroom. "Everything's fine, babe."

"Teddy," she said, "I don't know why . . ."

"We'll find out tomorrow," he said soothingly.

"But what was he doing . . ."

"Tomorrow," Teddy said.

"But what was he . . ."

She couldn't finish her sentences. She sat on the bed, suddenly feeling her exhaustion, overwhelmed by it.

"I'll stay on the couch," he said. "I don't want you alone tonight." He looked at her, chucked her on the chin. "Don't worry about a thing, babe."

He reached over, and took the QAR out of her hand. She released it unwillingly. "We'll just put this right here," he said, setting it on the bedside table. He was talking to her as to a child.

"Teddy, it's important . . ."

"I know. It'll be there, when you wake up. Okay?"

"Okay."

"Call if you need anything." He left, closing the door.

She looked at the pillow. She had to get out of her clothes, to get ready for bed. Her face hurt; she didn't know what had happened to it. She needed to look at her face.

She picked up the QAR and stuck it behind the pillow. She stared at the pillow, then lay down on it, and closed her eyes.

Just for a moment, she thought.

# FRIDAY

# GLENDALE

6:30 A.M.

*Something was wrong.*

Casey sat up quickly. Pain streaked through her body; she gasped. She felt a burning sensation in her face. She touched her cheek, and winced.

Sunlight poured through her window onto the foot of the bed. She looked down at twin arcs of grease on the bedspread. She still had her shoes on. She still had her clothes on.

She was lying on top of the bedspread, fully dressed.

Groaning, she twisted her body, swung her feet to the floor. Everything hurt. She looked down at the bedside table. The clock said six-thirty.

She reached behind the pillow, brought out the green metal box with a white stripe.

The QAR.

She smelled coffee.

The door opened, and Teddy came in in his boxer shorts, bringing her a mug. "How bad is it?"

"Everything hurts."

"I figured." He held the coffee out to her. "Can you handle this?"

She nodded, took the mug gratefully. Her shoulders hurt as she lifted it to her lips. The coffee was hot and strong.

"Face isn't too bad," he said, looking at her critically. "Mostly on the side. I guess that's where you hit the mesh . . ."

She suddenly remembered: the interview.

"Oh Jesus," she said. She got off the bed, groaning again.

"Three aspirins," Teddy said, "and a very hot bath."

"I don't have time."

"Make time. Hot as you can stand."

She went into the bathroom and turned on the shower. She looked in the mirror. Her face was streaked with grime. There was a purple bruise that started by her ear and ran back behind her neck. Her hair would cover it, she thought. It wouldn't show.

She took another drink of coffee, removed her clothes, got into the shower. She had bruises on her elbow, on her hip, on her knees. She couldn't remember how she had gotten them. The stinging hot spray felt good.

When she came out of the shower, the telephone was ringing. She pushed open the door.

"Don't answer that," Casey said.

"Are you sure?"

"There's no time," she said. "Not today."

She went into the bedroom to dress.

She had only ten hours until her interview with Marty Reardon. Between now and then, she had only one thing she wanted to do.

Clear up Flight 545.

# NORTON/DDS

7:40 A.M.

Rob Wong placed the green box on the table, attached a cable, pressed a key on his console. A small red light glowed on the QAR box.

"It's got power," Wong said. He sat back in his chair, looked at Casey. "You ready to try this?"

"I'm ready," she said.

"Keep your fingers crossed," Wong said. He pushed a single key on the keyboard.

The red light on the QAR box began to flicker rapidly.

Uneasily, Casey said, "Is that . . ."

"It's okay. It's downloading."

After a few seconds, the red light glowed steadily again.

"Now what?"

"It's done," Wong said. "Let's see the data." His screen began to show columns of numbers. Wong leaned forward, looking closely. "Uh . . . looks pretty good, Casey. This could be your lucky day." He typed rapidly at the keyboard for several seconds. Then he sat back.

"Now we see how good it is."

On the monitor, a wire-frame aircraft appeared and rapidly filled in, becoming solid, three-dimensional. A sky-blue background appeared. A silver aircraft, seen horizontally in profile. The landing gear down.

Wong punched keys, moving the aircraft around so they saw it from the tail. He added a green field running to the horizon, and a gray runway. The image was schematic but effective. The airplane began to move, going down the runway. It changed attitude, the nose raising up. The landing gear folded into the wings.

"You just took off," Wong said. He was grinning.

The aircraft was still rising. Wong hit a key, and a rectangle opened on the right side of the screen. A series of numbers appeared, changing quickly. "It's not a DFDR, but it's good enough," Wong said. "All the major stuff is here. Altitude, airspeed, heading, fuel, deltas on control surfaces—flaps, slats, ailerons, elevators, rudder. Everything you need. And the data's stable, Casey."

The aircraft was still climbing. Wong hit a button, and white clouds appeared. The plane continued upward, through the clouds.

"I figure you don't want to real time this," he said. "You know when the accident occurred?"

"Yes," she said. "It was about nine-forty into the flight."

"Nine-forty elapsed?"

"Right."

"Coming up."

On the monitor, the aircraft was level, the rectangle of numbers on the right stable. Then a red light began to flash among the numbers.

"What's that?"

"Fault recording. It's, uh, slats disagree."

She looked at the aircraft on the screen. Nothing changed.

"Slats extending?"

"No," Wong said. "Nothing. It's just a fault."

She watched a moment longer. The aircraft was still level. Five seconds passed. Then the slats emerged from the leading edge.

"Slats extending," Wong said, looking at the numbers. And then, "Slats fully extended."

Casey said, "So there was a fault first? And then the slats extended afterward?"

"Right."

"Uncommanded extension?"

"No. Commanded. Now, plane goes nose up, and—uh-oh—exceeding buffet boundary—now here's the stall warning, and—"

On the screen, the airplane nosed over into a steep dive. The white clouds streaked past, faster and faster. Alarms began to beep, flashing on the screen.

"What's that?" Casey said.

"The plane's exceeding the G-load envelope. Jeez, look at him."

The airplane pulled out of the dive, and began a steep climb. "He's going up at sixteen . . . eighteen . . . twenty-one degrees," Wong said, shaking his head. "Twenty-one degrees!"

On commercial flights, a standard rate of climb was three to five degrees. Ten degrees was steep, used only in takeoffs. At twenty-one degrees, passengers would feel as if the plane were going straight up.

More alarms.

"Exceedences," Wong said again, in a flat voice. "He's stressing the hell out of the airframe. It's not built to take that. You guys do a structure inspect?"

As they watched, the plane went into a dive again.

"I can't believe this," Wong said. "The autopilot's supposed to prevent that—"

"He was on manual."

"Even so, these wild oscillations would kick in the autopilot." Wong pointed to the box of data to one side. "Yeah, there it is. The autopilot tries to take over. Pilot keeps punching it back to manual. That's crazy."

Another climb.

Another dive.

In all, they watched aghast as the aircraft went through six cycles of dive and climb, until suddenly, abruptly, it returned to stable flight.

"What happened?" she said.

"Autopilot took over. *Finally.*" Rob Wong gave a long sigh. "Well, I'd say you know what happened to this airplane, Casey. But I'm damned if I know *why.*"

# WAR ROOM

9:00 A.M.

A cleaning crew was at work in the War Room. The big windows overlooking the factory floor were being washed, the chairs and the Formica table wiped down. In the far corner, a woman was vacuuming the carpet.

Doherty and Ron Smith were standing near the door, looking at a printout.

"What's going on?" she said.

"No IRT today," Doherty said. "Marder canceled it."

Casey said, "How come nobody told me that—"

Then she remembered. She'd turned her beeper off, the night before. She reached down, turned it back on.

"CET test last night was damn near perfect," Ron said. "Just as we said all along, that's an excellent airplane. We only got two repeated faults. We got a consistent fault on AUX COA, starting five cycles in, around ten-thirty; I don't know why that happened." He looked at her, waiting. He must have heard that she had been inside the hangar the night before, at about that time.

But she wasn't going to explain it to him. At least, not right now. She said, "And what about the proximity sensor?"

"That was the other fault," Smith said. "Out of

twenty-two cycles we ran during the night, the wing proximity sensor faulted six times. It's definitely bad."

"And if that proximity sensor faulted during flight . . ."

"You'd get a slats disagree in the cockpit."

She turned to leave.

"Hey," Doherty said. "Where are you going?"

"I've got to look at some video."

"Casey: Do you know what the hell is going on?"

"You'll be the first to know," she said. And she walked away.

As swiftly as the investigation had stalled the day before, she felt it coming together. The QAR had been the key. At last she could reconstruct the sequence of events on Flight 545. And with that, the pieces of the puzzle were falling rapidly into place.

As she walked to her car, she called Norma on her cell phone. "Norma, I need a route schedule for TransPacific."

"Got one right here," Norma said. "It came over with the FAA packet. What do you want to know?"

"Flight schedule to Honolulu."

"I'll check." There was a pause. "They don't go into Honolulu," Norma said. "They only go to—"

"Never mind," Casey said. "That's all I need to know." It was the answer she had expected.

"Listen," Norma said, "Marder has called three times for you already. He says you're not answering your pager."

"Tell him you can't reach me."

"And Richman has been trying to—"

"You can't reach me," Casey said.

She hung up, and hurried to her car.

Driving in the car, she called Ellen Fong in Accounting. The secretary said Ellen was working at home again today. Casey got the number, and called.

"Ellen, it's Casey Singleton."

"Oh yes, Casey." Her voice was cool. Careful.

"Did you do the translation?" Casey said.

"Yes." Flat. No expression.

"Did you finish it?"

"Yes. I finished it."

"Can you fax it to me?" Casey said.

There was a pause. "I don't think I should do that," Ellen said.

"All right . . ."

"Do you know why?" Ellen Fong asked.

"I can guess."

"I will bring it to your office," Ellen said. "Two o'clock?"

"Fine," Casey said.

The pieces were coming together. Fast.

Casey was now pretty sure she could explain what happened on Flight 545. She could almost lay out the entire chain of causal events. With luck, the tape at Video Imaging would give her final confirmation.

Only one question remained.

What was she going to do about it?

# SEPULVEDA BOULEVARD

10:45 A.M.

Fred Barker was sweating. The air conditioner was turned off in his office, and now, under Marty Reardon's insistent questioning, sweat trickled down his cheeks, glistened in his beard, dampened his shirt.

"Mr. Barker," Marty said, leaning forward. Marty was forty-five, handsome in a thin-lipped, sharp-eyed way. He had the air of a reluctant prosecutor, a seasoned man who'd seen it all. He spoke slowly, often in short fragments, with the appearance of reasonableness. He was giving the witness every possible break. And his favorite tone was that of disappointment. Dark eyebrows up: How could this be? Marty said, "Mr. Barker, you've described 'problems' with the Norton N-22. But the company says Airworthiness Directives were issued that fixed the problems. Are they right?"

"No." Under Marty's probing, Barker had dropped the full sentences. He now said as little as possible.

"The Directives didn't work?"

"Well, we just had another incident, didn't we. Involving slats."

"Norton told us it wasn't slats."

"I think you'll find it was."

"So Norton Aircraft is lying?"

"They're doing what they always do. They come

up with some complicated explanation that conceals the real problem."

"Some complicated explanation," Marty repeated. "But aren't aircraft complicated?"

"Not in this case. This accident is the result of their failure to redress a long-standing design flaw."

"You're confident of that."

"Yes."

"How can you be so sure? Are you an engineer?"

"No."

"You have an aerospace degree?"

"No."

"What was your major in college?"

"That was a long time ago . . ."

"Wasn't it music, Mr. Barker? Weren't you a music major?"

"Well, yes, but, uh . . ."

Jennifer watched Marty's attack with mixed feelings. It was always fun to see an interview squirm, and the audience loved to watch pompous experts cut down to size. But Marty's attack threatened to devastate her entire segment. If Marty destroyed Barker's credibility . . .

Of course, she thought, she could work around him. She didn't have to use him.

"A Bachelor of Arts. In music," Marty said, in his reasonable tone. "Mr. Barker, do you think that qualifies you to judge aircraft?"

"Not in itself, but—"

"You have other degrees?"

"No."

"Do you have any scientific or engineering training at all?"

Barker tugged at his collar. "Well, I worked for the FAA . . ."

"Did the FAA give you any scientific or engineering training? Did they teach you, say, fluid dynamics?"

"No."

"Aerodynamics?"

"Well, I have a lot of experience—"

"I'm sure. But do you have *formal training* in aerodynamics, calculus, metallurgy, structural analysis, or any of the other subjects involved in making an airplane?"

"Not formally, no."

"Informally?"

"Yes, certainly. A lifetime of experience."

"Good. That's fine. Now, I notice those books behind you, and on your desk." Reardon leaned forward, touched one of the books that lay open. "This one here. It's called *Advanced Structural Integrity Methods for Airframe Durability and Damage Tolerance.* Pretty dense. You understand this book?"

"Most of it, yes."

"For example." Reardon pointed to the open page, turned it to read. "Here on page 807, it says, 'Leevers and Radon introduced a biaxiality parameter B that relates the magnitude of the T stress as in equation 5.' You see that?"

"Yes." Barker swallowed.

"What is a 'biaxiality parameter'?"

"Uh, well, it's rather difficult to explain briefly . . ."

Marty jumped: "Who are Leevers and Radon?"

"They're researchers in the field."

"You know them?"

"Not personally."

"But you're familiar with their work."

"I've heard their names."

"Do you know anything about them at all?"

"Not personally, no."

"Are they important researchers in the field?"

"I've said I don't know." Barker tugged at his collar again.

Jennifer realized she had to put a stop to this. Marty was doing his attack-dog routine, snarling at the smell of fear. Jennifer couldn't use any of this stuff; the significant fact was that Barker had been on a crusade for years, he had a track record, he was committed to the fight. In any case she already had his slats explanation from the day before, and she had softball answers to the questions she had asked herself. She tapped Marty on the shoulder. "We're running late," she said.

Marty responded instantly; he was bored. He jumped up. "I'm sorry, Mr. Barker, we have to cut this short. We appreciate your time. You've been very helpful."

Barker appeared to be in shock. He mumbled something. The makeup girl came up to him with wipes in her hand and said, "I'll help you get the makeup off . . ."

Marty Reardon turned to Jennifer. In a low voice he said, "What the fuck are you doing?"

"Marty," she said, answering him in the same low tones, "the CNN tape is dynamite. The story's dynamite. The public's scared to get on airplanes. We're fleshing out the controversy. Performing a public service."

"Not with this clown you're not," Reardon said. "He's a litigator's stooge. All he's good for is an out-of-court settlement. He doesn't know what the fuck he's talking about."

"Marty. Whether you like this guy or not, the plane has a history of problems. And the tape is fabulous."

"Yes, and everybody's seen the tape," Reardon said. "But what's the *story?* You better show me something, Jennifer."

"I will, Marty."

"You better."

Left unstated was the rest of the sentence: Or I'm going to call Dick Shenk and pull the plug.

## AVIATION HIGHWAY

### 11:15 A.M.

For a different look, they shot the FAA guy on the street, with the airport as background. The FAA guy was skinny and wore glasses. He blinked rapidly in the sun. He looked weak and bland. He was such a non-entity, Jennifer couldn't even remember his name. She felt confident he wouldn't hold up well.

Unfortunately, he was devastating about Barker.

"The FAA handles a great deal of sensitive information. Some is proprietary. Some is technical. Some is industry sensitive, and some is company sensitive. Since the candor of all parties is critical to our function, we have very strict rules about the dissemination of this information. Mr. Barker violated those rules. He seemed to have a great desire to see himself on television, and his name in the newspapers."

"He says, not true," Marty replied. "He says, the FAA wasn't doing its job, and he had to speak out."

"To attorneys?"

Marty said, "Attorneys?"

"Yes," the FAA guy said. "Most of his leaks were to attorneys bringing cases against carriers. He released confidential information to attorneys, incomplete information about investigations in progress. And that's illegal."

"Did you prosecute?"

"We're not able to prosecute. We don't have that authority. But it was clear to us that he was being paid under the table by lawyers to give them information. We turned his case over to the Justice Department, which failed to pursue it. We were pretty upset about it. We thought he should go to jail, and the attorneys with him."

"Why didn't that happen?"

"You'd have to ask Justice. But the Justice Department is made up of attorneys. And attorneys don't like to send other attorneys to jail. Sort of professional courtesy. Barker worked for attorneys, and they got him off. Barker still works for attorneys. Everything he says is designed to support or incite a frivolous lawsuit. He has no real interest in aviation safety. If he did, he'd still be working for us. Trying to serve the public, instead of trying to make a lot of money."

Marty said, "As you know, the FAA is currently under fire . . ."

Jennifer thought she'd better stop Marty now. There wasn't any point in continuing. She already intended to drop most of this interview. She'd use just the early statement where the FAA guy said Barker wanted publicity. That was the least damaging comment, and it would constitute a balanced response in the segment.

Because she needed Barker.

"Marty, I'm sorry, we have to get across town."

Marty nodded, thanked the guy immediately— another indication he was bored—signed an autograph for the guy's kid, and climbed into the limo ahead of Jennifer.

"Jesus," Marty said, as the limo pulled away.

He waved good-bye to the FAA guy through the window, smiled to him. Then he flopped back in the seat. "I don't get it, Jennifer," he said ominously. "Correct me if I'm wrong. But you don't have a story. You got some bullshit allegations by lawyers and their paid stooges. But you've got nothing of substance."

"We've got a story," she said. "You'll see." She tried to sound confident.

Marty grunted unhappily.

The car pulled out, and headed north to the Valley, toward Norton Aircraft.

## VIDEO IMAGING SYSTEMS

11:17 A.M.

"Tape's coming up now," Harmon said. He drummed his fingers on the console.

Casey shifted her body in the chair, feeling twinges of pain. She still had several hours before the interview. And she still couldn't decide how she would handle it.

The tape began to run.

Harmon had tripled the frames, the image moving in a jerky slow motion. The change made the sequence appear even more horrifying. She watched in silence as the bodies tumbled, the camera spun and fell, and finally came to rest at the cockpit door.

"Go back."

"How far?"

"As slow as you can."

"One frame at a time?"

"Yes."

The images ran backward. The gray carpet. The blur as the camera jumped away from the door. The glint of light off the open cockpit door. The hot glare from the cockpit windows, the shoulders of the two pilots on either side of the pedestal, captain on the left, first officer on the right.

The captain reaching toward the pedestal.

"Stop."

She stared at the frame. The captain was reaching, no hat, the face of the first officer turned forward, away from him.

The captain reaching his hand out.

Casey rolled her chair toward the console, and peered at the monitor. Then she stood, moved very close to the screen, seeing the scan lines.

There it is, she thought. In living color.

*But what was she going to do about it?*

Nothing, she realized. There was nothing she could do. She had the information now, but she could not possibly release it, and hold on to her job. But she realized she was probably going to lose her job anyway. Marder and Edgarton had set her up to do the press. Whether she lied, as Marder wanted her to do, or whether she told the truth, she was in trouble. There was no way out.

The only possible solution that Casey could see was not to do the interview. But she had to do it. She was caught in the middle.

"Okay," she said, sighing. "I've seen enough."

"What do you want to do?"

"Run another copy."

Harmon pressed a button on the console. He shifted in his chair, looking uncomfortable. "Ms. Singleton," he said. "I feel I have to mention something. The people who work here have seen this tape, and frankly, they're pretty upset."

"I can imagine," Casey said.

"They've all seen that guy on television, the attorney, who says you're covering up the real cause of the accident . . ."

"Uh-huh . . ."

"And one person in particular, a woman in reception, thinks we should turn this tape over to the authorities, or to the television stations. I mean, it's like the Rodney King thing. We're sitting on a bomb here. People's lives are at risk."

Casey sighed. She was not really surprised. But it presented a new issue, and she would have to deal with it. "Has that already happened? Is that what you're telling me?"

"No," Harmon said. "Not yet."

"But people are concerned."

"Yes."

"And what about you? What do you think?"

"Well. To tell you the truth, I'm bothered, as well," Harmon said. "I mean, you work for the company, you have your loyalties. I understand that. But if there really is something wrong with this airplane and people died because of it . . ."

Casey's mind was working fast again, thinking through the situation. There was no way to know how many copies of the tape had already been made. There was no way to contain or control events, now. And she was tired of the intrigue—with the carrier, with the engineers, with the union, with Marder, with Richman. All these conflicting agendas, while she was caught in the middle, trying to hold it together.

And now the damn tape company!

She said, "What's the name of the woman in reception?"

"Christine Barron."

"Does she know your company has signed a non-disclosure agreement with us?"

"Yeah, but . . . I guess she thinks her conscience takes precedence."

"I need to make a call," Casey said. "On a private line."

He took her to an office that wasn't being used. She made two telephone calls. When she came back, she said to Harmon, "The tape is Norton property. It is not to be released to anyone without our authorization. And you have signed a non-disclosure agreement with us."

"Doesn't your conscience bother you?" Harmon said.

"No," Casey said. "It doesn't. We're investigating this, and we'll get to the bottom of it. All you're doing is talking about things you don't understand. If you release this tape, you'll help a bottom-feeder lawyer sue us for damages. You signed an NDA with us. You violate it, and you're out of business. Keep it in mind."

She took her copy of the tape, and walked out of the room.

# NORTON QA

11:50 A.M.

Frustrated and angry, Casey stormed into her office at QA. An elderly woman was waiting for her. She introduced herself as Martha Gershon, in "media training." In person, she looked like a kindly grandmother: gray hair, tied up in a bun, and a beige, high-necked dress.

Casey said, "I'm sorry, I'm very busy. I know Marder asked you to see me, but I'm afraid that—"

"Oh, I realize how busy you are," Martha Gershon said. Her voice was calm, reassuring. "You don't have time for me, especially today. And you don't really *want* to see me, do you? Because you don't much care for John Marder."

Casey paused.

She looked again at this pleasant lady, standing there in her office, smiling.

"You must feel you've been manipulated by Mr. Marder. I understand. Now that I've met him, I must say I don't get a strong feeling of integrity from him. Do you?"

"No," Casey said.

"And I don't think he likes women much," Gershon continued. "And I suspect he's arranged for you to speak to the television cameras, in the hope that you would fail. Gosh, I'd hate to see that happen."

Casey stared at her. "Please sit down," she said.

"Thank you, dear." The woman sat on the couch,

her beige dress billowing around her. She folded her hands neatly in her lap. She remained utterly calm. "I won't take long," she said. "But perhaps you'd be more comfortable if you sat down, too."

Casey sat down.

"There's just a few things I'd like to remind you of," Gershon said, "before your interview. You know you'll be speaking to Martin Reardon."

"No, I didn't."

"Yes," she said, "which means you'll be dealing with his distinctive interviewing style. That will make it easier."

"I hope you're right."

"I am, dear," she said. "Are you comfortable now?"

"I think so."

"I'd like to see you sit back in your chair. There you go. Sit back. When you lean forward you appear too eager, and your body gets tense. Sit back, so you can take in what is said to you, and be relaxed. You might want to do that in the interview. Sit back, I mean. And be relaxed."

"All right," Casey said, sitting back.

"Relaxed now?"

"I think so," Casey said.

"Do you clasp your hands together like that on the desk, usually? I'd like to see what happens if you place your hands apart. Yes. Rest them on the desk, just like you're doing. If you close your hands, it makes you tense. It's so much better when you just stay open. Good. Does that feel natural?"

"I guess so."

"You must be under great strain now," Gershon said, clucking sympathetically. "But I've known Martin Reardon since he was a young reporter. Cronkite disliked him. Thought Martin was cocky and insubstantial. I fear that assessment has proved accurate. Martin is all tricks and no substance. He's not going to give you any trouble, Katherine. Not a woman of your intelligence. You'll have no trouble at all."

Casey said, "You're making me feel wonderful."

"I'm just telling you how it is," Gershon said lightly. "The most important thing to remember with Reardon is that you know more than he does. You've worked in this business for years. Reardon has literally just arrived. He probably flew in this morning, and he will fly out again tonight. He's bright, facile, and a quick study, but he does not have your depth of knowledge. Remember that: you know more than he does."

"Okay," Casey said.

"Now, because Reardon has almost no information at his disposal, his chief skill is manipulating the information you give him. Reardon has a reputation as a hatchet man, but if you watch how he behaves, he's actually a one-trick performer. And this is his trick. He gets you to agree with a series of statements, so you are nodding, yes, yes—and then he hits you with something out of left field. Reardon's done that his whole life. It's amazing people haven't caught on.

"He'll say, You're a woman. Yes. You live in

California. Yes. You have a good job. Yes. You enjoy life. Yes. So why did you steal the money? And you've been nodding along, and suddenly you're flustered, you're off-balance—and he's got a reaction he can use.

"Remember, all he wants is that one-sentence reaction. If he doesn't get it, he'll double back, and ask the question another way. He may return to a subject again and again. If he keeps raising a particular topic, you'll know he hasn't gotten what he wants."

"Okay."

"Martin has another trick. He will make a provocative statement, and then pause, waiting for you to fill the vacuum. He'll say, Casey, you make airplanes, so you must *know* the planes are unsafe . . . And wait for you to answer. But notice he hasn't actually asked a question."

Casey nodded.

"Or he will repeat what you say, in a tone of disbelief."

"I understand," Casey said.

"You *understand?*" Gershon said, surprised, raising her eyebrows. It was a pretty good imitation of Reardon. "You see what I mean. You will be goaded to defend yourself. But you don't have to. If Martin doesn't ask a question, you needn't say anything."

Casey nodded. Not saying anything.

"Very good." Gershon smiled. "You'll do just fine. Just remember to take all the time you want. The interview is taped, so they'll cut out any pauses. If you don't understand a question, ask him to clarify it. Martin is extremely good at asking vague questions that provoke specific answers. Remember: he doesn't really know what he's talking about. He's just here for the day."

"I understand," Casey said.

"Now. If you're comfortable looking at him, do that. If you're not, you might choose a point somewhere near his head, like the corner of a chair, or a picture on the wall behind him. And focus on that instead. The camera won't be able to tell you're not really looking at him. Just do whatever you need to do to keep your concentration."

Casey tried it, looking just past Gershon's ear.

"That's good," Gershon said. "You'll do fine. There's only one more thing I can tell you, Katherine. You work in a complex business. If you try to explain that complexity to Martin, you'll be frustrated. You'll feel he isn't interested. He'll probably cut you off. Because he *isn't* interested. A lot of people complain that television lacks focus. But that's the nature of the medium. Television's not about information at all. Information is active, engaging. Television is passive. Information is disinterested, objective. Television is emotional. It's entertainment. Whatever he says, however he acts, in truth Martin has absolutely no interest in you, or your company, or your airplanes. He's paid to exercise his one reliable talent: provoking people, getting them to make an emotional outburst, to lose their temper, to say something outrageous. He doesn't really want to know about airplanes. He wants a media *moment*. If you understand that, you can deal with him."

And she smiled, her grandmotherly smile. "I know you'll do just fine, Casey."

Casey said, "Will you be there? At the interview?"

"Oh no," Gershon said, smiling. "Martin and I have a long history. We don't much care for each other. On the rare occasions we find ourselves in the same location, I'm afraid we tend to *spit*."

## ADMINISTRATION

1:00 P.M.

John Marder was sitting at his desk, arranging the documents—props—for Casey to use in her interview. He wanted them complete, and he wanted them in order. First, the parts record for the counterfeit thruster cowl on the number-two engine. Finding that part had been a stroke of luck. Kenny Burne, for all his bluster, had done something right. A thruster cowl was a big-bone part, something everybody could relate to. And it was definitely counterfeit. Pratt and Whitney would scream when they saw it: the famous eagle on their logo had been printed backward. More important, the presence of a counterfeit part could throw the entire story in that direction, and it would take the heat off—

His private phone rang.

He picked it up. "Marder."

He heard the hissing crackle of a satellite phone. Hal Edgarton, calling from the company jet on his way to Hong Kong. Edgarton said, "Has it happened yet?"

"Not yet, Hal. Another hour."

"Call me, as soon as it's over."

"I will, Hal."

"And it better be good news," Edgarton said, and he hung up.

# BURBANK

### 1:15 P.M.

Jennifer was fretting. She had had to leave Marty alone for a while. And it was never a good idea to leave Marty alone during a shoot: he was a restless, high-energy guy, and he needed constant attention. Someone had to hold his hand and fuss over him. Marty was like all the on-camera talent at *Newsline*—they might once have been reporters, but now they were actors, and they had all the traits of actors. Self-centered, vain, demanding. They were a pain in the ass, is what they were.

She also knew that Marty, for all his bitching about the Norton story, was at bottom just worried about appearances. He knew the segment had been put together fast. He knew it was down and dirty. And he was afraid that when the segment was cut, he'd be fronting a lame story. He was afraid his friends would make snide comments about the story over lunch at the Four Seasons. He didn't care about journalistic responsibility. He just cared about appearances.

And the proof, Jennifer knew, was in her hands. She had only been gone twenty minutes, but as her Town Car rolled up to the location, she saw Marty pacing, head down. Troubled and unhappy.

Typical Marty.

She got out of the car. He came right over to her, started to make his complaint, started to say he thought they should bail on the segment, call Dick, tell him it wasn't working . . . She cut him off.

"Marty. Look at this."

She took the videotape she was carrying, gave it to the cameraman, and told him to play it back. The cameraman popped it into the camera while she went over to the small playback monitor that sat on the grass.

"What is it?" Marty said, standing over the monitor.

"Watch."

The tape began to play. It started with a baby on the mother's lap. Goo-goo. Ga-ga. Baby sucking her toes.

Marty looked at Jennifer. His dark eyebrows went up.

She said nothing.

The tape continued.

With the glare of the sun on the monitor, it was hard to see in detail, but it was clear enough. Bodies suddenly tumbling through the air. Marty sucked in his breath as he watched, excited.

"Where did you get this?"

"Disgruntled employee."

"An employee of?"

"A video shop that does work for Norton Aircraft. A solid citizen who thought it should be released. She called me."

"This is a Norton tape?"

"They found it on the plane."

"Unbelievable," Marty said, watching the tape. "Un-believable." Bodies tumbling, the camera moving. "This is shocking."

"Isn't it fabulous?"

The tape continued. It was good. It was all good—even better than the CNN tape, more kinetic, more radical. Because the camera broke free and bounced around, this tape conveyed a better sense of what must have happened on the flight.

"Who else has this?" Marty said.

"Nobody."

"But your disgruntled employee may . . ."

"No," Jennifer said. "I promised we'd pay her legal bills, as long as she didn't give it to anybody else. She'll sit tight."

"So this is our exclusive."

"Right."

"An *actual tape* from *inside* Norton Aircraft."

"Right."

"Then we've got a fabulous segment here," Marty said.

Back from the dead! Jennifer thought, as she watched Marty go over to the fence, and start to prepare for his stand-up. The segment was saved!

She knew she could count on Marty to cut the crap. Because, of course, this new tape added nothing to the information already in the can. But Marty was a pro. He knew their segments lived and died on the visuals. If the visuals worked, nothing else mattered.

And this tape was a grabber.

So Marty was cheerful now, pacing back and forth, glancing at Norton Aircraft through the fence. The whole situation was perfect for Marty, a tape obtained from inside the company, with all the innuendo of stonewall and cover-up. Marty could milk that for all it was worth.

While the makeup girl retouched his neck, Marty said, "We should probably send that tape to Dick. So he can tease it."

"Done," Jennifer said, pointing to one of the cars heading down the road.

Dick would have it within an hour. And he would cream when he saw it.

Of course he would tease it. He'd use bits of it to promote Saturday's show. "Shocking new film of the Norton disaster! Terrifying footage of death in the skies! Only on *Newsline,* Saturday at ten!"

They'd run that sucker every half hour until showtime. By Saturday night, the whole country would be watching.

Marty ad-libbed his stand-up, and he did it well. Now they were back in the car, heading toward the Norton gate. They were even a few minutes ahead of schedule.

"Who's the company contact?" he said.

"Woman named Singleton."

"A woman?" Dark eyebrows up again. "What's the deal?"

"She's a vice-president. Late thirties. And she's on the investigation team."

Marty held out his hand. "Give me the file and the notes." He started to read through them, in the car. "Because you realize what we have to do now, don't you, Jennifer? The segment's all moved around. That tape runs maybe four, four-thirty. And you may show parts of it twice—I would. So you won't have much time for Barker and the others. It's going to be the tape, and the Norton spokesman. That's the core of the piece. So there isn't any choice. We have to nail this woman, cold."

Jennifer said nothing. She waited, while Marty thumbed through the file.

"Wait just a minute here," Marty said. He was staring at the file. "Are you kidding me?"

"No," Jennifer said.

"This is dynamite," Reardon said. "Where'd you get it?"

"Norton sent it to me in a background package, three days ago, by accident."

"Bad accident," Marty said. "Especially for Ms. Singleton."

# WAR ROOM

2:15 P.M.

Casey was crossing the plant, heading over to IAA, when her cell phone rang. It was Steve Nieto, the Fizer in Vancouver.

"Bad news," Nieto said. "I went to the hospital yesterday. He's dead. Cerebral edema. Mike Lee wasn't around, so they asked me if I could identify the body, and—"

"Steve," she said. "Not on a cell phone. Send me a telex."

"Okay."

"But don't send it here. Send it to FT in Yuma."

"Really?"

"Yes."

"Okay."

She hung up and entered Hangar 4, where the tape strips were laid out on the floor. She wanted to talk to Ringer about the pilot's hat they'd found. That hat was critical to the story, as it was now becoming clear to Casey.

She had a sudden thought, and called Norma. "Listen, I think I know where that fax came from about the in-flight magazine."

"Does it matter?"

"Yes. Call Centinela Hospital at the airport. Ask for a stewardess named Kay Liang. And this is what I want you to ask her. Better write it down."

She spoke to Norma for several minutes, then hung up. Immediately, her cell phone rang again.

"Casey Singleton."

Marder screamed, "Where are you, for Chrissakes?"

"Hangar Four," she said, "I'm trying to—"

"You're supposed to be *here*," Marder screamed. "For the interview."

"The interview's four o'clock."

"They moved it up. They're here *now*."

"Now?"

"Yes, they're all here, the crew, everybody, they're setting up. They're all waiting for you. It's *now*, Casey."

Which was how she found herself in the War Room, sitting in a chair, with a makeup woman daubing at her face. The War Room was full of people, there were guys setting up big lights on stands, and taping sheets of cardboard to the ceiling. Other men were taping microphones to the table, and to the walls. There were two camera crews setting up, each with two cameras—four cameras in all, pointing in opposite directions. Two chairs had been arranged at opposite sides of the table, one for her, one for the interviewer.

She thought it was inappropriate that they were taping in the War Room; she didn't know why Marder had agreed to it. She thought it was disrespectful that this room, where they worked and argued and struggled to understand what happened to planes in flight, had been turned into a prop for a television show. And she didn't like it.

Casey was off-balance; everything was happening too fast. The makeup woman kept asking her to keep her head still, to close her eyes, then open them. Eileen, Marder's secretary, came over and thrust a manila folder in her hands. "John wanted to make sure you had this," she said.

Casey tried to look at the folder.

"Please," the makeup woman said, "I need you to look up for a minute. Just a minute, then you can go."

Jennifer Malone, the producer, came over with a cheerful smile. "How's everything today, Ms. Singleton?"

"Fine, thanks," Casey said. Still looking up for makeup.

"Barbara," Malone said, to the makeup woman. "Make sure you get the, uh . . ." And she waved her hand toward Casey, a vague gesture.

"I will," the makeup woman said.

"Get the what?" Casey said.

"A touchup," the makeup woman said. "Nothing."

Malone said, "I'll give you a minute to finish here, and then Marty should be in to meet you, and we'll go over the general areas we're covering, before we start."

"Okay."

Malone went away. The makeup woman, Barbara, continued to daub at Casey's face. "I'm going to give you a little under the eyes," she said. "So you don't look so tired."

"Ms. Singleton?"

Casey recognized the voice at once, a voice she'd heard for years. The makeup woman jumped back, and Casey saw Marty Reardon standing in front of her. Reardon was in shirtsleeves and a tie. He had Kleenex around his collar. He held out his hand. "Marty Reardon. Nice to meet you."

"Hi," she said.

"Thanks for your help with this," Reardon said. "We'll try to make it as painless as possible."

"Okay . . ."

"You know of course we're on tape," Reardon said. "So if you have a bobble or something, don't worry; we'll just cut it. If at any time you want to restate an answer, go ahead and do that. You can say exactly what you want to say."

"Okay."

"Primarily we'll be talking about the TransPacific flight. But I'm going to have to touch on some other matters as well. Somewhere along the line, I'll ask about the China sale. And there'll probably be some questions about the union response, if we have time. But I don't really want to get into those other issues. I want to stay with TransPacific. You're a member of the investigation team?"

"Yes."

"All right, fine. I have a tendency to jump around in my questions. Don't let that bother you. We're really here to understand the situation as best we can."

"Okay."

"I'll see you later, then," Reardon said. He smiled, and turned away.

The makeup woman moved back in front of her again. "Look up," she said. Casey stared at the ceiling. "He's very nice," the makeup woman said. "A sweet man, underneath it all. *Dotes* on his children."

She heard Malone call out, "How much more time, guys?"

Someone said, "Five minutes."

"Sound?"

"We're ready. Just give us the bodies."

The makeup woman began to powder Casey's neck. Casey winced, feeling twinges of pain. "You know," the woman said, "I have a number you can call."

"For what?"

"It's a very good organization, very good people. Psychologists mostly. And extremely discreet. They can help you."

"With what?"

"Look left, please. He must have hit you pretty hard."

Casey said, "I fell."

"Sure, I understand. I'll leave my card, in case you change your mind," the makeup woman said, using the powder puff. "Hmm. I better get some base on that, to take the blue out." She turned back to her box, got a piece of sponge with makeup on it. She began to daub it onto Casey's neck. "I can't tell you how much I see, in my line of work, and the woman always denies it. But domestic violence has to be stopped."

Casey said, "I live alone."

"I know, I know," the makeup woman said. "Men count on your silence. My own husband, Jeez, he wouldn't go into counseling. I finally left with the kids."

Casey said, "You don't understand."

"I understand that when this violence is going on, you think there's nothing you can do. That's part of the depression, the hopelessness," the makeup woman said. "But sooner or later, we all face the truth."

Malone came over. "Did Marty tell you? We're mostly doing the accident, and he'll probably start with that. But he may mention the China sale, and the unions. Just take your time. And don't worry if he jumps around from one thing to another. He does that."

"Look right," the makeup woman said, doing the other side of her neck. Casey turned to the right. A man came over and said, "Ma'am? Can I give you this?" and he thrust a plastic box into her hands, with a dangling wire.

"What is it?" Casey said.

"Look right, please," the makeup woman said. "It's the radio mike. I'll help you with it in a minute."

Her cell phone rang, in her purse on the floor beside her chair.

"Turn that off!" someone shouted.

Casey reached for it, flipped it open. "It's mine."

"Oh, sorry."

She brought the phone to her ear. John Marder said, "Did you get the folder from Eileen?"

"Yes."

"Did you look at it?"

"Not yet," she said.

"Just lift your chin a little," the makeup woman said.

On the telephone, Marder said, "The folder documents everything we talked about. Parts report on the reverser cowl, everything. It's all there."

"Uh-huh . . . Okay . . ."

"Just wanted to make sure you're all set."

"I'm all set," she said.

"Good, we're counting on you."

She clicked the phone off, turning the power switch off.

"Chin up," the makeup woman said. "That's a girl."

When makeup was finished, Casey stood, and the woman brushed her shoulders with a little brush, and put hair spray in her hair. Then she took Casey into the bathroom, and showed her how to thread the mike wire up under her blouse, through her bra, and clip it to her lapel. The wire ran back down inside her skirt, then back up to the radio box. The woman hooked the box to the waistband of Casey's skirt, and turned the power on.

"Remember," she said. "From now on, you're live. They can hear whatever you say."

"Okay," Casey said. She adjusted her clothes. She felt the box pinching at her waist, the wire against the skin of her chest. She felt cramped and uncomfortable.

The makeup woman led her back into the War Room, holding her by the elbow. Casey felt like a gladiator being taken into the arena.

Inside the War Room, the lights were glaring. The room was very hot. She was led to her seat at the table, told to watch she didn't trip over the camera cables, and helped to sit down. There were two cameras behind her. There were two cameras facing her. The cameraman behind her asked her to please move her chair an inch to the right. She did. A man came over and adjusted her microphone clip, because he said there was clothing noise.

On the opposite side, Reardon was attaching his own microphone without assistance, chatting with the cameraman. Then he slipped easily into his chair. He looked relaxed, and casual. He faced her, smiled at her.

"Nothing to worry about," he said. "Piece of cake."

Malone said, "Let's go, guys, they're in the chairs. It's hot in here."

"A camera ready."

"B camera ready."

"Sound ready."

"Let's have the lights," Malone said.

Casey had thought the lights were already on, but suddenly, new harsh lights blazed down at her, from all directions. She felt as if she were in the middle of a glaring furnace.

"Camera check," Malone said.

"Fine here."

"We're fine."

"All right," Malone said. "Roll tape."

The interview began.

# WAR ROOM

### 2:33 P.M.

Marty Reardon met her eyes, smiled, and gestured to the room. "So. This is where it all happens."

Casey nodded.

"This is where the Norton specialists meet to analyze aircraft accidents."

"Yes."

"And you're part of that team."

"Yes."

"You're vice-president of Quality Assurance at Norton Aircraft."

"Yes."

"Been with the company five years."

"Yes."

"They call this room the War Room, don't they?"

"Some do, yes."

"Why is that?"

She paused. She couldn't think of any way to describe the arguments in this room, the flares of temper, the outbursts that accompanied every attempt to clarify an aircraft incident, without saying something he could take out of context.

She said, "It's just a nickname."

"The War Room," Reardon said. "Maps, charts, battle plans, pressure. Tension under siege. Your company, Norton Aircraft, is under siege at the moment, isn't it?"

"I'm not sure what you're referring to," Casey said.

Reardon's eyebrows went up. "The JAA, Europe's Joint Aviation Authority, is refusing to certify one of your aircraft, the N-22, because they say it's unsafe."

"Actually, the plane's already certified but—"

"And you're about to sell fifty N-22s to China. But now the Chinese, too, are said to be concerned about the safety of the planes."

She didn't get angry at the innuendo; she focused on Reardon. The rest of the room seemed to fade away.

She said, "I'm not aware of any Chinese concerns."

"But you *are* aware," Reardon said, "of the reason *behind* these safety concerns. Earlier this week, a very serious accident. Involving an N-22 aircraft."

"Yes."

"TransPacific Flight 545. An accident in midair, over the Pacific Ocean."

"Yes."

"Three people died. And how many injured?"

"I believe fifty-six," she said. She knew it sounded awful, no matter how she said it.

"Fifty-six injured," Reardon intoned. "Broken necks. Broken limbs. Concussions. Brain damage. Two people paralyzed for life . . ."

Reardon trailed off, looking at her.

He hadn't asked a question. She said nothing. She waited, in the glaring heat of the lights.

"How do you feel about that?"

She said, "I think everyone at Norton feels very great concern for air safety. That's why we test our airframes to three times the design life—"

"Very great concern. Do you think that's an adequate response?"

Casey hesitated. What was he saying? "I'm sorry," she said. "I'm afraid I don't follow—"

"Doesn't the company have an obligation to build safe aircraft?"

"Of course. And we do."

"Not everyone agrees," Reardon said. "The JAA doesn't agree. The Chinese may not agree . . . Doesn't the company have an *obligation* to fix the design of an aircraft which it *knows* to be unsafe?"

"What do you mean?"

"What I mean," Reardon said, "is that what happened to Flight 545 has happened before. Many times before. On other N-22s. Isn't that true?"

"No," Casey said.

"No?" Reardon's eyebrows shot up.

"No," Casey said, firmly. This was the moment, she thought. She was stepping off the cliff.

"This is the first time?"

"Yes."

"Well then," Reardon said, "perhaps you can explain this list." He produced a sheet of paper, held it up. She knew from across the room what it was. "This is a list of slats episodes on the N-22, going back to 1992, right after the plane was introduced. Eight episodes. Eight separate episodes. TransPacific is the ninth."

"That's not accurate."

"Well, tell me why."

Casey went through, as briefly as she could, the way Airworthiness Directives worked. She explained why they had been issued for the N-22. How the problem had been solved, except for foreign carriers that had failed to comply. How there had not been a domestic incident since 1992.

Reardon listened with continuously raised eyebrows, as if he had never heard such an outlandish thing before.

"So let me see if I understand," he said. "In your view, the company has followed the rules. By issuing these air directives, which are supposed to fix the problem."

"No," Casey said. "The company *has* fixed the problem."

"Has it? We're told slats deployment is the reason people died on Flight 545."

"That's incorrect." She was now dancing on a tightrope, working a fine and technical line, and she knew it. If he asked her, Did the slats deploy? she would be in trouble. She waited breathlessly for the next question.

Reardon said, "The people who told us the slats deployed are wrong?"

"I don't know how they'd know," Casey said. She decided to go farther. "Yes, they're wrong."

"Fred Barker, former FAA investigator, is wrong."

"Yes."

"The JAA is wrong."

"Well, as you know, the JAA is actually delaying certification over noise emissions, and—"

"Let's just stay with this for a moment," Reardon said.

She remembered what Gershon had said: *He's not interested in information.*

"The JAA is wrong?" he said, repeating the question.

This called for a complicated answer, she thought. How could she put it briefly? "They're wrong to say the aircraft is unsafe."

"So in your opinion," Reardon said, "there is absolutely no substance to these criticisms of the N-22."

"That's correct. It is an excellent aircraft."

"A well-designed aircraft."

"Yes."

"A safe aircraft."

"Absolutely."

"You'd fly in it."

"Whenever possible."

"Your family, your friends . . ."

"Absolutely."

"No hesitation whatsoever?"

"That's right."

"So what was your reaction, when you saw the tape on television from Flight 545?"

*He'll get you saying yes, then hit you from left field.*

But Casey was ready for it. "All of us here knew that it was a very tragic accident. When I saw the tape, I felt very sad for the people involved."

"You felt sad."

"Yes."

"Didn't it shake your conviction about the aircraft? Make you question the N-22?"

"No."

"Why not?"

"Because the N-22 has a superb safety record. One of the best in the industry."

"One of the best *in the industry* . . ." Reardon smirked.

"Yes, Mr. Reardon," she said. "Let me ask you. Last year, forty-three thousand Americans died in automobile accidents. Four thousand people drowned. Two thousand people choked to death on food. Do you know how many died in domestic commercial transports?"

Reardon paused. He chuckled. "I must admit you've stumped the panel."

"It's a fair question, Mr. Reardon. How many died in commercial aircraft last year?"

Reardon frowned. "I'll say . . . I'll say a thousand."

"Fifty," Casey said. "Fifty people died. Do you know how many died the year before that? Sixteen. Fewer than were killed on bicycles."

"And how many of those died on the N-22?" Reardon asked, eyes narrowed, trying to recover.

"None," Casey said.

"So your point is . . ."

"We have a nation in which forty-three thousand people die every year in cars, and nobody worries about it at all. They get into cars when they're drunk, when they're tired—without a second thought. But these same people are panicked at the thought of getting on an airplane. And the reason," Casey said, "is that television consistently exaggerates the real dangers involved. That tape will make people afraid to fly. And for no good reason."

"You think the tape shouldn't have been shown?"

"I didn't say that."

"But you said it will make people afraid—for no good reason."

"Correct."

"Is it your view tapes such as these should not be shown?"

She thought: Where is he going? Why is he doing this?

"I didn't say that."

"I'm asking you now."

"I said," Casey replied, "that those tapes create an inaccurate perception of the danger of air travel."

"Including the danger of the N-22?"

"I've already said I think the N-22 is safe."

"So you don't think such tapes should be shown to the public."

*What the hell was he doing?* She still couldn't figure it out. She didn't answer him; she was thinking hard. Trying to see where he was going with this. She had a sinking feeling she knew.

"In your view, Ms. Singleton, should such tapes be suppressed?"

"No," Casey said.

"They should *not* be suppressed."

"No."

"Has Norton Aircraft ever suppressed any tapes?"

Uh-oh, she thought. She was trying to figure out how many people knew of the tape. A lot, she decided: Ellen Fong, Ziegler, the people at Video Imaging. Maybe a dozen people, maybe more . . .

"Ms. Singleton," Reardon said, "are you personally aware of any other tape of this accident?"

*Just lie,* Amos had said.

"Yes," she said. "I know of another tape."

"And have you seen the tape?"

"I have."

Reardon said, "It's upsetting. Horrifying. Isn't it?"

She thought: *They have it.* They'd gotten the tape. She would have to proceed very carefully now.

"It's tragic," Casey said. "What happened on Flight 545 is a tragedy." She felt tired. Her shoulders ached from tension.

"Ms. Singleton, let me put it to you directly: Did Norton Aircraft suppress this tape?"

"No."

Eyebrows up, the look of surprise. "But you certainly didn't release it, did you."

"No."

"Why not?"

"That tape was found on the aircraft," Casey said,

"and is being used in our ongoing investigation. We didn't feel it appropriate to release it until our investigation is completed."

"You weren't covering up the well-known defects of the N-22?"

"No."

"Not everyone agrees with you about that, Ms. Singleton. Because *Newsline* obtained a copy of that tape, from a conscience-stricken Norton employee who felt that the company *was* covering up. Who felt the tape should be made public."

Casey held herself rigid. She didn't move.

"Are you surprised?" Reardon said, his lips in a curl.

She didn't answer. Her mind was spinning. She had to plan her next move.

Reardon was smirking, a patronizing smile. Enjoying the moment.

*Now.*

"Have you yourself actually seen this tape, Mr. Reardon?" She asked the question in a tone that implied the tape didn't exist, that Reardon was making it all up.

"Oh yes," Reardon said solemnly, "I have seen the tape. It's difficult, painful to watch. It is a terrible, damning record of what happened on that N-22 aircraft."

"You've seen it all the way through?"

"Of course. So have my associates in New York."

So it had already gone to New York, she thought. Careful.

*Careful.*

"Ms. Singleton, was Norton *ever* planning to release that tape?"

"It's not ours to release. We'd return it to the owners, after the investigation was completed. It would be up to the owners to decide what to do with it."

"After the investigation was completed . . ." Reardon was shaking his head. "Forgive me, but for a company *you say* is committed to flight safety, there seems to be a consistent pattern of cover-ups here."

"Cover-ups?"

"Ms. Singleton, if there was a problem with the airplane—a serious problem, an ongoing problem, a problem the company knew about—would you tell us?"

"But there is no problem."

"Isn't there?" Reardon was looking down now, at the papers in front of him. "If the N-22 is really as safe as you say, Ms. Singleton, then how do you explain this?"

And he handed her a sheet of paper.

She took it, glanced at the paper.

"Jesus Christ," she said.


Reardon had his media moment. He had gotten her unguarded, off-balance reaction. She knew it would look bad. She knew there was no way for her to recover from it, no matter what she said from this point on. But she was focused on the paper in front of her, stunned to see it now.

It was a Xerox of the cover sheet of a report done three years ago.

### PRIVILEGED INFORMATION—
### FOR INTERNAL USE ONLY

NORTON AIRCRAFT
INTERNAL REVIEW ACTION COMMITTEE
EXECUTIVE SUMMARY
UNSTABLE FLIGHT CHARACTERISTICS OF
N-22 AIRCRAFT

And following was a list of the names of the committee members. Beginning with her name, since she had chaired the committee.

Casey knew that there was nothing improper about the study, nothing improper in its findings. But everything about it, even the name—"Unstable Flight Characteristics"—appeared damning. It was going to be very difficult for her to explain.

*He's not interested in information.*

And this was an internal company report, she thought. It should never have been released. It was three years old—not that many people would even remember it existed. How had Reardon gotten it?

She glanced at the top of the page, saw a fax number, and the name of the sending station: NORTON QA.

It had come from her own office.

How?

Who had done it?

Richman, she thought, grimly.

Richman had placed this report in the packet of press material on her desk. The material Casey had told Norma to fax to *Newsline*.

How had Richman known about it?

Marder.

Marder knew all about the study. Marder had been program manager on the N-22; he'd ordered it. And now Marder had arranged for the study to be released while she was on television, because—

"Ms. Singleton?" Reardon said.

She looked up. Back into the lights. "Yes."

"Do you recognize this report?"

"Yes, I do," she said.

"Is that your own name at the bottom?"

"Yes."

Reardon handed her three other sheets, the rest of the executive summary. "In fact, you were the chairman of a *secret committee* inside Norton that investigated 'flight instabilities' of the N-22. Isn't that right?"

How was she going to do this? she thought.

*He's not interested in information.*

"It wasn't a secret," she said. "It's the kind of study we frequently conduct on operational aspects of our aircraft, once they're in service."

"By your own admission, it's a study of flight instabilities."

"Look," she said, "this study is a good thing."

"A good thing?" Eyebrows up, astonished.

"Yes," she said. "After the first slats incident four years ago, there was a question about whether the aircraft had unstable handling characteristics, in certain configurations. We didn't avoid that question. We didn't ignore it. We addressed it head-on—by forming a committee, to test the aircraft in various conditions, and see if it were true. And we concluded—"

"Let me read," Reardon said, "from your own report. 'The aircraft relies upon computers for basic stabilization.'"

"Yes," she said. "All modern aircraft use—"

"'The aircraft has demonstrated marked sensitivity to manual handling during attitude change.'"

Casey was looking at the pages now. Following his quotes. "Yes, but if you'll read the rest of the sentence, you will—"

Reardon cut in: "'Pilots have reported the aircraft cannot be controlled.'"

"But you're taking all this out of context."

"Am I?" Eyebrows up. "These are all statements from *your* report. A secret Norton report."

"I thought you said you wanted to hear what I had to say." She was starting to get angry. She knew it showed, and didn't care.

Reardon leaned back in his chair, spread his hands. The picture of reason. "By all means, Ms. Singleton."

"Then let me explain. This study was carried out to determine whether the N-22 had a stability problem. We concluded it did not, and—"

"So you say."

"I thought I was going to be allowed to explain."

"Of course."

"Then let me put your quotes in context," Casey said. "The report says the N-22 relies on computers. All modern aircraft rely on computers for stabilization in flight. The reason is not because they can't be flown by pilots. They can. There's no problem with that. But the carriers now want extremely fuel-efficient aircraft. Maximum fuel efficiency comes from minimal drag, as the aircraft flies through the air."

Reardon was waving his hand, a dismissing gesture. "I'm sorry, but all this is beside—"

"To minimize drag," Casey continued, "the aircraft has to hold a very precise attitude, or position in the air. The most efficient position is slightly nose up. The computers hold the aircraft in this position during ordinary flight. None of this is unusual."

"Not unusual? Flight *instabilities?*" Reardon said.

He was always shifting the subject, never letting her catch up. "I'm coming to that."

"We're eager to hear." Open sarcasm.

She struggled to control her temper. However bad things were now, it would be worse if she lost her temper. "You read a sentence before," she said. "Let me finish it. 'The aircraft has demonstrated marked sensitivity to manual handling during attitude change, *but this sensitivity is entirely within design parameters and presents no difficulty to properly certified pilots.*' That's the rest of the sentence."

"But you've admitted there is sensitive handling. Isn't that just another word for instability?"

"No," she said. "Sensitive does not mean unstable."

"The plane can't be controlled," Reardon said, shaking his head.

"It can."

"You did a study because you were worried."

"We did a study because it's our job to make sure the aircraft is safe," she said. "And we are sure: it *is* safe."

"A secret study."

"It wasn't secret."

"Never distributed. Never shown to the public . . ."

"It was an internal report," she said.

"You have nothing to hide?"

"No," she said.

"Then why haven't you told us the truth about TransPacific Flight 545?"

"The truth?"

"We're told your accident team *already has* a preliminary finding on the probable cause. Is that not true?"

"We're close," she said.

"Close . . . Ms. Singleton, do you have a finding, or not?"

Casey stared at Reardon. The question hung in the air.

"I'm very sorry," the cameraman said, behind her. "But we have to reload."

"Camera reloading!"

"Reloading!"

Reardon looked as if he had been slapped. But almost immediately he recovered. "To be continued," he said, smiling at Casey. He was relaxed; he knew he had beaten her. He got up from his chair, turned his back to her. The big lights clicked off; the room seemed suddenly almost dark. Somebody turned the air-conditioning back on.

Casey got up, too. She pulled the radio mike off her waist. The makeup woman came running over to her, holding out a powder puff. Casey held up her hand. "In a minute," she said.

With the lights off, she saw Richman, heading for the door.

Casey hurried after him.

# BLDG 64

### 3:01 P.M.

She caught him in the hallway, grabbed him by the arm, spun him around. "You son of a bitch."

"Hey," Richman said. "Take it easy." He smiled, nodded past her shoulder. Looking back, she saw the soundman and one of the cameramen coming out into the hallway.

Furious, Casey pushed Richman backward, shoving him through the door to the women's room. Richman started to laugh. "Jeez, Casey, I didn't know you cared—"

Then they were in the bathroom. She pushed him back against the row of sinks. "You little bastard," she hissed, "I don't know what the hell you think you're doing, but you released that report, and I'm going to—"

"You're going to do nothing," Richman said, his voice suddenly cold. He threw her hands off him. "You still don't get it, do you? It's *over,* Casey. You just blew the China sale. You're *finished.*"

She stared at him, not understanding. He was strong, confident—a different person.

"Edgarton's finished. The China sale's finished. And you're finished." He smiled. "Just the way John said it would happen."

Marder, she thought. Marder was behind it. "If the China sale goes, Marder will go, too. Edgarton will see to that."

Richman was shaking his head, pityingly. "No, he won't. Edgarton's sitting on his ass in Hong Kong, he'll never know what hit him. By noon Sunday, Marder'll be the new president of Norton Aircraft. It'll take him ten minutes with the Board. Because we've made a much bigger deal with Korea. A hundred and ten aircraft firm, and an option on thirty-five more. Sixteen billion dollars. The Board will be thrilled."

"Korea," Casey said. She was trying to put it together. Because it was a huge order, the biggest in the history of the company. "But why would—"

"Because he gave them the wing," Richman said. "And in return, they're more than happy to buy a hundred and ten aircraft. They don't care about sensationalistic American press. They know the plane's safe."

"He's giving them the *wing?*"

"Sure. It's a killer deal."

"Yeah," Casey said. "It kills the company."

"Global economy," Richman said. "Get with the program."

"But you're gutting the company," she said.

"Sixteen billion dollars," Richman said. "The minute that's announced, Norton stock'll go through the roof. Everybody gets well."

Everybody but the people in the company, she thought.

"This is a done deal," Richman said. "All we needed was somebody to publicly trash the N-22. And you just did that for us."

Casey sighed. Her shoulders dropped.

Looking past Richman, she saw herself in the mirror. Makeup was pancaked around her neck, and now it was cracking. Her eyes were dark. She looked haggard, exhausted. Defeated.

"So I suggest," Richman said, "that you ask me, very politely, what you should do next. Because your only choice now is to follow orders. Do as you're told, be a good girl, and maybe John will give you severance. Say, three months. Otherwise, you're out on your fucking ass."

He leaned close to her.

"Do you understand what I'm saying?"

"Yes," Casey said.

"I'm waiting. Ask politely."

In her exhaustion, her mind raced, examining the options, trying to see a way out. But she could see no way out. *Newsline* would run the story. Marder's plan would succeed. She was defeated. She had been defeated from the very beginning. Defeated from the first day Richman had shown up.

"I'm still waiting," Richman said.

She looked at his smooth face, smelled his cologne. The little bastard was enjoying this. And in a moment of fury, of deep outrage, she suddenly saw another possibility.

From the beginning, she had tried so hard to do the right thing, to solve the problem of 545. She had been honest, she had been straight, and it had just gotten her into trouble.

Or had it?

"You have to face facts, here," Richman said. "It's over. There's nothing you can do."

She pushed away from the sink.

"Watch me," she said.

And she walked out of the room.

## WAR ROOM

### 3:15 P.M.

Casey slipped into her seat. The soundman came over and clipped the radio pack to the waist of her dress. "Say a few words for me, will you please? Just for level."

"Testing, testing, I'm getting tired," she said.

"That's fine. Thank you."

She saw Richman slip into the room, and stand with his back to the far wall. He had a faint smile on his face. He didn't look worried. He was confident there was nothing she could do. Marder had made a huge deal, he was shipping the wing, he was gutting the company, and he'd used Casey to do it.

Reardon dropped into his seat opposite her, shrugged his shoulders, adjusted his tie. He smiled at her. "How you holding up?"

"I'm okay."

"Hot in here, isn't it?" he said. He glanced at his watch. "We're almost finished."

Malone came over, and whispered in Reardon's ear. The whispering continued for some time. Reardon said, "Really?" and his eyebrows went up, then he nodded several times. Finally he said, "Got it." He began to shuffle his papers, going through the folder in front of him.

Malone said, "Guys? We ready?"

"A camera ready."

"B camera ready."

"Sound ready."

"Roll tape," she said.

This is it, Casey thought. She took a deep breath, looked expectantly at Reardon.

Reardon smiled at her.

"You're an executive at Norton Aircraft."

"Yes."

"Been here five years."

"Yes."

"You're a trusted, highly placed executive."

She nodded. If he only knew.

"Now there is an incident, Flight 545. Involving an aircraft *you say* is perfectly safe."

"Correct."

"Yet three people died, and more than fifty were injured."

"Yes."

"The footage, which we've all seen, is horrifying. Your Incident Review Team has been working around the clock. And now we hear you have a finding."

"Yes," she said.

"You know what happened on that flight."

*Careful.*

She had to do this very, very carefully. Because the truth was she didn't know; she just had a very strong suspicion. They still had to put the sequence together, to verify that things had happened in a certain order: the chain of causation. They didn't know for sure.

"We are close to a finding," Casey said.

"Needless to say, we're eager to hear."

"We will announce it tomorrow," Casey said.

Behind the lights, she saw Richman's startled reaction. He hadn't been expecting that. The little bastard was trying to see where she was going.

Let him try.

Across the table from her, Reardon turned aside, and Malone whispered in his ear. Reardon nodded, turned back to Casey. "Ms. Singleton, if you know now, why wait?"

"Because this was a serious accident, as you yourself said. There's already been a great deal of unwarranted speculation from many sources. Norton Aircraft feels it is important to act responsibly. Before we say anything publicly, we have to confirm our findings at Flight Test, using the same aircraft that was involved in the accident."

"When will you flight test?"

"Tomorrow morning."

"Ah." Reardon sighed regretfully. "But that's too late for our broadcast. You understand that you're denying your company the opportunity to respond to these serious charges."

Casey had her answer ready. "We've scheduled the flight test for five A.M.," she said. "We'll hold a press conference immediately afterward—tomorrow at noon."

"Noon," Reardon said.

His expression was bland, but she knew he was working it out. Noon in LA was 3:00 P.M. in New York. Plenty of time to make the evening news in both New York and Los Angeles. Norton's preliminary finding would be widely reported on both local and network news. And *Newsline,* which aired at 10:00 P.M. Saturday night, would be out-of-date. Depending on what emerged from the press conference, the *Newsline* segment, edited the night before, would be ancient history. It might even be embarrassing.

Reardon sighed. "On the other hand," he said, "we want to be fair to you."

"Naturally," Casey said.

# NORTON ADMINISTRATION

### 4:15 P.M.

"Fuck her," Marder said to Richman. "It doesn't make any difference what she does now."

"But if she's scheduling a flight test—"

"Who cares?" Marder said.

"And I think she's going to let the news crews film it."

"So what? Flight Test will only make the story worse. She has no idea what caused the accident. And she has no idea what will happen if she takes that TransPacific plane up. They probably can't reproduce the event. And there may be problems nobody knows about."

"Like what?"

"That aircraft went through very severe G-force loads," Marder said. "It may have undetected structural damage. Anything can happen, when they take that plane up." Marder made a dismissive wave. "This changes nothing. *Newsline* airs from ten to eleven Saturday night. Early Saturday evening I'll notify the Board that some bad publicity is coming our way, and we have to schedule an emergency meeting Sunday morning. Hal can't get back from Hong Kong in time. And his friends on the Board will drop him when they hear about a sixteen-bil-lion-dollar deal. They've all got stock. They know what the announcement will do to their shares. I'm the next president of this company, and nobody can do a thing to stop it. Not Hal Edgarton. And certain-ly not Casey Singleton."

"I don't know," Richman said. "I think she may be planning something. She's pretty smart, John."

"Not smart enough," Marder said.

## WAR ROOM

4:20 P.M.

The cameras were packed up; the white foam sheets removed from the ceiling, the microphones unclipped; the electrical boxes and camera cases removed. But the negotiations dragged on. Ed Fuller, the lanky head of Legal, was there; so was Teddy Rawley, the pilot; and two engineers who worked on FT, to answer technical questions that arose.

For *Newsline,* Malone now did all of the talking; Reardon paced in the background, occasionally stopping to whisper in her ear. His commanding presence seemed to have vanished with the bright lights; he now appeared tired, fretful, and impatient.

Malone began by saying that since *Newsline* was doing an entire segment on the Norton N-22, it was in the interest of the company to allow *Newsline* to film the flight test.

Casey said that presented no problem. Flight tests

were documented with dozens of video cameras, mounted both inside and outside the plane; the *Newsline* people could watch the entire test on monitors, on the ground. They could have the film afterward, for their broadcast.

No, Malone said. That wouldn't be sufficient. *Newsline*'s crews had to actually be on the plane.

Casey said that was impossible, that no airframe manufacturer had ever allowed an outside crew on a flight test. She was, she said, already making a concession to let them see the video on the ground.

Not good enough, Malone said.

Ed Fuller broke in to explain it was a question of liability. Norton simply couldn't allow uninsured nonemployees on the test. "You realize, of course, there is inherent danger in flight test. It's simply inescapable."

Malone said that *Newsline* would accept any risk, and sign waivers of liability.

Ed Fuller said he would have to draw up the waivers, but that *Newsline*'s lawyers would have to approve them, and there wasn't time for that.

Malone said she could get approval from *Newsline*'s lawyers in an hour. Any time of the day or night.

Fuller shifted ground. He said if Norton was going to let *Newsline* see the flight test, he wanted to be sure that the results of that test were accurately reported. He said he wanted to approve the edited film.

Malone said that journalistic ethics forbade that,

and in any case there wasn't time. If the flight test ended around noon, she would have to cut film in the truck and transmit it to New York at once.

Fuller said the problem for the company remained. He wanted the flight test portrayed accurately.

They went back and forth. Finally Malone said she would include thirty seconds of unedited comment on the outcome of the flight by a Norton spokesperson. This would be taken from the press conference.

Fuller demanded a minute.

They compromised on forty seconds.

"We have another problem," Fuller said. "If we let you film the flight test, we don't want you to use the tape you obtained today, showing the actual incident."

No way, Malone said. The tape was going to be aired.

"You characterized the tape as having been obtained from a Norton employee," Fuller said. "That's incorrect. We want the provenance accurately stated."

"Well, we certainly got it from someone who works for Norton."

"No," Fuller said, "you didn't."

"It's one of your subcontractors."

"No, it's not. I can provide you with the IRS definition of a subcontractor, if you like."

"This is a fine point . . ."

"We have already obtained a sworn statement from the receptionist, Christine Barron. She is not an employee of Norton Aircraft. She is not, in fact, an employee of Video Imaging. She is a temp from an agency."

"What's the point here?"

"We want you to state the facts accurately: that you obtained the tape from sources outside the company."

Malone shrugged. "As I said, this is a fine point."

"Then what's the problem?"

Malone thought for a minute. "Okay," she said.

Fuller slid a piece of paper across the table. "This brief document conveys that understanding. Sign it."

Malone looked at Reardon. Reardon shrugged.

Malone signed it. "I don't understand what all the fuss is about." She started to push it back to Fuller, and paused.

"Two crews, on the aircraft, during the flight test. Is that our agreement?"

"No," Fuller said. "That was never the agreement. Your crews will watch the test on the ground."

"That won't work for us."

Casey said that the *Newsline* crews could come to the test area; they could film the preparations, the takeoff and landing. But they couldn't actually come on the plane during the flight.

"Sorry," Malone said.

Teddy Rawley cleared his throat. "I don't think you understand the situation, Ms. Malone," he said. "You can't be walking around filming inside the airplane, during a flight test. Everybody on board has to be strapped in in a four-point harness. You can't even get up to pee. And you can't have lights or bat-teries, because they generate magnetic fields that might disrupt our readings."

"We don't need lights," she said. "We can shoot available light."

"You don't understand," Rawley said. "It can get pretty hairy up there."

"That's why we have to be there," Malone said.

Ed Fuller cleared his throat. "Let me be entirely clear, Ms. Malone," he said. "Under no circumstances is this company going to allow your film crew on board that aircraft. It is absolutely out of the question."

Malone's face was rigid, set.

"Ma'am," Rawley said, "you've got to realize, there's a reason we test over the desert. Over large uninhabited spaces?"

"You mean it might crash."

"I mean we don't know what might happen. Trust me on this: you want to be on the ground."

Malone shook her head. "No. We must have our crews on board."

"Ma'am, there's going to be big G-forces—"

Casey said, "There'll be thirty cameras all over the plane. They'll cover every possible angle—cockpit, wings, passenger cabin, everywhere. You're getting exclusive use of the film. No one will know your cameras aren't getting the footage."

Malone glowered, but Casey knew that she had made the point. The woman only cared about the visuals.

"I want to place the cameras," she said.

"Uh-uh," Rawley said.

"I have to be able to say our cameras are on board," Malone said. "I have to be able to say that."

In the end, Casey hammered out a compromise. *Newsline* would be allowed to position two locked-down cameras, anywhere in the plane, to cover the test flight. They would take the feed directly from these cameras. In addition, they would be allowed to use footage from other cameras mounted in the interior. Finally, *Newsline* would be allowed to shoot a stand-up with Reardon outside Building 64, where the assembly line was located.

Norton would provide transportation for the *Newsline* crews to the Arizona test facility later in the day; would put them up in a local motel; would transport them to the test facility in the morning; and back to LA in the afternoon.

Malone pushed the paper back to Fuller. "Deal," she said.

Reardon was looking fretfully at his watch as he left with Malone to shoot the stand-up. Casey was alone with Rawley and Fuller in the War Room.

Fuller sighed. "I hope we've made the right decision." He turned to Casey. "I did what you asked, when you called me earlier from the video company."

"Yes, Ed," she said. "You were perfect."

"But I saw the tape," he said. "It's dreadful. I'm afraid that whatever the flight test shows, that tape will be the only thing anybody remembers."

Casey said, "If anybody ever sees that tape."

"My concern," Fuller said, "is that *Newsline* will run that tape no matter what."

"I think they won't," Casey said. "Not when we get through with them."

Fuller sighed. "I hope you're right. High stakes."

"Yes," she said. "High stakes."

Teddy said, "You better tell them to bring warm clothing. You, too, babe. And another thing: I watched that woman. She thinks she's going to get on the plane tomorrow."

"Yeah, probably."

"And you, too, right?" Teddy said.

"Maybe," Casey said.

"You better think about this real good," Teddy said. "Because you saw the QAR video, Casey. That airplane exceeded its design G-loads by a hundred and sixty percent. That guy subjected the airframe to forces it was never built to withstand. And tomorrow I'm going to go up and do it again."

She shrugged. "Doherty checked the fuse," she said, "they've X-rayed and—"

"Yeah, he checked," Teddy said. "But not thoroughly. Ordinarily, we'd go over that fuselage for a month, before we put it back in active service. We'd X-ray every join on the plane. That hasn't been done."

"What are you saying?"

"I'm saying," Teddy said, "that when I put that aircraft through those same G-force loads, there's a chance that the airframe will fail."

"You trying to scare me?" Casey said.

"No, I'm just telling you. This is serious, Casey. Real world. It could happen."

## OUTSIDE BLDG 64

### 4:55 P.M.

"No aircraft company in history," Reardon said, "has ever permitted a television crew on a flight test. But so important is this test to the future of Norton Aircraft, so confident are they of the outcome, that they have agreed to allow our crews to film. So today, for the first time, we will be seeing footage of the actual plane involved in Flight 545, the controversial Norton N-22 aircraft. Critics say it's a death-trap. The company says it's safe. The flight test will prove who's right."

Reardon paused.

"Done," Jennifer said.

"You need something for the cut?"

"Yeah."

"Where do they do the test, anyway?"

"Yuma."

"Okay," Reardon said.

Standing in afternoon sun, before Building 64, he looked down at his feet and said, in a low, confidential voice, "We are here, at the Norton test facility in Yuma, Arizona. It's five o'clock in the morning, and the Norton team is making final preparations to take Flight 545 into the air." He looked up. "What time's dawn?"

"Damned if I know," Jennifer said. "Cover it."

"All right," Reardon said. He looked down at his feet again, and intoned. "In the early predawn, tension mounts. In the predawn darkness, tension mounts. As dawn breaks, tension mounts."

"That should do it," Jennifer said.

"How do you want to handle the wrap?" he said.

"You've got to cover it both ways, Marty."

"I mean do we win, or what?"

"Cover it both ways to be sure."

Reardon looked down at his feet again. "As the aircraft lands, the team is jubilant. Happy faces all around. The flight is successful. Norton has made its point. At least for now." He took a breath. "As the aircraft lands, the team is muted. Norton is devastated. The deadly controversy over the N-22 continues to rage." He looked up. "Enough?"

She said, "You better give me an on-camera about the controversy continues to rage. We can close with that."

"Good idea."

Marty always thought it was a good idea for him to appear on camera. He stood erect, set his jaw, and faced the camera.

"Here, in this building where the N-22 is built, no . . . Behind me is the building where . . . no. Hold on." He shook his head, faced the camera again.

"And yet, the bitter controversy over the N-22 will not die. Here, in this building where the aircraft is made, workers are confident that it is a safe, reliable aircraft. But critics of the N-22 remain unconvinced. Will there be another harvest of death in the skies? Only time will tell. This is Martin Reardon, for *Newsline,* Burbank, California."

He blinked.

"Too corny? Too much on the money?"

"Great, Marty."

He was already unclipping his mike, removing the radio pack from his belt. He pecked Jennifer on the cheek. "I'm out of here," he said, and sprinted to the waiting car.

Jennifer turned to her crew. "Pack up, guys," she said. "We're going to Arizona."

# SATURDAY

# NORTON TEST FACILITY
# YUMA, ARIZONA

4:45 A.M.

A thin streak of red was starting to appear behind the flat range of the Gila Mountains to the east. The sky overhead was deep indigo, a few stars still visible. The air was very cold; Casey could see her breath. She zipped up her windbreaker and stamped her feet, trying to stay warm.

On the runway, lights shone up at the TransPacific widebody, as the FT team finished installing the video cameras. There were men on the wings, around the engines, by the landing gear.

The *Newsline* crew was already out, filming the preparations. Malone stood alongside Casey, watching them. "Jesus it's cold," she said.

Casey went into the Flight Test Station, a low Spanish-style bungalow beside the tower. Inside, the room was filled with monitors, each displaying the feed from a single camera. Most of the cameras were focused on specific parts—she found the camera on the right locking pin—and so the room had a technical, industrial feeling. It was not very exciting.

"This isn't what I expected," Malone said.

Casey pointed around the room. "There's the cockpit. High mount down. Cockpit, facing back at the pilot. You see Rawley there, in the chair. The interior cabin, looking aft. Interior cabin, looking forward. Looking out on right wing. The left wing.

Those are your main interiors. And we'll also have the chase plane."

"Chase plane?"

"An F-14 fighter follows the widebody all through the flight, so we'll have those cameras, too."

Malone frowned. "I don't know," she said, in a disappointed voice. "I thought it would be more, you know, glitzy."

"We're still on the ground."

Malone was frowning, unhappy. "These angles on the cabin," she said. "Who will be in there, during the flight?"

"Nobody."

"You mean the seats will be empty?"

"Right. It's a test flight."

"That isn't going to look very good," Malone said.

"But that's how it is on a test flight," Casey said. "This is how it's done."

"But it doesn't *look* good," Malone said. "This isn't compelling. There should be people in the seats. At least, in some of them. Can't we put some people on board? Can't I go on board?"

Casey shook her head. "It's a dangerous flight," she said. "The airframe was badly stressed by the accident. We don't know what will happen."

Malone snorted. "Oh, come on. There aren't any lawyers here. How about it?"

Casey just looked at her. She was a foolish kid who knew nothing about the world, who was just interested in a *look,* who lived for appearances, who skimmed over surfaces. She knew she should refuse.

Instead, she heard herself say, "You won't like it."

"You're telling me it's not safe?"

"I'm telling you that you won't like it."

"I'm going on," Malone said. She looked at Casey, her expression an open challenge. "So: How about you?"

In her mind, Casey could hear Marty Reardon's voice, as he said, *Despite her repeated insistence that the N-22 was safe, Norton's own spokesperson, Casey Singleton, refused to board the plane for the flight test. She said that the reason she wouldn't fly on it was . . .*

What?

Casey didn't have an answer, at least not an answer that would work for television. Not an answer that would *play.* And suddenly the days of strain, the effort to try and solve the incident, the effort to contrive an appearance for television, the effort to make sure she didn't say a single sentence that could be taken out of context, the distortion of everything in her life for this unwarranted intrusion of television, made her furious. She knew exactly what was coming. Malone had seen the videos, but she didn't understand they were real.

"Okay," Casey said. "Let's go."

They went out to the plane.

# ABOARD TPA 545

5:05 A.M.

Jennifer shivered: it was cold inside the airplane, and under fluorescent lights, the rows of empty seats, the long aisles, made it seem even colder. She was faintly shocked when she recognized, in places, the damage that she had seen on the videotape. This was where it happened, she thought. This was the plane. There were still bloody footprints on the ceiling. Broken luggage bins. Dented fiberglass panels. And a lingering odor. Even worse, in some places the plastic panels had been pulled off around the windows, so that she could see the naked silver padding, the bundles of wires. It was suddenly all too clear that she was in a big metal machine. She wondered if she had made a mistake, but by then Singleton was gesturing for her to take a seat, right in the front of the center cabin, facing a locked-down video camera.

Jennifer sat beside Singleton and waited as one of the Norton technicians, a man in coveralls, tightened the shoulder harness around her body. It was one of those harnesses like the stewardesses wore on regular flights. Two green canvas straps came over each shoulder, meeting at the waist. Then there was another wide canvas strap that went across her thighs. Heavy metal buckles clamped it all in place. It looked serious.

The man in coveralls pulled the straps tight, grunting.

"Jeez," Jennifer said. "Does it have to be that tight?"

"Ma'am, you need it as tight as you can stand it," the man said. "If you can breathe, it's too loose. Can you feel the way it is now?"

"Yes," she said.

"That's how you want it when you put it back on. Now here's your release here . . ." He showed her. "Pull that now."

"Why do I need to know—"

"Case of emergency. Pull it, please."

She pulled the release. The straps sprang away from her body, the pressure released.

"And just do it up again yourself, if you don't mind."

Jennifer put the contraption back together, just as he had done it before. It wasn't difficult. These people made such a fuss about nothing.

"Now tighten it, please, ma'am."

She pulled the straps.

"Tighter."

"If I need it tighter, I'll tighten it later."

"Ma'am," he said, "by the time you realize you need it tighter, it'll be too late. Do it now, please."

Alongside her, Singleton was calmly putting the harness on, cinching it down brutally. The straps dug into Singleton's thighs, pulled hard on her shoulders. Singleton sighed, sat back.

"I believe you ladies are prepared," the man said. "You have a pleasant flight."

He turned, and went out the door. The pilot, that Rawley character, came back from the cockpit, shaking his head.

"Ladies," he said. "I urge you not to do this." He was looking mostly at Singleton. He almost seemed to be angry at her.

Singleton said, "Fly the plane, Teddy."

"That's your best offer?"

"Best and final."

He disappeared. The intercom clicked. "Prepare to close, please." The doors were closed, clicked shut. *Thunk, thunk.* The air was still cold. Jennifer shivered in her harness.

She looked over her shoulder at the rows of empty seats. Then she looked at Singleton.

Singleton stared straight ahead.

Jennifer heard the whine of the jet engines as they started up, a low moan at first, then rising in pitch. The intercom clicked. She heard the pilot say, "Tower this is Norton zero one, request clearance for FT station check."

*Click.* "Roger zero one, taxi across runway two left contact point six."

*Click.* "Roger, tower."

The plane began to move, rolling forward. Out the windows she saw the sky was lightening. After a few moments, the plane stopped again.

"What are they doing?" Jennifer asked.

"Weighing it," Singleton answered. "They weigh

before and after, to guarantee we've simulated fly-ing conditions."

"On some kind of scale?"

"Built into the concrete."

*Click.* "Teddy. Need, uh, about two feet more on nose."

*Click.* "Hang on."

The whine of the engines increased. Jennifer felt the plane inch forward slowly. Then it stopped again.

*Click.* "Thank you. Got it. You're at fifty-seven two seven GW and CG is thirty-two percent MAC. Right where you want to be."

*Click.* "Bye, guys." *Click.* "Tower zero one request clearance for takeoff."

*Click.* "Cleared runway three contact ground point six three when off the runway."

*Click.* "Roger."

Then the plane began to roll forward, the engines increasing from a whine to a full deep roar, the sound building until it sounded louder to Jennifer than any engines she had heard before. She felt the thump of the wheels going over the cracks in the runway. And then suddenly they had lifted off, the plane going up, the sky blue out the windows.

Airborne.

*Click.* "Oh-kay, ladies, we are going to proceed to flight level three seven zero, that's thirty-seven thousand feet, and we are going to circle there between Yuma station and Carstairs, Nevada, for the duration of this excursion. Everybody comfy? If you look to your left, you will see our chase plane coming alongside."

Jennifer looked out and saw a silver jet fighter, glinting in the morning light. It was very close to their aircraft, close enough to see the pilot wave. Then suddenly it slid backward.

*Click.* "Uh, you probably won't see much more of him, he'll be staying high and behind us, out of our wake, the safest place to be. Right now we are coming up on twelve thousand feet, you may want to swallow, Ms. Malone, we're not creeping up like the airlines."

Jennifer swallowed, heard her ears pop loudly. She said, "Why are we going up so fast?"

"He wants to get to altitude quickly, to cold soak the plane."

"Cold soak?"

"At thirty-seven thousand feet, the air temperature is minus fifty degrees. The airplane is warmer than that right now, and different parts will cool off at different rates, but eventually on a long flight—such as a long Pacific crossing—all the parts of the plane will reach that temperature. One of the questions for the IRT is whether the cable rigging behaves differently at cold temperature. Cold soaking means putting the plane up at altitude long enough to cool it down. Then we begin the test."

"How long are we talking?" Jennifer said.

"Standard cold soak is two hours."

"We have to sit here for two hours?"

Singleton looked at her. "You wanted to come."

"You mean we spend two hours doing nothing?"

*Click.* "Oh, we'll try to amuse you, Ms. Malone," the pilot said. "We're now at twenty-two thousand feet and climbing. It'll be another few minutes to cruise altitude. We are at two eighty-seven KIAS and we will stabilize at three forty KIAS which is point eight Mach, eighty percent of the speed of sound. That's the usual cruise speed for commercial aircraft. Everybody comfy?"

Jennifer said, "Can you hear us?"

"I can hear you and see you. And if you look to your right, you can see me."

A monitor in the cabin in front of them came on. Jennifer saw the pilot's shoulder, his head, the controls arrayed in front of him. Bright light out the window.

Now they were high enough that full sunlight streamed in through the windows. But the interior of the plane was still cold. Because she was sitting in the center of the cabin, Jennifer could not see the ground out the windows.

She looked at Singleton.

Singleton smiled.

*Click.* "Ah, okay, we are now at flight level three seven zero, Doppler clear, no turbulence, a beautiful day in the neighborhood. Would you ladies please unbuckle your harnesses, and come to the cockpit."

What? Jennifer thought. But Singleton was already taking hers off, standing up in the cabin.

"I thought we couldn't walk around."

"It's okay right now," Singleton said.

Jennifer climbed out of her harness, and walked with Singleton up through first class, to the cockpit. She felt the faint vibration of the airplane beneath her feet. But it was quite stable. The door to the cockpit was open. She saw Rawley in there, with a second man he didn't introduce, and a third who was working with some instrumentation. Jennifer stood with Singleton just outside the cockpit, looking in.

"Now Ms. Malone," Rawley said. "You interviewed Mr. Barker, didn't you?"

"Yes."

"What did he say was the cause of the accident?"

"He said the slats deployed."

"Uh-huh. Okay, please watch carefully. This is the flaps/slats handle here. We are at cruise speed, cruise altitude. I am now going to deploy the slats." He reached his hand forward to the thing between the seats.

"Wait a minute! Let me get strapped in!"

"You're perfectly safe, Ms. Malone."

"I want to sit down, at least."

"Then sit down."

Jennifer started back, then realized that Singleton was remaining standing by the cockpit door. Staring at her. Feeling foolish, Jennifer went back and stood by Singleton.

"Deploying slats now."

Rawley pushed the lever down. She heard a faint rumble that lasted a few seconds. Nothing else. The nose tilted, steadied.

"Slats are extended." Rawley pointed to the instrument panel. "You see the speed? You see the altitude? And you see that indicator that says SLATS? We have just duplicated the exact conditions that Mr. Barker insists caused the death of three people, on this very same aircraft. And as you see, nothing happened. The attitude is rock solid. Want to try again?"

"Yes," she said. She didn't know what else to say.

"Okay. Slats retracting. This time, maybe you'd like to do it yourself, Ms. Malone. Or maybe you'd like to walk over and look at the wings, see what actually happens when the slats extend. It's kind of neat."

Rawley pressed a button. "Ah, Norton station, this is zero one, can I have a monitor check?" He listened a moment. "Okay, fine. Ms. Malone, move a little forward, so your friends can see you on that camera up there." He pointed up to the ceiling of the cockpit. "Give 'em a wave."

Jennifer waved, feeling foolish.

"Ms. Malone, how many more times would you like us to extend and retract the slats to satisfy your cameras?"

"Well, I don't know . . ." She was feeling more foolish by the minute. The flight test was starting to seem like a trap. The footage would make Barker look like a fool. It would make the whole segment look ridiculous. It would make—

"We can do this all day, if you like," Rawley was saying. "That's the point. No problem deploying the slats at cruise speed on the N-22. Plane can handle it fine."

"Try it once more," she said, tightly.

"That's the handle there. Just flip that little metal cover up, and pull it down about an inch."

She knew what he was doing. Putting her in the shot.

"I think you'd better do it."

"Yes, ma'am. Whatever you say."

Rawley pulled the lever down. The rumbling occurred again. The nose went up slightly. Exactly as before.

"Now," Rawley said, "we've got the chase plane getting views for you showing the slats extending, so you'll have exterior angles showing all the action. Okay? Slats retracting."

She watched impatiently. "Well," she said. "If the slats didn't cause this accident, what did?"

Singleton spoke for the first time. "How long has it been now, Teddy?"

"We've been up twenty-three minutes."

"Is that long enough?"

"Maybe. Could happen any minute now."

"What could happen?" Jennifer said.

"The first part of the sequence," Singleton said, "that caused the accident."

"The first part of the sequence?"

"Yes," Singleton said. "Nearly all aircraft accidents are the result of a sequence of events. We call it a cascade. It's never one thing. There's a chain of events, one after another. On this aircraft, we believe the initiating event was an erroneous fault reading, caused by a bad part."

With a sense of dread, Jennifer said, "A *bad part?*"

She was immediately recutting the tape in her mind. Getting around this awkward point. Singleton had said it was the initiating event. That didn't have to be emphasized, especially if it was just a link in the chain of events. The next link in the chain was equally important—probably more important. After all, what had happened on 545 was terrifying and spectacular, it involved the whole airplane, and it was surely unreasonable to blame it on a *bad part.*

"You said there was a chain of events . . ."

"That's right," Singleton said. "Several events in a sequence that we believe led to the final outcome."

Jennifer felt her shoulders drop.

They waited.

Nothing happened.

Five minutes went by. Jennifer was cold. She kept glancing at her watch. "What exactly are we waiting for?"

"Patience," Singleton said.

Then there was an electronic ping, and she saw amber words flash on the instrument panel. It said SLATS DISAGREE.

"There it is," Rawley said.

"There *what* is?"

"An indication that the FDAU believes the slats are not where they're supposed to be. As you see, the slats lever is up, so the slats should be stowed. And we know they are. But the airplane is picking up a reading that they are not stowed. In this case, we know the warning is coming from a bad proximity sensor in the right wing. The proximity sensor should read the presence of the retracted slat. But this sensor's been damaged. And when the sensor gets cold, it behaves erratically. Tells the pilot the slats are extended, when they're not."

Jennifer was shaking her head. "Proximity sensor . . . I'm not following you. What does this have to do with Flight 545?"

Singleton said, "The cockpit on 545 got a warning that something was wrong with the slats. Warnings like that happen fairly frequently. The pilot doesn't know whether something is really wrong, or whether the sensor is just acting up. So the pilot tries to clear the warning; he runs out the slats and retracts them."

"So the pilot on 545 deployed the slats, to clear the warning?"

"Yes."

"But deploying the slats didn't cause the accident . . ."

"No. We've just demonstrated that."

"What did?"

Rawley said, "Ladies, if you will please take your seats, we will now attempt to reproduce the event."

# ABOARD TPA 545

6:25 A.M.

In the center passenger cabin, Casey pulled the harness straps over her shoulders and cinched them tight. She looked over at Malone, who was sweating, her face pale.

"Tighter," Casey said.

"I already did—"

Casey reached over, grabbed her waist strap, and pulled as hard as she could.

Malone grunted. "Hey, for Christ's—"

"I don't much like you," Casey said, "but I don't want your little ass getting hurt on my watch."

Malone wiped her forehead with the back of her hand. Although the cabin was cold, sweat was running down her face.

Casey took out a white paper bag, and shoved it under Malone's thigh. "And I don't want you throwing up on me," she said.

"Do you think we'll need that?"

"I guarantee it," Casey said.

Malone's eyes were flicking back and forth. "Listen," she said, "maybe we should call this off."

"Change the channel?"

"Listen," Malone said, "maybe I was wrong."

"About what?"

"We shouldn't have come on the plane. We should have just watched."

"Too late now," Casey said.

She knew she was being tough with Malone because she was frightened herself. She didn't think Teddy was right about the airframe cracking; she didn't think he was foolish enough to go up in a plane that hadn't been thoroughly checked. He had hung around every minute of the tests, during the structural work, the CET, because he knew in a few days he was going to have to fly it. Teddy wasn't stupid.

But he was a test pilot, she thought.

And all test pilots were crazy.

*Click.* "All right, ladies, we are initiating the sequence. Everybody strapped in tight?"

"Yes," Casey said.

Malone said nothing. Her mouth was moving, but she wasn't saying anything.

*Click.* "Ah, chase alpha, this is zero one, initiating pitch oscillations now."

*Click.* "Roger zero one. We have you. Initiate on your mark."

*Click.* "Norton ground, this is zero one. Monitor check."

*Click.* "Check confirm. One to thirty."

*Click.* "Here we go, fellas. Mark."

Casey watched on the side monitor, which showed Teddy in the cockpit. His movements were calm, assured. His voice relaxed.

*Click.* "Ladies, I have received my slats disagree warning, and I am now extending the slats to clear the warning. Slats are now extended. I am out of the autopilot now. Nose is up, speed decreases . . . and I now have a stall . . ."

Casey heard the harsh electronic alarm, sounding again and again. Then the audio warning, the recorded voice flat and insistent: "Stall . . . Stall . . . Stall . . ."

*Click.* "I am bringing the nose down to avoid the stall condition . . ."

The plane nosed over, and began to dive.

It was as if they were going straight down.

Outside the scream of the engines became a shriek. Casey's body was pressing hard against the harness straps. Sitting beside her, Jennifer Malone began to scream, her mouth open, a single unvarying scream that merged with the scream of the engines.

Casey felt dizzy. She tried to count how long it was lasting. Five . . . six . . . seven . . . eight seconds . . . How long had the initial descent been?

Bit by bit, the plane began to level, to come out of the dive. The scream of the engines faded, changed to a lower register. Casey felt her body grow heavy, then heavier still, then amazingly heavy, her cheeks sagging, her arms pressed down to the armrests. The G-forces. They were at more than two Gs. Casey now weighed two hundred and fifty pounds. She sank lower in the seat, pressed down by a giant hand.

Beside her, Jennifer had stopped screaming, and now was making a continuous low groan.

The sensation of weight decreased as the plane started to climb again. At first the climb was reasonable, then uncomfortable—then it seemed to be straight up. The engines were screaming. Jennifer was screaming. Casey tried to count the seconds but couldn't. She didn't have the energy to focus.

And suddenly she felt the pit of her stomach begin to rise, followed by nausea, and she saw the monitor lift off the floor for a moment, held in place by the straps. They were weightless at the peak of the climb. Jennifer threw her hand over her mouth. Then the plane was going over . . . and down again.

*Click.* "Second pitch oscillation . . ."

Another steep dive.

Jennifer took her hand away from her mouth and screamed, much louder than before. Casey tried to hold on to the armrests, tried to occupy her mind. She had forgotten to count, she had forgotten to—

The weight again.

Sinking. Pressing.

Deep into the chair.

Casey couldn't move. She couldn't turn her head.

Then they were climbing again, steeper than before, the shriek of the engines loud in her ears, and she felt Jennifer reach for her, Jennifer grabbing her arm. Casey turned to look at her, and Jennifer, pale and wild-eyed, was shouting:

"Stop it! Stop it! *Stop it!*"

The plane was coming to the top of the rise. Her stomach lifting, a sickening sensation. Jennifer's stricken look, hand clapped to her mouth. Vomit spurting through her fingers.

The plane going over.

Another dive.

*Click.* "Releasing the luggage bins. Give you a sense of how it was."

Along both aisles, the luggage bins above the seats sprang open, and two-foot white blocks spilled out. They were harmless neoprene foam, but they bounced around the cabin like a dense blizzard. Casey felt them strike her face, the back of her head.

Jennifer was retching again, trying to pull the bag from under her leg. The blocks tumbled forward, moving down the cabin toward the cockpit. They obscured their view on all sides, until one by one, they began to fall to the floor, roll over, and remain there. The whine of the engines changed.

The sinking drag of added weight.

The plane was going up again.

The pilot in the F-14 chase plane watched as the big Norton widebody streaked upward through the clouds, climbing at twenty-one degrees.

"Teddy," he said over the radio. "What the hell are you doing?"

"Just reproducing what's on the flight recorder."

"Christ," the pilot said.

The huge passenger jet roared upward, breaking through cloud cover at thirty-one thousand feet.

Going up another thousand feet, before losing speed. Approaching stall.

Then nosing over again.

Jennifer vomited explosively into the bag. It spilled out over her hands, dribbled onto her lap. She turned to Casey, her face green, weak, contorted.

"Stop it, *please* . . ."

The plane had started to nose over again. Going down.

Casey looked at her. "Don't you want to reproduce the full event for your cameras? Great visuals. Two more cycles to go."

"No! *No* . . ."

The plane was diving steeply now. Still looking at Jennifer, Casey said, "Teddy! Teddy, take your hands off the controls!"

Jennifer's eyes widened. Horrified.

*Click.* "Roger. Taking my hands off now."

Immediately the plane leveled out. Smoothly, gently. The scream of the engines abated to a constant, steady roar. The foam blocks fell to the carpet, tumbled once, and did not move.

Level flight.

Sunlight streamed through the windows.

Jennifer wiped vomit from her lips with the back of her hand. She stared around the cabin in a daze. "What . . . what happened?"

"The pilot took his hands off the stick."

Jennifer shook her head, not understanding. Her

eyes were glazed. In a weak voice she said, "He took his hands off?"

Casey nodded. "That's right."

"Well then . . ."

"The autopilot is flying the plane."

Malone collapsed back in her seat, put her head back. Closed her eyes. "I don't understand," she said.

"To end the incident on Flight 545, all the pilot had to do was take his hands off the column. If he had taken his hands away, it would have ended immediately."

Jennifer sighed. "Then why didn't he?"

Casey didn't answer her. She turned to the monitor. "Teddy," she said, "let's go back."

## YUMA TEST STATION

### 9:45 A.M.

Back on the ground, Casey went through the main room of the Flight Test Station, and into the pilots' room. It was an old, wood-paneled lounge for test pilots from the days when Norton still made military aircraft. A lumpy green couch, faded gray from sunlight. A couple of metal flight chairs, pulled up to a scratched Formica table. The only new object in the room was a small television, with a built-in tape deck. It stood beside a battered Coke machine, with a taped card that said OUT OF ORDER. In the window, a grinding air conditioner. It was already blazing hot on the airfield, and the room was uncomfortably warm.

Casey looked through the window at the *Newsline* crew, walking around Flight 545, filming it as it sat on the runway. The aircraft gleamed in the bright desert sun. The crew seemed lost, not certain what to do. They aimed their cameras as if composing a shot, then lowered them again immediately. They seemed to be waiting.

Casey opened the manila folder she had brought with her, and looked through the sheets of paper inside. The color Xeroxes she asked Norma to make had turned out rather well. And the telexes were satisfactory. Everything was in order.

She went to the television, which she had ordered brought out here. She pushed a tape into the deck, and waited.

Waited for Malone.

Casey was tired. Then she remembered the scope. She rolled up her sleeve, and pulled off the four circular bandages arranged in a row on the skin of her arm. Scopolamine patches, for motion sickness. That was why she had not vomited on the plane. She had known what she was in for. Malone had not.

Casey had no sympathy for her. She just wanted to be finished. This would be the last step. This would end it.

The only person at Norton who really knew what she was doing was Fuller. Fuller had understood immediately when Casey had called him from Video

Imaging. Fuller recognized the implications of releasing the tape to *Newsline*. He saw what it would do to them, how they might be boxed in.

Flight Test had done that.

She waited for Malone.

Five minutes later, Jennifer Malone came in, slamming the door behind her. She was wearing a pair of flight test coveralls. Her face was washed, her hair pulled back.

And she was very angry.

"I don't know what you think you proved up there," she said. "You had your fun. Taped the show. Scared the shit out of me. I hope you enjoyed it, because it isn't going to change a fucking thing in our story. Barker is right. Your plane has slats problems, just like he says. The only thing he's missing is that the problem occurs when the autopilot's off. That's all your little exercise demonstrated today. But our story isn't changed. Your plane's a deathtrap. And by the time we air our story, you won't be able to sell one of those planes on *Mars*. We're going to bury your shitty little airplane, and we're going to bury you."

Casey did not speak. She thought: She's young. Young and stupid. The harshness of her own judgment surprised her. Perhaps she'd learned something from the tough older men at the plant. Men who knew about power, as opposed to posturing and strutting.

She let Malone rant awhile longer, and then she said, "Actually, you're not going to do any of that."

"You fucking watch me."

"The only thing you can do is report what actually happened on Flight 545. You may not want to do that."

"You wait," Malone said, hissing. "You fucking wait. It's a fucking deathtrap."

Casey sighed. "Sit down."

"I'll be goddamned if I will—"

"Did you ever wonder," Casey said, "how a secretary at a video house in Glendale knew you were doing a story on Norton? Had your cell phone number, and knew to call you?"

Malone was silent.

"Did you ever wonder," Casey said, "how Norton's attorney could have found out so quickly you had the tape? And then have gotten a sworn statement from the receptionist that she'd given it to you?"

Malone was silent.

"Ed Fuller walked in the door of Video Imaging just a few minutes after you walked out, Ms. Malone. He was worried about running into you."

Malone frowned. "What is this?"

"Did you ever wonder," Casey said, "why Ed Fuller was so insistent you sign a document saying you didn't obtain the tape from a Norton employee?"

"It's obvious. The tape's damaging. He doesn't want the company to be blamed."

"Blamed *by whom?*"

"By . . . I don't know. The public."

"You better sit down," Casey said. She opened the file.

Slowly, Malone sat.

She frowned.

"Wait a minute," Malone said. "You're saying that secretary didn't call me, about the tape?"

Casey looked at her.

"Then who called?" Malone said.

Casey said nothing.

"It was *you?*"

Casey nodded.

"You *wanted* me to have that tape?"

"Yes."

"*Why?*"

Casey smiled.

She handed Malone the first sheet of paper. "This is a parts inspection record, stamped off by a PMI at the FAA yesterday, for the number two inboard slats proximity sensor on Flight 545. The part is noted to be cracked, and defective. The crack is old."

"I'm not doing a parts story," Malone said.

"No," Casey said. "You're not. Because what flight test showed you today is that any competent pilot could have handled the slats warning initiated by the bad part. All the pilot had to do is leave the plane in autopilot. But on Flight 545, he didn't."

Malone said, "We already checked that. The captain of 545 was an outstanding pilot."

"That's right," Casey said.

She passed her the next piece of paper.

"This is the crew manifest submitted to the FAA

with the flight plan, on the date of departure of Flight 545."

| | | |
|---|---|---|
| John Zhen Chang, Captain | 5/7/51 | M |
| Leu Zan Ping, First Officer | 3/11/59 | M |
| Richard Yong, First Officer | 9/9/61 | M |
| Gerhard Reimann, First Officer | 7/23/49 | M |
| Thomas Chang, First Officer | 6/29/70 | M |
| Henri Marchand, Engineer | 4/25/69 | M |
| Robert Sheng, Engineer | 6/13/62 | M |

Malone glanced at it, pushed it aside.

"And this is the crew manifest we got from TransPacific the day after the incident."

| | |
|---|---|
| JOHN ZHEN CHANG, CAPTAIN | 5/7/51 |
| LEU ZAN PING, FIRST OFFICER | 3/11/59 |
| RICHARD YONG, FIRST OFFICER | 9/9/61 |
| GERHARD REIMANN, FIRST OFFICER | 7/23/49 |
| HENRI MARCHAND, ENGINEER | 4/25/69 |
| THOMAS CHANG, ENGINEER | 6/29/70 |
| ROBERT SHENG, ENGINEER | 6/13/62 |

Malone scanned it, shrugged. "It's the same."

"No, it's not. In one, Thomas Chang is listed as a first officer. In the second list, he appears as an engineer."

Malone said, "A clerical error."

Casey shook her head. "No."

She passed another sheet.

"This is a page from the TransPacific in-flight

magazine, showing Captain John Chang and his family. It was sent to us by a TransPacific flight attendant, who wanted us to know the real story. You will notice his children are Erica and Thomas Chang. Thomas Chang is the pilot's son. He was among the flight crew of Flight 545."

Malone frowned.

"The Changs are a family of pilots. Thomas Chang is a pilot, qualified on several commuter aircraft. He is not type certified to fly the N-22."

"I don't believe this," Malone said.

"At the time of the incident," Casey continued, "the captain, John Chang, had left the cockpit and walked to the back of the plane for coffee. He was aft when the accident occurred, and severely injured. He underwent brain surgery in Vancouver two days ago. The hospital thought it was the first officer, but his identity has now been confirmed as John Zhen Chang."

Malone was shaking her head.

Casey handed her a memo:

```
FROM: S. NIETO, FSR VANC
TO: C. SINGLETON, YUMA TEST FAC

HIGHLY CONFIDENTIAL

AUTHORITIES NOW CONFIRM THE POST-
MORTEM IDENTIFICATION OF INJURED
CREW MEMBER IN VANCOUVER HOSPITAL
AS JOHN ZHEN CHANG THE CAPTAIN OF
TRANSPACIFIC FLIGHT 545.
```

"Chang wasn't in the cockpit," Casey said. "He was in the back of the plane. His hat was found there. So someone else was in the captain's chair, when the incident occurred."

Casey turned on the television, started the tape. "These are the concluding moments of the video-tape which you obtained from the receptionist. You see the camera falling toward the front of the plane, and twisting to eventually lodge in the cockpit door. But before it does . . . here!" She froze the frame. "You can see the flight deck."

"I can't see much," Malone said. "They're both looking away."

"You can see that the pilot has extremely short hair," Casey said. "Look at the picture. Thomas Chang has close-cropped hair."

Malone was shaking her head, strongly now. "I just don't believe this. That visual is not good enough, you have a three-quarter profile, it doesn't identify, it doesn't say anything."

"Thomas Chang has a small stud in his ear. You can see it in this magazine photo. And on the video, you can see the same stud catch the light, right there."

Malone was silent.

Casey pushed another piece of paper across to her.

"This is a translation of the Chinese voice communications in the cockpit as recorded on the tape you have. A great deal of it is unintelligible because of the cockpit alarms. But the relevant passage is marked for you."

| 0544:59 | ALM | stall stall stall |
| 0545:00 | F/O | what (unintelligible) you |
| 0545:01 | CPTN | am (unintelligible) correct the |
| 0545:02 | ALM | stall stall stall |
| 0545:03 | F/O | tom release the (unintelligible) |
| 0545:04 | CPTN | what do (unintelligible) it |
| 0545:11 | F/O | tommy (unintelligible) when (unintelligible) must (unintelligible) the |

Casey took the paper back. "That's not for you to keep, or refer to publicly. But it corroborates the videotape in your possession."

Malone said, in a stunned voice, *"He let his kid fly the plane?"*

"Yes," Casey said. "John Chang permitted a pilot who was not type-certified to fly the N-22. As a result, fifty-six people were injured and four people died—including John Chang himself. We believe that the aircraft was on autopilot, and Chang left his son momentarily in charge of the flight. That was when the disagree warning occurred, and the son extended the slats to clear it. But the son panicked, overcorrected, and porpoised. Eventually we believe

Thomas Chang was knocked unconscious by the severe movements of the airplane, and the autopilot took over."

Malone said, "On a commercial flight, some guy lets his fucking kid fly the plane?"

"Yes," Casey said.

"*That's* the story?"

"Yes," Casey said. "And you have the tape in your possession that proves it. Therefore you are aware of the facts. Mr. Reardon stated on camera that both he and his colleagues in New York have watched the tape in its entirety. So you have seen this shot of the cockpit. I have now informed you what that shot represents. We have provided you with corroborating evidence—not all the evidence, there's more. We have also demonstrated in flight test that there is nothing wrong with the aircraft itself."

"Not everyone agrees . . ." she began.

"This is no longer a matter of opinion, Ms. Malone. It is a matter of fact. You are undeniably in possession of the facts. If *Newsline* does not report these facts, which you are now aware of, and if it makes any suggestion whatsoever that there is anything wrong with the N-22 aircraft based on this incident, we will sue you for reckless disregard and malicious intent. Ed Fuller is very conservative, but he thinks we will certainly win. Because you acquired the tape that proves our case. Now, would you like Mr. Fuller to call Mr. Shenk and explain the situation, or would you prefer to do it yourself?"

Malone said nothing.

"Ms. Malone?"

"Where's a phone?" she said.

"There's one in the corner."

Malone got up, and walked over to the phone. Casey headed for the door.

"Jesus Christ," Malone said, shaking her head. "The guy lets his kid fly a plane full of people? I mean, how can that happen?"

Casey shrugged. "He loves his son. We believe he's allowed him to fly on other occasions. But there's a reason why commercial pilots are required to train extensively on specific equipment, to be type certified. He didn't know what he was doing, and he got caught."

Casey closed the door, and thought: *And so did you.*

# YUMA

## 10:05 A.M.

"Jesus fucking Christ," Dick Shenk said. "I got a hole in the show the size of Afghanistan and you're telling me you've got a *bad parts* story? Featuring Yellow Peril Pilots? Is that what you're telling me, Jennifer? Because I'm not going to run with that. I'll get murdered. I'm not going to be the Pat Buchanan of the airwaves. Fuck that noise."

"Dick," she said. "It doesn't really play that way. It's a family tragedy, the guy loves his son, and—"

"But I can't *use* it," Shenk said. "He's *Chinese.* I can't even *go near* it."

"The kid killed four people and injured fifty-six—"

"What difference does that make? I'm very dis-appointed in you, Jennifer," he said. "Very, *very* disappointed. Do you realize what this means? This means I have to go with the gimp Little League segment."

"Dick," she said. "I didn't cause the accident, I'm just reporting the story . . ."

"Wait a minute. What fresh bullshit is this?"

"Dick, I—"

"You're reporting your ineptitude, is what you're reporting," Shenk said. "You fucked up, Jennifer. You had a hot story, a story I wanted, a story about a crappy American product, and two days later you come back with some horseshit about a whack. It's not the airplane, it's the pilot. And maintenance. And *bad parts.*"

"Dick—"

"I warned you, I didn't want bad parts. You fucked this one to death, Jennifer. We'll talk Monday."

And he hung up.

# GLENDALE

11:00 P.M.

*Newsline's* closing credits were running when Casey's phone rang. An unfamiliar, gruff voice said, "Casey Singleton?"

"Speaking."

"Hal Edgarton here."

"How are you, sir?"

"I'm in Hong Kong, and I've just been told by one of my board members that *Newsline* did not run a Norton story tonight."

"That's right, sir."

"I'm very pleased," he said. "I wonder why they didn't run it?"

"I have no idea," Casey said.

"Well, whatever you did, it was obviously effective," Edgarton said. "I'm leaving for Beijing in a few hours, to sign the sales agreement. John Marder was supposed to meet me there, but I'm told that, for some reason, he hasn't left California."

"I don't know anything about that," she said.

"Good," Edgarton said. "Glad to hear it. We'll be making some changes at Norton in the next few days. Meanwhile I wanted to congratulate you, Casey. You've been under a lot of pressure. You've done an outstanding job."

"Thank you, sir."

"Hal."

"Thank you, Hal."

"My secretary will call to arrange lunch when I get back," he said. "Keep up the good work."

Edgarton hung up, and then there were other calls. From Mike Lee, congratulating her, in guarded tones. Asking how she managed to kill the story. She said she had nothing to do with it, that *Newsline* for some reason had decided not to run it.

Then there were more calls, from Doherty, and

Burne, and Ron Smith. And Norma, who said, "Honey, I'm proud of you."

And finally Teddy Rawley, who said he happened to be in the neighborhood, and wondered what she was doing.

"I'm really tired," Casey said. "Another time, okay?"

"Aw, babe. It was a great day. Your day."

"Yeah, Teddy. But I'm really tired."

She took her phone off the hook, and went to bed.


# GLENDALE

### Sunday, 5:45 P.M.

It was a clear evening. She was standing outside her bungalow, in the twilight, when Amos came up with his dog. The dog slobbered on her hand.

"So," Amos said. "You dodged a bullet."

"Yes," she said. "I guess so."

"Whole plant's talking. Everyone's saying you stood up to Marder. Wouldn't lie about 545. That true?"

"More or less."

"Then you were stupid," Amos said. "You should have lied. *They* lie. It's just a question of whose lie gets on the air."

"Amos . . ."

"Your father was a journalist; you think there's some kind of truth to be told. There isn't. Not for years, kid. I watched those scum on the Aloha incident. All they wanted was the gory details. Stewardess gets sucked out of the plane, did she die before she hit the water? Was she still alive? That's all they wanted to know."

"Amos," she said. She wanted him to stop.

"I know," he said. "That's entertainment. But I'm telling you, Casey. You were lucky this time. You might not be as lucky next time. So don't let this become a habit. Remember: they make the rules. And the game's got nothing to do with accuracy, or the facts, or reality. It's just a circus."

She wasn't going to argue with him. She petted the dog.

"Fact is," Amos said, "everything's changing. Used to be—in the old days—the media image roughly corresponded to reality. But now it's all reversed. The media image is the reality, and by comparison day-to-day life seems to lack excitement. So now day-to-day life is false, and the media image is true. Sometimes I look around my living room, and the most real thing in the room is the television. It's bright and vivid, and the rest of my life looks drab. So I turn the damn thing off. That does it every time. Get my life back."

Casey continued to pet the dog. She saw headlights in the darkening night swing around the corner, and come up the street toward them. She walked to the curb.

"Well, I'm rambling," Amos said.

"Good night, Amos," she said.

The car came to a stop. The door flung open.

"Mom!"

Her daughter jumped into her arms, wrapping her legs around her. "Oh, Mom, I *missed* you!"

"Me too, honey," she said. "Me too."

Jim got out of the car, handed Casey the backpack. In the near darkness, she couldn't really see his face.

"Good night," he said to her.

"Good night, Jim," she said.

Her daughter took her hand. They started back inside. It was growing dark, and the air was cool. When she looked up, she saw the straight contrail of a passenger jet. It was so high, it was still in daylight, a thin white streak across the darkening sky.

5TH STORY of Level 1 printed in FULL
format
COPYRIGHT TELEGRAPH-STAR, INC.

HEADLINE: NORTON SELLS 50 WIDEBODY JETS
TO CHINA
TAILS TO BE MANUFACTURED IN SHANGHAI
CASH FLOW AIDS DEVELOPMENT OF FUTURE
JET.
UNION LEADERS CRITICIZE LOSS OF JOBS.

BYLINE: JACK ROGERS

BODY:
Norton Aircraft today announced they
have closed the sale of fifty N-22 widebody jets to the People's Republic of
China. According to Norton president
Harold Edgarton, the agreement signed yesterday in Beijing calls for delivery of
the jets over the next four years. Under
the terms of the agreement, there will be
a so-called "offset" of work to China,
which will require the N-22 tails to be
constructed at a factory in Shanghai.
The sale represents a coup for the
beleaguered Burbank manufacturer, and a
bitter defeat for Airbus, which had lob-
bied heavily, both in Beijing and
Washington, for the sale. According to
Edgarton, the fifty Chinese jets, combined
with the further sale of twelve N-22s to
TransPacific Airlines, will give Norton
the cash flow it needs to continue development of the N-XX widebody, to address
the twenty-first century market.

# AIRFRAME

News of the offset agreement produced anger in some quarters of the Burbank company. UAW leader Don Brull criticized the offset agreement, noting, "We're losing thousands of jobs every year. Norton is exporting the jobs of American workers to make their sale. I don't think it's good for our future."

When asked about the loss of jobs, Edgarton stated that "offsets are a fact of life in our industry, and have been for many years. The fact is, if we don't make the agreement, then Boeing or Airbus will. I think it is important to look to the future, and the new assembly lines that will come with the N-XX widebody."

Under the agreement, Edgarton emphasized, China had an option for thirty additional jets. The Shanghai factory would begin its work in January of next year.

News of the sale ends speculation that much-publicized recent incidents involving the N-22 might prevent the Chinese purchase. Edgarton noted, "The N-22 is a proven aircraft with an excellent safety record. I think the Chinese sale is a tribute to that record."

---

DOCUMENT ID: C\LEX 40\DL\NORTON


TRANSPACIFIC BUYS NORTON JETS
TransPacific Airlines, the Hong
Kong—based carrier, today ordered twelve
Norton N-22 widebody jets, giving further
proof that the Asian market is the growth
segment for the aircraft industry.


EXPERT WITNESS BITES HAND THAT DIDN'T
FEED HIM
Controversial aviation expert Frederick
"Fred" Barker sued Bradley King for failing to pay promised "holding fees" for his
anticipated courtroom appearances. King
could not be reached for comment.


AIRBUS CONSIDERS KOREAN PARTNERSHIP
Songking Industries, the industrial con-
glomerate based in Seoul, has announced
they are negotiating with Airbus Industrie
of Toulouse to manufacture major subassem-
bly components of the new A-340B stretch
derivative. Recent speculation has cen-
tered on Songking's continuing efforts to
establish an aerospace presence in world
markets, now that long-rumored secret
negotiations with Norton Aircraft in
Burbank have apparently broken down.


SHENK TO BE HONORED AT HUMANITARIAN FETE
Richard Shenk, producer of "Newsline,"
has been named Humanitarian Producer of
the Year by the American Interfaith
Council. The Council promotes "humane
understanding among the peoples of the

world" in contemporary media. Shenk, cited
for his "outstanding life-long commitment
to tolerance," will be honored at a banquet on June 10 at the Waldorf Astoria. A
star-studded industry audience is expected
to turn out.

MARDER TAKES CONSULTING POST
   In a surprise move, John Marder, 46, has
left Norton Aircraft to head The Aviation
Institute, an aerospace consulting firm
with close ties to European carriers.
Marder assumes his new position effective
immediately. Coworkers at Norton praised
the departing Marder as "a leader of
deep integrity."

U.S. JOBS EXPORTED—A DISTURBING TREND?
   Responding to the recent sale of fifty
Norton jets to China, William Campbell
claimed that American aviation companies
will export 250,000 jobs over the next
five years. Since much of this export is
financed by the Commerce Department's Ex-
Im Bank, he says, "It's unconscionable.
U.S. workers aren't paying taxes to have
the government assist American companies
to take away American jobs." Campbell
cites the Japanese corporate concern for
their workers as strikingly different from
the behavior of American multinationals.

RICHMAN ARRESTED IN SINGAPORE
   A youthful member of the Norton clan was
arrested today by police in Singapore on
charges of narcotics possession. Bob
Richman, 28, is being held by authorities

awaiting arraignment. If convicted under the nation's draconian drug laws, he faces the death penalty.

SINGLETON HEADS DIVISION
Harold Edgarton today named Katherine C. Singleton as the new head of Norton Aircraft's Media Relations Division. Singleton was formerly a vice-president for Quality Assurance at Norton, which is headquartered in Burbank.

MALONE TO JOIN "HARD COPY" STAFF
Veteran news producer Jennifer Malone, 29, ends four years with "Newsline" to join the staff of "Hard Copy," it was announced today. Malone's departure was described as resulting from a contract dispute. Malone said, "'Hard Copy' is what's happening now, and I am just thrilled to be part of it."

# AIRFRAME

---

## AIRCRAFT INCIDENT REPORT

REPORT NO:           IRT-96-42

TODAY'S DATE:        18 April
MODEL:               N-22
INCIDENT DATE:       08 April
OPERATOR:            TransPacific
FUSELAGE NO:         271
REPORTED BY:         R. Rakoski, FSR HK
LOCATION:            Pacific Oc
REFERENCE:           a) AVN-SVC-08764/AAC

SUBJECT:             <u>Severe Pitch Oscillations in
                     Flight</u>

### DESCRIPTION OF EVENT:

Reportedly during cruise flight a "Slats Disagree" warning appeared on the flight deck, and a member of the flight crew extended the slats in an attempt to clear the warning. Subsequently the aircraft experienced severe pitch oscillations and lost 6,000 feet altitude before control was returned to the autopilot. Four persons died, and fifty-six were injured.

### ACTION TAKEN:

Inspection of the aircraft revealed the following damage:

1. The interior cabin sustained substantial damage.
2. The Number 2 IB slats proximity sensor was faulty.
3. The Number 2 slats locking pin was found to be non-PMA.
4. The Number 1 engine thruster panel was found to be non-PMA.
5. Several other non-PMA parts were identified for replacement.

Review of human factors revealed the following:

1. Flight deck procedures require added carrier scrutiny.
2. Foreign repair procedures require added carrier scrutiny.

The aircraft is in the process of being repaired. Internal procedures are being reviewed by the carrier.

David Levine
Technical Integration
Product Support
Norton Aircraft Company
Burbank, CA

**LARGE PRINT EDITIONS**

## Look for these and other Random House Large Print books at your local bookstore

Ben Artzi-Pelossof, Noa, *In the Name of Sorrow and Hope*
Berendt, John, *Midnight in the Garden of Good and Evil*
Brinkley, David, *David Brinkley*
Byatt, A. S., *Babel Tower*
Crichton, Michael, *The Lost World*
Cruz Smith, Martin, *Rose*
Daly, Rosie, *In the Kitchen with Rosie*
Flagg, Fannie, *Daisy Fay and the Miracle Man*
Flagg, Fannie, *Fried Green Tomatoes at the
      Whistle Stop Cafe*
Follett, Ken, *A Place Called Freedom*
Fulghum, Robert, *From Beginning to End*
Grimes, Martha, *Hotel Paradise*
Hepburn, Katharine, *Me*
Krantz, Judith, *Spring Collection*
Koontz, Dean, *Intensity*
Landers, Ann, *Wake Up and Smell the Coffee!*
Lindbergh, Anne Morrow, *Gift from the Sea*
Mayle, Peter, *Anything Considered*
Michener, James A., *Mexico*
Mother Teresa, *A Simple Path*
Patterson, Richard North, *The Final Judgment*
Phillips, Louis, editor, *The Random House Large Print
      Treasury of Best-Loved Poems*
Pope John Paul II, *Crossing the Threshold of Hope*
Powell, Colin with Joseph E. Persico, *My American
      Journey*
Shaara, Jeff, *Gods and Generals*
Truman, Margaret, *Murder at the National Gallery*
Tyler, Anne, *Ladder of Years*